BATMAN™

NO MAN'S LAND

BATMAN

NO MAN'S LAND

A NOVEL

GREG RUCKA

BATMAN CREATED BY BOB KANE

POCKET BOOKS

New York   London   Toronto   Sydney   Singapore   Gotham City

POCKET BOOKS, a division of Simon & Schuster Inc.
1230 Avenue of the Americas, New York, NY 10020

ISBN: 0-671-03828-1

First Pocket Books hardcover printing January 2000

10   9   8   7   6   5   4   3   2   1

Book design by Richard Oriolo

Printed in the U.S.A.

RRDH/✖

F
Ruck

Batman: No Man's Land was primarily adapted from the story serialized in the following comic books, originally published by DC Comics:

Batman: No Man's Land #1 (March 1999)
Batman #560–574 (December 1998–February 2000)
Detective Comics #727–741 (December 1998–February 2000)
Batman: Shadow of the Bat #80–94 (December 1998–February 2000)
Legends of the Dark Knight #116–126 (April 1999–February 2000)

With additional material adapted from or inspired by:

Batman Chronicles #16–18 (April, July, and October 1999)
Batman: Harley Quinn (September 1999)
Batman: No Man's Land #0 (October 1999)

These comic books were created by the following people:

GROUP EDITORS
Dennis O'Neil
Mike Carlin

EDITORS
Jordan B. Gorfinkel
Matt Idelson
Scott Peterson
Darren Vincenzo

ASSOCIATE EDITOR
Joseph Illidge

ASSISTANT EDITOR
Frank Berrios

WRITERS
Steven Barnes
Bronwyn Carlton
Paul Dini
Chuck Dixon
Ian Edgington
Bob Gale
Jordan B. Gorfinkel
Alan Grant
Devin K. Grayson
Larry Hama
Janet Harvey
Lisa Klink
Dennis O'Neil
Kelley Puckett
Greg Rucka

PENCILLERS
Jim Aparo
Jon Bogdanove
Mat Broome
Mark Buckingham
Rick Burchett
Sergio Cariello
Guy Davis
Mike Deodato
D'Israeli
Dale Eaglesham
Yvel Guichet
Paul Gulacy
Dan Jurgens
Rafael Kayanan
Greg Land
Alex Maleev
Jason Minor
Tom Morgan
Jason Pearson
Pablo Raimondi
Roger Robinson
William Rosado
Paul Ryan
Damion Scott
Frank Teran
Phil Winslade

INKERS
Eduardo Barreto
Sal Buscema
Robert Campanella
Randy Emberlin
Wayne Faucher
John Floyd
Drew Geraci
James A. Hodgkins
Andy Lanning
Mark McKenna
Jaime Mendoza
Sean Parsons
James Pascoe
David Roach
Matt Ryan
Bill Sienkiewicz
Batt and Aaron Sowd
Phil Winslade

To Corrina Joan Rucka,

My mother, who taught me to read;

and

To Dennis O'Neil,

The Master, who inspired me to write.

ACKNOWLEDGMENTS

IN A WORK SUCH AS THIS, THE DEBTS ARE profound and the list is long . . . so buckle up.

First, foremost, and always . . . a debt of gratitude to Bob Kane and Bill Finger. It's an honor to be part of the legacy.

At DC Comics and Pocket Books, special thanks to the editorial team who allowed this book to happen—Charlie "Chas Man" Kochman, Elisabeth "Spicey" Vincentelli, and Marco "MX" Palmieri. Additional gratitude to the on-deck circle at both houses, particularly to Trent Duffy, Sandy Resnick, Larry Ganem, Dorothy Crouch, and Scott Shannon.

Much admiration and appreciation for the real Bat-squad, in downtown Gotham City (. . . or is this Metropolis?): Jordan B. Gorfinkel (who had the bright idea in the first place), Darren Vincenzo, Joseph Illidge, Frank Berrios, Matt Idelson, Mike Carlin, Eddie Berganza, Willie Schubert, Arlene Lo, Patty Jeres, Ivan Cohen, and Scott Nybakken. A fond farewell to David Vinson—you will be missed.

To the writers who make Batman come to life: Paul Dini, Chuck Dixon, Bob Gale, Alan Grant, Larry Hama, Doug Moench, and Devin K. Grayson, as well as the countless others, too talented to forget, and too many to be named herein.

Thanks, always and in abundance, to my agent David Hale Smith, for joining me in my love of comics.

Special note of thanks to Mark "Boomer" Waid for knowing not only what Batman keeps in his Utility Belt, but which compartment it's in, to boot.

From the trenches, and for keeping my back: Nicolo, Max, Jessie, and Han.

To the Rom: See you on the rooftop express. Bella loves you.

To Mike Rucka, for knowing exactly what the Richest Man in the World would have for dinner, and for knowing how to spell it.

Finally, to Jennifer, who's sassier than Barbara Gordon.

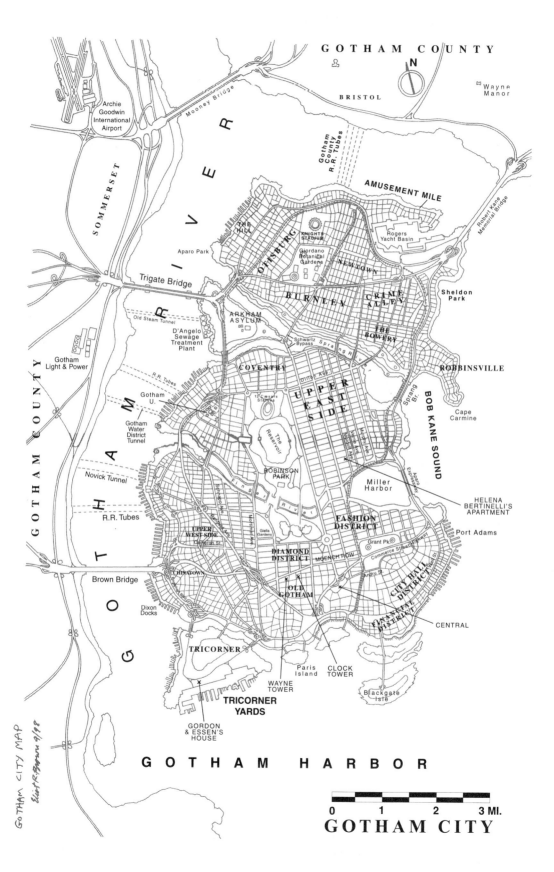

BATMAN

NO MAN'S LAND

ORACLE

Dear Dad—

This is harder than I thought it would be.

This is me breaking the silence and telling the secrets.

I wish there was another way to do this, and I pray that you'll never read these words, and the many words sure to follow. But someone has to keep the chronicle, someone has to record and remember, and the only person left who can do it is me.

The problem is, to tell it right I can't hold anything back—not for myself, not for him, not for any of us—no half-truths, no dodges, no feints, not even the parts that will hurt.

This, as they say, is the proverbial "it."

All or nothing, for us like it is for Gotham.

It means I have to strip the masks away. It means I have to betray secrets shared in confidence or learned through treachery. It means nothing is sacred.

I'm trying very hard not to think about what might come, how you'll react if you ever do read these words. I'm trying very hard not to think about your righteous anger, or about how you'll curse me for keeping so much from you for so long. I'm trying very hard not to think about the proud man you are, and how humiliated you'll feel. I know you as you know me, Commissioner; you'll think you were played for a fool.

But Dad, you've never been a fool. Never to me. Never to him.

I really, really, *really* hope that no one else will ever read this but me.

Because, if you're reading this, it means we lost.

It means Gotham City really and truly is dead.

And probably me along with it.

My name was Batgirl, once.

Now I'm called Oracle.

But my name is really Barbara Gordon.

First mask removed.

I had to get that out of the way up front, because you have to understand my *bona fides*, such as they are. You have to believe that I know what I'm talking about, that when I say such-and-such happened, or Batman and Joker did this or that, I'm reporting the facts, as best I can. When I say that I *know* what's going on, you must trust that I am telling you the truth, all of it.

You must believe that you can believe me.

As Batgirl, I learned Gotham City like the back of my gloved hand. The Gotham that Fodor's doesn't write about, the Gotham that lives between criminal madness and ultimate despair. I know things. For example, I know that the sewer grate on the north side of the intersection at Middaugh and Cohen is a false one, not on any city record, installed by a certain vigilante to allow for immediate access to a cache of equipment if he's ever low on Batarangs as he's passing through.

I know, too, that if you dive off what was once the Babylon Towers with a good cable and perfect aim, you can loop your throw around the statue of the Zion Lion thirty feet below, the one that sits atop the GCBC building. If you do it right, your arms will feel like they're leaving their sockets the hard way, but if you keep your grip and your nerve, you can swing all the way to the penthouse apartments overlooking Victory Square.

I know that if you do it wrong, you'll hit the ground so hard they'll need a sponge to get you out of your costume.

I know that, if you do this at 2337 hours Monday through Friday, you can clear the next three rooftops in time to land atop the J Street el as it slows to turn up Broadway. On Saturdays, you've got to do it three minutes earlier.

At least, you could before the Cataclysm.

As Oracle, my knowledge is even greater, though perhaps more abstract. Given time and a computer or six, I can find just about any piece of information stored in any electronic system, anywhere on the planet, provided I can hack my way in. And I can hack my way in like I designed the code myself.

Usually.

Remember back three years, when the Gotham Knights made it to the World Series? Remember how all the cameras went down at the bottom of the ninth for three seconds, just as Malone was pitching on a full count to the Meteors?

Oops.

More than that, I've got records like you wouldn't believe, from places you wouldn't imagine. Scanned documents from two hundred years ago up to the latest burn of the *Complete Who's Who* CD. I know how to research, and I know how to investigate. I'm a spymaster to give George Smiley a run for his money, know what I mean?

I should be. I learned it from two of the best there are.

And yes, Dad, one of them's you.

I read back over this so far, and I realize that, though those two alter egos may be me at my best, Barbara Gordon is the woman at its heart.

She's the most important part of this, in a way.

She is, after all, the girl who was raised in Gotham City, the girl who sneers at New Yorkers who talk about their tough town. She's the girl who tells the Metropolis jokes.

Me.

As much Gotham City as anyone, in a way. As much as you, Dad. As much as any of your cops.

As much as Batman himself.

I'm looking out the window now, which is not really a window at all. I'm not in my apartment, not exactly; I'm through the secret door in the wall where you normally hang your coat, in my control room, my command post. This is where Oracle lives. I'm surrounded by monitors and mini-towers, computers running on battery power charged by the solar cells I've stockpiled. I've got a satellite phone with a T3 connection and uplink, I've got flashlights and rope, even a couple of nonlethal weapons—a *tonfa*, a sawed-down baseball bat, a collapsible baton—and one rifle, in case things get really nasty.

I've got two portable heaters and a blanket, and I'm using all three, and I'm still freezing my ass off.

I'm looking at the worst winter in Gotham City's history, and it's not the weather that did it, or even Mother Nature.

I can see the flashes of light as the charges go off, demolishing the Brown Bridge, cutting off this island city from the rest of the United States of America.

As of exactly seven minutes ago, we're no longer citizens of the U.S.A. As of exactly seven minutes ago, Gotham City officially became a No Man's Land.

Everyone who could go, has. As for the rest of us, now we couldn't leave even if we wanted to.

How did we come to this?

They were asking the same question on *Nightline* and *The News Hour*. They recounted the contagion that devastated the city three years ago, then the second outbreak that picked up where the first one had left off. They talked about how tens of thousands of Gothamites died, about the repeated impositions of martial law. They talked about the eroding economic, social, and cultural bases as people fled this city for greener pastures, relocating to Blüdhaven or Boston or Metropolis or—God forbid—Hub City.

Gotham, they all sadly admitted, was pretty much a write-off even before the Cataclysm.

Oh, and how they *love* to talk about the Cataclysm, Dad! A whopping 7.6 earthquake with an epicenter not ten miles from downtown, the fires burning for days, the massive loss of life. As far as tragedies go, let's be honest, the media couldn't have asked for better. Gotham City was front-page news around the world that morning, you can bet Aunt Mae's girdle on that.

Put all the tragedies together, one after the other, and we've got a death toll in the hundreds of thousands, easy.

I'm looking out the window and I want to laugh, because, let's be frank . . . the Cataclysm, that was just insult to injury.

What happened next, when you think about it in that light, wasn't so hard to believe. I mean, after Mother Nature, there was really only one thing worse that could happen to Our Fair City.

Politics.

No money for Gotham, said Congress. No money for Gotham, said the Senate. Federal funds in excess of one hundred billion dollars would be needed to rebuild the civic infrastructure, that was the sound bite. And then the number climbed higher—not one hundred, one-twenty—not one-twenty, one-fifty. . . .

We became the nation's latest scapegoat and, in a way, wasn't it about time?

We're the murder capital of the country, or at least, we used to be, when we were part of the country. According to the FBI—and I know this, trust me—we outscored every other city in the nation with our stats.

Highest incidence of crimes against property per capita? Gotham City. Highest incidence of robbery-homicide per capita? Gotham City. Assaults? Gotham City. Rapes? Gotham City. Kidnapping, arson, hell, even auto theft? Gotham City.

If that wasn't enough—and for the politicos, it wasn't—next came the parade of lunatics. Two-Face and Mr. Freeze. Ivy and Clayface. Mr. Zsasz, the Riddler, the Penguin . . . and, of course, their favorite madman, the son of a bitch who put a bullet through my spine, who put me in this wheelchair for the rest of my life:

The Joker.

Where the politicians went, then, the nation followed. Gotham City, the new Sodom. Let it burn. Let it rot. Let it crumble.

Even our favorite son, Bruce Wayne, couldn't save us from the might of Washington. The billionaire playboy, the inheritor of the Wayne fortune, the wayward president of Wayne Enterprises, Wayne Technologies, and Wayne Development. Even with the billions of dollars from the companies bearing his name that Wayne poured into both cities at once, Gotham and D.C., he couldn't keep the President from signing into law the Federal Declaration of No Man's Land.

Bruce Wayne . . .

Here comes another mask removed. The big one. Brace yourself.

Dad, Bruce Wayne is the Batman.

Seriously.

He told me once how it happened, or, more specifically, why it happened. Perhaps you've already figured it out.

I can't imagine what it was like, to be him. To be eight years old and on the way home from a night at the movies. To have your mother holding one hand, your father holding the other. To let go, laughing, to jump out in front of them, wheeling, swinging the imagined sword of Zorro.

To see the fear crossing the face of your parents as a shadow fell from behind you.

To turn and see the man with the gun.

To see him shoot. To smell the cordite.

To watch your mother and father die on the sidewalk in front of you.

To wonder why they had to die, to wonder why they'd left you alone.

To wonder at a world that could allow such a thing to happen.

. . .

But Bruce Wayne is gone now, and the Batman with him. I suppose that shouldn't mean anything—so many don't even believe he exists—but this time it feels . . . *different.*

It feels like maybe he really is gone.

That maybe Batman and Bruce Wayne both have done the sensible thing, the sane thing.

Maybe they got out while they could.

I don't want to believe it. Gotham City needs him now as much as he has ever needed Gotham City.

I don't want to believe he's abandoned us.

But he hasn't been seen in days. I would have heard something by now.

I *should* have heard something by now.

For the first time since as long as I can remember, there is no Batman.

And I'm scared, Dad.

I'm really scared.

PROLOGUE

SIX OF THEM STOOD ON THE SUNKEN roof of the GCPD Central Precinct, almost in a perfect line, just shy of the edge. All faced west, toward the Gotham River, and with the height of the Precinct building and the rest of the shattered skyline before them, their view was almost entirely unobstructed. In the distance, shrouded in the thin mist that rose from the water, helicopters flew low along the far shore, halogen beams drawing white lines through the air. Behind them, on its mount, sat the broken floodlight that could paint the clouds with the silhouette of a giant bat.

It was brittle-cold, the middle of winter, but there had been no snow yet, not even at Christmas. The air was dry and the wind was strong and from the north and it made the condensation from their breathing look more like smoke than steam, whipped away as quickly as it was exhaled. All breathed through their mouths, trying to minimize the assault of scent from the traumatized city—the rotten food, the sewage, the smoke.

They stood quietly, waiting, each with their own thoughts, hands thrust deep into pockets or folded under armpits, shifting from foot to foot in an attempt to stay warm. Two of them, in the center, held hands.

At 11:50 exactly, the man on the end, the one dressed in tactical gear and wearing a black ball-cap with the GCPD badge stitched to its face, said, "Ten minutes, Jim."

James Gordon, at the center of the line, his wife's hand in his own, said, "Thank you, Bill."

Somewhere across the river, in the mass of floodlights camped on the far shore, a Klaxon began blaring. They watched as ant-sized soldiers in toy-sized trucks burst into a sudden frenzy of movement. A voice, distorted by amplification, drifted across the water. None of them could make out the words; all knew what was being said.

Gordon tightened his grip on his wife's hand, not so much to reassure her as to keep himself in check. In his mid-fifties, with hair now more gray than brown and a face that had lines etched from a thousand different crime scenes, he had been a police all of his adult life since leaving the Marine Corps. His career had started in Chicago, a young rookie on a rough force, but just over ten years ago he had moved to Gotham City, a new lieutenant in a department wallowing gleefully in its own corruption.

It was—and he knew this—the single most important decision of his life. Looking out at the city now, he found himself remembering the city then.

He had arrived and almost immediately hated the new job, hated the people he was forced to work with even more. He had hated the crime and apathy and desperation that seemed stamped on every street of his new home. He had hated the arrogance of the public servants who had turned their backs on the people.

But Gordon had fallen immediately in love with Gotham herself, with the vibrancy of the city, with its character and its history. Gotham was an American city, with streets full of people of every color, stores that catered to every culture. Gotham had a pulse, a heartbeat, a soul. Its buildings stood tall and bold, as if reaching for the heavens in the light of day, art deco architecture a block from Bauhaus, a street from neo-classical, abutting the baroque. Gotham had glamour and sass, yet the brassiness of a longshoreman beneath it all. Gordon loved it. Within days of his arrival, he'd known he would never leave, indeed, that he could not. He'd known that Gotham was to be his city. He'd known he would serve her, come what may.

Within a year Gordon had made captain and overseen the purging of one of the most corrupt police forces in the nation's history. He had made new enemies and new allies, and all but destroyed his first marriage. He had met Sarah Essen—the woman whose hand was even now his anchor—and Harvey Dent, the friend who too soon became a foe.

But if those were all important, vital facts to who he was now, there was one other.

His first year in Gotham had been the first year of the Batman, as well.

Sarah gave his hand a squeeze, almost reflexive reassurance, jerking Gordon back from the past. He looked away from the National Guard encampment on the far shore, at the miles of razor wire and tank barricades that had been assembled across the already-mined river, to look at her. Twelve years his junior, twice as pretty as when they'd first met; looking at her he could feel his heart beat just a little faster. For a moment, the temptation to bury his face in her hair, to hide in the familiar feel of her skin, was overpowering.

But it wouldn't do, and he knew that. Not in front of his people, certainly. They were looking to him for leadership and strength, and, after all, he was *still* the Commissioner of Police.

At least for another seven minutes or so.

His people. It almost made him smile as he looked at the line on either side of him, at those cops who, like himself, had decided to stay behind for one reason or another.

At the far end of the line, Renee Montoya, Detective Third Class and the only other woman in the rooftop group aside from Sarah. Born and raised in Gotham, the child of Dominican immigrants,

Montoya was one of the best on his force, and he had a paternal pride in her. He had promoted her himself, overseen her assignments and training. At times, he felt as fond of Renee Montoya as he did of his own daughter, Barbara.

Standing beside Montoya, her partner Detective Sergeant Harvey Bullock. Sarah liked to call him the Bulldog—never when Harvey could hear, of course—and Gordon thought that it was more than just an apt physical description of the overweight cop. Nobody more stubborn, nobody more tenacious, nobody more potentially offensive in the whole of the GCPD than Bullock. A hell of a police.

Then Sarah Essen, Lieutenant. Their marriage had seen more rocks dug up than a quarry, and there were times when Gordon wondered if they kept returning to each other simply because no one else would have them. She was more than his wife and more than his friend and more than his lover; Sarah, he thought, was his equal.

How could he not love her most of all for that?

That was on his left. On his right, the remaining two of the GCPD hierarchy. Hugh Foley, the latest addition to the GCPD officer corps. A lieutenant in Vice/Bunko, Gordon knew Foley as a competent administrator, good with the public and the media. Quiet in the ranks, one of the many men under Gordon's command, hardly distinguishable from so many of the others. Looking at him now, Gordon had to admit he had no idea why Foley had decided to stay behind with the rest of them.

And then the end of the line, where Captain William Pettit, head of the GCPD Quick Response Team, stood, binoculars in one hand, watch in the other. Another former soldier, Pettit had served in Gotham's own war for several years now, responsible for training and commanding a unit where hostage takings and shoot-outs were only twenty-four hours apart on a good day. As far as tactical support, Gordon couldn't think of anyone better.

We six, Gordon thought. We six, and down below another four dozen wearing the Blue, and what the hell are we thinking anyway? Do we really think we can make a difference?

"Five minutes," Pettit said.

"Suppose it's too late to change our minds about this, huh?" Foley asked.

"Not if you run for it. You sprint—"

"—you might make it as far as Brady Avenue before the charges start going off," Bullock said, the sneer in his voice. "Go for it, Foley."

"Quiet," Gordon said.

Sarah gave his hand another squeeze.

The problem, as far as Helena Bertinelli was concerned, was with her watch.

It was a good watch, and she knew that. A Rolex, shock-resistant and waterproof and accurate like you wouldn't believe. That wasn't the problem.

It was that she had to wear the damn thing on her wrist, even when she was in costume. Even when she was the Huntress. There was just no other accessible place to put it where she could reach it in a hurry. In a pouch on her belt, for instance, would require both having a free hand and the time to reach it. So it stayed on her wrist, below the launcher on her forearm that fired razor-sharp spikes with a blast of compressed air, and she had long ago resigned herself to all the problems that created; Helena couldn't even count how many times she'd had to have the watch crystal repaired. Not to mention the pain that came from blocking a punch with a lump of metal wrapped around your wrist.

The Batman, she was certain, did not wear a watch to work.

No, he had some fancy heads-up display in that Kevlar-lined cowl of his, something that kept perfect time, tied to the atomic clock in Colorado, and that was visible day or night but never obscured his vision. All Helena had behind the domino mask she wore as the Huntress were third-generation starlight lenses, and they only worked half the time.

The Batman didn't have any of these problems. The Batman had all of the cool equipment, and all the training to use it.

And what the Batman had he shared only with a chosen few, and long ago he had made it clear that Helena Bertinelli was not one of those. Sure, they were both vigilantes in a city where crime was as common as cars, but as far as he was concerned, the similarities ended there. She wasn't Robin and she wasn't Nightwing and she wasn't welcome in the club, and that, it seemed, was that.

He had laid it all out for her once, almost two years before, when she had been crouching on the roof of a warehouse overlooking Miller Harbor. Surveillance on a group of mafia soldiers, getting ready to move some heroin off the docks. She hadn't even known he was there until he'd spoken, making her jump half out of her costume.

"Huntress," he'd said, just the one word to start, and the tone of it made the hair on the back of her neck stand. Then he'd looked pointedly at the crossbow she was holding.

"I've got this," Helena had answered. "I don't need your help."

"No one dies tonight," he'd said. Just like that. Just like he was laying down the law.

It had made her angry, suddenly, the judgment in his voice, the command. "Unlike you, I shoot back."

"That's the problem," the Batman had said, already turning away.

"Don't do that! Don't walk away from me!" She'd gotten to her feet without thinking, blowing the hiding place, blowing the hours of surveillance. "I've been out here every night for a year! We do the same thing! How dare you presume to judge me?"

The movement had been so quick she hadn't even seen it, the blur of cape so fast it might have been shadow. And then the crossbow was out of her hand and he'd tossed it across the rooftop, not bothering to look, face-to-face with her. It was the first time she'd been that close to him, been able to see that there truly was a man beneath the cowl. His jaw was strong, and his lips thin, drawn tight as he spoke.

"You kill," the Batman had hissed.

She'd surprised herself by finding her voice. "Yes."

"Not in my city."

"Is that why you don't like me? That when some four-time loser with murder on his mind pulls a gun on me, I'm not afraid to drop him? Is that it?"

His jaw had clenched further. It was like ice when he spoke. "Yes."

"That's not what this is about!"

"That's *all* that this is about," he'd said, and the tone had stunned her, the way his voice had dropped, and once again she could imagine the man beneath the cowl. But before she'd been able to respond he'd already turned, and then was gone, dropping off the roof with a snapping of his cape and a flutter that . . . well, that honestly had sounded like bat wings.

Helena had known better than to try to follow him, and that had been that for a while, until only a year ago when the Malfatti thing had come up and she'd found herself sharing the case with the Batman's protégé, Nightwing. They had ended up teaming together by accident more than anything else, Nightwing coming up from his usual beat of Blüdhaven—sixty miles south of Gotham—to cover for the Batman who was mysteriously out of town on business. Before she'd known what had happened, they were sharing clues and facts.

Then they'd shared her bed.

After the case was done, she'd told herself it was a one-time thing. They had both been alone in Gotham, and it was a thrill and a comfort and nothing more. Certainly, Nightwing had tried to be a gentleman about the brief affair, which in its own way was pretty funny. He'd refused to even let slip his real name, which she had teased him about mercilessly. There they'd been, for God's sake, masks as off as they could get, and still he'd tried to protect his identity.

She knew why. She knew it wasn't for him. It was for the Batman. Whoever he really was, Nightwing would rather die than betray that confidence. She hadn't pressed. She respected that.

Still, she found herself thinking about Nightwing more often than she'd ever thought she would. Even now, she wondered where he was.

She realized she'd been staring at her watch for over a minute now, not registering what the hands were telling her.

Five to midnight.

Five minutes until all hell breaks loose, she thought. Five minutes until Gotham City becomes persona non grata to the rest of the U.S. of A.

She let the cuff fall back into place, smiling despite herself.

Like me.

It wasn't strictly analogous, she knew that. But she felt a perverse camaraderie with Gotham, suddenly. They were both alone, they were both unwanted, and both would fight on against the odds. She wrapped her cape around herself a little tighter, trying to stay warm, then leaned back into the shadows.

Not in my city.

She checked her watch again.

Three minutes to go.

Not your city any longer, she thought. Not after midnight. After midnight, this concrete jungle becomes a truly savage place, and the creatures that walk it will be different beasts entirely. After midnight there's no Gotham City, only a No Man's Land.

She touched the cross at her throat, the one part of her costume as the Huntress that carried over into the life of Helena Bertinelli. She said a quick Our Father.

Then she took a deep breath and prepared to go hunting.

The voices were getting to him, which was vaguely puzzling since, every day and for as long as he could recall, the voices had always been his. But he was relatively sure that the voices he was hearing now, though of course they concerned him, were not, actually, his own.

He turned his head on his pillow and listened.

Yep.

Voices. In the hall, outside the cells.

"Keep it down out there!" he shouted. "Some of us have to go to work in the morning!"

Somewhere outside, down the hall, someone laughed. Whether it was one of the simpleton guards or another of his comrades in arms, he wasn't certain.

"You're too kind," he said, dryly.

The cell was dark—the lights went off at 9:00 P.M., rain or shine, didn't matter what you might be doing at the time—and no illumination leaked through the door, but he guessed it had to be near midnight. Once, way back when, after that damned winged rodent—and honestly the most *unappreciative* audience *ever*—had captured him, he'd been put in a cell with a window. The window had been barred, of course, but at least at night he could see the stars, and when he stood on the commode he could look down at the grounds. And whenever he had slipped while on the commode, his foot had gotten stuck in the toilet, and that had been funny. *Really* funny.

Toilet jokes were always funny, after all.

Then he had pushed Dr. Nybakken's head through the bars in an attempt to remove his ears, to sort of, you know, peel them off. It had worked, but the doctor's skull had been crushed as a result, which was actually doubly funny, and worth it. The look on the guard's face when he came in that time and saw the doctor just dangling there, death rattle and all, limbs jerking around all crazy like that. Then the guard had turned and seen him sitting there on his cot, looking innocent as could be. Just the Joker, minding his own business.

And wearing Dr. Nybakken's ears, of course.

Now *that* was funny.

The memory of it made Joker laugh.

None of the voices told him to shut up.

He pivoted off the bed, then did a pratfall while getting up, tripping over his own feet and taking a header into the far wall. It was still pitch-black and there was no one to see it, but it was worth a laugh, and Joker thought he pulled it off quite well.

"Thank you, ladies and gentlemen," he said, sincerity flooding his voice. "I'll be here all week."

Springing up, he dusted himself off and went for the door. He put his hands out in front of him, thinking to settle himself against it, to feel for the seam in the center, eye-level, where the little sliding surveillance window was. He didn't put too much pressure on the door at all.

But it swung open, and the shift took him utterly by surprise, and he did another pratfall, this one unintentional, out into the corridor.

"Clumsy," Harvey Dent told him.

Joker got up quickly, then exaggeratedly dusted himself off. Harvey's presence in the hall surprised him. Normally, when Harvey was in the hall, there were orderlies in hot pursuit. With cattle prods, more often than not.

But the hallway was empty.

"Harv," Joker said, extending an arm and slapping the larger man on the back. "What the hell is going on here, old son?"

Harvey reached and removed Joker's hand as if it were coated with poison, then turned to look at him full on. Joker got his big grin out, fixing it in place. He needed it, because, honestly, Harvey was crazy, and you could literally see it on his face. Back before the dawn of time, Harvey Dent had been the Gotham City D.A., and then a mobster—Joker couldn't remember who it was, Marcelli, Marconi, Macaroni, didn't matter—had thrown a lovely bottle of perfectly good acid at him. Harvey, not being a total fool, had turned away, but the result was that half of his face—the left side—was puckered and red and purple and all greasy crinkles, even around his left eye, which bulged like someone was trying to shove it out of his head from within. The acid had even caught his hair, burning the scalp so that the only thing that grew on that side was wiry and white.

Joker had no problem with that side of Harvey Dent's face.

It was the other side, the one that was still handsome and charming, blue eyed and brown haired, with the noble brow and strong nose, that was the side he couldn't stand.

Frankly, it made Joker's bowels rumble.

Harvey Dent, or Two-Face as Harvey preferred half the time, glared back at him.

"Shouldn't there be an alarm by now?" Joker asked.

Harvey shook his head and started down the hall. Joker, after a moment, followed. It was awfully quiet, he decided. Even the voices —the other voices—had stopped.

He couldn't help noticing that a lot of the cell doors were open and their occupants missing, and he moved on, checking the names. The Ventriloquist was gone—probably searching for a log to carve into Scarface, the dummy gangster that was a man in his own right; so was Roman Sionis, another member of the Horribly Scarred Brigade, who was so damn hideous he normally wore a mask made from—Joker loved this part—his mother's ebony funeral coffin, and thus went around telling everyone to call him Black Mask.

Joker stopped at Pamela Isley's room, peering in, perplexed. Pam was a kick—Poison Ivy, lovely girl, a kiss that could kill—but the thing was, the cell was bare. Not even her appalling fern that she kept in that old pot, or the single rose that the doctors let her keep. All gone.

"Um, Harvey?" Joker asked. "Where's Pam?"

"Come on," Dent said, ignoring the question. "I need to find a coin."

Joker sighed and followed. Find a coin, find a coin, it was always the same. "Check O'Malley's desk. I heard him saying something about laundry money after I came back from my last shock therapy."

Harvey grunted, moving down the hall and stopping at the orderly's desk.

"Now, shock therapy," Joker went on. "That's a buzz, if you get my gist. I mean, it'll really make you sit up at attention, really get you charged up for your day. Shock treatment, in fact, has to be——"

"Shut up," Harvey said, but the tone had changed, and Joker saw that now, in his hand, was a nice and shiny half-dollar. It made him grin. Harvey had finally left, and now Two-Face was in the house.

"What was O'Malley doing with your coin?" Joker asked.

"This isn't *my* coin. This is *a* coin. It'll do."

"Where's *your* coin?"

Two-Face looked wistfully past Joker's shoulder, a look that Joker found more than a little silly. "Gave it to a cop," he said.

Joker laughed. "Oh, Harvey, stop it! You *gave* it to a cop? Which one?"

"You know Montoya? Detective Montoya?"

"He's the fat slob one who smells like Spamburgers and is always smoking stogies?"

"No, that's her partner, Bullock. I'm talking about the other one, the lady one, in Major Crimes."

Joker thought, wrinkling his brow. When he wrinkled his brow, he thought perhaps he could get his forehead to touch his nose, but that didn't work. Then his brow smoothed.

"Oh, yeah, her," Joker said. "She's mighty fine, ain't she, Harv? Nudge nudge, wink wink, know what I mean?"

Two-Face took a quick step and grabbed Joker by the collar of his shirt, pulling him in and up so that their noses were almost touching. Joker grinned maniacally, not so much because he was maniacal, but because there wasn't much else he could do. Of the two of them, Two-Face was the stronger by far, and in a straight battle of strength against strength, Joker knew he'd be a loser every time. But then again, Joker would never stand for a fair fight. Fighting fair wasn't funny; it was boring.

Two-Face growled at him. "You talk about her like that, I'll feed you each of your teeth. Rectally."

Joker kissed the tip of Two-Face's nose. "Tag, you're it."

Two-Face turned the growl to a snarl and pushed him away, then flipped the coin in his hand. Joker waited respectfully for the result. Two-Face caught the coin, slapping it down on the back of his hand.

"Follow me," Two-Face said.

"Oh, of course!" said Joker, stopping just long enough at the desk to find himself a pair of scissors. He snipped the air with them experimentally a couple of times, working his way down the hall, and wondering what Two-Face would do when they hit the security doors. Those doors, those were always the problem in each and every escape plan, the great massive steel things that slammed shut automatically when the alarm sounded. Four hundred pounds apiece, if not more, and Joker knew that personally. They'd swung shut on him on more than one occasion.

He was vaguely irritated to see that the doors, were, in fact, open.

"Someone," Joker remarked, "forgot to close the door."

"You're an idiot," Two-Face said without looking back.

Joker tried to remember how to look wounded, failed, and contemplated burying the scissors in Two-Face's back.

"Don't," Two-Face warned.

"Don't what?"

"Don't stab me with the scissors, Clown."

"Clown? I'm not the one who looks like Pruneface!" Joker said. After a beat, just long enough to set up the gag, he added, "Ever read *Dick Tracy*?"

"Shut," said Two-Face, "up."

Joker snipped the air again, continued to follow Two-Face down the hall, then out into reception, at which point a couple of things struck him in quick succession. First, no one was working reception. No nurses. No orderlies. No security guards. No Dr. Jeremiah Arkham. Second, it wasn't simply that the asylum seemed to be empty, he was now getting the distinct impression that it was deserted. And third, and perhaps most important, the front doors were wide open.

"This has to be some sort of joke," he said.

"No Man's Land," Two-Face said. "The earthquake. Gotham City totaled. Any of these ring a bell?"

Joker frowned and snipped at the air again, thoughtfully. He didn't like being condescended to, but the problem was that Two-Face was almost always condescending, and he had the impression that if he stabbed him now, he wouldn't get the answer to his questions.

Two-Face continued. "Government's called it quits on Gotham. Closed off the city. Blowing the bridges at midnight."

Something tickled at the back of Joker's brain for a moment, and he chewed his lip, trying to draw the idea out. It wasn't coming, though, so Joker turned to the nearest wall and bashed his forehead against the cinder block.

"Ah!" Joker said. "What Dr. Quinzel said!"

"Who?" Two-Face demanded.

Joker rubbed his forehead, trying to massage the rest of the memory free. The earthquake, Dr. Quinzel had talked about it in one of their last sessions. About how the city was a mess, how the asylum was going to be abandoned. Then Dr. Quinzel had cried, because she didn't want to leave Joker. She told him that Dr. Arkham was calling institutions all over the country, trying to get the patients placed in new facilities. But no one wanted to take them, Joker remembered. No one wanted Poison Ivy or Two-Face or Joker.

He tried to get his lower lip to quiver with the memory. And now, here they were. Well, at least here Joker and Two-Face were. Who cared about Poison Ivy?

Or Dr. Quinzel for that matter?

Joker checked the clock on the wall over the receptionist's desk. His favorite, Betsy, wasn't there. That was a pity, because now that he had the scissors he'd have really liked to talk with her about the way she cut her hair.

The clock read 11:58. Because it was dark out, Joker felt safe in adding, "P.M." to the calculation.

"Everyone with an ounce of sense has left town already," Two-Face was saying. "Dr. Arkham programmed the doors to open at 11:55. Figures this way we're all stuck in Gotham, can't get off the island."

"Can we?" Joker asked hopefully.

"Not unless you want an Apache gunship firing missiles down your throat, no."

Joker snipped at the air again, crestfallen, then suddenly brightened. "Wait! You mean . . . ?"

Two-Face nodded slowly, as if trying to teach a very slow child.

"It's all ours?" Joker finished, awed.

"You got it, buddy."

"Gotham?"

"All of it."

"Ours?"

"Yes."

Joker craned his neck slowly to look past Two-Face, out at the barren grounds of Arkham Asylum. Beyond the fence, through the trees, down the hill, he could see where the Sprang River was flowing beneath the Schwartz Bridge. He felt his heart starting to race. All thoughts of stabbing Two-Face to death had vanished.

"And Batman?" Joker was almost afraid to ask.

"He's staying. He has to." Two-Face's bulging left eye glinted with barely contained glee. "He's too crazy to leave. He's locked in here with us."

For a moment, Joker honestly thought he might cry with the joy of it. The whole city, his to play with. No government, that meant no cops. No cops, that meant no law. And no law . . .

"Victims," he sighed happily.

Two-Face scowled. "You're crazy. I'm going. See you around, Clown."

Joker watched as Two-Face went down the steps, crossed the manicured lawn to the front gate, and then disappeared from view. Joker sighed again and stepped out into the cold air, settling down at the top of the steps. He snipped at the air dreamily, gazing at the city.

"I'll wait awhile," he said to no one in particular.

Pettit began counting down from five.

Across the river, half a second later, Gordon heard the amplified voice doing the same.

"One," Pettit said, and before he was finished they saw the flash as the Brown Bridge exploded, the demolition charges firing in perfect sequence. Farther upriver, they heard other explosions, saw the light as the TriGate Bridge blew. The Gotham River bubbled as beneath it, each of the subway and rail tunnels suddenly imploded, water rushing to fill the space.

The last electric lights winked out.

The sound of the detonations echoed through the broken streets.

From within the city, there was absolute silence.

Gordon let go of his wife's hand and stepped forward, then turned to face the line of people—the line of *his* people. From inside his jacket he produced his shield, holding it so that they all could see.

Make it good, he thought.

"Gotham City is gone," he said. "There's no such thing as the GCPD from here on out.

"But we're still police, and we're still here. So it's up to us, now, to make it work. It's up to us alone to keep what we have, what we value, safe.

"No Man's Land won't last. You know it, I know it. Eventually, Washington will come to its senses. Eventually, those bridges will be rebuilt.

"Until then, this shield—all our shields—they're only worth the person wearing them."

He pinned his badge to his shirt, feeling the heavy metal drag on the fabric.

"As long as we can wear these, we'll make it," he said.

For a moment no one moved, and Gordon thought that he'd tanked it. He'd never been good at public speaking. Even after ten years of media hounds looking for sound bites he'd never gotten it down.

Then Sarah was pinning her badge to her shirt, then Pettit, then Montoya, and suddenly all of them were wearing their gold shields, all looking at him, waiting for what would happen next.

"Time to protect and to serve," Gordon said, and he headed for the door off the roof, back downstairs.

On the way his eyes went to the broken Bat-Signal, where the shattered bulb sat in dark shadow.

Don't let us down, he thought.

We need you now more than ever.

PART ONE

ORACLE

[NOTE: I'm truncating here, so if it seems a little choppy, that's why. Most of the last 288 entries have been mix-and-match, three months of getting my bearings and pretty much doing what we've all been, just trying to figure out what the hell is going on.

In other words, it's a summary of sorts, and I make no pretense to artistry here. Cut your girl a break. :-)]

Dear Dad—

After ninety days of No Man's Land, I have come to the following conclusion:

Anarchy is mankind's natural state.

I don't think even the most jaded social anthropologist could've anticipated how quickly it would happen, how quickly the "tribes" would form. Within one week of Black Monday—the day the bridges blew and NML began—this block alone, where I now write, changed hands three times, gangs that came and went so quickly I don't even remember their names. Since then it's settled down somewhat, as I understand it has all across the city. As of this moment, I *think* I live in Street Demonz territory, but I can't be sure. Either them or the LoBoys.

The difference is academic, because aside from their tags and colors, their rule is pretty much the same. They tromp along the streets, demanding that everyone they see give them either food or goods in exchange for their "protection." That's about as evolved as they've gotten—they've yet to truly discover the entrepreneurial spirit, unlike many of their compatriots throughout the city.

Ah, yes, their compatriots, Gotham's own Rogues Gallery. God knows how it happened, but someone let them out of Arkham sometime during that first week. So, in addition to the poor, the disenfranchised, and the stubborn, we've got the lunatics roaming the streets. I've been trying to keep tabs on them. . . .

Which I suppose begs the question, how exactly am I doing that? I haven't been outside of the Clock Tower in months now, through no fault of my own. The elevators are, of course, shut down, and though I like to think that I'm in excellent shape, there's no way I'm going to get myself and the chair down twenty floors, then back up again. And even if I were to make it to the lobby, then what? Wheelchairs and broken asphalt don't exactly mix, especially when you add fallen masonry to the equation.

Answer is, I've got people loyal to me. Some of them I had before the quake, agents on the ground who run errands and gather intelligence. Oracle's Eyes, I've taken to calling them.

Right now I've got eight of them, all outfitted with two-way radios, maps of the city, and emergency rations. They report to me daily, either in person or via radio, and they trust me and I trust them. If I need anything, they're who I turn to. . . .

—EXCERPT—

. . . there's one agent, though, she's something else. Can't be older than 16, if a day. Pretty young woman, Eurasian, very smart. And functionally mute, in that she seems incapable of using language. I've gone through all of my resources trying to determine if there is a language or code she might know, but it's gotten us nowhere. And she has been singularly unhelpful in aiding me, offering only the odd grunt and groan and whistle. No words at all. I don't know if it's a psychological or physiological trauma, but I'm beginning to suspect she was never *taught* how to speak or read or write. I've been working with her a couple times a week, trying to teach her some basic verbal skills, but it's slow going. She's been unable to give me her name—though whether that's because she doesn't have one, doesn't know it, or doesn't like it, I've no clue.

I've taken to calling her Cassandra.

Communications difficulties with her notwithstanding, Cassandra has become, in the last couple months, one of my most reliable people. She's fast and strong and very sneaky, and to top it all off she's fairly imaginative, so that her reports end up being a somewhat entertaining game of charades, aided by scraps of paper and pencils. She's a horrible artist, but I understand her concepts more often than not, so we're getting by.

She was in here this morning—she's actually the only one I've let into the Control Room. Reported that she had been in TriCorner, and I asked if she'd seen you, showed her that picture of us from when I graduated GSU, and she nodded and smiled. Reported that she'd seen you yelling at some of your men.

"That's him all right," I told her.

I suppose you know this already, too, but Cassandra tells me that the people in your territory don't refer to you all as the GCPD anymore. Now you're the Blue Boys, with a tag and everything. I have to say, the thought of you spray-painting the side of a building with *your* gang's tag, that made me laugh aloud. . . .

—EXCERPT—

. . . taken this long, but I now have a working map. Aside from where I am in Old Gotham, which, as I've already explained, changes hands depending on the day of the week, I've been able to locate some others:

1. Two-Face is confirmed at City Hall, either residing there or in the Criminal Courts Building. It makes a strange kind of sense that he would head there. By all accounts his numbers are small, and he seems to be behaving himself thus far. . . .

2. Scarface and the Ventriloquist have set up shop somewhere on the West Side, below the Meat District. Scarface has anywhere between five and fifteen enforcers, all of whom are armed. He's had work gangs clearing rubble since Day 22, looking to salvage anything he can. I suspect he's mostly after food and equipment, those essentials that we all need to survive, and that are all in short supply. . . .

3. Black Mask is proving to be harder to locate. From what little I've been able to learn, he's wandering the city, gathering people to him. To what end I don't know. Unlike the others thus far, he seems to have no fixed "territory" to speak of, and no interest in claiming any, either. I can't tell if he's just gone all the way around the bend, or if he's honestly searching for something. . . .

4. Poison Ivy has apparently disappeared into Robinson Park. That's all I know.

5.   Nobody knows where Joker is. I suppose hoping he died in the quake is too much to ask for, so the only conclusion I can draw is that he's biding his time. . . .

—EXCERPT—

. . . bringing us to the Penguin. Oswald Cobblepot was out on bail pending trial for trafficking in illegal goods at the time of the quake, as you know. In the ensuing chaos he disappeared. Now he's back, and I have to confess, I think he's adapted to the No Man's Land faster than any of the rest of us did.

He's set himself up in the remains of the Davenport Tower, in—surprise—the Fashion District. From there, he's running a combination bazaar and cabaret, and apparently is *the* man to see if you're looking for a particular item. My agents tell me that, unlike just about everyone else in town, he *will* accept payment in the form of cash and/or precious objects, i.e., art, jewelry, etc. Since these are things of no value whatsoever to the rest of the NML, he's doing booming business.

Why he's bothering to collect such items I can't begin to guess, but I have a sneaking suspicion that Penguin, unlike the rest of us, knows a way out of here. One of my agents, Vanessa, has even suggested that Penguin is working an active pipeline to the rest of the world, shipping out his booty in exchange for supplies with which he can then trade for more goods, and so on. Seems reasonable, but I've found no evidence to prove the assertion.

And while I'm talking about the criminals, I might as well bring up Huntress. I've never been sure how much you know about the newest addition to Gotham's Vigilante Set, but I am *not* a fan of hers. For the record, her real name is Helena Bertinelli, and yes, you read that right. The same Helena Bertinelli whose father was Don Franco Bertinelli, *capo di tutti capi* of Gotham's Five Families way back when. The same Helena Bertinelli who watched her whole family murdered before her eyes when she was eight years old.

You might think that, given the similarities between what happened to her and what happened to Bruce, I'd be more inclined to cut her some slack on the vigilante front. But that's where the similarity between Huntress and Batman ends, Dad; for Helena Bertinelli, it's about vendetta; for Bruce Wayne, it's about making certain that no one ever, ever again suffers what he went through.

I've received a report stating that Huntress has confined her zone to one block in the Upper East Side, just away from the harbor. Not coincidentally, this is the block in which she makes her home, so I'm less inclined to believe she's discovered altruism as much as enlightened self-interest. . . .

—EXCERPT—

Which brings us, logically, to Him.

Ninety days, and no sign. Ninety days, and no Batman.

I've told my agents to keep an eye out, an ear open, that I want to know the moment there's the faintest whisper that he's on the move. He's got to be here, I know it. But what he's waiting for, I've got no idea.

He wouldn't abandon us, Dad.

That's what I keep telling myself, at any rate.

This morning Vanessa called to report a new tag in Dooley Square, one she hadn't seen before. Dooley Square. On my map, that's Xhosa territory, an orange tag of crossed spears.

"No," Vanessa says to me. "Not this one."

"Well, whose is it?"

"His," she says. "It's the Bat, boss."

ONE

IT HAD TAKEN THEM A WEEK OF WORK to get this far, digging out the site only at night, trying to stay safe from watching eyes. The two moved rubble and dug in silence, working mostly by feel. Each of them had more cuts and scrapes on their hands than they could count, and their fingers were numb from the effort and the cold of the air and the bite of the frozen snow.

The elder of the two, Paolo, was only twenty-one. His brother, Nicky, was nineteen. They had arrived in Gotham during the summer, immigrating illegally with their parents, and for a while it had looked good for all of them.

Then the earthquake came, and the tenement they were living in, the room they shared with two other families, was buried under twenty tons of concrete and iron from the building next door. The bodies were never recovered.

When No Man's Land came, they stayed more out of fear than anything else. There had been soldiers on the bridges, on the roads, in the tunnels. Soldiers with guns, and both Paolo and Nicky had bad memories of soldiers with guns from their childhood in Colombia. As far as they were concerned, the soldiers meant one of two things: either they'd be shot, or they'd be deported. And being deported, that amounted to being shot.

So they stayed.

It had to be past midnight when Nicky heard his brother speak for the first time in hours, the hoarse whisper of excitement.

"I found it," Paolo hissed in Spanish. "I found a way in, look."

Nicky moved, checking where his brother pointed. It was a clear night, with half a moon, and in the light and past the shadows he could see where Paolo was indicating, a small opening, just big enough to wriggle through. And inside, the prize, a whole Jiffy Junior convenience store, a mother lode of treasure. Canned goods, batteries, flashlights, aspirin, soda, chips, bread, cigarettes, beer . . .

"You remember what we do," Paolo whispered. "You go in, you grab what you can, we cover it up again, then take it to Penguin. He'll take care of us. But we don't tell him where we found it, we keep this our secret."

"I remember," Nicky snapped. "Of course I remember."

"Keep your voice down."

Nicky frowned, then took the flashlight his brother handed him. It was their prized possession, and they had only turned it on once since they'd found it, just to make certain the batteries worked. Now Nicky held it tightly in one hand as he got on his knees, and crawled through the tiny opening.

The stink inside was awful, and almost immediately he wanted to throw up. He told himself it was spoiled milk and meat, and not a body. He told himself it didn't matter if it was a body, because the dead had it easy right now. He convinced himself to keep going, and managed to work his way out of the hole, dropping down inside the wreckage of the store. His feet splashed in something when he landed, he didn't know what. It was entirely black inside but for the broken circle of moonlight leaking in from above.

Nicky turned on the flashlight, then turned it off again.

Jiffy Junior stores were open twenty-four hours a day, seven days a week. They never closed. That was their motto, he knew that.

There had been customers inside when the earthquake hit.

From above, he heard his brother's voice. "Nicky? Are you all right?"

Nicky tried to answer, caught another whiff of the air, and now there was no way to pretend it was anything but death. He felt his stomach buckle, swallowed hard, and managed the words.

"There are bodies," he told his brother.

"Ignore them," Paolo hissed. "Hurry, Nicky. We don't want to be caught."

"I know that. Shut up, I'm looking."

Paolo shut up.

Nicky switched on the flashlight again, panning the beam carefully past the corpses, toward the fallen racks. He went for the batteries first, then for the cigarette lighters on the counter. He stuffed his pockets full of all the small things he could find, tiny tins of Imodium and aspirin, bandages, matches, whatever would fit, before switching to the backpack. He was smart about it, he thought, taking another backpack, rolling it up tightly and putting it in the first. Everyone needed a backpack in the No Man's Land. Everyone had to carry all their possessions with them.

Then he went to the racks, quickly examining the cans, taking only those that were still sealed. Ravioli, soup, beans, tuna, all into the backpack. Two cans of Soder Cola, and another two cans of Brew Beer. He put more and more into the backpack until he was afraid the seams would split, and only then did he stop, zipping the pack as closed as he could make it, then moving back to the hole.

"I'm coming up," he whispered, pushing the backpack into the opening with a shove. Then he turned back, letting the flashlight track one last time through the store. He switched it off, but the image stayed, the crushed bodies still lit in his mind. He whispered a quick prayer, then climbed back into the hole.

It wasn't Paolo waiting for him when he came out. It was someone else, a big man, bald, and behind him were three others, one of them already going through the backpack, the other two holding Paolo by the arms. In the moonlight, Nicky could see where his brother was bleeding at the mouth, and it made his stomach shrink. Then the big man was pulling him to his feet, and showing him the pointed end of a machete.

"This is Demonz territory," the man said. "You've just been caught stealing. I should cut off your hands, that's what I should do."

Nicky fumbled for the words in English and managed, "It's not stealing."

The big man laughed and shoved him back with his free hand. "Empty your pockets, let's see what you brought us."

Nicky glanced at his brother, saw Paolo's jaw clenched tight, more rage than fear in his eyes. It crept into Nicky, as well.

"No. It's ours."

The man looked at Nicky, surprised at the defiance, then sighed, cutting at the air with the blade. "You just broke Demonz law, kid."

Nicky realized that he was going to die, and started another prayer, hoping to finish it before the machete came back down. He watched the blade go up, the moonlight catching its edge, watched it start to fall.

Then the blade was gone and the man was holding his hand where it was now bleeding, and there had been a noise, something hard hitting something meat. Nicky heard another sound, turned his head toward it, and saw the shape, and his heart stopped for a second, because he knew what it was.

He had never seen it before, no one he knew had, and some people had even told him it was a lie, made up by the police, to scare the criminals.

But Nicky had always known it was true, and he knew what it was.

So did the big man.

The shape moved, passing Nicky faster than a shadow hit by light, and there was another sound, and the big man made a noise of pain, and fell backward.

The shape spoke.

"Leave them alone."

And Nicky thought there was something wrong, then, because he'd never imagined the voice would sound like that.

The big man tried to get up, and the shape moved again, and Nicky heard the snap of another kick. The man made more noise, and then the shape had grabbed him by the shirt, was turning, and the big man was stumbling away while the others stood stunned. Even Paolo, Nicky thought, looked stunned.

But Paolo had never believed.

The shape kept moving, another rustle of shadow, and the gang member who had taken the backpack dropped it, spilling the contents all on the ground. The other Street Demonz, who had been holding Paolo, moved forward, trying to attack.

But you cannot attack a shadow, Nicky thought, and as if to prove him right, their blows landed in empty air. There was another rustle, and the shape was behind them, had one of the men by the arm, had hit him twice in the face, then was pitching him sharply away. Another of the gang members was passing Nicky, as if trying to flee, and the shape turned, and Nicky got a good look then, just for an instant, as the shape reached out as if its arm were impossibly long. The man pitched forward into the street with a cry, then stumbled back up and ran.

The shape pivoted, but the last of the Demonz had already fled.

"Batman," Paolo said.

Nicky tried to find his voice, to say, no, no, not Batman, at least, not like we were told, but the shape was already crouching at the backpack, replacing the spilled cans, then offering the bag to Nicky. When the arms moved, the cape billowed back, and Nicky saw the shape in the shadow, the yellow outline of the bat on the black chest.

A woman's chest.

Nicky took the bag, staring.

"Are you all right?"

He tried to speak, failed utterly, and simply nodded.

"TriCorner is held by the GCPD. You'll be safer there," the woman said, and then she raised an arm and there was a sound, and it was as if the Batwoman were flying away.

Gone. Just like that.

After a time, Nicky looked back to his brother, saw Paolo was still staring up at the sky, where the woman had disappeared. Then Paolo lowered his eyes, and Nicky saw the understanding there, the awe.

Without another word, the boys began heading south, toward TriCorner.

It began to snow.

TWO

THE SNOW HAD STARTED FALLING SOME-
time the previous night, and by morning had accumulated enough that Renee Montoya was afraid of slipping as she made her way from the Blue Boy blockade on Kelso
Avenue, TriCorner, south down Bonafe. It was the third snow in less
than a week, and it made her scowl, made her think the Almighty
was playing games with Gotham in general and her in particular.

Middle of March and it's still snowing.

It wasn't helping her mood.

Montoya sighed, moving forward into the blast of condensation
she had created, trying to figure out what it all meant. The gnawing
in her gut, she knew what it was, it was worry. Trying to articulate
it, that was harder.

It had happened that morning, when she had been checking posts on the east edge of their territory, along Cooper. Essen and Gordon had joined her on the rounds, just making certain everyone had everything they needed. One of the nearly fifty patrol cops who had remained, a young guy named DeFilippis, had caught up to them outside of a ruined music store. He'd been obviously excited, almost jumping up and down.

"Sir! Sir! I've got something to show you!"

Montoya had seen it on the officer's face, the excitement, the dance in the brown eyes. Whatever it was he wanted to show Gordon, DeFilippis was certainly thrilled about it.

"It's over here," DeFilippis had said, indicating a rooftop across the way. "On the roof. Follow me."

So they had all followed, Gordon's brow furrowed in a mixture of amusement and curiosity.

DeFilippis had flown up the stairs, was already on the roof when they stepped out into the light snow. The building had been some sort of insurance office, brick and old, and relatively solid. From the roof, there was a nice view of TriCorner, even with the weather.

"Well?" Gordon had asked.

With a flourish, DeFilippis had yanked back the tarp concealing a small heap of metal in the center of the roof. Maybe four feet in diameter, a makeshift searchlight, and over the cracked lens, cobbled together from scraps of broken metal, the unmistakable shape of the bat.

Montoya had recognized what it was instantly, started grinning. Unlike most of the GCPD, she had seen the Batman up close, knew he was real. And she understood what the young cop was trying to do, and she understood exactly why it mattered. She hadn't been out of the academy a week before she'd snuck up to the roof of Central to see the real Bat-Signal, just to prove to herself it was there, that when things got really bad, it would burn in the sky.

DeFilippis had started talking, excitedly throwing a switch. There was a grinding of a small motor and a crackling, and the light had come on, and in daylight it wasn't much to see, but that didn't matter at all, really. The light glowed pale and weak, but come the night, everyone looking would be able to see it.

"I used a low voltage quartz bulb," DeFilippis was saying in a rush. "And then some car batteries that still had charge, mounted the whole thing on a steering mechanism and then routed it through this switch and——"

"No," Gordon had said, and the tone in his voice had frozen Montoya in place. Essen had given her husband a look of almost anger, but before she could speak the Commissioner had moved forward, two long, quick strides and was nearly on top of the light.

Then he'd raised his foot and brought it down on the fragile, cracked glass, and turned the lens into a thousand shards. The bulb crackled and went out.

Montoya had been utterly stunned.

Gordon had stepped back, a half hop, setting his foot again on the roof. Specks of blood were visible on the cuff of his pants. He'd turned and leveled his gaze at DeFilippis, whose mouth was still open in surprise.

"We don't need this," Gordon had growled. "We don't need it because he's not coming, do you understand that, Officer DeFilippis? He's not coming!"

DeFilippis had been speechless, then drew himself to attention and answered, "Yes, sir. I understand, sir."

"Good."

"Commissioner," Montoya had said. "How do you know?"

"He'd have been here by now."

"But maybe he hasn't shown up because we haven't called."

Gordon had looked at her sadly, pushing his glasses back up the bridge of his nose. Essen's mouth had formed a tight line as she focused on her husband. Montoya could see the disapproval in her look.

"No, Renee," Gordon said. "He gave up on Gotham like everyone else. He took the easy way out."

Montoya had looked at Essen for help, but Sarah had simply shaken her head almost imperceptibly. Don't, the look had said, it's not worth it, and Renee realized that Essen had had this conversation with her husband before.

Renee had tried anyway.

"But . . . wouldn't it be a good idea to make people think he was around, at least?"

"Why bother?" Gordon had responded. "Why raise false hope?"

Essen's look had said, I told you so.

Before Montoya could think of a counter, Gordon had stepped back, making certain he could address all of them, DeFilippis included. "We have to make our way through this without him," the Commissioner had said. "No more myths and legends. This time it's up to us. This time it's the GCPD that puts the fear into the criminals. We're taking back Gotham. Us. Understood?"

Montoya and DeFilippis both answered, "Yes, sir." Essen hadn't moved, all but glaring at her husband.

Gordon's frown had deepened, and he'd headed back for the stairs, DeFilippis following. Montoya had moved next to Essen, keeping her voice low as they followed the men down, anxious for an explanation. If Jim Gordon, as Commissioner, was her boss, then Sarah Essen, as the Major Crimes Unit shift commander, was her leader, and Renee Montoya trusted the lieutenant implicitly.

"Why is he so upset about Batman?" Montoya had asked.

"Be careful about that," Essen had cautioned. "It's gotten so you can't even say the name in his presence."

"I thought . . . I thought they were friends."

Essen had stopped on the stairs, looking at Montoya. "They were."

"And?"

"And it's been three months, Renee." Essen had checked the stairs, making certain her husband was out of earshot. "No Batman. Jim's not unreasonably feeling abandoned."

"Maybe . . . maybe there's a reason, you know. . . ."

Essen had sighed. "Does it matter? The damage is done. Friends have to trust one another, don't they? And Jim doesn't trust him anymore."

From outside, they'd heard Gordon's bellow, questioning if they were coming.

"Right down," Essen had shouted back, then smiled sympathetically at Montoya.

"Do you think he's right?" Montoya had asked. "Do you think Batman is really gone?"

"If he's not, I don't envy the person who gets to break the news to Jim," Essen had said, and then turned and continued down.

. . .

That was the thing, Montoya thought, that was the thing of it all. The Batman had betrayed their trust.

She hadn't really considered that he was gone until that moment on the roof when Gordon had said the words. Her experiences with the Batman had been limited at best. She'd seen him a handful of times at crime scenes, a shadow that spoke to the officer in charge and then vanished. Once he'd even spoken directly to her, asked if a ballistics report had come back.

Given that, it wasn't unusual for her to go months without seeing a sign of him.

But if the Commissioner hadn't seen him either, well, that meant something else.

She tried to imagine what it would be like to call the Batman your friend. She couldn't.

No wonder Gordon feels betrayed, she thought, digging her hands deeper into the pockets of her parka. She kept her head down, watching her footing as she picked her way through the rubble-strewn street.

A fire was burning in a metal garbage can on the corner, a small group huddled around it, and Montoya exchanged a thin smile with them, counting her blessings. She, at least, had good winter clothes to keep her warm, and she knew that, in the grand scheme of No Man's Land, she could count herself lucky on that front.

Since the beginning of the month, Day 62, she had personally seen the bodies of eleven people claimed by the cold.

But the Blue Boys—she hated the name—had been lucky. Outfitting themselves with what was left of the GCPD's stores, settling in TriCorner, they'd started out the NML ahead of the game. Clothes, food, shelter, even ammunition . . . while none of those things were abundant, at least in the Blue Boy neck of the woods, all were available. Elsewhere on the island, she knew, others weren't as lucky.

Not for the first time, she thanked God that her parents and brother had made it out before the bridges had been blown.

Bullock was waiting for her outside the house, talking with the two men on duty. Each of the guards was dressed in damaged riot gear, the dark navy fabric of the GCPD torn and peeling in places on the armor, showing the hardened plastic and Kevlar beneath. Each

held a shotgun casually in their hands. Montoya wondered if the
shotguns were loaded; her own sidearm was empty, had been now for
weeks, and Pettit was diligent in rationing ammunition. According
to the QRT leader, bullets were now worth their weight in gold.

One of the guards noted her approach, and Bullock turned to
greet her, pulling the stick he'd been gnawing on from his mouth. He
was long past the nicotine withdrawal stage of his stogie habit, she
knew that, and suspected he sucked on the surrogate cigars more to
maintain his image than anything else. He turned his head and spat
out a sliver of wood, then grinned at her.

"Howdy, Pard," Bullock said.

"Howdy, Pard," Montoya responded. "I'm late?"

Harvey shrugged, a gesture that had become more pronounced
with the twenty-odd pounds he'd lost since the start of the NML.
The weight loss, not unexpected, had still been sudden enough that
his skin had yet to catch up. Beneath the now-baggy clothes, she
thought he looked more like a bloodhound than ever before.

"Waiting on you," he said. "How's the Kelso Blockade?"

"Fine. Some Street Demonz formed up at the end of the opposite block last night, but nothing came of it." Montoya gestured to
the house with a tilt of her head. "Shall we?"

"Ladies first."

She grinned at that, because it was so far from the truth. For as
long as she'd partnered with Harvey Bullock, gender had never been
an issue. She'd always appreciated that of him. He'd never cared she
was a woman, that she was Latina, that Spanish was her first tongue,
or that she was young—almost too young by department standards—for a detective. Harvey had only cared that she could do the
job. Once she'd proven that, he'd made it plain they were equals.

He held the door for her as she went into the house, felt the
slight change of temperature against her face. There was no electricity or gas in the Gordon/Essen home—none working anywhere
on the island that she knew of—but the shelter was sturdy and well
insulated, and retained what warmth the fireplace generated. Built
before the First World War, the house was brick and wood, and like
a handful of others in the neighborhood, had managed to survive the
earthquake relatively unscathed.

They made their way down the long hall, silently, Montoya looking again at the framed photographs on the walls, as she always did. Pictures of Gordon and Essen at different functions, civic award ceremonies. One of them on vacation in Hawaii, maybe during their honeymoon. Another of Gordon hugging his daughter, Barbara, at her graduation from Gotham State University.

Again, Montoya found herself thinking of her own family, glad that they were safe and well. Her parents had owned a bodega in Burnley, on the southern part of the north island. More commonly called Spanish Burnley, it had been an immigrant community since the dawn of time, the Gotham equivalent of New York's South Bronx. Though she knew her old neighborhood was probably full of people who could use a hand, she'd had no opportunities to make it that far north since Black Monday. The journey was now an all but impossible one, through at least ten differently held territories—and some of those territories, she knew, wouldn't let a cop through alive.

She and Bullock entered the War Room, the rec room where the Commissioner had once run his model trains. Now the trains were gone, the space cleared for chairs, with a city map of Gotham tacked to the far wall. The others were waiting, Essen, Pettit, and Foley, with Gordon standing opposite his wife.

"Take a seat," Gordon told them as they entered.

"How's Kelso holding?" Pettit asked.

"Fine," Montoya answered. "They could use more ammunition, but the border's secure."

Pettit nodded. "See what I can do."

Gordon cleared his throat, and they all put their attention on him.

"Situation report, as of today, Day 90," Gordon said. "TriCorner is ours. We've made it a week now without any incursions from the Street Demonz or the LoBoys, and it looks like most of our residents seem content with the protection we're providing. Right now we're still holding with twenty-three officers fit for duty, plus another fifty-odd residents who have expressed their desire to help. Pettit's been working with them for the last month now, and he informed me this morning that he thinks they're ready for action."

"Ready and waiting," Pettit said, grinning. "Just point and shoot, Jim."

Gordon nodded slowly, then smoothed his mustache. "We're ready for the next phase."

"Which would be?" Foley asked.

"Old Gotham, everything between here and Central. I want it all back."

Montoya kept her mouth from dropping open in surprise. Back to Central, to the main precinct, over a mile from the edge of TriCorner. And to secure that much area they'd have to take out both the Demonz *and* the LoBoys, combined numbers of over a hundred men who didn't feel any need to fight fair, who had long since given up any pretense of civilized behavior.

She glanced around the room, at the faces and reactions. Essen had obviously seen this coming, and was still sitting calmly. Pettit looked positively delighted. At her side, Harvey just grunted.

Foley, frowning, said, "I think it's a bad idea, Commissioner."

"What would you suggest?"

"Shoring up our own territory should be the priority. Making sure we can defend what we've got here."

Pettit turned in his chair to address Foley. "We're not playing a defensive game anymore, Hugh. That's old-style cop-think you're using. We're on offense now."

"Bill is right," Gordon said. "As the GCPD, we were a reactive force for the most part. What we're talking about now is being proactive, plain and simple. The Demonz and the LoBoys, they're just biding their time. Sooner or later, one of them will incorporate the other, and when that happens, you know they'll head south. We've got to hit them first."

"But Central's miles away. There's no point in reclaiming it," Foley said softly. "Any gear that was there has long since been looted, you know that."

"It's our HQ," Pettit said. "It's where the Blue Boys need to be. The propaganda value of having the GCPD back where they belong could do wonders. Or would you rather have some class-A skel going through your desk drawers and wandering around in our colors? Don't be so gutless, Hugh."

Foley stiffened, cheeks ranging with color. "It's not gutless. It's practical. It at least acknowledges our situation."

"Meaning what?" Gordon asked.

"Meaning I think you've got an ulterior motive here, Commissioner. Your daughter lives near Central, doesn't she?"

Montoya saw the line of Gordon's jaw tighten for a moment, the muscles flexing. "She does."

"So maybe this is less about propaganda and taking what's 'ours' than it is about you wanting to protect what's *yours*. And if that's the case, you could at least acknowledge it."

"Gladly," Gordon said. "I want to protect my daughter, I make no bones about it. There's nothing ulterior in that, Hugh. It's called being a father."

"There are too many of them," Foley said, quieter, changing his tack. "We can't take them all on. We'd lose what's left of our ammunition. We'd lose men."

"I have no intention of launching a frontal assault or losing our people."

"Well, they're not just going to surrender to us when they see the badges we're all wearing."

"Yes they will. If we pick the right moment . . . no, if we *make* the right moment."

Montoya cleared her throat. "And that would be what, sir?"

He looked at her, and she saw the corner of his mouth turn down slightly. "We're going to get them to kill each other off. We're going to incite them to war. And when it's over, when they've blown their strength and lowered their numbers, that's when we'll move."

Montoya wasn't quite certain she'd heard him correctly, but Pettit was speaking, saying, "That's *beautiful*, Jim, that's perfect! I couldn't have come up with better myself."

"It's pragmatic, that's all, Bill."

Bullock pulled the stick from his mouth. "Am I hearing you right, Commish?"

Gordon's look was as serious and solemn as any Montoya had seen on him before. It was the look she'd marked on him at crime scenes, where innocents lay dead at the hands of madmen. He knew exactly what he was saying, she realized. He'd already thought this through, had been thinking on it for a while now. Whether or not she agreed with the decision, she knew it was one the Commissioner had reached only through long consideration.

As if to confirm, Gordon said, "Yes, Harvey. We're going to get them to kill one another."

"You can't be serious," Foley managed.

"You have a better way?" Pettit asked.

"We're talking about manipulating people to commit murder, Bill!"

Pettit shook his head, almost amused, almost condescending. "We're at war. Out there, beyond TriCorner, it's chaos, plain and simple. We're the only order left in this burg, and if we want the burg to survive, it's up to us to impose it on the rest of the island. And the only way to do that is by being stronger, by being meaner."

Montoya heard Bullock settling in the chair beside her, the sound of his teeth digging farther into the stick in his mouth. Essen was still motionless in her seat, listening. Foley had looked back to the Commissioner. No one spoke.

"Then we start tonight," Gordon said. "Dismissed."

She was in the backyard, sitting on the cold concrete steps down from the cracked sliding glass door, eating her lunch, when he found her.

"Renee," Gordon said, settling next to the detective. "How's the meal?"

She held up the can of vegetarian chili for him to see. "Passable, sir. Cooked in the can, gives it that extra-tinny flavor."

Gordon smiled briefly at the bad joke, eyes surveying his garden. Since the start of the No Man's Land he'd put considerable effort into the yard, preparing it, optimistically, for spring. Montoya had been with him when, last month, they'd gone through the wreckage of a Yards and Yards Home Supply store, looking for tools and supplies. She had left carrying axes, shovels, and pry bars. The Commissioner had left with boxes of vegetable seeds and six books on gardening.

Right now, as far as Montoya could tell, the garden had a long way to go before it would ever yield fruit.

She ran her metal spoon around the can a final time, licking it off. She set the can aside, then used the edge of a bandanna to clean the spoon before stowing it back in her inside pocket. She heard the end of it clink against the silver half-dollar in her pocket, the one she had taken from Two-Face just weeks before the No Man's Land was declared. For an instant her mind wandered to him, the man who was, somewhere beneath the scarring and insanity, still Harvey Dent. She didn't understand why he'd given her the coin, and she understood less why she kept it. As currency it was useless, not even a real half-dollar, but instead a gag coin, double-headed. One of the sides had been defaced, scraped and burnt, turned into what Two-Face called "the bad side." The other held the representation of Liberty.

"I want you to come with me tonight," Gordon was saying, and his voice pulled her attention back. "I want to cross into the Demonz territory, see if we can get the ball rolling."

"Me, sir?"

Gordon nodded, still looking at his garden, as if expecting it to bloom before his eyes.

"Don't you want to take Pettit?" Montoya asked. "Don't you think he'd be better for this than I would?"

"Bill's excellent in a fight, absolutely. But he's not very subtle, and we need to make certain this doesn't get traced back to us. Wouldn't do to have the Demonz and LoBoys uniting to take us on."

"Still . . ."

He looked at her, those blue eyes that were almost gray and always made her think of her own father. "I'm not going to take Sarah. If it goes wrong, that would be the entire command structure gone, and I won't risk that. I can't take Foley for obvious reasons. And Bullock, well . . . he's never been the quietest soul on the force."

Montoya tried not to laugh. Calling Harvey Bullock quiet was like calling him refined. An out-and-out lie.

"We'll leave from the Kelso Blockade at midnight," Gordon said, rising.

"Yes, sir," Montoya said, and then she was alone in the garden again.

After a second, she took the badge off her jacket, examining it. She blew a breath on the gold metal, polished it against the leg of her jeans.

Then she put it in her jacket pocket.

She wouldn't wear it tonight.

THREE

THE GIRL ORACLE HAD NAMED CASSANDRA was looking at the map in her hand, trying to determine where, exactly, she now stood in Gotham City. Most of the street signs were long gone, and block-counting, her personal tactic, only worked if she could absolutely concentrate. She supposed it was her own failing, that if she had lived in Gotham long enough, even if she had lived here before the quake, she would know the city better. As it was, she had slipped in just prior to the detonations on Black Monday, sneaking past the blockades and barely making it off the Brown Bridge before it had blown sky-high.

She had come to Gotham because, honestly, she felt it was the safest place for her.

She frowned down at the map one last time, then resolved she must be somewhere on the Upper East Side, and since that was where Oracle wanted her to be, she relaxed.

"Black Mask is up there, somewhere," Oracle had told her that morning. "See if you can locate him, find out what he's up to."

Simple enough, Cassandra thought.

She continued north, working along the sides of the quake-damaged buildings, waiting for the sun to finish its descent. She could smell a fire burning somewhere, pungent, and voices ahead of her in the distance. She lowered into a crouch, moving from shadow to shadow, just as her father had taught her, feet silent on the broken concrete and asphalt.

The voices were getting louder, and then one of them shouted.

She heard a woman scream, and Cassandra stopped dead, both her hands coming to her ears, cupping them with palms out. She turned her head slowly, trying to locate the source, and then the scream came again, louder, terrified, and Cassandra got a bearing and began to run. The broken ground was uneven and could be tricky, and twice during her first weeks in the NML she had almost twisted her ankles. But that was months ago now, and she had long since adapted—again, as her father had taught her—learning to use the ground to her advantage. She was certain she could now run faster than ever.

The scream sounded a final time, and Cassandra came around the corner of a shattered diner, turning to an alley, leaving the shadows and then stopping short even as the sound died.

She had expected a victim, a fight, a conflict.

What she saw she knew instantly as a trap, and it made a sudden heat of shame burn her cheeks.

The woman who had been screaming was at the end of the alley, wrapped in layers of rags, torn blankets tied around a jacket, all to keep out the cold. Late thirties, white, and mean looking, and it wasn't just the fact that she was holding a composite bow drawn back and ready to put its arrow in Cassandra's chest that was the alarming thing. The woman's face was a mass of scars, lines visible in the dusk, puffy skin that looked alternately lacerated and burnt. The woman's mouth itself looked as if it had been cut, blackened scabs that shone with fresh blood at both sides.

From behind her, Cassandra heard movement out of the rubble, at least three people, and none of them so stupid as to be within striking distance.

"Dinner time," the scarred woman said, and she loosed the arrow.

Cassandra went down, letting her left leg take her weight as she spun to see the men behind her. Three of them, all with faces carved up like the woman's, all dressed in the same fashion. The arrow sliced the air over her head, hitting the chest of the man who had stood behind her.

The other two men were moving up on her, and she knew, could almost feel, where the woman at the end of the alley was nocking another arrow.

Using her left leg, Cassandra sprang up, high, going into the kick intuitively, and the heel of her foot connected with the jaw of the nearest man. Still in the jump she twisted from her hips, bringing her right leg up and around, pinwheeling in the air and feeling her other foot connect with the remaining man. The contact rushed along the bone, a solid strike, and she went back down, hands out, over, springing up again facing the end of the alley in time to hear the woman with the bow scream once more.

Another figure was in the alley, now, between them, cloaked in a purple that in the shadow turned to black. Cassandra found her balance instantly, returning to ready, arms up, pulling another breath through her nose. The figure turned and beyond her, on the ground, the woman with the bow was clutching at her hand.

Through the back of the woman's palm, Cassandra saw the spike of metal, wet with blood.

The cloaked figure absently kicked at the woman, catching her in the stomach, and Cassandra's own gut trembled. She moved her mouth, wanting to make the figure stop, but already it was over. Now the figure was moving forward, and Cassandra suddenly recognized her, remembering the pictures that Oracle had shown her only a week before. The masks, Oracle had called them, trying to stress their obvious importance. And this was one of them, Cassandra remembered, one of the bad ones, according to Oracle.

"Criminal," Oracle had warned. "Stay away from her."

The figure stopped in front of her, cape billowing back, and Cassandra's eyes flicked to the glint of the cross at the woman's throat.

"There'll be more of them," the Huntress said. "They stick close together, in packs. Follow me."

Huntress went past, ignoring the men on the ground, the one with the arrow in his chest already visibly dead. Cassandra followed her out of the alley, across the street. Huntress knew how to run on the broken ground, too, she noted, leading the way through rubble and shadow to a building, cracked but still standing. The sun had finally set, and the sky was turning almost the same shade as the Huntress's costume.

Sheltered, in shadow, Huntress turned to look at her.

"Injured?"

Cassandra shook her head.

"Need a moment? Catch your breath?"

Cassandra shook her head once more, then opened her mouth. She tried for "thank you," one of the phrases that Oracle had been teaching her, but managed only a broken croak and squeak.

Behind the mask, Huntress's eyes widened slightly. "Did they cut you? Are you all right?"

Cassandra put the fingers of her right hand over her mouth, trying to show that it wasn't that she didn't want to speak, but that she didn't know how. For a moment, Huntress stared at her, and then Cassandra saw her make the connection.

"You're mute?"

It was more complicated than that, but Cassandra nodded, knowing that it would be nearly impossible to explain the how and the why. And even if she could explain those two things, she would have to explain the rest, the darkness of it all, and the evil, and she didn't want to tell anyone that. Not ever.

What she wanted was to forget it all, actually.

"I haven't seen you before," Huntress was saying. "Not in this neighborhood, at least. Are you lost?"

Cassandra shook her head, pulling out the map. She pointed at the section of Old Gotham, just below the Diamond District.

Huntress misunderstood. "No, no, you're up here, now, see?" With a gloved finger, she indicated the street they were on.

Cassandra nodded, quickly replacing the map in her pocket, then turning to face Huntress again. She thought for a moment, then presented both hands, palms up. She looked at Huntress, smiling, then brought her hands together, lacing the fingers.

"You're welcome," Huntress said.

Cassandra grinned.

"But it looked like you didn't really need my help," Huntress amended. "You need a place to stay for the night? I know some safe spots. I've been protecting a block just east of here. There's warmth and shelter and food there, if you'd like."

The offer was tempting. It would be nice to be warm for a little while, and she was hungry, hadn't eaten since that morning, when Oracle had made her a bowl of instant oatmeal. Cassandra started to nod, and then she balked.

Criminal. Stay away from her.

Huntress was looking at her with an almost maternal concern now, and it surprised Cassandra, the sudden softness in the eyes behind the mask. But it didn't matter. It wasn't enough.

Oracle was counting on her. Find Black Mask, that was the job. Cassandra had to do the job, and then, maybe, she could think about being warm and fed.

Cassandra shook her head.

The softness Cassandra thought she'd seen in the Huntress's eyes vanished like vapor. Then Huntress was looking again at the ruined street, ready to return to business.

"Remember, only one block east of here," Huntress said softly. "That's where you'll find me. Come back if you need anything."

Cassandra nodded, and then Huntress moved past her, out of the shadow and into the newly forming night.

"Take care of yourself, kid," Huntress said.

Cassandra moved her mouth to try the words, really pushing the air past her sore and stripped vocal cords, feeling the clumsy shuffle of her tongue against the back of her teeth and on the roof of her mouth. She shut her eyes for an instant, to concentrate, to make the extra effort.

"Guh byh-eeee," she managed, the words coming out as if written on thin tissue and dropped onto a bonfire, crackling into nothingness almost immediately.

But Huntress was already gone, and Cassandra closed her mouth, knowing that no one had heard her at all.

FOUR

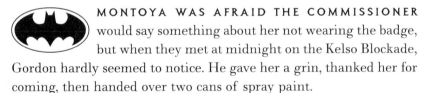MONTOYA WAS AFRAID THE COMMISSIONER would say something about her not wearing the badge, but when they met at midnight on the Kelso Blockade, Gordon hardly seemed to notice. He gave her a grin, thanked her for coming, then handed over two cans of spray paint.

"Demonz is red, LoBoys is gold," Gordon said. "Make sure you know which is which."

"Absolutely, sir."

"Good. You armed?"

"I've got my Glock, sir. Two shots left."

Gordon grunted and rummaged through his coat pockets, then handed over another seven 9mm bullets, which he dropped into Montoya's hand. "Don't use them all in one place," he said mildly.

Montoya took the rounds, surprised, then set about loading her pistol, asking, "Where did you find these? I thought we'd used up all of the nines. . . ."

"Pettit," Gordon said. "Don't know where he keeps finding them. He presented me with almost a hundred rounds of .38 and 9 millimeter before the meeting this morning."

Montoya nodded, not truly listening, as she slipped the magazine back into her gun and chambered her first round. Loaded, she set the safety, holstered the gun, and turned her attention expectantly back to Gordon.

"Badge," Gordon said. "Where's your shield, Detective?"

Montoya swallowed. "Thought it . . . thought it would be best if I didn't wear it tonight, sir. It didn't feel right."

Gordon studied her for several long seconds, apparently considering her answer. "Fair. Hopefully you'll put it back on come morning."

"That's my plan, sir."

"All right. Let's go."

It was easier than either of them expected to cross from TriCorner into Old Gotham, and they slunk past the Demonz checkpoint on the Westward Bridge without noise or hesitation. They moved north another two blocks, shadowing one another from either side of the street, until they reached the outskirts of one of the many settled pockets in the territory. Demonz tags were painted at random intervals, each a stylized red "D" with a curved devil's tail and horns, usually one every two blocks or so, sometimes more. Whenever Montoya spotted one she would stop, checking Gordon's position, then the safety of the street. Then she'd produce her can of gold paint, the ball bearing inside it rattling with obvious noise. Two lines first, through the Demonz tag, and then beside it a quick, bold "LB" to implicate the LoBoys. The hiss of the paint flying under pressure sounded like a shout in her ears.

When they reached O'Neil Avenue, Gordon gestured to her from across the street, urging her out of the shadows. Cans concealed in her jacket, Montoya moved forward, and Gordon met her halfway. Side by side, they continued along the street.

"Nothing to be afraid of," Gordon said. "Just two folks out for a stroll."

"In the middle of the night in the middle of No Man's Land," Montoya said.

"They won't notice. Trust me, they've got other things to worry about."

They continued along O'Neil, deeper into the heart of Demonz territory. The tags here were farther apart. Every so often Montoya heard vague noises in the distance, sometimes movement from inside the buildings, sometimes the thread of voices tripping down from above. The night was clear, the half-moon bright, and small packets of snow shone white-blue along the ground, mounded against the broken pavement.

They fell into the shadows of larger buildings, turning along Brady, heading northeast now. In the gap between two fallen buildings Montoya saw the outline of the Clock Tower, still easily a mile or more away. Moonlight shone off the still intact stained glass on the giant clock face, and she felt herself grinning without realizing it.

"Can't believe it's still standing," the detective whispered.

"Built by Wayne Enterprises," Gordon said softly. "Turns out Wayne buildings were the only ones built earthquake proof."

"Lucky for your daughter."

The Commissioner nodded slightly, then stopped, and she heard him draw a deep breath through his nose. A fraction later she caught the scent, too: an open fire, the unmistakable odor of burnt paper. They slowed at the corner, peeking around to see the remains of the Gotham City Public Library main branch, a small mob gathered silently in front. The men and women stood in a large circle at the foot of the steps, warming themselves with a fire on the open ground. As Montoya looked, one of the men added more fuel to the fire—they were burning books, and a sharp heaviness drove against her heart, suddenly, forcing her to look away.

"Makes my stomach turn, too," Gordon whispered.

"We should stop them."

"We can't stop them. Not now. Maybe, when we're here, when we control this land, maybe then." Gordon settled his gaze on Montoya. "But right now it would only make us targets."

She nodded.

"Come on, let's find what we're after and get out of here."

It took another twenty minutes before they reached the border zone of the territories, Martin Luther King, Jr. Boulevard, running north to the south end of Robinson Park, out of sight. Tags were becoming plentiful once more, and they had to slow their progress, taking each as it came, methodical in the defacement. Montoya tried not to dwell on the irony, to think of how many teens she had busted while on the beat for doing exactly what she and the Commissioner did now.

At Twelfth and Schreck they found a large Demonz tag, almost six feet high.

"Border sign," Montoya whispered.

"We do this one, then head back," Gordon said. "That should get them riled."

The relief surprised her, and Montoya nodded quickly, careful with her can. She drew the lines through the tag, feeling the nozzle on the spray can digging into her index finger. The light wouldn't confirm it, but she was certain her fingertip was coated in the gold paint.

She had just finished painting the "B" in the LoBoys tag when she heard the voice.

"You two sure as hell don't look like LoBoys."

Montoya turned, saw that Gordon had already done the same, but both held off on going for their weapons. There was no point.

There were five of them, all men, the eldest no more than thirty, if that, though in the night light it was hard to tell. Their jackets were salvaged denim, painted. Horns and tails. Two had machetes, another an ax. The remaining two had shotguns. All of them had shaved their heads.

The one with the ax said, "Doesn't matter. The penalty for trashing the Demonz is death." He turned his head slightly, lowering his voice, speaking to the other four. "Kill the geezer, try to keep her alive. She might be fine in the light."

Gordon hadn't moved. In her periphery, Montoya could see his hand waiting at his hip, knew what he was waiting for. If the shotguns were loaded, they didn't stand a chance of drawing in time, they'd be dead before their weapons cleared their holsters.

But now it was just a chance they were going to have to take.

She swung her hand back, knocking the edge of her coat away to clear her holster, just as she'd done a thousand times before in drills, in practice, and she felt the world become slow with the sudden feed of adrenaline, and as always the strange clarity came with it. Gordon was doing the same, she knew, and speaking, or rather shouting, and the man with the shotgun pointed at her; his mouth was shaped like a bow, a soft shape, she thought, for a killer. The air was clean, she realized, much cleaner than it had ever been in Gotham before the No Man's Land, and sure, it stank like hell in places, but at least the pollution was gone, and that wasn't so bad, really, was it? And dammit, but she was sorry, really sorry, that she wouldn't be seeing her parents and little brother again.

Then the man with the mouth like a bow turned red and wet and was falling, and the other man with a shotgun was doing the same, and Montoya had just now taken her gun out of its holster, and she was wondering how Gordon got to be so damn fast on the draw. Must have been Chicago, she thought, must have been learned in Chicago, and she had her weapon up and her finger on the trigger and she was feeling the kick of the gun in her hand.

And all five men were dead, and she and the Commissioner were still breathing, still standing. A man was coming out of the shadows beyond the bodies, slinging an M16 back over his shoulder, and Montoya moved her weapon to track him, opened her mouth to challenge his approach.

"Pettit," Gordon said.

Captain Billy Pettit grinned, and his mustache and the light made him look almost feral to Montoya's eyes. "Hope you don't mind, Commissioner. Figured it was time to take a little initiative."

"You've been following us all night?"

Pettit's grin grew, and he cast a quick glance at Montoya. It must be the adrenaline, she thought. *That's why he looks like this is one big joke.*

"I just couldn't sleep, Jim, knowing that you and Renee were out here without anyone to cover your backs," Pettit said. "I was just tossing and turning, thinking that maybe spray paint alone just wouldn't be enough to start our little war."

Gordon didn't say anything.

Pettit's expression faded to neutral. "Was I wrong, Commissioner?"

"No." Gordon's voice was soft.

Pettit nodded, then bent to the nearest body, taking it by the feet and dragging it toward the retagged wall. "Little help here, Renee?"

Montoya holstered her weapon, and the three of them moved the bodies beneath the LoBoy tag. When they were finished, Montoya crossed herself.

"Now that's how to incite a war," Pettit said. "Bodies. Of course, this is all for nothing if their comrades-in-arms, so to speak, don't see what those degenerate LoBoys have done." He flashed a grin of white teeth at Montoya. "Shouldn't be a problem, though. Between the gunfire and a little added incentive."

Montoya wasn't certain she wanted to know the answer, but she asked anyway. "Like what?"

Pettit cupped his hands to his mouth, tilting his body back. "Demonz!" he shouted, and the word echoed and bounced along the broken buildings. "Come out and play!"

Gordon muttered something, reaching out to touch Montoya, and she turned to follow him, suddenly sprinting down the block, into LoBoy territory. Pettit was right behind her, and over his footsteps she heard others, farther back, louder. Then they stopped and she knew the bodies had been seen, heard the sound of the voices climbing in rage.

In another nest of shadow they stopped, Montoya crouched between Pettit and Gordon.

"Good start," Pettit said. "Means nothing if the LoBoys don't join 'em, though."

"This way," Gordon said, and they began sprinting again, dodging the rubble, trying to keep their footing on the treacherous pavement.

Behind them, Montoya heard more shouts, someone cursing

them as LoBoys, and then she couldn't concentrate on the words but only on staying upright on the terrain, vaulting over fallen masonry, skidding, then righting herself again and continuing to run. Stealth was gone. Now it was the hare leading the hounds, hopefully straight into another pack of dogs.

She wasn't even sure where they were anymore as she came around another corner. Gordon and Pettit were behind her now, and she saw the fires burning farther down the street, the figures around them, and the LoBoy tag on the brick across from her. She stopped, felt Pettit bump into her a moment later, then Gordon was at her side again.

"LoBoys," Montoya said, scanning the ground. A shattered piece of brick caught her eye, and she grabbed it, pulling her arm back and then taking a couple of stutter-steps forward, throwing it hard. The brick flew, bouncing off the hood of a rusted and stripped car, and the group of LoBoys turned.

"Chick, chick, chick," Pettit mocked, pulling Montoya back into the shadows.

The LoBoys turned to them and began menacing their way along the street.

"Up," Gordon whispered, indicating the fire escape in the alley behind them. The ladder had been lowered already, and the Commissioner was reaching toward it. "Out of their way."

Montoya followed him up, Pettit on her heels. She held her breath as they crossed the grating on the third floor, hearing the metal creak, feeling the rust peel and stick to her hands as she used the railing. Of the buildings that were still standing, few of them engendered her trust, but the thought of falling to the street and landing between the Demonz and the LoBoys kept her moving. Gordon had made it to the roof and extended a hand to her, which Montoya ignored, pulling herself over the edge and onto the sunken tar-paper surface. Pettit appeared only a couple of seconds later.

All of them crouched again, peering over the edge, catching their breath. The voices were drifting up to them: anger, curses. Montoya thought the number of the two groups looked roughly even, maybe six or seven to a side. All were brandishing weapons, and she heard the accusations start.

And then one of the Demonz swung a baseball bat, and Montoya heard the sound of bone shattering, heard it climb the six stories to where they were hiding, and she didn't want to watch anymore. She turned away from the edge, putting her back to the short retaining wall. Her stomach was in knots, and her hands were shaking slightly, and she wanted something to drink to drive the dryness from her mouth. She knew it wasn't just adrenaline that was making her feel sick.

"Congratulations," Pettit said, still watching eagerly. "We've just started a war."

FIVE

HIS BRIDE WAS WAITING FOR HIM WHEN
Gordon got home, and as always, it made him smile
and feel lighter, if only for a moment. Sarah waited
until he was through the door, past where Weir and DeFilippis stood
guarding the house, and then followed him down the hall to their
bedroom. He took off his coat and tossed it over the back of the chair,
then stooped to pick up the can of spray paint that had fallen from
his pocket. He sat on the edge of the bed and took off his shoes, then
removed the holster from his belt, setting it on the table to the side.

Then he stood up and took his wife in his arms.

"Bad, huh?" Sarah asked gently.

Gordon swallowed, fought for a moment for the words, then nodded, felt her lips brushing his cheek, then finding his mouth. He took

the kiss like it was water, like he was dying of thirst. For a while, he thought maybe he could never get enough.

Later, staring at the ceiling, feeling Sarah's heart beating against his chest, safe in their bed, he almost thought it would be okay.

She moved, drawing a hand along his chest, nuzzling his neck for a second. He almost didn't hear her when she spoke.

"Tell me," she said.

"We're going to have to pay," he said after a moment, and his voice surprised him, how young he sounded to his own ear. "What we did . . . I wish I could be sure, Sarah. I wish I could be sure I was doing the right thing."

"When have any of us ever had that luxury?" she asked gently. "When the married cop and the single detective began their affair, who was sure then?"

He smiled. "I'm sure now."

"Hindsight is twenty/twenty, Jim."

"Pettit is sure."

"Pettit is narrow. He knows what he knows, and that's all he needs. Black and white makes him happy."

"Maybe a black and white view of the world is what we need now."

"Maybe."

Gordon sighed, tightened his grip slightly on Sarah, felt her settle against him. Her leg was long and warm and for a moment he thought he could concentrate just on that.

"You can't be sure, Jim," she said gently. "It's not who you are."

"I know. But . . . I have to wonder, how far will it go? How far will *we* have to go?"

"How far are you prepared to take it?"

"I don't know."

He felt her body shiver for a moment with a restrained chuckle, the soft laugh he adored. "Yes, you do. How far will a father go to protect his daughter?"

"All the way."

"Right," she said, agreeing.

He turned in the bed, touching her face with his hand, then his lips. "I'll go all the way," he said.

She grinned. "Again?"

He had to laugh. "I'm old, remember? Twice in a night is too much for this old warhorse."

"Let's test that theory," Sarah said, moving to cover his body more fully with her own. He watched her face cloud for a moment again, the seriousness return. "Jim. We do what we have to in order to survive. That's the rule of nature. Until we have survival, we can't have civilization."

"If this is foreplay, it's not working."

"You get foreplay in a second. For now, listen to me." She lowered her head, her nose touching his, eyes locked on his own. "We're going to make it, hon. We'll make it."

"I believe you."

"You should. I'm a cop, I'm honest and trustworthy and my word is my bond."

"Less word, please. More bond."

"Thought you were too old."

"I'm feeling younger every second."

"Is that what you're feeling?"

"That's my story and I'm sticking to it."

Her brow creased in mock concentration, and he felt her move gently against him. "In that case, Commissioner, I think further investigation is in order."

"Carry on, Lieutenant," Gordon said.

"Love you, cop boy."

"Love you, too, shamus."

ORACLE

Dear Dad—

No one knows which side started it.

Woke up three days ago, suddenly the war was on, Demonz versus LoBoys.

My Eyes tell me it's bloody. They tell me it's personal, that on the ground, the "civilians" know enough to stay out of the way, behind their closed doors and hidden in their shelters. On the street, the gangs roam, armed and angry, looking for another fight.

The body count is unknown. I expect it's pretty high. Without medical facilities and care, casualties turn to fatalities as a matter of course. The LoBoys on the street below have taken to burning their dead, pretending it's the bodies of their mortal enemies, the hated Demonz. Nobody watching buys it.

Rumor is that the Demonz are doing the exact same thing, claiming their own dead as that of the LoBoys.

What I'm finding fascinating—and you'll forgive the academic in me rearing its head here—is the way the propaganda war has manifested. I doubt anyone on either side could explain their behavior as such, much less define what the word itself means, but they have fallen into the techniques quickly, mastering them at the most basic level.

For hours yesterday, a group of LoBoys went up and down the street below, explaining how, when the Demonz come, the women will be raped, the children will be raped, and the men will be raped and eaten. The Demonz, we are told, are cannibals, barbarians, monsters. And for that reason, we need the LoBoys.

They're here to protect us, after all.

And, I suppose, in a fashion, they do believe that.

All the same, it's failed them. Doors stay shut, windows stay boarded. Only LoBoys have been seen on the streets for the last few days.

No Man's Land we may be, but we're still Gotham, and most of us just don't want to get involved.

Cassandra reported this morning that you and your crew are on the move. She drew me a picture of a badge, and then a building. I'm assuming that means you're headed for Central.

If that's true, maybe I'll see you soon. I hope so. I miss you and Sarah.

Cassandra also spent fifteen minutes or so scribbling on the scraps of paper, drawing tags and then crossing them out, redrawing different tags. Then she was pointing at the picture of the badge. It took me a while before the neuron fired.

If I'm understanding what she's trying to tell me, Dad, I really don't know what to say. I really don't know how to respond.

Hopefully, I'll have a chance to get the answer from you in person.

The tally on the bat-tags has grown, now eleven of them, scattered throughout the city. No one has seen the Batman, though, so I really don't know what to make of the tags at this point. It occurred to me last night as I was failing to sleep that it's most likely not him at all, but rather a different gang, trying to capitalize on the strength of the symbol, the currency of myth.

I still haven't heard from him.

Is it arrogant of me to think he'd call, that he'd let me know he was here? I don't think it is, really . . . I've helped him more times than either of us could recall in the past few years, I know that. I've been a major source of information for him in the past. I have, quite honestly, been part of the team.

He'd call me, wouldn't he?

I was Batgirl, after all. He'd call, he'd let me know he was here.

But he hasn't, and I don't know what that means. I honestly don't know what to make of that. Maybe he really did leave us here alone, leave Gotham to its misery . . .

No, see, I don't buy that.

So maybe he's hurt, or even dead.

But I don't buy that, either.

Some nights I look out my window, and I think there is a weight hanging over us all. We're all waiting for something to happen, for something to change this status quo of one hundred—odd days.

Then I realize I'm waiting for him.

He *must* be here.

He must.

SIX

GARRETT WAS NOT, IN HIS OWN OPINION, a bad person. A criminal, certainly, he'd be the first to admit that. But a bad person, no. He was just a guy using what talents he had to make ends meet, that's all it was. Before NML, he'd been a thug, a petty bruiser, working for the Lindsey Crew in the Bowery. Steady work, it kept him in beer money, and he could spend his days practicing his pool game and rebuilding his Camaro—a '67, bloodred, the kind of car that got him plenty of dates. At nights he'd go where his old boss, Lindsey, sent him. Sometimes Garrett would carry a gun, but more often than not a crowbar or baseball bat would do the trick nicely. Garrett never hit more or harder than he needed to, and he never enjoyed it. He was not, and he was always quick to point this out, one of those Arkham nuts that got off on inflicting damage.

But that was before. Then 8.4 or 7.8 or however much of Richter's scale had come to visit Gotham, and that was the end of Lindsey's Crew, buried under the remnants of the Otis Auto Supply Warehouse, where they had all hung out. When the National Guard finally found them, Garrett was the only one still conscious. Lindsey himself had been alive, but died three days later in a mobile hospital from his injuries.

For a while after that, especially when the word came down that the ol' U.S. of A. was pulling Gotham's plug, Garrett had seriously considered bugging out, maybe even going straight. He had a sister in Metropolis who worked at a diner, and she'd told him the joint was looking for a short order cook, and hell, Garrett could've done that.

He'd actually been packing what was left of his stuff when Fowler came to visit. Fowler, who was so skinny it seemed like the guy was nothing but walking bones. Fowler, who always seemed to know what sort of petty crime needed to be done.

"The Penguin would like to offer you a job," Fowler had said.

Easier than going straight, that's for sure.

Working for Penguin was different from working for Lindsey, in that Penguin was smart. Really smart. Had every angle covered, had plans inside of plans. Garrett dug that, and had great respect for Penguin. They were a lot alike, Garrett thought. Not in the brains department or anything like that, but because they each knew what they did best, and didn't pretend. Garrett, over six foot two and mostly muscle, knew what his assets were. Same could be said of Penguin, with his malformed and squat little body. Penguin needed Garrett's muscle for busting heads and for other stuff, too.

"My friend," Penguin had said to him. "Look at this city and tell me what you see."

Garrett prided himself on honesty. "Rubble," he'd said.

Penguin had made that strange clucking noise he sometimes did, the one Garrett began to realize was like a chuckle. "Opportunity, my friend, opportunity. For when the federal government in its glorious short-sightedness calls an end to Gotham City as we know it, we will be the first pioneers of a brave new world. Gotham shall be our oyster."

"Never much cared for oysters, Mr. Cobblepot," Garrett said.

"Don't interrupt, my lad," Penguin snapped.

Garrett had shut his mouth. He was good at following orders, he knew that.

"The business opportunities for the enterprising entrepreneur in this forsaken urban sprawl will be lucrative. A man—a smart man— could find himself rich beyond the dreams of avarice, richer than a Bruce Wayne, richer even, dare I say it, than a Lex Luthor!" Penguin arched the eyebrow above his monocle, making certain Garrett was following. And Garrett was; Penguin was talking about being really rich.

"Rich is good," Garrett said.

Penguin's eyebrow had fallen, and the cigarette holder clamped between his teeth canted downward. Penguin frowned, his small and dark eyes focusing intently on Garrett for a moment longer. He was barely half Garrett's height, though almost Garrett's weight, with a long nose that tapered to an almost painfully sharp point at its end. For a moment, Garrett was afraid Penguin would peck at him with the nose.

"Not the sharpest stick in the bundle, are you, Garrett?" Penguin finally asked.

"No, sir, Mr. Cobblepot."

"But you follow orders, I'm told, and are strong, yes?"

"Yes, sir, Mr. Cobblepot."

"And manners are always a plus." Penguin sighed. "Very well, Garrett. Stick with Fowler, he'll tell you what we'll need."

Tonight, what Penguin needed was someone to prove if the bridges and river were mined. Fowler's plan—and once he had explained it to Garrett it had made a kind of sense—had been to find people in the No Man's Land, people all alone that no one would miss. Then Garrett and Fowler would take these people—one at a time, of course—and put them on the bridges or whatnot, or throw them into the water. And if the people blew up, well, then, they would have not only proven that such routes were, indeed, mined, but they would have also disarmed one of those same mines in the process.

"Disarmed?" Garrett asked.

"Well, detonated, more like," Fowler said. "But the principle is the same."

"I don't know," Garrett said slowly. "It seems kind of . . . mean."

"You think it's mean?"

"Kinda, yeah."

"Would you rather it be you?"

Garrett shook his head.

"So then, if it isn't you, how is that mean?" Fowler asked.

"Gimme a sec."

"Garrett, you're a stump, you know that? Come on, let's go find Murphy, then we can get to work."

Garrett, Fowler, and Murphy waited in cover by the Robert Kane Memorial Bridge, watching the shadows growing longer as the night fell. Garrett was cold, and kept opening and closing his hands in an attempt to get them warm again. The gloves Penguin had given him were too small—almost all gloves were too small for Garrett—and he'd traded them to Slick Cindy three weeks back for two issues of *Girl World*. Far as Garrett was concerned, he'd come out on top in that deal.

"There's one," Murphy whispered. "That guy, there. Think he'll do?"

Garrett looked where Murphy was indicating, even though he knew darn well Murphy wasn't talking to him, but to Fowler. Murphy was just another of Penguin's crew and had worked with Fowler before the NML. Murphy had made it plain he thought Garrett was a stump, too, and always ignored him when they were out on business for Penguin.

Murphy was pointing at a man maybe two hundred yards away, ambling along the embankment of the Gotham River. The fading light made it hard to pick him out, but one thing was clear to Garrett right away, and that was that the man was old. Really old, like stooped and withered and probably really wrinkled, to boot.

Garrett didn't like old people. They smelled.

"He'll do," Fowler said. "Come on."

Garrett followed as Murphy and Fowler began working their way toward the man. About fifty yards away, Garrett realized the man was singing. It took him another second to realize the man wasn't singing in English.

Murphy stopped about ten feet away from the man, blocking his retreat. Fowler moved to block the front, which left Garrett to take the middle. This close he could see the old man had a beard, long and gray like Santa Claus's, only this guy was thin, and wearing a real hat, with like a broad brim instead of a stocking thing with a puffball on it. For a moment, Garrett wondered what he'd do for Christmas.

"Where you headed, man?" Fowler was asking.

"Nowhere," the old man said. His voice was thin, accent like he was from New York, maybe Brooklyn.

"Nah, you don't want to do that," Fowler said. "Nowhere, that's a waste of time. Especially when you could be going somewhere instead. Want to do that? Do something useful with us?"

"No."

"Okay, well, how about you say yes and we don't kill you right here?" Fowler asked, and he pulled out his knife, which was the signal for Garrett and Murphy to pull out their knives as well. That was one of the things you got when you worked for Penguin—a really good knife; Penguin made sure his guys had only the best.

The old man didn't look up, but he stopped moving, not even shuffling to keep warm.

"Got his attention there, I think," Murphy said.

"Oh, yeah. So this is the deal, old man. We're going up on the bridge. And you're gonna cross it. Now I know what you're thinking, you're thinking that the bridge is broken. This is true. So you're going to go off the bridge and into the water."

Fowler nodded to Garrett, and Garrett moved forward and put a hand on the old man's shoulder and started moving him. The old guy was taller than Garrett had first thought, but still stooped, and he moved without resisting.

Fowler led the way onto the bridge, Garrett followed with the old man, Murphy took up the rear. Together they walked up the embankment onto the cracked asphalt of the bridge, heading toward the broken segment. The Gotham River flowed by slowly over a hundred feet below. Garrett wondered if it would freeze again this year. The river had frozen once when he was a kid, and he'd played hockey on the ice with a couple friends.

When they reached the edge, Fowler said, "You're getting a chance to leave Gotham, old man. Can you swim?"

"Not in there," the old man said. "Mines in there."

"Hey, not so dumb after all," Murphy said.

"That's right," Fowler said. "The river is supposed to have mines in it. And you're gonna find out if that's true or not. If there's no mines, figure you swim to safety, you escape. If there is mines, then you get blown to hell, and there'll be one less mine for the next guy we toss in. So this is what we call a win-win situation, see?"

"Not for me," the old man said.

"Well, no. But that's too bad for you, then, isn't it?"

The old man nodded slowly, as if accepting what Fowler had said, and then with a speed that surprised Garrett, spun and brought his right hand up, then back down, breaking first Garrett's grip and then Garrett's nose.

Garrett howled in pain and reached for the man as he tried to move away. Fowler and Murphy had the knives out again, but Garrett wanted the old guy now, wanted him alone, and he closed his fist around the man's beard and yanked.

The beard came off in his hand, and Garrett looked at the face of the man and for almost a second couldn't understand what he was seeing. Then he realized the beard was a fake, and that the man, while old, wasn't more than sixty, and that the man's eyes were clear and smart, and not crazy at all.

"Wha—" said Garrett.

Then it all happened at once.

There was a snapping sound, like a whip cracking, and then a shadow had taken Murphy's knife, and Murphy was on the ground with his eyes closed. Fowler had grabbed the man, but when the shadow moved forward, he let go of him and tried to run. The old man, off balance, fell back against Garrett. Garrett closed his grip on instinct, putting his knife to the man's throat.

The shadow raised an arm quickly, throwing something small and black that whistled past Garrett's head. Then Fowler made a noise and fell flat, and the shadow was coming forward.

And it had horns. And wings. And claws. And was as big as Garrett himself, and moving like it didn't need to touch the ground at all.

It was the Bat.

Garrett felt his stomach trying to slide down his legs.

"Let him go."

The words seemed to rattle around the inside of Garrett's chest. When he answered, he was shocked by what he said.

"Like hell."

The Batman moved forward again, and Garrett pressed the blade against the old man's throat.

"I'll kill him. I don't want to, but I'll do it. You let me pass."

"Let. Him. Go."

Garrett thought, tried to do it quickly, trying to find a way out.

He shoved the old man toward the ledge, and off the side of the bridge, then lunged. He thought it was a good plan. He thought it would give him time.

He was wrong.

The Batman moved, cape swirling up into the man's path and the old man caught it, used it to swing around behind the Batman, staying safely on the bridge. Garrett lunged with the knife and the Batman moved out of the way effortlessly, and as Garrett passed he felt a sudden sting in his wrist, then a dull pain on his neck.

Garrett hit the ground flat, his head aching, the knife now gone. He rolled quickly onto his back, trying to get up once more, and the Batman loomed over him. Garrett saw the boot coming down.

Then he saw darkness.

SEVEN

IT WASN'T TRULY A CAVE AT ALL, BUT rather an abandoned Gotham Power and Electric Company substation in Newtown. But through the false wall at the south side there was a small flight of stairs, and at the bottom of that another door, and then, beyond, the place Bruce Wayne was currently resting his head. He didn't like thinking of it as a Batcave, but then, he'd never cared much for calling the true cave that either. As it was, though, the true cave was buried under the ruins of Wayne Manor, a house that had stood for over two hundred years only to be felled in an instant by Nature's whimsy.

This Batcave was only one of several throughout Gotham, a network of bolt-holes and command posts he had constructed after his back had been broken a few years back by the man who called himself Bane. Bane had defeated Batman, had nearly killed him, and Bane had done it all by wearing Batman down, chipping away at him until there was nothing left with which the Batman could fight.

Never again, Batman had vowed. Never that unprepared again.

Thus the many satellite caves.

The Batman stepped back, throwing the switch for the gasoline generator, then activating the lights. The space was cramped, used for both work and rest. Medical supplies and other equipment were neatly stacked along one far wall. A worktable ran the length of another, the metal surface covered with bits and pieces of equipment, extra spools of monofilament, a scattering of pocket explosives, miniature tear gas, and smoke grenades. A squat radio with handset rested near the edge, switched off.

The paraphernalia of the Batman.

Batman turned, checking the progress of his companion on the stairs, watching as Alfred Pennyworth entered and then moved past him. Somewhere in his sixties, tall, thin, and eminently proper, Alfred took the small room in archly, the coat he'd been wearing in disguise folded properly over his left arm, the false beard and broad-brimmed hat in one hand.

"Very nice, Master Bruce," Alfred said. "You've done wonders with the place."

"Thank you, Alfred." Bruce Wayne pulled back the cowl, feeling in that instant of exposure the weight that always returned to his heart. He watched as the older man set the coat and hat on the nearest cot, then turned back to look at him. Bruce knew the look, the combat-medic look that Alfred had turned on him every night when Batman returned to the true cave. More than a survey of damage, it was a look that spoke volumes. It was, more often than not, a paternal look, and there were times when Bruce savored it.

There were times when he hated it from his core.

Alfred Pennyworth had been one of Thomas and Martha Wayne's dearest friends. When Bruce was orphaned at eight, it was Alfred who took care of him, and since that time, Alfred had always been there. Alfred had been Bruce's tutor and confidant and, certainly, the greatest gentleman's gentleman one could ever have asked for. He was an able medic, a gifted actor, a learned scholar of life.

But he was not, and could never be, Bruce Wayne's father. And both men knew that.

For nearly a minute they stood in silence looking at one another. Then Alfred coughed discreetly into his hand.

"I had begun to fear, Master Bruce, that the homing transmitter was defective."

"No." Bruce moved to the table, began unfastening the Utility Belt around his waist, laying it out on the surface, checking its compartments. "I was."

"I beg your pardon, sir?"

"I was, Alfred. I have to relearn how to move in Gotham. Broken cornices, rubble, collapsed rooftops . . . it's forcing me to slow down." He stopped respooling the monofilament for a moment. "I hope it's not Gotham trying to tell me something."

"Given the length of your absence, sir, I had thought you would have worked past such thoughts already."

"I thought I had, too."

"You have only been back a scant few weeks," Alfred said mildly. "And tonight was your first foray in your . . . work clothes, shall we say? It could have gone much worse."

"You nearly died."

"But I did not." The older man sighed. "As always, you demand too much of yourself."

"I've been away nearly three months," Bruce said. "Three months I wasted, searching my own soul instead of fighting for Gotham's."

"After every battle, a time is required to recover. After a defeat, sir, the recovery is inevitably longer. I know you well enough to say with certainty that you never waste time."

Bruce smiled almost without meaning to. "The night wasn't a total failure," he conceded.

"No, indeed," Alfred agreed, turning to the workbench and using a handkerchief from his pocket to dust quickly before leaning back against it. "We have learned that I am a brilliant actor who can masquerade effectively as a senile old coot."

"We knew that already," Bruce said softly.

"I beg your pardon, sir?"

"We know that Penguin is interested in clearing the waterways. That means that whatever pipeline he has to the outside world—assuming he *does* have one—isn't by water. That means he must have access to a tunnel."

"A plausible conclusion, Master Bruce."

For a moment, neither of the men said anything. Bruce finished restocking the stores on the Utility Belt.

"I was away too long," he finally said. "The rules have changed. That man, the one who held the knife to you on the bridge . . . he should have run. They've forgotten me, Alfred."

Alfred shook his head, a bare smile. "No, sir. It is simply that there are now things in Gotham which scare them more than the Batman."

Bruce considered the older man's words for several seconds, then began fastening the belt in place once more.

"Sir?" The concern in Alfred's voice was almost surprisingly clear. "Do you intend to go out again?"

"Night's young. A lot to do."

"Shall I wait for your return here?"

"No. You said Leslie is still in the city."

"Indeed she is, sir. Dr. Thompkins has maintained a small neutral zone in the northeast of the city, where she tends the sick and injured as best she can. It is widely referred to as the 'MASH Sector.'"

Bruce nodded slightly. Dr. Leslie Thompkins, like Alfred, had been a friend of his parents. A passionate humanitarian and physician, Bruce wasn't surprised at all to have learned that Leslie had remained behind in the No Man's Land, attempting to provide medical services to any and all who could reach her.

"Leslie's a remarkable woman."

"I would be a fool to disagree, sir," Alfred said.

"Head there. I'll contact you when I can." Bruce turned to face his butler. "I'm sorry I was slow tonight, Alfred."

"Better late than never, Master Bruce. It was nice seeing you back in action. You looked, dare I say, quite good. Did it feel good?"

"No, Alfred." Bruce pulled the cowl back into place, felt the comfort of the mask tight around his face. "It felt great."

. . .

It did feel great, and that was his greatest comfort as the Batman moved back into the night, quickly climbing the shattered lines of rubble until he reached those still-stable rooftops that gave him a view of the city spreading out around him. *His* city.

Looking over the wrecked terrain, Batman thought he could feel tears coming to his eyes, and for a moment felt sentimental and even foolish. He turned north and deployed his jumpline, swinging across the collapsed ruin of what had been a mosque, moving quickly, feeling the comfort that came from familiar motion.

When the rumors had begun that the government was planning to abandon Gotham, Bruce Wayne had gone to Washington to plead his city's case. It had been a horrible experience for him, one where he had felt exceptionally off balance, and certainly out of his element. To the public eye Bruce Wayne was a joke; a billionaire layabout more concerned with shaving strokes off his notoriously bad golf game and dating as many beautiful women as quickly as possible than dabbling in issues of politics. For the most part, it was an image that had served Bruce well, had kept his true identity well hidden from the world.

In Washington, though, it had worked *too* well, and Bruce Wayne's heartfelt pleas were dismissed out of hand. He had been utterly and completely helpless, a feeling he had known only once before in his life. It was the feeling that had led him onto the streets of Gotham every night for ten years, that had driven him for almost three times that long. It was the feeling that had ultimately created the Batman.

He stopped, crouching carefully on the edge of a slumped roof overlooking what had been Park Row. When he was a boy, Park Row had been one of the nicest parts of town, a collection of high-priced town houses and elegant shops, restaurants, and theaters. All manner of Gothamites could be found walking the neighborhood's streets, and at night the lights had shone on men and women and children who laughed and rejoiced in the glory of their city. Park Row was where Thomas and Martha Wayne took their little son to the movies, where they'd promised to take him for ice cream after the show.

Even before the Cataclysm, though, Park Row had declined to

become what was universally referred to throughout Gotham as Crime Alley. The shops had closed, the town houses had been replaced by blocks upon blocks of substandard housing. Its alleys and streets, once clean and alive with laughter, had turned dark and foreboding. Trash had littered the streets, and the laughter had fled, chased away by the cries of suffering addicts, the sounds of violence, ultimately, by the screams of victims.

To the Batman, there had been one scream, nearly twenty-five years before, that had started it all.

He moved from the rooftop, dropping silently onto the rubble below. Clinging to the shadows, he made his way up the block, and then left. He knew the way perfectly, having traveled it literally a thousand times before, and when he reached the mouth of the alley, he stopped.

It had been here that it all started. It had been here that Thomas and Martha Wayne had been murdered, here that Bruce felt for the first time the utter capriciousness of life. Looking now at where his parents had lain, bleeding to death so many years ago, the Batman felt that helplessness again.

His parents had died before him, and Bruce had been powerless to stop it. That single thing, more than any other, had created the Batman. He had dedicated his life to a mission; what Bruce Wayne suffered that night no one else ever would.

It was a fool's quest, and he knew it, doomed to failure before it had even begun. He could not police a planet, could barely police his own city. Yet he did it anyway, night after night, fighting through despair, returning again and again to the battle that consumed him.

He did not think of himself as noble, nor even as driven. It was far more complicated, and yet far simpler, than that.

He was the Batman. He had no other choice.

Until, at least, Congress had made him feel eight years old once more, had again delivered the lesson that life could not be controlled, and that even Bruce Wayne's billions, even the Batman's brilliance, could be brushed aside by apathy and self-interest. If Bane had broken his back once more, it would have hurt him less.

It seemed, three months before, not just a setback, but a resounding defeat, indeed, a rout. It had crushed his spirit, and thus injured, Bruce

Wayne and the Batman had both retreated. It was the kind of blow that didn't just call into question one's own actions, but one's own *life*.

While Alfred remained behind in Gotham, using his considerable skills to gather intelligence for the day when the Batman would return, Bruce fled the country, throwing himself with seeming abandon into the role of playboy and dilettante. In fact, he had been building an alibi that would allow Bruce Wayne to vanish for the months, if not years, it would take the Batman to restore Gotham.

In Monaco, Bruce had gambled with petty monarchs and corpulent executives; in Rio he had danced with supermodels and partied with rock stars; in Hong Kong he had acquired two new companies and bought another Learjet. And all the while, he had planned, trying to see what he had done wrong, trying to discover what he could do to make it right again.

The petty monarchs and executives, they could help bring political pressure on the President of the United States. One of the rock star's personal trainers was an accomplished Capoeira *mestre*. The two companies he acquired each had proprietary construction technology that would aid an eventual rebuilding of Gotham. And he had contacted Lucius Fox, the man he had handpicked to be Wayne Enterprises's CEO, and he had told him that all of the Wayne empire's formidable resources were to be brought to bear for one purpose: the redemption of Gotham.

"The public," Bruce had told Lucius. "It will all come down to the public. That's where we need to start."

"How?" Lucius had said.

"I don't know. Buy ads. Television, newspaper, radio. Hire lobbyists. Anything. But we have to get the public on Gotham's side."

"It'll take time, Bruce. And a lot of money. A hundred million, at least, just to do what you're talking about."

"It's my home, Lucius," Bruce had said, and then pretended he was wanted at the pool to pour more suntan lotion on the back of someone named Kitty.

It had taken, in the Batman's opinion, much too long to get his act together, to put his plan into motion. Too long since he had set foot on his home ground.

Now he had been in Gotham for just over a week, watching and waiting, walking the different neighborhoods, learning the new dynamic of the No Man's Land. The tagging intrigued him; the bat-tag he had seen, in particular, had raised his eyebrow. He had resisted the urge to jump pell-mell into the fray, instead making contact with Alfred, learning what the gentleman's gentleman had to tell.

Finally, the Batman felt ready to face the helplessness head-on.

A dog was barking nearby, and the sound drew Batman's attention back to the present, away from the alley. The sound seemed alien, and he realized that since returning to Gotham he had seen no dogs at all, nowhere on the streets.

The barking grew louder and more desperate, and Batman moved toward the sound, taking the rooftops again, staying silent on the dark and empty street. The noise was deceptive in the stillness of the city, at first seeming merely around the next corner, but Batman had gone six blocks before finally homing in on the source. From the edge of a rooftop he looked down.

It was an adult Airedale, standing in the middle of the street, its tail stiff and its head lowered as it guarded its master, a boy of perhaps fifteen. The two were surrounded by a group of men, all in salvaged and torn winter clothes, all holding makeshift weapons of one kind or another. Across the street from where he had perched, Batman could make out a spray-painted tag on one of the opposite buildings, the crossed spears of the Xhosa.

"Looks like dinner," one of the men below was saying. He held a baseball bat, its end wrapped in barbed wire.

The Airedale's head dipped lower, growling. The boy began backing away, then halted as he realized that he and his pet had been surrounded. His voice drifted up to where Batman had perched, thin with fear.

"Leave my dog alone," the boy said.

"Weren't talking about no dog," the one with the bat said.

Normally, Batman would have waited a second or two longer, timing his entrance to best effect just before any violence could begin. But what he was seeing now made him angry, and he'd had enough. He launched himself off the rooftop with a leap, gathering the edges of his cape in each hand, letting the air fill the ballistic fabric. The move served two purposes. First, it slowed his descent enough to keep him from any injury. Second, it threw his silhouette over the gathered Xhosa, and put the fear of God into them. The moon had risen already, and in its light the shadow of cape and cowl fell over the assembly the way a storm cloud blocks the sun.

Two of the Xhosa had enough time to register what was happening. They shouted out warnings, and Batman heard the boy gasp. Then he was down, driving his feet into the back of the nearest of the Xhosa as he landed, knocking the man flat to the ground and driving the breath from him. Without stopping Batman continued forward, breaking into the center of the circle, his right hand dipping around beneath his cape and appearing again holding three Batarangs.

He turned and threw all three with his right, ducking as the Xhosa with the barbed-wire bat took a swing at his head. Batman heard the shouts as the Batarangs hit their marks, breaking fingers and disarming the men. Without bothering to look, Batman snapped off a side kick that caught the one with the bat cleanly in the stomach and knocked him to the ground.

One of the Xhosa was already running, and of the three Batman had hit with the Batarangs two of them were turning to flee as well. The one with the bat was now on his back, disarmed. Of the four remaining, one was going for the boy with a machete; the other three were directing their attention at Batman, all wielding blunt objects—two pipes and another bat, this one aluminum.

There was no choice to make, and Batman sprang forward to protect the boy. He felt the blows of the other Xhosa swing past him, then the explosion of pain as one of them connected with his torso. He was certain he'd cracked his ribs again, but it didn't matter. He was still up, and the machete was coming down, and the Batman got his forearm in the way of the blade, felt the collision as the metal bashed into the Kevlar and titanium weave reinforcement of his glove. The nerves in his arm shouted, and again the Batman ignored the message, driving the heel of his right palm into the Xhosa's chin.

Batman turned back to see two of the remaining gang members lunging forward. The Airedale, snarling, had bit into the back of the other's leg, bringing him to the ground. Batman waited a fraction of a second, letting each of the remaining Xhosa commit to their attacks. Then, with their balance changing, Batman moved, bringing his fist up and into the first's sternum, slamming home a kick to the stomach of the second. Both men went down breathless, each temporarily stunned.

The Airedale made a horrible whine, almost a shriek, and Batman turned to see that the one with the barbed-wire bat had gotten his weapon to hand once more, had struck the dog on its hindquarters. The boy, enraged, was already on the man, beating at his head and neck. Batman reached quickly, pulling the boy back, and then, with his free hand, delivered a final, savage punch to the remaining Xhosa's face.

It was suddenly silent but for the sobbing breath of the boy, and the gentle whine of the dog.

Batman let the boy go, crouching quickly beside the animal. The barbed wire around the bat had torn at the dog's skin, and blood was flowing, but Batman could tell quickly that the blow had broken no bones and that the wound looked far more serious than it was. From his Utility Belt he took a bandage and pressed it against the wound, petting the dog as he did so.

"What's your name?" he asked the boy.

The boy, still sobbing, needed some time before he could stammer out, "Matt."

The Batman nodded and scooped the dog up, cradling the Airedale against his chest. "Matt. Are you alone here?"

"I . . . my . . . my parents died in . . . in the 'quake. Is . . . is Sophie going to be all right?"

"Sophie will be fine. Where are you living?"

"I don't have a . . . anywhere I can. Anywhere that's safe."

Batman looked at the boy, thinking, and then realized that the look was easily mistaken for an imposing one, and so looked away down the street, instead. After another second, he began walking north along the street, still carrying the dog. "Follow me."

Matt scurried over the broken pavement, catching up. "Where are we going?"

"Sophie and you need a safe place to stay," Batman said. "I have a friend who is a doctor. You can stay with her."

Together, with Batman still carrying the dog, they made their

way north, to Leslie Thompkin's MASH Sector. For a long time, neither of them spoke.

Then Matt asked, "Are you . . . uh . . . are you really . . . *him*?"

"Him?"

"Batman."

"Yes."

For several more seconds the boy was silent, thinking hard.

"Cool."

ORACLE

Dear Dad—

I woke up yesterday morning thinking I was late for school. I was hearing your voice, and I sat up in the darkness of my apartment, in the bitter cold, and for a second I honestly thought I was thirteen once more.

Then I remembered where I was, and I started to lie back down, and I heard your voice again.

It was just before dawn, the light beginning to streak in across the ceiling, past the ice that's been forming on the inside of my windows every night. I reached for my glasses, fumbled myself to the side of the bed, and hoisted my drowsy keister into the chair. The only reason I was sure I was awake was that I was so damn cold I knew I couldn't still be under my blankets.

I rolled to the window and had to open it to look out, and then it was really clear, your voice, coming through some megaphone from down below, maybe a block away at the most.

"There's a new gang on the street! The Blue Boys, the GCPD! Street Demonz, LoBoys, you're in *our* territory now! Surrender!"

Over and over again, variations on the same theme. Your voice, big and echoing down the block. Across the street I saw doors and windows opening, people pulling back their barricades and risking glances outside, listening. At the end of the block, I watched a group of Street Demonz break around the corner running like the whole department was after them with hats and bats. Then you guys appeared, and for a second that's almost exactly what it did look like.

At least, if your department had switched to baseball bats and makeshift clubs, instead of riot batons and .38 Specials.

"Attention!" you were shouting. "We are the police! We're here to maintain the order! Help us rid your streets of these gangsters! Now's the time to rise up! Now's the time to take back what's yours!"

It was like magic, Dad.

Like magic.

"There aren't many women who can say that a war was fought on their behalf," you said after I finally got you to stop hugging me.

I thought maybe you were joking at first, but the look in your eyes said that you weren't, and you almost made me cry. Sarah was standing right behind you, and she was smiling, and when you moved she gave me a hug and a kiss on the cheek.

"Care to step outside?" she asked.

"Are you kidding?" I said. "I haven't been out of this damn apartment since the earthquake. If you're willing to carry me down eighteen floors, I'm willing to go outside."

"Your father will carry you," she said. "I'll take the chair."

And you did, you picked me up and carried me down eighteen flights of stairs, and when we got out front and I was back in the wheelchair, you handed me a can of blue spray paint and pointed at the Demonz tag on the side of the Clock Tower.

"Would you like to do the honors?" you asked.

You have no idea how big a kick I got out of spraying that big, blue "GCPD" on the side of my own home. And the people watching, all my neighbors who had been living under siege just like myself for the last three months, they loved it, too. I thought they were going to put you and Sarah on their shoulders and march you through the streets, they were so happy.

Then Bullock came over and said, "The neighborhood's been secured. We've got

Demonz and LoBoys in a temporary holding area on the next block for now. Pettit's getting antsy."

"I'll come over," you said, and you gave my hand a squeeze and promised you'd be right back, and off you went, Sarah with you.

I sat there for a minute, just grinning at the street, breathing the fresh winter air. It hurt my lungs it was that cold, but God, it felt good. I'd been cooped up for so long, I couldn't get enough of it. The sidewalk was cracked in places, but pretty clear, and I started rolling along, and it wasn't really that I meant to follow you, but in the end I have to admit that's what I was doing.

I came around the corner and I heard Foley talking to Bullock.

". . . all our lives for the sake of his daughter, Harvey. He got damn lucky."

"Luck, hell," Bullock said. "It was strategy. It was tactics."

"It was pure recklessness." Foley was practically spitting. "Sanctioning murder. He should be ashamed to call himself a police."

"He doesn't call himself a police, Foley. He calls himself Commissioner."

Foley opened his mouth to shoot off something else, and that's when he saw me. I wish I could say that the way he went pale, or the way he muttered sorry, or the way he slunk off made me feel better.

I wish I could.

But I can't.

I thought that was the low point of the day, the counter to the delight in seeing you and Sarah.

I was wrong.

Around midnight one of my agents called in, Alex. He's been pretty reliable for me, and he's another of my sneaks, in that he's good at sticking to the shadows and getting in close to where the action is. I've no reason to doubt the veracity of his reports.

When you and Sarah left today, I knew you were trying to figure out what to do with the Demonz and LoBoys that had been taken prisoner. Jailing them was obviously out of the question. The jail itself is in ruins, and it's not like you can spare anyone to guard these guys twenty-four hours a day, seven days a week. And that doesn't even touch on the resource drain it would be.

Alex reported that you and Pettit had been arguing about how to proceed for most of the evening, and that you finally made a decision a little after dark. You and Pettit went over to the holding area.

Alex says that you used that megaphone of yours again, and you gave all the LoBoys and all the Demonz one hour to clear the territory.

"If any of you are found here after that, the penalty is death," you said.

Then Pettit drew his weapon, put it to the head of the nearest LoBoy, and splattered his brains all over the street.

Just to prove that you guys were serious.

I know he did it without your permission, Dad. I know that. I know you would never have sanctioned a murder in cold blood.

You're a cop, after all. You're the best cop.

You're my hero, Dad.

Tell me he did it without your permission.

My radio woke me eight minutes ago, a squawk from the one frequency I've kept clear for the last 104 days. The frequency I've been praying would go active.

I had been dreaming about what I was like when I had my legs, or at least, when my legs would listen to my brain. I had been dreaming of the nights when I could almost fly, when I felt beautiful and powerful and did good. Dreaming myself as I had been, as Batgirl. In my dream, Gotham had been whole and vibrant, the lights of the city bright. I moved from rooftop to air to rooftop again, and I was happy and certain and feeling so very much alive.

And then I heard his voice, and I opened my eyes, and it was him, on the radio.

"I'm back. Just thought you'd like to know."

The way he said it, it was like he'd just gone down to the corner for some groceries and been delayed. That's the way he said it.

"It was you, then," I said. "Putting the tags up in Dooley Square."

"Tags?"

"Bat-tags, yellow paint. Your symbol."

"I haven't been to Dooley Square."

"Then who was it?" I asked, but there was no response, just static, and I realized he'd cut the connection.

I'm looking at the dawn of NML Day 104, and I'm beginning to think that things aren't getting better.

I'm beginning to think they're about to get worse.

A lot worse.

EIGHT

JAMES GORDON WAS WORKING IN THE garden, trying to get frozen earth out of a terra cotta flowerpot. His fingers hurt, and his back, and Sarah had already told him to come inside and go to bed, that it was past midnight, but he knew there was no point to it. If he went to bed he'd stay awake, replaying the moment in his head. If he went to bed he'd close his eyes, and if he closed his eyes, he'd see it all again.

The LoBoy's look of surprise that turned to horror in the instant before Pettit pulled the trigger.

The look in his eyes the moment after the bullet had burst through brain and bone, and the LoBoy had realized he was dead.

Gordon was clenching his jaw without meaning to, and he had to force himself to relax. Not a LoBoy, he thought. Just a boy. Not older than twenty, at the most. Some scared twenty-year-old kid who tried to survive the No Man's Land by being tough, finding safety in numbers, and doing what the rest did.

How was that any damn different from what he and the rest of the GCPD were doing right now?

He set the pot down, realizing the attempt was futile. The earth was staying put, despite his best intentions. He looked up at the clear sky, the starlight so much brighter in the cold air. After one, now, at least.

He heard scraping from the far side of the garden, the sounds of pebbles rattling on the ground. More rats running along the edge, looking for food. He and Sarah had found a couple inside in the last few weeks, searching for scraps in the empty kitchen. Gordon doubted they'd had any luck.

It was Pettit, that was the damn problem. Simply giving the declaration, telling them to stay out, warning them if they ever came back they'd be killed—Pettit had insisted that wasn't enough.

"They have to know you mean it, Commissioner," Pettit had said.

And Gordon had responded, "I do."

He hadn't been lying.

But Pettit had killed the boy anyway, and when Gordon, almost spitting in his fury, had demanded why, the response had been unequivocal, almost reasonable.

"Now they believe us. Now they'll run all over the city, telling everyone they meet that the Blue Boys aren't to be messed with. They'll say we've lost it, and that anyone who crosses us is looking for a world of hurt. Now they'll leave us alone."

Pettit was right, of course. The words would not have been enough. It was the action that sold them.

But it didn't make Jim Gordon feel any better.

The rats had stopped their scrabbling, and there was another sound, soft, and Gordon realized he wasn't alone in the garden any longer. He rose slowly, taking his time to ease his right hand to his hip, and started to turn for the door back to the house. There was another sound, the slight noise of a foot readjusting on the cold earth, and he could pinpoint it now. He pivoted, drawing, and as he did so he thought that perhaps it might be Batman and not some LoBoy out for revenge, in which case Gordon wouldn't shoot, but he sure as hell would give the vigilante a piece of his mind.

"Working the graveyard shift, Commissioner?"

The voice came from the corner away from the house, deep in the shadow beneath the leafless plum tree. Gordon couldn't make out the shape of the speaker. But he knew the voice, and he cocked the pistol in his hands, holding it steady.

"How did you get in here?"

"Simple. Your men are too tired, too terrified, and too few. You've all had a long week, haven't you? All that running around, chasing the Demonz and the LoBoys . . . and then that little execution in the street. Didn't know you had that in you, Jimmy."

"Give me a reason I don't drop you where you stand," Gordon said.

"I'll give you two. First, you haven't heard what I have to say. Second, you're still the law."

Gordon adjusted his grip, breathing carefully.

"Want me to continue?" the voice asked.

"I'm listening."

"We can help each other, Jim."

"Forget it. You're psychotic."

When the man laughed, it was the laugh Gordon remembered, and it made chills run down his spine.

"One man's psychotic is another man's visionary," the voice said reasonably. "Besides which, if we're going to bring up the issue of sanity, what kind of police lets his wife and crippled daughter stay in this godforsaken hellhole? Anyone with half a brain quit while the going was good. All that's left in Gotham are the degenerates, the same people you'd never have thought twice about rousting before NML.

"But here you are, Jimmy, with no legal jurisdiction and no powers of the state behind you. Why'd *you* stay?"

"Someone had to," Gordon said. "Law must be maintained. There has to be order."

"Exactly! Justice must prevail, even in a lawless land. That's why I'm here. We're two of a kind, Commissioner. Anarchy has forged some strange allies here. Why not us?"

Gordon swallowed, feeling the ache in his triceps from holding the gun steady for so long. "Because you're a killer," he whispered.

"Really? Then the joke's on you, isn't it?"

"What do you mean?"

"Don't play coy. I heard about your stunt with the Demonz and the LoBoys, playing them off against each other while you and yours sat back and watched." The voice stopped for a second. When it resumed, its tone was friendly. "It was a good move. Tactically brilliant. Ruthless. I liked it."

"This is war," Gordon spat.

"I know."

"Desperate times call for desperate measures."

"Jim, you're preaching to the choir, here. You've got nothing to lose by hearing me out."

Gordon looked at the shape in the shadows, saw both hands come up, palms out and empty. The ache in his arms was fierce, now, and the pain in his back was getting worse. With a shock, he realized that he was feeling truly old.

He put his thumb on the hammer and uncocked the pistol, lowering the weapon to point at the ground.

"Talk," Gordon said. "I'll listen."

Sarah was asleep when he crawled into bed, finally, just before dawn. Gordon tried to settle in without disrupting her, and he'd finally forced his body to relax, letting his head truly sink back into the pillow, when she rolled to look at him.

"Jim?"

"Go back to sleep."

"I thought I heard voices," she said, softly. "In the garden."

Gordon shook his head slightly, putting an arm around his wife, and she moved in closer and he felt her warmth chasing the chill away from his own body.

"Was someone out there?" Sarah asked, sleepily.

"No, shamus. Just me."

She yawned. "Must have dreamt it."

"Must have."

He felt her breathing lengthen and grow regular once more, and he knew she had fallen back asleep, probably had never truly woken at all. In the morning, the odds were she wouldn't remember the conversation ever taking place.

James Gordon stared at the ceiling.

When he closed his eyes, he saw the boy's face.

NINE

 THE WOMAN WHO HAD MADE HERSELF into the new Batgirl had never known all that much about Black Mask. But it seemed to her that, this time, the criminal had finally gone off the deep end.

She knew the man who had once called himself Roman Sionis had started life as a spoiled and rich brat, heir to the Sionis cosmetics fortune, an empire of makeup and perfumes created by Roman's parents. She knew that somewhere along the line, little Roman had become obsessed with masks—both literal and figurative. She was hazy on a lot of the details, but some stuck in memory—the fact that Sionis's face had been horribly burnt in a chemical fire, one that had left his skin shiny and black; the fact that Sionis had fashioned his mask from the lid of his mother's ebony coffin; the fact that Sionis, upon creating himself as Black Mask, had gathered to him those criminals he could, calling them the False Face Society; that the False Face Society had been some of Gotham's worst and most diehard felons, all of them masked, all of them eager to do violence in the name of their work.

For a couple of years, despite Sionis's clearly slipping grip on sanity, he had ruled the Gotham underworld, had even managed to expand operations as far south as Blüdhaven, down the coast. Crazy he might have been all along, but it hadn't gotten in his way.

Not anymore, she thought.

For the better part of a week now, every night after finishing her other duties and donning the costume, the new Batgirl had headed out from her home and worked her way along the East Side, trying to track Black Mask's movements, or if not him precisely, at least the movements of his gang. The Street Demonz and LoBoys had been taken down finally by the GCPD, and she felt it was time to expand her purview, as well; time to take down another of the warlords, and try to keep Gotham from spiraling entirely into the pit.

She had chosen Black Mask as her target for a couple of reasons, not the least of which being he was a "named" criminal, and she wanted that cachet. She wanted it in spades, so everyone in Gotham would know that the Bat still haunted the night, and that criminals had damn well better beware. She didn't know if Batman himself was ever coming back—if indeed he was truly gone, rather than just lying low—but she knew the power of the symbol, what the Bat meant to Gotham, and she was going to make certain nobody forgot.

So that was the first reason for her choice. The second was more practical. Black Mask's followers had been appearing more and more frequently in what she considered to be her neck of the woods, and their appearances were consistently unpleasant. The followers were maybe as crazy as Black Mask himself, self-mutilated men and women who dressed in rags and tatters, fresh scars showing on every inch of their exposed flesh. From what Batgirl had heard, they were collecting people; to what end she did not know.

But those reasons aside, there was one other, just as important and certainly more motivating, at least for her. If and when the Batman came back, she wanted to be able to look him in the eye, to make it perfectly clear that she was, if not his equal, at least worthy of playing on the same team.

If she could take down Black Mask, that would do it. If she did that, he'd have no choice but to accept her.

She harbored no illusions about how the Batman would respond to her. By donning the mantle of the Bat without his permission, indeed, without his knowledge, she had issued a challenge. And she knew enough about him to know he wouldn't like that. His partners in the past—Robin and Nightwing—they had been authorized help, trained by him personally. Even with that she knew for a fact that they were ridden hard, that Batman demanded as much from them as from himself. In his book, there was no room at all for failure. You could do the job or you couldn't, and that was the end of the discussion.

So the new Batgirl would show him just how well she could do the job.

She'd tracked a group of Black Mask's followers from Puckett Park on the Upper East Side all the way to where the Sprang River separated the north and south parts of the island that was Gotham. There had been six of them in the group, all in the same mixture of torn rags and tatters, and all with horrible mutilations to their faces and arms. Most had shaved their heads, and a couple had managed makeshift piercings through their skin, thin strips of metal that dangled and glinted in the night, swaying from their faces.

Batgirl watched as they entered the remnants of St. Vincent's off what had once been Dillon Avenue, waited another twenty seconds, and then slid through the shadows until she was close enough to get a look inside. Light was flickering from within. One source, she thought, probably a single fire. There was the soft sound of voices.

Inside, beyond the pews, she saw the group seated together around the fire. One of them was handing out bundles from a small cloth bag. She watched as each of the followers speared their bundle on the end of a long spike, then held it over the fire. The stink of burning fur assaulted her.

Rats, she thought. They're eating rats.

She held still for almost another minute, watching, then resolved that the group would be staying put for some time. Her back was exposed, too, and that made her very uncomfortable, and so she stepped silently away, scaling the side of a nearby building, testing the wall as she climbed. Up top, she turned and settled in to watch the entrance of the church. They'd be coming out soon, probably when it was darker. She'd follow them if she could, and maybe they'd lead her to Black Mask himself, and maybe, just maybe, she could figure out his agenda.

Didn't make sense, she thought again. In a city where more of the structures have collapsed than are still standing, Black Mask is having his folks burn down those that remain.

And it wasn't even that he was going after all of the standing structures; the fact that she had her current perch and that they were inside St. Vincent's right now was proof of that. No, it seemed to be only certain buildings. She had heard from someone in the MASH Sector that a whole mob of Black Mask's followers had descended on the old Embassy Orient and driven out all of the squatters. And then they'd burnt the place to the ground, destroying the shelter used by over sixty of Gotham's refugees.

From what Batgirl had heard, there had been over fifty people in Black Mask's mob. Practically an army in the No Man's Land, and terrifying to contemplate even for a moment. Fifty of the mutilated monsters, all descending on the Embassy Orient. It was a miracle no one had died.

"Nice costume."

Batgirl stiffened, taking her time to turn, telling herself she had known this was coming all along. She forced herself to meet his eyes, but he wasn't ready for the stare-down yet. He looked her over slowly, starting with the boots, then tracking up until he reached her fully concealed face.

"Glad you approve," she said. She did a good job keeping her voice neutral, and thought she sounded nearly as arrogant and dis-passionate as he.

"I don't," Batman said.

"Gotham needed a Bat. You weren't around."

"Where I've been and why, those reasons are my own."

She thought he sounded almost defensive, and that gave her confidence that she had made the right choice in donning the costume. She took a step closer, and now he was meeting her eyes.

"But now you're back," she said. "And you're going to need help."

"No."

"You're wrong."

His voice was harder, though no louder. "Then I'll learn that on my own."

She adjusted her stance, reminding herself to hold her ground. "I've been doing this for weeks now. It's made a difference."

"The work or the symbol?" He never looked away from her, and behind the mask his eyes were hidden, but she was certain they were locked on her own.

"The Bat is a powerful image, as you know," she said. "Very primal. Very potent. It's made things . . . easier."

He didn't say anything.

"If you tell me to take it off, I will." She made it sound matter-of-fact, not a concession, simply an agreement. "But I won't stop the work."

He nodded slowly, as if accepting the concession and the terms. Then he gestured to her waist with his chin, where the can of spray paint was affixed to her belt. "The tagging. That's been you?"

"Yes."

"It's a good idea. I intend to adopt it."

"Thanks."

He looked past her for a moment, to the horizon. "You're right about one thing. This city does need a Bat."

"Maybe more than one."

His head came back to her quickly, and for a moment she thought she'd pushed it too far, that she'd blown it. But when he spoke, his tone was the same level one, all restraint and control.

"Don't disgrace the symbol."

"Then I'm approved?"

"No," he said. "But you're not disapproved."

"Fair enough. For now."

Batman turned, the cape billowing back for a moment as he stepped up to the edge of the roof. Without looking back, he said, "Keep your watch on Black Mask. I'll be in touch."

And then he stepped off into the air, and fell into the darkness.

TEN

CHRISTINA WEIR HAD BEEN A COP FOR eight years before the No Man's Land was declared; she loved her job, and she was damn good at it. That was why she'd stayed in Gotham. She was GCPD. It was what she was supposed to do. Even before Gordon and Essen had announced that they were staying behind on Black Monday, even before the other officers—DeFilippis and Montoya and Bullock and the rest—all threw their lot in with the Commissioner, she had decided to stay.

She'd had absolutely no intention of falling in love as a result of the decision.

During the battle against the Demonz and the LoBoys over a week before, she'd waded to the front and kicked some serious ass. She'd even saved a couple of lives. DeFilippis's, when a Demonz skel tried to bury a hatchet in the young cop's head—Weir had stopped that action with a knee to the groin—then Bullock's, when the LoBoys had started in with the arrows and she'd pushed him out of the line of fire. She'd almost been too slow then: A shaft of wood had pierced Bullock's coat.

"Harvey, Jesus," she'd said, and Bullock had laughed and pulled back the fabric to show where the arrow had passed through the clothing but missed his skin.

"I'm only half the man I once was," he'd told her, pulling on his baggy overcoat to illustrate the weight he'd lost in the last few months. "You keep jumping on me like this, Weir, I'm gonna accuse you of sexual harassment."

She'd blushed and scrambled off him, thinking that he knew, because, after all, he was a detective. But Bullock's expression hadn't changed and she had known that she was being paranoid. There was no way any of them knew, she had been certain. She and DeFilippis had been careful.

By then the fighting had moved on and she'd had to rush to catch up. They'd taken back Central, then Old Gotham, and then Pettit had gotten out of hand. She didn't want to dwell on that, but it soured the victory. She didn't want to call what Pettit had done murder, but she sure as hell couldn't think of another way to put it.

That night she had wanted to find Andy again, wanted to sneak another few minutes of warmth in his arms, but it hadn't worked out. She'd been on post outside of the Gordon home until past midnight, and he'd been out at Central, getting things squared away. Just wasn't possible, and she'd known that, but it had made her moody anyway, and when Donnelly had tried to get her talking about baseball that night on post she hadn't even responded. She'd gone back to her shelter before three, the gutted remnants of what had once been a liquor store, eaten a cold dinner of Beefaroni straight from the can, removed her boots and body armor, slid into the sleeping bag, and put her head down on the pillow.

Then she'd raised it again, wondering what was making such a hard lump. She'd found her flashlight, flicked it on just long enough to move the pillow and take a look, and beneath the pillow she'd found a small, miraculously intact music box. When she opened it, it had played "Lara's Theme" from *Doctor Zhivago*.

She'd gone to sleep listening to it play.

. . .

"You're late, Chris," Donnelly said to her the next morning when she returned to post.

"I know," Weir said, falling into position beside the front door of the house, feeling her stomach quaver. "Had a can of Beefaroni before bed last night and shot the whole thing back out again this morning."

Officer Donnelly looked at her with some concern. "That's not good. I've got some canned tuna if you want. It tastes okay, and it's pretty mild."

She shook her head. "Not really hungry, Brian."

He shrugged. "Commissioner wanted to see you."

"Why?"

"He didn't say. He's in the garden."

She looked over her shoulder at the closed front door of the house. "Now?"

"Said as soon as you arrived."

Her stomach turned from uneasy to honestly sour. "Be right back," she said, heading inside.

"Word of advice, Chris," Brian called after her. "Don't say the name, 'Batman.' Andy says it's poison."

"Yeah, he told me," she muttered, already too worried about what it might mean to be summoned to the garden. She had nothing but respect for Gordon, thought of him as a gifted police and a strong leader, but—and she knew this already—if he knew about her and DeFilippis and he wanted it to stop, she was going to have to tell him to keep out of it. She'd spent more than a month thinking about it already, and while she understood the department's policy against fraternization, she hardly felt it was an issue. And the fact was, if Gordon went there, she'd call him on it. It was the pot and the kettle, as far as she was concerned.

He was at the workbench when she came in, chipping away at the frozen earth inside a clay pot, but he stopped when he saw her enter, saying, "Chris, come on in."

She came down the steps and stopped a respectful ten feet away, keeping her face blank. She'd been a patrol officer before the NML, a sergeant, but she knew the detective tricks well, and she knew how to keep a poker face.

Gordon studied her for a moment, almost stern, then asked, "How are you feeling?"

"Fine, sir."

"Good, good. I heard about what you did, Chris."

She kept her mouth shut.

"It was fine work," Gordon finished. "In the last week alone I've had six people tell me that you retook Central pretty much single-handed. Montoya, Lee, Bullock . . . all of them have gone out of their way to tell me what a fine job you did."

Despite her best efforts the surprise leaked out. "Sir?"

"It's mostly because of that that I wanted to talk to you. You know that my daughter is still in the city, right?"

"Yes, sir. She lives in the Clock Tower."

Gordon frowned slightly. "Yes, she does. And she refuses to leave. I told her I'd be happier if she was in TriCorner with the rest of us, and she just wouldn't listen. About as stubborn as her old man, I guess."

Weir nodded, not knowing what to say.

"We've got that area pretty much secured," Gordon went on. "But I'm a father and I'm nervous, and that's why I wanted to talk to you." He wiped his dirty hands against his pants, trying to clean them, then looked back at her. His smile was apologetic. "I want you to take five officers, draw arms and ammunition from Pettit, and get a flare gun. And I'd like you to organize the protection around the Clock Tower."

She wasn't entirely certain she understood. "You want me to protect the Tower?"

"Not just the Tower, no, but of course that's a large part of it. You've seen the map. The border is holding, but that's the outer edge. It abuts on Penguin's territory, and Two-Face is to the east, as well. I want a fixed observation post, and I want to make certain my daughter is relatively protected. You're the best person for the job, Chris."

"Thank you, sir."

"If there's any trouble, send up a flare. Otherwise, I trust you to handle whatever may arise."

Weir nodded. "Yes, sir. Thank you, sir."

Gordon stuck out his hand. "No, Chris. Thank you."

ELEVEN

BLACK MASK LOOKED AT THE MAN hanging over the oil drum. The man's feet had been tied to a length of good rope, the rope slung across the rafters, and the effect was like that of a piñata, dangling at a crowded party. The fire from the oil drum was already singeing the man's hair, and his sweat sizzled when it splashed down against the heated metal.

Black Mask removed the blindfold and took the man's face in his hands, tenderly. He tried to do it the way his mother had before she'd died, before he'd changed from Roman Sionis into the deformed and reborn man he was now. He tried to do it with love, because he wanted the man to truly understand.

"Do you see?" Black Mask asked.

"Go to hell," the man spat.

Black Mask shut his eyes for a moment and sighed. This was not really an unexpected response, but he had hoped for more understanding, for less drastic measures. He let his hands slip from the man's face, turning to face the congregation spread out before him. They filled the hall, lit by the burning makeshift torches. He saw the faces of his flock, the scars on each and every one of them. All those scars on the outside, showing the world the truth of what was within each and every one of them.

"He does not yet see," Black Mask said, his voice filling the space, echoing.

The congregation let out a great moan of sadness, nearly fifty voices together in their shared sympathy for the man's plight.

"He believes nothing has changed," Black Mask said. "He believes that the lie can continue. But we know better, do we not? We know better now. Once, yes, once I hid behind a mask myself. Once I covered my scars, my true face. I played games, pretending to greatness. I played games, pretending to rule crime.

"And in one instant I saw it was all false. In that instant, the mask was destroyed.

"In that instant, Gotham fell. For the house built on a foundation of sand, it will collapse under its own weight, surely. Thus Gotham collapsed, its shining façades giving way to the broken soul it concealed.

"What they called an earthquake, we now know was more, a warning."

Black Mask moved around to stand beside the dangling man, still addressing the congregation. From his pocket he removed the straight razor he had used to reveal his own true face, the very blade that had cut the mask from him once and for all. With it he had drawn the lines across the face blackened and burnt so many years before, making cuts that turned the shining and smooth skin into the patchwork of pieces that represented his soul.

"All of us must show our true face or pay the price."

"Amen," said the congregation.

"He must see."

"He must see," echoed the congregation.

"We make the cuts . . ." Black Mask said, reaching out with the blade.

". . . that open our souls," the congregation finished.

Black Mask made the cuts. Blood spattered and sizzled into the flames.

When the man's screams subsided, Black Mask leaned close enough to feel the heat searing at the too sensitive skin on his face. "Do you see?" he asked.

The man was crying, tears mixing with the blood racing along the split skin of his face.

Black Mask smiled and addressed the congregation once more.

"He sees," he said.

"Hallelujah," the congregation cried.

He raised an arm, pointing out the shattered windows of the building in the distance, still standing arrogantly against the broken skyline of the No Man's Land.

"We destroy the lies," he cried. "What has been revealed must remain uncovered. What still stands as a mask must be torn down. Those people who are blind, they must be made to see. Those buildings that still stand, they too must fall. For Gotham to be redeemed, all of its scars must show. Look upon the affront to us, know it for what it is."

The congregation turned, each set of eyes settling on the building in the distance, the tower with the giant clock.

"Do you see?" Black Mask demanded.

"We see," the congregation murmured.

"And shall you act?"

"We shall act."

"Then prepare yourselves well, for the time is short. We will march soon. We will burn it down. And God help anyone who tries to protect the lies.

"Amen."

"Amen."

TWELVE

"BLACK MASK HAS TAKEN THREE MORE buildings in the last two days," Batgirl said. "But each time I arrive, he and his followers have already vanished. I don't know where he's hiding, I don't know where he's working from."

"How many men does he have?" Batman demanded.

"I don't know that, either. I've heard reports of sixty, probably more. It's a cult of some sort, that's about all I've figured out so far. It's . . . it's pretty bad."

"Meaning?"

"Meaning that everywhere he's struck, he's left people either dead or mutilated. Cuts, mostly, but some branding. Uniformly to the face."

Batman nodded, then reached for the canisters resting on the workbench and offered one to her. "Tear gas," he said. "Very potent, special mixture. Use it sparingly."

"I will. Thanks."

"What can you tell me about the buildings?"

"They've all been tall, over six stories."

"Built by Wayne Enterprises," Batman said. It wasn't a question.

"Wayne buildings are the only big ones still standing in Gotham. He was the only builder smart enough to quake-proof his structures. 'Course, at the time, everyone thought it was just another example of his remarkable stupidity."

"Then he was lucky," Batman said, spreading a map of the city on the now-cleared worktable. "Show me where the buildings were."

She drew a line with her gloved finger, down along the East Side, toward the south and Old Gotham. "Consistently been moving south."

"He's going for the Clock Tower."

"You think?"

"I know. It represents Gotham. It was built by Wayne Enterprises. Roman Sionis hates Wayne. If the Clock Tower is not his next target, it's certainly on the short list." He looked up from the map. She felt the glare from behind his hidden eyes, and found herself wondering what she might have done wrong. "You're going to stop him. He will not take the Clock Tower. Is that understood?"

"I'll try, but—"

"Don't try. Keep it from happening." He held the gaze, then added, "And stay out of sight."

"I can do one or the other, not both."

"Then you're not worthy of the mantle." He pivoted silently, moving to the stairs that would lead out of the basement and back into the night. "Prove me wrong."

Batgirl watched him leave. After a time, she realized her fists were clenched, and she forced her fingers open, felt the circulation returning to her hands. Batgirl cursed him softly under her breath, and then began gathering the equipment she'd need for the job.

THIRTEEN

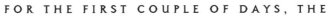 FOR THE FIRST COUPLE OF DAYS, THE
posting went fine. Weir set up a rotating schedule out-
side of the Clock Tower, three shifts of two cops each,
herself included. Gordon let her take Donnelly as her second in command, and he ran the day shift, while Weir took the second shift. Way
she figured it, they'd stick to the schedule as it was for a week, then
swap around so she could get some daylight time in, too. That way it
would be fair, and that way none of the cops would become complacent.

Pettit had granted them all five shells for their shotguns, and
Weir had drawn a flare gun, too, as requested. It was the emergency
beacon, only to be fired off if things really started to go sour.

She settled into position, watching the sunset. Turner was on post
with her, another rookie, like Donnelly, but one who had yet to dis-

tinguish himself in her eyes. Andy had referred to him a couple of times as "the minnow," and looking at him now, Chris had to suppress a grin. Turner was thin and tall and towheaded, and he looked like a worried fish the way his eyes wandered up and down the street.

Her stomach was still bothering her, had been throughout the week. For a while she'd thought it was the water, that maybe it wasn't as purified as the Blue Boys had hoped, but no one else seemed to be reacting to it. For now, she was grinning and bearing it. Worse came to worst, she'd try to make her way up the East Side to the MASH Sector, maybe see the doctor there. If in fact there was a doctor there; the MASH Sector was really nothing more than a rumor as far as she knew, but it seemed plausible that one doctor in all of Gotham City would have been just crazy enough to remain.

The dark finally crept its way in, and the night turned colder. Not as bad as it had been even a week before, and Weir wondered if spring was finally en route. That'd be nice, she thought. A little warmth, something to melt the snow away.

Weir heard it before Turner, and for a moment she thought it was the sound of drums, like some Revolutionary War party was approaching from the distance. But as the noise grew it also became more distinct, and she heard the metal undertone to it, the thudding rhythmic and almost immediately frightening. Through the rubble, it was impossible to determine which direction it was coming from.

"What is that?" Turner asked.

"Shut up." She brought the shotgun up to her shoulder, chambering the first round, using the barrel to guide her search as she swept the length of the street.

Doors were closed. No one was out.

It was getting louder.

"What the hell is that?" Turner asked again, more insistently, and Weir could see where he, too, had brought his weapon to his shoulder.

"I don't know."

"Fire the flare!" he hissed.

"No, not yet. Not until we know what it is."

"Whatever it is, it's not good," Turner insisted. "Come on, Chris, fire the flare. We need reinforcements."

She shook her head, digging the butt of the weapon against her shoulder. She wasn't going to cry wolf; she wasn't going to ask for help until she was damn certain help was needed.

The noise, which had continued to grow, suddenly stopped.

Silence ran down the length of the street, the No Man's Land quiet that Weir heard in the night. The city without noise, no voices, no engines, at times seemed without life itself. Absolute.

That scared her more than the noise did.

Then they appeared at the ends of the street as if by magic, and she thought perhaps her eyes were playing tricks on her. The darkness, perhaps, that was what made them look so awful, so completely pitiless and horrifying. Even at the distance, the faces seemed grotesque, marred, and evil.

One of the figures stepped forward, and she saw he was holding a pistol, a big one, maybe a .357.

"Surrender," Black Mask said. "Or die."

From her angle, Batgirl saw Black Mask leading the larger of the two groups to the north end of the block. Thirty-three of his followers, all of them armed with the weaponry of the NML, bats and clubs and axes and knives. They had only one firearm among them, she was certain, and that was the pistol in Black Mask's hand.

Makes sense, she thought. With the gun, he's in control. Anyone else with a gun, they're a threat.

She checked the harness, making certain the straps were tight, fitted properly. She hoped to God that the wings would hold. She hoped to God she could control her descent and make the right kind of entrance, the entrance that would cut the head off the beast. There was only one way to do this now, and whether Batman approved of it or not, she would go through with it.

It burned her, though, that he had left her to this without explanation. After all, if protecting the Clock Tower was important, why wasn't he there, too? She didn't even understand the reason behind it—as far as Batgirl knew, the Clock Tower was just another building that had somehow managed to keep from falling in the quake.

She'd ask Batman about it later, after it was over. If she still could.

She watched the cops at the foot of the tower reacting as they realized Black Mask had flanked both ends of the block, and that their retreat was cut off. The taller of the two, the male, had turned as if to run, then balked. She heard the woman below shouting something to him, but the other cop didn't seem to hear, or if he did, he didn't seem to care, because he threw down his shotgun and ran.

"Charming," Batgirl muttered.

The remaining cop had put her back to the front of the building.

From the north end of the street, the sound of Black Mask's shout rose to her ears.

"We have come to reveal Gotham's true face," Black Mask proclaimed. Even from on high, she heard him clearly. All else below was silence. He pointed at the Tower, almost at where Batgirl herself was crouched, just above the clock face. "This affront to the No Man's Land, we will destroy it! And all within shall see, shall remove their masks, or else they shall suffer for it."

Just below her, inside the tower, Batgirl heard the sound of a window creaking open, watched as the barrel of a rifle slipped out, glinting in the night. Her surprise was only momentary; clearly people were living in the tower. That someone at the top was about to play sniper was totally unexpected.

Batman would never forgive her if she let Black Mask die.

Without another thought, she pushed off the roof, curling her knees against her chest, and dropped through the air like a cinder block into a pond.

"Turner! You bastard!" Weir shouted.

But there was no point. He was already gone.

At both ends of the street, the mobs began to advance.

Weir dropped the shotgun and went for the flare, and as she did she heard the report, the distinctive explosion of a magnum round, and she felt her leg snap back and the total numbness run from her hip to her foot. She knew she was on her side, felt the cold stairs in front of the Clock Tower digging into her body. Weir knew she had taken a round. And she knew she had the flare gun in her hand.

She fired, watching the white streak race into the sky.

On the street, the converging groups froze, tracking the ascending light.

The flare reached its apex and went out, and for a half second there was only more darkness, and Weir heard someone laughing in the mob.

Then the flare detonated, and everything was suddenly bathed in shattering white light, the shadows falling suddenly, sharp and long around the block. And Weir opened her mouth as the shape, lit by the flare from above, resolved, and she saw the giant wings of a descending bat. Its shadow slid silently over her, across to the mob, and the laughter stopped.

Again, there was only silence.

Then someone screamed.

Weir fumbled for her shotgun, took her eyes off the sky long enough to find the weapon, and tried to reach it. The pain in her leg ran like electricity along the bone, and she bit down on her lip and told herself that the noises she was hearing weren't hers, the screams weren't her own. She lurched, grabbing the gun, rolling and looking for the shot, and again she froze at what she saw.

Smoke had enveloped the space where the mobs were converging, and people were falling back, coughing and crying and running, men and women alike, all with the same horribly mutilated faces. Standing in the middle, clouds spiraling past him, stood Black Mask, gun up, firing at the giant bat descending on him. The wings alone stretched sixteen feet, at least, and as she watched, Weir saw them collapse and a figure drop from between them, cape billowing back and up, landing perhaps twenty feet from the mob, already straightening.

"You can back down or you can fall down," the Batgirl shouted, and the voice if not the shape confirmed it for Weir, that it was in fact a woman facing down Black Mask. "But if you fall down, you won't be getting up again."

"No more masks!" Black Mask screamed, and he swung the gun and fired again, and the Batgirl had leapt, it seemed to Weir, impossibly high and impossibly far, and she had come down again now with a kick, and Black Mask was on the ground. The Batgirl whirled, the edges of the cape climbing up, catching another of the mob along the head with its edge, and Weir thought the cape had to have been weighted, the way the man went down, unconscious, without a sound.

Then the Batgirl was on Black Mask, yanking him up for the

crowd to see, but as Weir looked she realized that the crowd was already retreating. He tried to strike her, and the blow was blocked, almost casually, and then the Batgirl was hitting him, once, again, again, again, and Black Mask was going down once more. Before he hit the ground, however, she caught him, throwing him over her shoulder and then diving forward, into the smoke.

Weir held her breath, tracking the shotgun along the length of the street, blinking back the tears that were now filling her eyes.

It seemed to her to have ended as quickly as it had begun.

The smoke was already dissipating, revealing bodies on the ground, their coughs and moans pathetic. The last of the mobile members of Black Mask's mob disappeared into the darkness.

The pain in her leg suddenly intensified and she gasped audibly, dropping the shotgun and clutching her wounded leg. Blood had soaked through her pants. Wincing, she felt along the wound.

She heard the sounds of running feet and scrabbled for the shotgun once more, looking up to see not more of Black Mask's mob, but instead Gordon and Montoya and Bullock racing down the street toward her. More cops were following, and she saw DeFilippis, and he caught her eyes, but she kept herself from calling his name.

"Weir!" Gordon shouted.

"Sir . . . "

He didn't stop, just nodded at her and then continued through the open doorway, and she understood the look on his face. She understood it, because it seemed to her DeFilippis had the same one, but was pointing it at her. She heard the Commissioner say that Montoya should follow him, that Bullock should secure the area, and the others ran inside.

DeFilippis made it to her first, on his knees and at her side, pushing past Bullock who mumbled something about priorities.

"The hell did this to you?" DeFilippis asked.

"Black Mask," she said. "He's gone. He's . . . he's gone."

She looked at him, at the way he was staring at her, then glanced past his shoulder at the other cops, now moving along the street. She looked back to him, wanting to say something more, but not wanting to betray what they had.

He said, "Hell with it," and then he kissed her.

She thought she heard Bullock say, "Well, I'll be damned."

ORACLE

Dear Dad—

You didn't have to break the door down, you know?

I understand that you were worried, but you really didn't have to break the door down.

It's easier, incidentally, to be angrier at you about that than at him about *her.*

And I'm livid, let me tell you. I could just spit.

A *new* Batgirl?

I sit in this chair and there's a *new Batgirl?*

Damn right I'm angry.

The noise had gotten my attention, that's what did it, that sound of them marching and banging their metal and maybe they were chanting, too; I don't know what the hell it was. But I looked out the window and there were over fifty of them, Dad, at both ends of the street, and I knew it was Black Mask leading them, knew it even before I used my binoculars to confirm it.

Two cops and one of them turned rabbit, leaving the other, Sergeant Weir, to block the door. I mean, what was she supposed to do? Threaten to arrest them?

I've kept the rifle for years, Dad. Always the weapon of last resort, I've never even fired the damn thing. Bought it in case it ever became the one situation, the one justification, where a life had to be taken to preserve another, an innocent's. It felt like poison in my hands. It didn't sit right on my shoulder, and I could barely see through the scope at first.

But I had to kill him, that's what I told myself. They were following Black Mask, and if I took him from them, that was the only way I thought I could protect Weir and the others still living in my building. And myself.

Because, let's face it, while your little girl is no slouch in the hand-to-hand department, even in this here chair, there ain't no way I'm going to win in a fight against fifty.

Have you ever looked through the scope on a rifle and seen a man, oblivious to you, and known you could kill him with just one pound of pull from your right index finger? You never talk about the war. Maybe you know it too well. . . .

I didn't like that feeling, Dad. It made me want to vomit.

But I'd taken the safety off, and I'd let my breath out, and I'd lined up the shot best as I could . . .

. . . and then *she* flew by.

You can't know what it felt like. I don't think *anyone* can know what that moment felt like.

Watching her swooping down, wearing those wings, the glider wings—the glider wings I helped design, for God's sake!—that made her look so big and terrifying and powerful. Watching her drop the canister of tear gas, the handful of smoke pellets. The way she cut loose from the wings and dropped onto the scene, like she'd been doing it forever, like she was made for it, like . . .

Like she was me.

I hated her absolutely in that moment. I was so angry, I couldn't speak, I couldn't even breathe, I just moved the scope onto her head and I thought about it.

Forgive me, but I honestly thought about it for an instant. I honestly thought about punishing her for making me feel the way I did then.

But I didn't.

I set the rifle down and I took off my glasses and I started crying.

. . .

When you showed up you saw I'd been crying and because you are the World's Greatest Dad, you thought it was because I was terrified. You were partly right, I had been, but that wasn't it. It's unfortunate, because you were worried enough you wanted to stay, to make certain I was feeling all right, and I felt like I had to practically shove you out the door before I could do what I needed to.

But I saw the look on your face, Dad. When you asked me what had happened.

"Black Mask," I said. "He ran away before you got here."

You didn't believe me for an instant. Maybe you thought it had been the Batman, that he had appeared and saved me in the nick of time. Maybe that's why you looked so angry. There was no time or way to explain it, though.

After you left, I went back into the control room and got on the radio. I tried for two hours to raise him on his frequency, demanding that he talk to me and getting no answer whatsoever. Finally I broke out one of my solar NiCads and plugged it into the infrared projector I've been using for sensor tests. I cut out a stencil, the shape of a bat, and I went to the window and I turned it all on, shining my invisible Bat-Signal at the sky. Faint, nearly useless, invisible to the whole city. But if the Batman looked up for a moment with those IR lenses of his switched on, maybe, just maybe, he'd see me.

I sat there all night, I sat there until dawn waiting for him to show up.

I'd finished cursing him with every name in the book when I heard him behind me, in my control room.

"Barbara."

I swung that chair around so fast your head would've spun, Dad.

He didn't even move, standing half in the shadows at the other end of the room, like some cross between a gargoyle and a nightmare. I glared at him, trying to find the words, and I could feel my cheeks getting hot and my chest getting tight.

"Did you think I wouldn't find out?" I asked, and it came out fast and much more petulant than I'd care to admit, and then it was all racing out and I was getting louder and louder and by the end I was almost screaming at him. "Did you think I honestly wouldn't care that someone else is out there being me? Did you even think about it at all? How dare you? How dare you do this to me?"

He still didn't move. It was like he had turned to marble, absolutely untouchable, emotionless. Then he said, "You know it wasn't as simple as that."

"No! No, I do not know that. What I know is that there's now someone else out there, someone who isn't me! And she's got what I *made*, she's got what I *was*." I took the projector and shoved it to the floor, and the crashing noise was almost satisfying, and for a moment I wanted to kick it and get that noise again, and then I remembered that I couldn't do that. Wouldn't ever be able to do that again. Never.

He moved out of the shadow, coming forward. His jaw had softened. "My options have been limited, Barbara. It was like this when I . . . when I returned."

I glared at him. "Returned. So you did leave after all. You did turn your back on us."

"I never turned my back. I needed to prepare. I needed to think."

"Three months, Batman. Three months. While you were thinking we were here, fighting."

"I know."

"You didn't give her the job?" I asked. "You're saying she took it on all by herself?" He nodded.

"So it was her doing the tagging?"

"At first, yes."

"Who is she? Just tell me that."

"I can't."

I rolled in close, glared up at him. "I can find out. You know I can. You're not the only detective in the No Man's Land."

"Yes, you can find out." He put a hand out, on my shoulder, and then he crouched so we were at eye level, and when he did that I felt the anger just slip away, and then all I felt was sad. He was still looking at me. "But what will it prove?"

"Nothing," I said, and my voice was getting thin with the emotion, and my eyes hurt, and it wasn't from staring at my terminals all day. I turned my head away, looking at the window, the window where I'd held the rifle, the window where the other Batgirl had dropped past me like she knew all of my tricks already, and maybe knew them better than I ever had.

I felt his hand move from my shoulder to my chin, and he turned my face back to look at him, and then I really did want to cry. He'd only ever touched my face one time before, when I was in the hospital after Joker shot me. I remembered waking up then, in the darkness, and being so scared and hurting so much, hearing the machines hissing and the EKG buzzing. He had touched my cheek then, the feel of his hand inside that glove, so gentle. It made me think of you, Dad.

"No pain I've ever caused you was my choice," he said, and he sounded different, maybe even tired. "I've never wanted you hurt. I know that makes no difference."

He moved his hand away.

"I need you to trust me," he said.

"I've always trusted you," I said. "And you know I always will."

PERSONAL
Entry #385—NML Day 140
0610 Zulu

Dear Dad—

Looks like we've all been busy the last few weeks, huh? And now spring has sprung, and there's been almost a calm in the No Man's Land for a while.

Which is normally what one gets before a storm, I suppose.

Updates abound. I've got reports from all my Eyes throughout the city, and some of it gives me hope. But, being a cynic, I don't expect it to last.

I don't understand exactly what's going on between you and the Batman, I've got to tell you that. Now that he's back, I'd have thought the two of you would have put your heads together and taken on the task of bringing law and order back to Gotham.

Instead, I hear stories that you've had your Blue Boys removing any bat-tags they find. That your people paint over them, or scrape them off, or otherwise obliterate them. I'm not certain if I think you're being petty, or if it's that you really think a bat-tag does more harm than good.

Ironic, though. In one quarter of the time it took you and yours to take TriCorner and Old Gotham, he's managed to secure almost all of the Upper East Side, and a fair portion of Burnley as well. On my map, that makes him the second-largest landowner in Gotham currently, after Two-Face. That puts you Blue Boys in a comfortable third place.

Of course, he's been so successful for four very specific reasons, none of which apply to you. First, he's got this Batgirl helping him, and while I don't much care for the fact that she's out there, I have to admit she's been doing a damn fine job thus far. It's the thus far, of course, that I'm worried about. I took some notes based on what I saw of her in action back on Day 124, and I checked it against my files, and I have a pretty solid idea of who is behind that full-face mask right now. And if I'm right, she had damn well better keep that mask on if she knows what's good for her.

That's one.

Second, since Black Mask had been working his way south along the East Side, and since he had started in Burnley, he'd pretty much crushed all of the minor gangs that had stood in his way. Once he was taken down, it was relatively easy for the Batman to take that territory as his own. How he and Batgirl are managing to cover it all I don't know, but so far they've been pretty successful.

Third, and this one even caught me by surprise, apparently Batman has worked out some sort of arrangement with Penguin, a nonaggression pact. I'm not entirely clear on the details or even how it came about, though Alex, one of my Eyes, reported that Batman had crashed one of Penguin's "fetes" and pretty much took on the whole house.

And he won.

Then he pulled Penguin off into the shadows, and when he was done speaking with him the nonaggression pact was in place, and that was pretty much that. It's worked out well so far. Penguin's territory abuts the Batman's along the Upper East Side. I'm sure Penguin was getting nervous about his northern border, and I'm just as sure the Batman didn't want to deal with Penguin launching an offensive from his south. Détente at its finest, I suppose.

Fourth and finally . . .

Well, he's the Batman. And the word is spreading that he's back. And the minor players, they seem to have figured out that it's time for them to clear the field.

FOURTEEN

ON DAY 143 ANOTHER WAR COUNCIL was held in the Gordon/Essen home in TriCorner, this time in the garden, rather than the rec room. Spring had come into Gotham quickly and already the temperature was beginning to climb from tolerable to pleasant, and it wouldn't be long after that, Montoya knew, before they hit humid-as-hell unbearable.

But on this late May day, under a clear blue sky and comforted by a slight breeze, it was perfect spring, and Montoya wanted to enjoy it.

Gordon's garden had exploded in the last few weeks, frozen and dead earth coming rampantly alive with a riot of leaf, vine, and petal. He had planted too much too close together, and now the plants fought one another for space in the soil, trying to reach for light while slaking an ever-present thirst. In another few weeks, the battle would be over, the losers uprooted, the winners entrenching further to wait out the summer. Only the plum tree looked to be above it all, leafy and just beginning to form its fruit.

They sat in chairs brought from inside the house, Montoya between Essen on her left and Bullock on her right, with Foley and then Pettit extending out. Gordon stood with his back to the tree, using its shade. All of them wore short sleeves but Foley, who was still managing to maintain a jacket-and-tie look, even after so long. Montoya had to hand it to the man; he had the courage of his convictions.

"A little over a month ago we liberated Old Gotham and reclaimed Central," Gordon said. "We've survived the worst that the winter had to offer us, and we've done it without suffering unacceptable losses of personnel or matériel. Current intelligence puts us sharing the No Man's Land with a handful of minor gangs—the Xhosa, Lynx, and the like—and some of the heavy hitters.

"It's the heavy hitters we need to discuss. Bill, you have an analysis?"

Pettit rose and took the rolled map from where it lay on the potting shelf, spread it out on the brick patio in front of them, weighting its edges with flowerpots. He used the knife from his belt to indicate positions on the paper.

"Tactically, we're exposed as hell right now," he said with a frown. "Basically, we can be hit at any time from any side except from behind, and that's only because we've got the ocean to our back. Not good if we have to retreat. To the west we have the minor gangs, and right now they're acting as a buffer against whatever lunatics may be on the Upper West Side—reports are that Victor Fries is up there, and maybe that psychopath Zsasz.

"To our north we've got Penguin, basically between the edge of Old Gotham and the south side of Robinson Park. He's got more territory, as well, on the east of the park, which is acting as a buffer for his back, so he can free up more men to put on our border."

"He's not worried about the park?" Foley asked.

Pettit looked pointedly at Bullock, who cleared his throat and said, "Uh, Poison Ivy's in the park, Hugh. And since Ivy can control plants, and since she doesn't like people, she's pretty much being left alone. Nobody's going in or out. All we know about that situation is that, um, a certain masked individual apparently went into the Heart of Darkness there at the beginning of May, and when he came out a couple days later, deliveries of fresh produce began making their way throughout the city."

"Batman was in the park?" Foley asked.

Montoya winced, watching the Commissioner, expecting an eruption of some bile, something to acknowledge the mention. Gordon kept his attention fixed on the map and didn't make a sound.

"That's what we heard," Bullock said. "And there are freshies floating around the city to prove the point. Figure that Penguin worked out something with Ivy near the start of NML to keep his operation supplied with fruits and veggies . . . then you-know-who went in and, uh, renegotiated a less exclusive deal."

"Let's get back on point," Gordon said, looking up from the map and taking all of them in with his gaze. "We've got gangs to the west and Penguin to the north. It's the same problem we had with the Demonz and the LoBoys; it's just a matter of time before one of them decides they want our waterfront property."

"You're not suggesting the same solution we used before?" Foley asked. "Trying to facilitate another war?"

"Wouldn't work," Pettit said before Gordon could answer. "Word has spread by now about what went down. Can't get away with the same trick twice."

"So what are we going to do?"

They all looked at Gordon. "We've had minor incursions from the Xhosa already," the Commissioner began. "If Penguin pushes, we'll be fighting on two fronts."

"Three fronts," Montoya said. "Two-Face is to our east, and he'll attack first chance he gets."

Gordon looked at her, then nodded. "Renee's right. We need to secure a wider territory, insure our own survival. To this end I'm proposing a major offensive to take Penguin's territory to the north."

"Are you crazy?" Foley said.

"We put Robinson Park to our back, we secure our northern perimeter," Pettit said. "Tactically sound."

"Bullock just said that Ivy's in the park!" Foley said, getting to his feet. "Dear God, Bill, is that your idea of a safe perimeter?"

"And she hasn't come out, Hugh! Ivy's not the threat Penguin or Two-Face are."

Foley turned to Montoya, directing his appeal at her, Bullock, and Essen. "Then we should go after the gangs, after the Xhosa or the Lynx or whoever!"

"No," Gordon said again. "We need them as a buffer. We go after Penguin now, while we still have the manpower."

Foley spun back, and Montoya saw the man's cheeks coloring, his hands in fists. "He's got matériel, for God's sake, Commissioner! He's still got bullets!"

"Which we'll take from him."

"You'll get us all killed!"

Gordon stepped forward, nearly on top of Foley. "This is not open to debate, Hugh," he said evenly.

Montoya didn't move, none of them moved, watching. Finally Foley stepped back, his mouth twisting into a sour grimace, as if he were tasting the memory of a bad meal. He looked at each of them in turn, and when his eyes found Montoya's she didn't look away, trying to show her sympathy. But no one spoke and she saw his posture change, his shoulders slumping, and then Foley moved past the group, making for the door back into the house.

"You think you're a general," he said, looking back at Gordon. "But you're not. You're a bureaucrat who's playing at war, and we're going to pay the price."

Then he was out of sight, back inside the house.

"Are there any other objections?" Gordon asked. When no one spoke, he added, "Then that's all."

Pettit rose, saying, "I'll go talk to him, Jim."

Gordon nodded. Montoya got to her feet, waiting for Harvey, but before she was out of the garden she heard the Commissioner calling her name.

"Renee. Stay for a minute."

She stopped, looking at Bullock, who shrugged. Essen had held up in the doorway and was looking back at her with a confused expression.

"I need to talk to you alone," Gordon said.

Montoya watched Essen's face change, hardening slightly, and then the lieutenant had entered the house, Bullock with her. Montoya turned back around to face Gordon, who was still looking at the map spread out on the brick patio. He had removed his glasses and was rubbing the skin at the bridge of his nose, and she could see the discoloration where the pads on the frames had rested so often and for so long. He replaced the glasses and sighed heavily.

"What do you think?" he asked. " And please, don't worry about hurting my feelings."

"I think Foley is right, sir. We don't have the manpower to go up against Penguin. Pettit handed out the last of our bullets two weeks ago, and he hasn't been able to find any more. Our offensive capability is seriously limited, now. We used up a lot of our supplies retaking Central and Old Gotham. And for an offensive like the one you're proposing, you're going to have to commit all of the cops. We can't use the civilians in the sectors, they wouldn't stand a chance, most of them."

"I know."

"Then you know we'll probably lose if we try to take Penguin on." She swallowed hard. "And if that happens . . ."

". . . if that happens, then chaos will rule Gotham until Judgment Day," the Commissioner concluded.

Montoya heard the sound of bees buzzing in the flowers nearby, and distantly, beyond the garden's walls, the bare hint of voices. Gordon was staring at his house, and she could tell whatever he was thinking, it was giving him no joy. She caught a wisp of fragrance on the air, the bright scent of the plum tree.

Gordon broke the silence. "Do you trust me, Renee?"

"Absolutely, sir."

He nodded and she thought that, somehow, her answer hadn't been the one he was hoping for, that he looked a little sadder than before, a little older, a little more tired.

"I need you to do something," he said. "It's not an easy thing. It's something that, if you're caught doing it, I'll deny I ever asked it of you. No one can know, do you understand?"

"Yes, sir," she said.

"If you refuse to do what I'm going to ask, I'll understand. No penalty, I swear, and I won't think less of you for it. Understand, I'm asking you because you're the best person for the job, and I think . . . I think you'll see that." He looked at Montoya, those eyes that made her think of her own father. "Am I clear?"

"Perfectly, sir." Curiosity was creeping into her voice, and she tried to shut it down. "You know I'll follow your orders, sir. You know I trust you."

He looked even sadder. "I do."

And he told her.

As a cop, Sarah Essen knew she was suspicious by nature. But that didn't make her feel any better about it, and it wasn't helping her now as she looked out the closed window into the backyard where her husband and Detective Renee Montoya were sitting together on the bench by the plum tree, heads bent, clearly deep in conversation. They'd been at it for almost twenty minutes now, and she knew she shouldn't be timing it, and she knew it shouldn't really bother her, but it did nonetheless.

It wasn't that she suspected her husband of cheating on her, though God knew that if precedent was the issue, it had already been established by the two of them ten years earlier. That wasn't it at all.

It was that whatever he was sharing with Montoya, he wasn't willing to share with her. That rankled. She and her husband had been lovers before becoming friends, and there was a time when communication between the two of them had all but broken down. It had taken time and effort for each of them to learn to communicate, to listen and speak to one another with respect and care. But they had managed. Yet there he was, her husband and friend and lover, clearly engaging Montoya in a confidence he had neglected to share with his own wife.

More than that, it made Essen nervous. No, that wasn't quite right.

It frightened her.

It meant that whatever he was telling Montoya now, he was afraid to share with the one person he'd been willing to share everything else.

That couldn't be good.

Now Montoya was rising, and so was Jim. He put a hand on the young detective's shoulder, a pat, more paternal than friendly, and Renee was turning, heading back into the house, toward her, head down.

"What's up?" Sarah asked.

Montoya shook her head. "Nothing. Just . . . it was nothing."

Sarah watched her continue past, then turned back to the window again. In the garden, Jim had sat once more on the bench, staring at the map still weighted down on the ground.

"Nothing," Sarah echoed.

Sure.

FIFTEEN

"AND WHERE IS HE?" THE PENGUIN demanded.

"Um . . . maybe he got, uh, held up, you know," Garrett offered.

"Garrett, my fine friend, do you know what a rhetorical question is?"

Garrett shook his head.

"It's a question asked without the expectation of an answer," the Penguin explained, fitting another cigarette to the end of the long ebony holder. "My question was a rhetorical one. You did not need to answer it. Light, if you please."

Garrett fumbled the Zippo out and snapped the flame to life quickly, bending to light the smoke. He was sincerely trying to be as helpful as possible, still grateful that Penguin hadn't given him the sack after the disaster on the bridge. All things considered, actually, Penguin had been remarkably forgiving.

"The Bat Factor," Penguin had said. "Impossible to predict, and useless to bemoan. The best one can do is anticipate and prepare, and then hope that the damnable flying rodent minds his own business for once in his miserable life."

Garrett had understood only half of that, but figured it meant his job was safe. And in fact, replacing the Zippo in his pocket and straightening once more to take in the street, he had to accept that his read was right. Here he was, almost a month later, standing on an empty street at the south edge of Penguin's territory, baseball bat slung over his back, acting as Cobblepot's personal bodyguard. And behind Garrett another twenty men, his to command if the Penguin demanded it.

Garrett still wasn't certain exactly why they were there, though.

Penguin shuffled in a small circle, head up and pushed almost comically forward, adjusting the monocle on his right eye. He was muttering to himself, too, and Garrett had to bite his tongue to keep from laughing.

The man looked like a short, fat, bird, and that's all there was to it. Only, no feathers.

It took another five minutes of Penguin's waddling, by which time Garrett thought he might have actually bitten through his tongue, before things started happening. Garrett saw the man first, coming up from the south end of the avenue, tall, and for a horrifying moment Garrett thought it was the Bat again, what with the way the man's overcoat flapped like a cape and how big the guy was and everything. But the color was wrong. Then Penguin saw the guy approaching, too, and blew a long exhale of smoke, and Garrett figured that this was who they had been waiting for.

The man continued to approach, and out of the rubble behind him came more figures, ten by Garrett's count, all armed with bats and clubs. He grinned. Twenty to ten, they'd win any fight easy.

"You're late," snapped the Penguin.

"Half the time," the man said, and Garrett got a look at his face, and got scared again.

It was one of the freaks.

"You have a proposal for me, Two-Face?" the Penguin asked, and he sounded bored. Garrett looked respectfully down at his employer. If Penguin was scared of the freak, he didn't show it.

"I do," Two-Face said. "One you're going to like."

"And what exactly do you have in mind, my bipartisan friend?"

"A solution to a mutual problem. We don't have to fight, Cobblepot—"

Penguin held up a gloved hand, then gestured in an arc that took in Two-Face's men. "If you're proposing a surrender, Harvey, I should caution you. By all reports my forces vastly outnumber yours."

He indicated Garrett and the men standing behind him.

Two-Face nodded. "But you can't attack me, can you, Cobblepot? You're supposed to play nice from here on out. You've cut a deal with the Batman."

Penguin drew himself up, the cigarette holder in his mouth going level. His voice was tight. "Only for as long as it serves me."

"I can give you his land," Two-Face said. "Keep those white gloves of yours nice and clean."

Penguin made the clucking noise. "Such largesse is unlike you, Harvey. Meaning, my confrere, what's in it for you?"

"You always were a smart bird. Meaning, you take pressure off my northern border. As you've said, I'm low on manpower, can't spare them for both defense and offense. You leave me alone, I can go west."

"Gordon's to your west. Him and those Blue Boys of his."

Two-Face grinned, and Garrett was sure he'd be seeing it in his nightmares until he was ninety.

"I'll destroy him," Two-Face said.

The cigarette holder moved in Penguin's mouth, bobbing up and down. Penguin said, "You do take it personally, don't you, Harvey? It's been quite some time since you and Gordon were seated at the same table."

"Some of us don't forget where we came from."

"Ah, yes, the noble police lieutenant and the crusading district attorney, I remember it well." Penguin removed the monocle, cleaning it against the edge of his waistcoat, then replacing it. "And you guarantee you can take care of the Bat?"

"Absolutely. Give me two days and a little help, I'll get it done."

"Help how?"

"Chloral hydrate."

"Easily acquired. What else?"

"Just one more thing," Two-Face said, glancing over Penguin's men and settling his look on Garrett. "I'll need some bait."

"Me?" Garrett said.

Penguin patted his forearm reassuringly. "Don't worry, my friend. Harvey will take good care of you."

The TallyMan, chief among Two-Face's lieutenants, was as flamboyant a killer as any who stalked the No Man's Land. Part of the costumed-criminal set, it was his Seussian top hat that marked him more than anything else. That, and the two revolvers he carried on him at all times, shining silver and more often out of their holsters than in them.

To Two-Face's mind, the TallyMan was a glorified hit man, nothing more, and he suffered him only because he could control him. But Two-Face did not like him, and when he saw that the TallyMan was waiting in front of City Hall, it made Two-Face angry.

"There's someone here to see you," the TallyMan said.

"Who?" Two-Face snarled.

"One of the Blue Boys, came over under a white flag."

"And you honored it?"

"Wasn't going to, but before I put a bullet in her head she showed me this."

The TallyMan opened his hand, and Two-Face saw that in the hollow of the man's palm was resting his real coin, the trick silver half-dollar he had gotten from his father years ago. He grabbed it quickly, then used his other hand to take the TallyMan by the throat, letting his index finger press into the carotid artery.

"You put a bullet in her?" Two-Face hissed. "Is that what I heard you just say, TallyMan?"

The TallyMan's eyes bulged slightly. "No," he managed. "No . . . she's . . . alive. . . ."

"Where?"

"In . . . the . . . holding . . . cells. . . ."

Two-Face released his grip, squeezing the coin in his fist, then striding up the courthouse steps. He tried not to run, but all the same he raced across the marble floor of the main hall, to the access stairway, passing the guards he had on duty without a second glance. He went down the stairs into the basement, three and four steps at a time, pushed through another door, then stopped just outside the barred one that marked the start of the holding cells. He took a deep breath and ran the fingers of both his hands through his hair, realized he was still gripping the coin.

What if she doesn't want to see me? he thought suddenly. What if . . . what if what if what if . . .

Don't go in there.

No, go in there.

No, she'll laugh at you. She'll mock you. She'll hurt you.

She won't. She's different. She understood.

You like her. And you think because you like her she likes us.

She could like us. She could.

No. She couldn't.

She could.

Have you looked in a mirror lately, Harvey? How could she like us?

She . . . could . . .

Don't make me laugh.

He looked at the coin in his hand.

Yeah, we'll have to flip for it.

Good heads we go in.

Good heads we go in, agreed. Bad heads—

I won't let you kill her.

Who said anything about killing her? Do we need to kill her? I don't want to kill her.

Then what? Bad heads, then what?

Bad heads . . . we send TallyMan in, he can find out what she wants.

TallyMan's a boor. He'll treat her like crap.

Then we'll kill TallyMan.

He considered, then nodded.

Flip it. Go ahead. Flip it. And don't cheat, Harvey. I'm not going anywhere, and I'm not taking my eyes off that coin.

He flipped the half-dollar, a move so practiced he didn't even need to consider the action, the placement of the coin, the roll of the shifting balance. His thumb caught the edge, a perfect end-over-end flip straight up, the disk tumbling so fast that it was impossible to predict its result. The coin rose to its apex and then for a mere fraction of a second seemed to dangle, caught between force and gravity, then began its descent.

He snatched it out of the air then slapped the coin down on the back of his other hand.

Go ahead. Read it and weep, Harvey.

He shut his eyes and moved his hand.

Look.

He looked.

Good heads.

Grinning, he slipped the coin back into his pocket, then ran both hands down the sides of his jacket, making certain he was presentable. He took the keys from the locker on the wall, then swung the barred door back, entering the long hall of cells.

"Detective Montoya?"

There was a moment of silence and he'd just begun to think that the TallyMan had lied to him, was playing games with him, when her voice came from the end of the hall.

"Here."

This time he did a better job keeping himself from running, feeling the butterflies fluttering in his gut. He knew what it was, he knew exactly what was going on, and he had gone through contortions over it several times in the last months, since before leaving Arkham, even. He was dimly aware of just how crazy the whole damn situation was.

He was Two-Face, after all. And Two-Face absolutely did not get crushes on anyone, let alone a GCPD detective. It was one thing for Harvey Dent to be carrying a torch; that had happened before more times than he could recount. When that happened, Two-Face's response had been entirely and savagely negative. The object of Harvey's affection had deserved only scorn, and Two-Face had actively sought to crush any interest or hope that might be growing in his counterpart's heart.

It was another thing entirely when Two-Face agreed with Harvey.

There she was in the cell, Detective Renee Montoya, wearing blue jeans and scuffed black boots and a dirty leather jacket and it was the first time he'd seen her in over six months, and he thought she looked lovely and almost exactly the same. Maybe just a little older, but the No Man's Land could do that to anyone, and really it only made her prettier. Her hair had gotten a little longer, too.

"Sorry about TallyMan," he said, unlocking the cell door. "He didn't know who you were. He didn't, uh . . . he wasn't rough or anything, was he?"

She waited until he had swung the door back, then joined him in the hall. "No rougher than I'm used to. I'm fine."

"You can call me Harvey."

Montoya nodded. "I'm fine, Harvey."

"Good." He tried another smile, and he thought maybe she gave him just a tiny little hint of one in return, and he felt the butterflies start really going nuts then. He had maybe five, six inches on her, and she was looking right back at him, not flinching or repulsed or anything like that, at least, not that he could tell.

Stop staring at her, you idiot.

"Would you, um . . . you want a drink or something? I've got a crate of Zesti Cola we salvaged from the Jiffy Junior down on Ander."

"No, thanks," she said.

"You, um . . . you wanted to talk to me? TallyMan said you wanted to talk to me, that you came in under a white flag and everything. Did you want to talk to me?"

"Commissioner Gordon sent me."

Two-Face felt momentarily crestfallen. Of course Gordon had sent her, why would she have come on her own accord? It must've been an order.

"Oh," he said. "Right."

She was still looking at him. "You know why he sent me?"

Two-Face sighed, then gestured to the end of the hall. "If we're going to talk business, let's move somewhere more comfortable. Don't want to keep you down here. You might think I was planning on keeping you prisoner or something."

When she smiled, he felt a little better. Together they left the holding area, going back up the stairs. He tried to walk beside her where he could, but on the stairs it was difficult, so he took the lead, thinking that would make her a little more comfortable. When they came out again into the main hall, TallyMan was waiting inside the foyer. Two-Face ignored him, waiting for Montoya to move up on his side, and then he pointed to the other flight of stairs, the big broad set that ran up to the gallery overlooking the atrium, beyond which were the courtrooms and judges' chambers.

They went up the stairs and into another hallway, passing more posted guards. He watched them carefully, noting which ones were staring at Montoya and which ones were minding their own business. Only a few of his men directed glances their way that made Two-Face feel a response was in order, but he'd deal with them later, after Montoya had left. He knew she was a cop, and that she'd dealt with plenty of violence in her life, but even so, he didn't want her to have to see it if things got ugly.

He had been using Judge Halsey's chambers for his quarters, and he held the door open for her, even risked putting a hand on her back, lightly, to sort of guide her inside. She didn't react in any way that he could see, and he figured that must mean she didn't mind, and he was grinning when he shut the door behind them. By the time he was crossing to the desk, though, he had it under control again. He retrieved two bottles of Zesti from his stash in the bottom drawer, opening them and then offering her one.

When she took her bottle, her right index finger touched his for a second, and it was warm, and it made a soft heat climb into his whole body.

"Thanks," she said.

Two-Face nodded. "So . . . uh . . . I assume the Commissioner has decided to take me up on my offer?"

"That's why I'm here."

"You can sit down, if you want to, Renee."

She took the chair opposite the desk. He had hoped she would go for the couch by the coffee table instead, so that he might be able to sit closer to her without it being so obvious.

Stupid useless moron idiot! You should have moved from behind the desk first, you dolt!

He perched on the corner of the desk.

At least she didn't mind me calling her Renee.

So far. You're such a pathetic loser, you know that...

"He told me about the offer you made," Renee said. "About . . . about helping us."

"And now?"

"He's planning something . . . something that he feels we can't do alone, and he's hoping you'll help."

"He wants to take the land between Old Gotham and the Park."

She looked surprised, but only for a second. "That's right."

"Penguin's land."

"Yes."

Two-Face sipped at his bottle of cola, then made a face, wishing suddenly for ice. He had suspected that Gordon would come around sooner or later, but not as soon as this. In a way it was a perfect opportunity, and gave his plan regarding the Batman a perfect symmetry.

"I can help," he told Montoya. "I can help a lot, actually. You guys will have to do all the hard work, of course, but if you're ready to move at midnight tomorrow—by which I mean be ready to attack—then I can guarantee you'll win. It won't be easy, there will be resistance, but you'll get that land."

"What kind of resistance?" Montoya asked.

"Penguin has a lot of men, Renee, and a lot of equipment. All I can do is make it so there aren't too many of those men in your way. But there will be some." He took another pull from his bottle. "You're going to take casualties. Not as many as Penguin will, to be sure; but then again, for people like Penguin that's not an issue. For people like you and the Commish, it might be."

Montoya was looking at the bottle in her hands, turning it back and forth, not drinking. He noticed that her fingers were bare, that she didn't wear any jewelry on her hands or even in her ears. He remembered seeing her with earrings once, small cubic zirconium studs that had shone brightly against her tan skin.

"People will die, Renee."

Her head moved in a bare nod.

"Anything else Gordon wanted you to ask about?"

"He wanted to know what you'd take in trade. What you wanted in return."

You. That would be fair, don't you think? You stay with us, here.

Not possible. Can't ask for that. That would be . . .

Prisoner.

Right.

It's an option.

No.

It's an option, Harvey.

No!

"Harvey?"

She was looking at him, and for another second he remained distracted, but this time by those brown eyes, the warmth in them. Gilda had had blue eyes, he remembered. His wife, before the accident and the world splitting into two halves. Gilda's eyes had been blue.

He thought he liked Montoya's eyes more.

"I'm sorry?" Two-Face said.

"What do you want for the help?"

"Nothing for now. Maybe later I'll contact Gordon, maybe then he can lend me a hand when I need one. Will you tell him that?"

"Sure."

"And . . ." he trailed off.

Oh, don't say it, you fool . . . she'll shoot you down you know she'll shoot you down . . .

"What?" Montoya asked.

"And I think that if Gordon wants to contact me again, you're the person he should send. Now that my men know who you are, I mean, that's probably safer. He should send you. Okay?"

"That's fine," she said, and there wasn't even a pause, like she had no trouble with the idea, like maybe she even wanted to see him again sometime.

"Good. I'll make certain TallyMan knows."

"I should head back . . . if we've only got until tomorrow night, we're going to have to get ready." She rose from the chair, still holding the untouched bottle of Zesti. "Thanks for meeting with me, Harvey."

"My pleasure," he said earnestly. He set his empty soda bottle next to the Lucite paperweight on the desktop, then stood. "You hardly touched your cola, Renee. What's the matter, you don't like Zesti?"

Montoya smiled sheepishly and he felt his heart all but melt. "Not really, sorry. I'm a Soder drinker mostly."

Brilliant, you're brilliant, you know that? Offering Zesti to a Soder drinker...

She handed the bottle back to him. "Maybe one of your men would like it."

Two-Face felt the charge again as his fingers touched hers for an instant, and nearly forgot to say, "Sure, I'm sure they will." He cleared his throat. "Let me walk you out?"

"Okay, if you like."

He put her bottle next to his on the desk, and together they left Judge Halsey's chambers, making their way back outside. He wanted to tell her that he'd picked Halsey's chambers for a reason, that back when he had served as Gotham City's District Attorney, Halsey had been known as the most honest judge on the bench. As Harvey Dent, he'd had a lot of respect for Halsey.

But he didn't say anything about that to Renee.

The sun was setting as they stepped outside, and Two-Face said, "Would you like an escort to the border? Make certain no one gives you any trouble?"

"I'll be all right," Montoya said.

"It's no bother."

She put her arm on his. "Really, Harvey, I'll be fine."

Then she headed down the stairs, across Courthouse Plaza, making her way west.

"Thanks for bringing the coin back," he called.

He couldn't hear her response, but she nodded and actually waved, and he stayed there, leaning against the cracked Ionic columns at the front of the courthouse, watching her go. Even after she was out of sight he stayed there.

Well?

Well what?

Well, that could have been worse.

She likes us.

You hope.

No, she does. She really does, I mean, she touched me, she put her hand on my arm and she touched me and . . . nobody's touched me . . . no woman has touched me, you know, like that, not since Gilda. Not since Gilda, that's a long time.

You're reading too much into it. You're setting yourself up for a fall.

No. No, there's . . . she's different. Admit it. Even you think she's different.

. . .

Admit it.

. . . yeah, you're right. Happy? You're right. She's different.

See? Wasn't so hard.

You're a fool, Harvey. You're a damn fool, and she's going to break our heart.

SIXTEEN

MONTOYA FOUND GORDON IN THE GARDEN, talking to his wife. For a moment before opening the sliding glass doors she hesitated, thinking to wait until they were done speaking. But it was already dark, and the clock was running, and there was really no time to waste.

She slid the door back and stepped out into the spring air, catching the whiff of flowers immediately, the cloying smell of rot from the near corner where one of the plants was obviously decaying. The conversation stopped, and both Gordon and Essen turned to look at her. Montoya could read the question in the Commissioner's face, but she kept herself from offering him any answer yet. Essen's look had a question, too, but it was an entirely different one.

"What?" Essen demanded.

"I need to speak to the Commissioner."

"Go ahead."

"Alone."

Essen sharpened her glare, then turned it from Renee back to her husband. Gordon said something softly that Montoya didn't catch, and Essen frowned. Montoya moved out of the way, letting the other woman past. Essen didn't spare her a second glance.

Montoya waited until the door had slid shut before moving closer. When she was within reaching distance of Gordon she stopped.

"What did he say?"

For a moment, Renee thought about lying to him. In her chest, her heart felt like it was on the verge of breaking.

"Midnight tomorrow," she heard herself say. "We need to be ready at midnight tomorrow. He'll back us up."

"What did he want for payment?"

Montoya shook her head. "He said he'd take the payment later. He said . . . he said he knew you'd come around and that he'd already taken care of it."

She watched Gordon's face change, the sadness creeping into something closer to concern. "He knew?"

"He wasn't surprised." She tried to make the distinction clear. "And he said if you have any further messages for him, you should send me."

"Did he treat you all right?"

"Fine."

"I am sorry, Renee."

She didn't know what to say to that, and so she just nodded and then left, heading back out of the garden and through the house without stopping. Essen was nowhere to be seen. Donnelly was on post with Beardsely outside, and she caught a snippet of their conversation, talking about when Pettit next wanted them to drill their hand-to-hand moves.

For her quarters, Montoya had taken over one of the bedrooms in a still-intact bungalow, sharing the house with a couple other female officers. In her room she pulled off her jacket, throwing it to the floor. Montoya was turning when she caught her reflection in the cracked mirror above the bureau. The badge, hanging on its chain around her neck, glimmered gold. Taking the badge off, feeling its weight in her hand, the coolness of the metal, she traced the shape of her number with the pad of her thumb.

Then she threw it at the mirror. The glass shattered, pieces broken yet still sticking in the frame, and her reflection broke, too.

Montoya sat on the bed and put her head in her hands, fighting the urge to cry.

They had sold their souls.

There was a knock at the door.

"Go away," she said, then realized she'd spoken in Spanish, and repeated it in English.

"Renee? It's Chris. You okay in there?"

"I'm okay, Sergeant."

"Heard glass breaking." The door opened a fraction, and Sergeant Weir stuck her blond head through the opening, concern stretched over her face. "Whoa. What happened to your mirror?"

"I broke it."

Weir pushed the door open farther. "You want to talk about it?"

I'd love to talk about it, Montoya thought. But I can't say a word, because I told the Commissioner I trusted him, and he trusts me, and he is my boss, and he is in charge, and so, no, I can't say a damn thing.

"Not really," Montoya said.

"You want to be alone?"

"Not really."

Weir chuckled, then came in and sat on the bed beside her. Montoya watched while her broken reflection was joined by pieces of the other woman's face.

"Nice job on the mirror," Weir said. "Think you can afford the seven years' bad luck?"

"Way my luck is running right now, it'd be an improvement."

"Oh, it can't be that bad."

"We're in the No Man's Land, remember? How good can it be?"

Weir shifted her weight slightly. "It's life, you know. Just harder now. But it's not all bad."

Her tone made Montoya shift from looking at Weir's reflection to look at Weir herself. The sergeant made a kind of half-laugh from her throat.

"What?" Montoya asked.

Weir hesitated. "You can't tell anyone."

Oh, Christ, Montoya thought. What is it about me? Either I'm keeping secrets that I want no part of, or I'm being flirted with by a horribly disfigured lunatic who wants to be my boyfriend.

"I'm pregnant," Weir said.

Renee thought her jaw was flapping in the breeze.

Weir laughed. "Yeah, that's kind of how I reacted."

"You're what?"

"Preggers. Knocked up. Bun in the oven. Family way. Me."

"You're sure?"

"Pretty sure. Thought I'd been eating bad food or something, that's why I kept throwing up, but . . . I'm so late now, and I'm starting to . . ." She looked at Montoya. "I'm pretty sure."

"I don't know if I should say congratulations or I'm sorry, Chris . . ."

"Yeah, it's a hell of a thing. Life, like I said."

"Can I ask . . ."

"Andy."

"Andy DeFilippis?"

Weir arched an eyebrow. "You don't approve?"

"Did I say that? I didn't say that."

"Then what was that tone, there, that shocked tone?"

"Never figured you'd go for a rookie."

"I'm in love with him," Weir said, explaining.

"That would do it. How long . . . I mean, when do you think you're due?"

"November, I think."

"Wow."

"Yeah. You can't tell anyone, Renee. I haven't even told Andy yet, and . . . it's just going to make things so complicated. I mean, where do you go to get prenatal care in the NML?"

"We've got to get you to Dr. Thompkins."

"I was thinking the same thing. Maybe by the end of the week."

The thought struck Renee hard. "Tomorrow night . . . where are you posted tomorrow night?"

"The Clock Tower."

"Good. Stay there, okay? Make sure you stay on that post."

"Why?"

Montoya shook her head. "Just trust me, please, Chris. Things are going to get hairy tomorrow night . . . you and Andy, you should both pull duty at the Clock Tower, all right?"

Weir cocked her head, curiosity and concern wrestling on her brow for a couple of seconds.

"Please," Montoya urged. "Trust me."

"Okay, tomorrow night I'll be at the Clock Tower," Weir said. "Wish you'd tell me why it's so important, though."

"Give it twenty-four hours, you'll find out."

SEVENTEEN

 IT HAD STARTED EARLIER THAT NIGHT, when Batgirl was alone in the pseudo-cave where she'd brought Black Mask nearly four weeks earlier, waiting for the Batman to return. The two-way radio set on the workbench had crackled, and then Oracle's voice, computer synthesized and distorted, had broken out of the static.

"Come in, Batman. Come in."

She'd taken the handset and answered, "Go ahead."

The pause had felt like ice was creeping out of the speaker, up the wire to the microphone in Batgirl's hand.

"Where is he?" Oracle had demanded.

"Not here."

"When's he due back?"

"I don't know."

"I have intel for him, he's going to want to hear it ASAP."

"Whatever you need to tell him, you can tell me."

Oracle had laughed, the synthesized voice rocking along octaves. Batgirl wasn't certain who, exactly, Oracle was. She'd heard some people speculate that there was no actual person who was Oracle, simply a group of people who forwarded information. Other theories were that it was an AI, or even a totally alien intelligence.

But that laugh, it made Batgirl think that Oracle was just another human being, some man or woman in a room somewhere, just as human as the rest of them. And the laugh told her something else. It told her that Oracle didn't like her at all.

Not one little bit.

"Cowl on a little too tight?" Oracle had said. "Brain needing a little more oxygen, maybe?"

"You don't like me," Batgirl had said. "Don't let it interfere with the job."

There had been the briefest of pauses, as if the computer generated voice on the other end was determining its answer, and then the voice said, "Of course I don't like you. I know who you really are. Tell him to contact me. Oracle out."

The connection had gone dead, leaving Batgirl holding the handset, frustrated and a little frightened.

If Oracle knew . . . then the Batman knew.

Until that point it had been easy to indulge in the self-deception, to believe that she had done a good enough job at concealing her identity to keep the Batman from finding out who she really was. But Oracle changed that with a sentence, and Batgirl put the handset back in place, knowing that, certainly, she wasn't fooling anyone except herself.

Batman was a detective, after all, considered by some the World's Greatest Detective, and even though Batgirl had been careful, she knew she hadn't been careful enough. She wondered, if, in fact, she ever could have been.

But the Batman hadn't said anything about it, hadn't challenged her or demanded an unmasking or a confession, none of it. As far as she could see, that meant he didn't have a problem with her wearing the cowl or the symbol. If he did, he would have said something by now, right?

It wasn't much of a comfort, but it was enough for her to grasp and hold, and she had no intention of letting it go.

She was good at this, she knew that. She was worthy of the Bat, had saved lives, had made a difference.

And if Oracle didn't like her, if Oracle wanted her out, well, Oracle could just lump it. The cape and cowl weren't Oracle's to bestow, and Batgirl wouldn't part with them that easily.

She was still thinking about it when the Batman returned, entering the garage with a bare nod of the chin that acknowledged her presence, then moving to the workbench where he removed his belt and began checking his stores. She watched him for almost a minute without speaking, waiting for him to say something, anything, but he didn't.

"Oracle called," she finally said.

"And?"

"And apparently I'm not good enough to pass along whatever message he, she, or it had for you."

He replaced the belt on his waist, then began checking the pockets hidden in his cape. "She," he said.

"Well, then, *she* didn't feel I could be trusted. Said she had intel. That's all I know."

He crossed to the radio set silently, almost effortlessly. Sometimes, she would watch him move and just wonder at the precision of it all, how there was never anything wasted in any of his motions or gestures. He took the handset up and flipped two switches, and she heard the crackle of the speaker.

The synthesized voice sparked from the speaker again. "Oracle."

"That was unprofessional."

"Don't talk to me about professional. I know who she is."

"That's irrelevant. You have intel for me?"

There was a brief silence, as if Oracle was computing how to proceed. Batgirl almost smiled behind her mask. Maybe all her worry was for nothing. Maybe it didn't matter to him at all.

"One of my Eyes reported something down by City Hall," Oracle said. "Confirmed via your new pal, Penguin. Two-Face is on the move."

"Penguin's paranoid," the Batman said. "Two-Face is on his southern border."

"True, but my agent confirms that something is going on. Something about trial by combat. Two-Face brand justice, sounds like."

"When?"

"Rumored for midnight."

"I'll check it out."

There was another pause, and when Oracle spoke again, the words more than the tone took Batgirl by surprise.

"You want to know what I think?" Oracle asked.

"No."

"I think it's a trap. Oracle out."

He replaced the handset, then moved to the doorway, looking out at the night. Batgirl rose.

"Midnight. That gives us about two hours to prepare," she said.

"I'm going alone."

Batgirl almost bit back the response. He had all but validated her to Oracle. She knew that what he'd allowed her to overhear in that conversation might well be as close to approval as she was ever likely to get. But she didn't imagine that Nightwing held his tongue when thinking that the Batman was about to make a mistake, and she knew she couldn't either.

"Oracle said it's a trap."

"No, Oracle said she thought it was a trap. We don't know."

"If it is a trap, you're going to need backup."

He still hadn't turned around, and his voice was low and even, his tone perfectly calm. "No. You stay here, protect our territory."

She thought, but didn't say, that there were over sixty square blocks in their territory. How she was supposed to protect it all by herself, she had no idea. He wasn't in the mood to listen to any questions from her anyway, she realized; he was already focusing on where he was headed and what he would do when he got there.

"I'll be back by dawn."

Batman stepped out onto the street. Batgirl followed him, and when she made it outside he'd produced his line and grapnel and was already halfway up the side of the wrecked building across from them.

"I'm counting on you," he said before he vanished. "Don't let me down."

EIGHTEEN

GARRETT DIDN'T KNOW THE WOMAN he was supposed to kill. He'd only met her five minutes before, just inside the courthouse, where Two-Face had explained exactly what they were supposed to do, and how the plan was supposed to work.

"It's got to look good," Two-Face warned. "Batman has to believe you're going for her blood."

"Go for her blood, gotcha," Garrett had said.

Two-Face's fist had come out suddenly, grabbing Garrett by a chunk of his hair. He had twisted his head back, forcing Garrett to look at him, directly into his bulging eye and his scarred, purple face.

"No," Two-Face had hissed. "*Pretend* to go for her blood. You actually hurt her, I'll eat your liver, understand?"

Garrett had tried to nod, but his range of motion had been severely limited by Two-Face's grip. His intention had come across, though, and Garrett had been let go, told to grab a bat and a length of chain, and head on down to the arena. The woman had taken an old longsword that she needed both hands to swing. She'd also taken a collapsible baton, a small syringe, and a bottle of something that Penguin had given Garrett to give to Two-Face. Chloral something or other. Not dope, at least not dope as Garrett knew it.

He didn't do drugs anyway. They slowed him down.

The arena wasn't really an arena at all, just a big cleared circle out in front of the Gotham City Courthouse, ringed with oil drum fires and spectators. There were maybe thirty people gathered, none of them faces that Garrett recognized, though he knew some of the tags. A couple of the folks were pretty badly mutilated, former followers of Black Mask. There were a couple of Demonz, too, and some of the crew that had worked for Scarface before the Bat had taken him down.

The woman went into the arena, dragging the sword after her. Garrett liked watching her move. She was pretty, and clean, and on top of that, she had really nice red hair and these hazel eyes that sort of turned green sometimes when he got a close look at them. He wondered if she was Two-Face's girl, or if maybe, after everything was over, he could ask her out.

One of Two-Face's crew, a guy calling himself TallyMan on account of how he kept a count of all the people he killed and who wore a pretty strange-looking hat, started shouting for everyone's attention. Garrett tried to tune him out, watching the pretty red-haired girl. She didn't look happy, and he tried smiling at her, and she saw him do it and scowled in return. It took Garrett another second to remember that they were pretending to fight, and that it had to look good, and that therefore he probably shouldn't be smiling at her.

He tried to look mean.

The TallyMan was getting really loud now, holding out one palm, and on it Garrett saw a single bullet, shining in the firelight.

". . . even a chance to win this wonderful, glorious, fully functional .45 caliber round, yes, ladies and gentlemen, that's one-hundred-eighty-five grains of guaranteed justice," the TallyMan was shouting. "Place your bets as tonight's guilty party is tried in the impartial court of the Kingdom of Two-Face. For the prosecution, tonight, at six feet and four inches in height, two hundred and twenty pounds, Alexander Garrett!"

The crowd applauded, and Garrett nodded and started to smile, then caught himself and scowled some more. The applause got louder.

"And for the defense, at five feet and eight inches, weighing in at a whopping one hundred and forty pounds sopping wet, Isabella Cheranova!"

The crowd began booing. Garrett heard someone shouting that the fix was in.

TallyMan ignored the hoots and hollers, and continued. "Charged with theft of food, two counts, intent to subvert Two-Face's authority, three counts, and finally, flight to avoid prosecution! A plea of not guilty having been entered, tonight's trial may now begin!"

The crowd roared, and Garrett took that as his cue to swing the bat. He started with a slow move, coming up, like he was going for her head, and she surprised him by turning in closer, so the blow went over her head. Then she was right in front of him, and before he'd realized what had happened, she'd put her knee in his stomach and caught him across the jaw with her forearm.

Garrett staggered back, getting angry. Isabella had backed off, now holding the sword in both hands, head down and those pretty eyes of hers looked mean suddenly. It occurred to Garrett that maybe she hadn't been listening when Two-Face had explained what was supposed to happen.

He came at her again with the bat, faster this time, and she used the sword to parry the blow, then kicked him in the thigh, and Garrett felt the block of muscle on his right leg go numb for a second. He shouted out something his mother told him he should never call a lady, then brought the chain down. She dived out of the way, and he followed with another swing of the chain, then a crisscross with the bat. She parried the second one, and it took her guard down, and Garrett cried out in triumph, whipping the chain around, catching the blade of her sword.

With a sharp tug, he disarmed her.

The crowd was going wild.

Without a second thought, Garrett brought the bat up again and then down and then his whole arm went numb and he couldn't keep his grip. Three small black metal bats were sticking into his forearm.

He started to shout and turn, and then he felt a boot hitting his back and Garrett was on the broken concrete, sliding on the ground. He tried to get up but felt the boot move, pressing into his jaw and he swiveled his eyes furiously, looking up and seeing a portion of the black cape, the clawed hand.

"That's enough!" the Batman said, and then he came off Garrett's head and grabbed Isabella. Garrett used both hands to get up; the one with the Batarangs in it hurt like hell but he tried anyway, hoping to grab the Bat by the cape or something, anything to keep him from getting away.

But already he was gone, taking the pretty girl with him, rising into the night sky. He saw them land on the rooftop of the courthouse, wondered how he could get up there in time.

Then he saw the Batman turn around, looking back down at them. Behind him, he saw Isabella moving, snapping out the collapsible baton.

Then she hit the Batman over the head with it, and Garrett, having been there himself, recognized the way that the Batman fell.

Out cold.

There were too many of them and it happened too quickly and Batgirl honestly didn't know what she was supposed to do to stop them.

She'd tried, though. For nearly an hour she'd tried, using the rooftops to keep pace with the scattered groups of Penguin's men as they advanced northward, into Bat territory, into the territory that he had ordered her to protect only hours earlier. But for every group she stopped, there was another to replace it, and she'd gone through all the stores on her belt already, all of the smoke and all of the tear gas and all of the flash-bangs. She had personally taken down eleven of Penguin's men by hand, and had the cuts and bruises to show for it, including one laceration that burned along her back every time she moved her left arm.

But still the men kept coming, and now she was exhausted and praying for daylight, for what she hoped would mean an end to the battle.

That, and she prayed for the Batman, that he would arrive, and soon, before it was all too late.

She was leaving the EMS Barracks, where she had gone hoping that she might find something—anything—that would give her an edge, when she saw Penguin himself waddling up Sixth Avenue, surrounded by almost twenty men. He looked complacent, self-satisfied, and it made her furious, filled her with a righteous anger that took her back onto the street and up the side of the first building she found. She stayed low, racing along the broken rooftops until she managed to get ahead of him at the corner of Sixth and Peterson, in front of the ruins of the Eagle Cinema.

Good coverage, she thought, at least her back wouldn't be exposed. She leapt from the rooftop, snapping the cape out to slow her descent. She landed in a roll and came up fast, stopping dead, shouting.

"Penguin!"

He raised a hand, gesturing for his men to stop. She watched as several readied arrows for their bows, noting positions. All of his men were armed, clearly ready for the battle. A couple even had firearms, pistols and rifles. One of them, standing beside Penguin, had a crossbow.

"Have you come to parlay, my dear?" Penguin asked. He used his umbrella to indicate the surrounding area, drawing a half circle in the air between them. "It's over, you must realize. This land is mine now."

"You have a truce with Batman! You can't—"

"Indeed, yes, and where is he? Hmm?" Penguin shook his head, as if explaining the situation to a very slow child. "Don't you see, my second-rate rodent? He's left you here to fight this battle on your own. I'd advise you to surrender now, while you still can. Or else you might just get your wings clipped."

"I think your men can testify it won't be that easy."

"Indeed. But then again, those men you've dealt with thus far didn't have bullets. Since I don't think you want a lead injection to the brain, I'm giving you one last chance. Surrender."

She opened her mouth to tell him where to stuff his last chance, and then she heard one of Penguin's men shouting for his attention from the back of the group. She watched while the crowd parted, and as all eyes turned she took the opportunity to free her Batarang from where it was hooked at the back of her belt, feeling the metal hard in her hand.

"How about a hostage?" one of Penguin's men was saying, and Batgirl saw that a man was forced to the front of the group, driven at spearpoint.

"Excellent," Penguin said.

The man was white, young, and thin, but evidently healthy. His beard and hair were black, and his eyes moved quickly, finding Batgirl, taking in everything.

One of Penguin's thugs pushed the man to the ground, holding a spear to the back of his neck.

"And what's your name, my fine fellow?" Penguin asked.

"Charlie," the man said. "Chas."

"Charlie, well, you've just distinguished yourself." Penguin moved his attention from Charlie back to Batgirl. "The situation is now slightly different. Instead of wasting a bullet, I have a far more compelling offer. Surrender or this poor fellow springs a sudden and fatal leak in the gray matter area."

"Go to hell," Batgirl said, and threw the Batarang. She knew as she let it go that it was a good throw, dead on target. The Batarang sailed over Charlie, over the head of the spear, and Batgirl jerked the line down, and the metal end dropped, wrapping tightly around the shaft. Another yank and the spear was out of the man's hands, and whoever Charlie was, he was good, because he was already running.

She went low, hearing Penguin shouting for his men to kill her, and she heard the gunshots, felt the whistle as a round punched into the Kevlar lining of her cape. There was only one tactic she could think of, the one that had worked with Black Mask, to go for the head of the dragon, such as it was. But Penguin was backing away, and the guard next to him, the one with the crossbow, was turning to track her. She came up at his side, reaching around his body for his arm, pivoting him with her until she had the shot lined up and then she forced the man's hand back on the trigger. The cable snapped forward with a crack almost as loud as the shots, and the quarrel flew and hit Penguin dead in the right thigh.

Penguin hollered in pain, pitching forward, using his umbrella to stay his fall, and then they all heard the shout, echoing, loud enough that it demanded everyone's attention.

"Cobblepot!"

Penguin's men turned to the source of the noise, and Batgirl used the chance to retreat, pulling back and then finding herself along-side Charlie, who had stopped in the shadows between two buildings, still watching. Without a word she put an arm around him, then used her last jumpline to hoist them on top of what remained of the Eagle Cinema. She let Charlie go, turning back in time to see Penguin's men clearing the street.

Two-Face was approaching, and behind him was a mob the size of which Batgirl had yet to see in the No Man's Land. Easily twice, maybe three times as many people as had been following Black Mask, and as much as ten times as many men than Penguin had on the street before her. Two hundred armed men and women, at least.

"Harvey," she heard Penguin say. "Come to lend a hand?"

"Leave. Now." Two-Face's voice echoed on the street.

"We had a deal, Harvey, you duplicitous—"

"You had a deal with Bats, too, didn't you? I'll explain, Oswald. This is me using you, you arrogant, waddling buffoon. Always so certain you've got every angle covered, always certain you're the smartest of the bunch. Not this time. This time you've been played like the loser you are. And while you're standing here, gaping at me and bleeding out from that wound in your thigh, Gordon and his cops just annexed your southern border, all the way to the Park."

Penguin tried to stand upright, using the umbrella as a crutch. Batgirl heard him murmuring something in response. Whatever it was, Two-Face laughed.

"That's right. It means that your territory, instead of doubling, just got cut in half. Now leave *my* territory before I have you killed."

Penguin stood utterly still for a moment, head down. Then he turned, and using the umbrella, walked painfully to his men at the side of the street. Two of his crew took him by the arms, and slowly they made their way past Two-Face's army, heading back down Sixth, southward again.

Batgirl heard a sharp whistle and looked down to see Two-Face waving at her from below. "Batman's tied up right now," he shouted. "Think he'll be surprised when he gets back?"

She glared at him, trying to think of something to say, something to do.

But there were two hundred men on that street behind him, and Batgirl knew there was nothing left that she *could* do.

She turned, making her way off the roof.

Batman's territory was lost.

NINETEEN

IT SURPRISED HER ONLY A LITTLE THAT Two-Face had been so correct. Not that Montoya had thought she'd been lied to—she knew, intuitively, that Two-Face wouldn't lie to her—but more that he'd been so unerringly accurate.

They'd beaten Penguin's men, forcing them to retreat east, back into the Fashion District. They'd uncovered seven different caches of equipment and food, including medical supplies, MREs, and ammunition.

And they had taken losses, eleven men dead, all of whom had worn the badge, and another seven wounded.

One of the wounded was Sarah Essen, who had taken a bullet to the ribs as they were rushing the Penguin blockade at MLK and

Thirty-eighth. She'd been in the front, three steps ahead of Montoya, with Foley coming up behind and the Commissioner in the lead, and the shots had been coming at irregular intervals, Penguin's men trying to make each bullet count.

And then Essen had gone down, and Montoya had thought at first that the lieutenant had tripped, and Renee stopped to help her back to her feet. Then she'd seen the blood.

"Commissioner!" Montoya had shouted. "Essen's hit!"

Gordon, already twenty feet ahead, had spun in place, waving Pettit's squad past him. His face had been the white of a sheet, and he'd rushed back to where Montoya was kneeling by Essen's side, had almost bodily moved Renee out of the way. He'd scooped his wife up, looking around frantically, then finally focused on Montoya again. She had seen the fear in his eyes, even behind the lenses of his glasses.

"Keep fighting," he'd said, and then he'd begun running south, making for the Clock Tower.

Montoya had done as ordered and kept fighting, falling in with Pettit's squad, the sixteen men that he'd been training day in and day out for the last couple months. All her other misgivings about Billy Pettit aside, Renee had been forced to admit that the QRT leader knew his stuff. His squad alone had cleared five of the seven blockades they'd encountered, and casualties among his men were nonexistent.

By three that morning the fighting was over, and the cleaning up had begun. Montoya and Bullock had begun locating the caches, taking inventory, and it was nearly five before she felt she had enough information to actually make a report to the Commissioner. She rushed back down MLK, making her way to the Clock Tower, carrying with her one of the trauma kits they'd recovered. Weir and DeFilippis were on post outside the building, and Renee had seen other cops moving around outside as well. A couple were lining up the bodies of the fallen, covering them with sheets.

She went inside, through the atrium to where the triage center had been set up. Barbara Gordon was there, hands stained with blood, rolling among the cots that had been lined up, checking on the wounded. Montoya recognized most of the sleeping faces, but didn't see Essen.

"Miss Gordon?" Montoya called. "Barbara?"

Barbara turned her chair, and with a quick flick of both wrists had crossed, then stopped, right in front of her. Montoya offered her the triage kit, saying, "We recovered this and another twenty or so like it from one of the caches. Thought it might be of some use."

Barbara used the back of one bloodstained hand to adjust her glasses, crinkling a small smile. "That's great, Renee, thanks."

"How's your stepmother?"

"Sarah's okay. It was a graze. The bullet took a piece of meat off her side, but that's it. She lost some blood and Dad's gonna have to be judicious with his hugs for a couple of weeks, but she'll be fine."

"I didn't see her anywhere," Montoya said, feeling the relief flood through her. "Started to worry, you know?"

"Dad took her back to TriCorner to get some rest. That was about an hour or so ago. He should be back any time."

"Okay, great, thanks."

She started to turn to head outside, but Barbara reached out a hand, touching her coat. "Detective?"

"Yes, Miss Gordon?"

"How'd it go?"

"We won," Renee said.

Which was true, wasn't it?

The Commissioner arrived a little before six, looking haggard and tired, and he gestured Montoya over as soon as he saw her. She left DeFilippis and Weir, and crossed the street to where Gordon was standing, staring at the line of covered bodies.

"Renee."

"Sir. How's Lieutenant Essen?"

"Cranky." He made a halfhearted laugh. "Gets cranky whenever she gets hurt. Makes it seem like it was her own fault, somehow, as if she did it on purpose."

"I doubt she wanted to get shot."

"That's pretty much what I said." He used his thumb and index finger to push his glasses up, rubbing the bridge of his nose. "I need you to go to him again, Renee."

"Sir." Her tone was flat.

"Just tell him . . . tell him it worked." His hand came down and the glasses fell once more into place. She could see the resolve in his face. "And then tell him we're through. We won't be dealing with him anymore."

She felt herself smiling. "Gladly, sir."

The sun had just finished rising when she made it to Civic Plaza, the gold light splashing across the broken pavement and ruined park, drawing long shadows up the steps of the building. Montoya crossed through a circle of oil drums that she presumed were used for holding fires at night, and stopped just across the street from the building. She counted six guards, all of whom were giving her their undivided attention.

"I need to see Two-Face," she called. "Tell him it's Montoya. Renee Montoya."

One of the guards turned and went inside, taking his time about it.

She waited. The sunlight was warm on her back, heating the leather of her jacket. After what felt like almost three minutes, she saw the guard return, Two-Face accompanying him. He came down the stairs, taking them several at a time, buttoning his suit jacket, a taupe-colored Armani with matching slacks and black loafers. There was no question, he was the best-dressed warlord in the city.

He misread her grin as he crossed the street, answered it with one of his own, smoothing down his tie with a free hand while extending the other to her for a shake. "Renee! Good morning!"

"Morning," she said. She took his hand, and the shake was precise and quick, and he didn't linger over it, which she appreciated. His hand was strong and big.

"Didn't expect to be seeing you again so soon," Two-Face said. "You want to come in? I was just about to have some breakfast. Got some oranges from Penguin last night, fresh juice. Got to love that."

She actually stopped to consider the offer—she couldn't remember the last time she'd had juice, let alone fresh orange juice, and the temptation for a second was almost irrationally overwhelming—before shaking her head. "I can't, I'm sorry," Montoya said. "I don't have a lot of time, actually. You were right about the fight. We lost some good people. I have to head back and help with the cleanup."

The unmarred side of his face registered the disappointment briefly. "Well, perhaps another time."

"Well, that's kind of what I need to talk to you about."

"Oh?"

"Yeah. The Commissioner sent me, wanted me to thank you for your help and your assistance last night. We're not really certain what part you played but, like I said, it turned out almost exactly as you predicted."

He shrugged modestly, and the gesture, paradoxically, reminded Montoya of how big a man Two-Face was. "It was nothing."

"So the Commissioner, you understand, he wanted me to thank you," Montoya went on. "And he wanted me to tell you that he feels the business between the two of you is completed, and he won't be bothering you anymore."

Two-Face blinked at her, once, slowly. "Does he now?"

Montoya nodded, felt the fear begin moving inside of her, fought to keep it from her face.

The right half of Two-Face's mouth closed, his lips coming together tightly. The movement pulled at the skin on the scarred side, drawing the flesh up and revealing half his teeth, even and white. It made him look terribly dangerous and terribly sad at the same instant, and Montoya could see as clearly as ever the two personalities battling.

The silence stretched.

"That means you won't be coming back, doesn't it?" Two-Face asked.

"I don't think the Commissioner's going to send me again, no."

"So . . . I won't be seeing you again, will I?"

"Probably not for a while. Not unless the Commissioner sends me, like I said."

Another slow nod. Another blink. In her peripheral vision, she saw Two-Face's hand dip into his coat pocket, coming out again with the half-dollar. He turned it end-over-end on his knuckles, bringing it to rest finally on his thumb, ready to toss.

"You should go," he said softly. "Before I throw the coin, you should go."

"Harvey . . ."

His shout filled the plaza, echoed and bounced off the rubble, off the steps of the courthouse.

"GO NOW!"

She took a step back, then another.

"Please," Two-Face hissed, and she saw the desperation in his clear eye, and that did it.

She turned and ran for her life.

I told you.

It wasn't her fault. You saw her, you saw the look on her face. She didn't want to hurt us.

The bitch—

Don't talk about her like that.

. . . sorry . . . you're right, it's not her, it's him, isn't it?

Yes.

Gordon.

Yes.

He knew . . . he knew all along. He never intended to honor our deal, he just wanted to use us.

Yes.

We went to him with an offer to help, an honest offer. And what did he do, Harvey? What did he do when we came to him with our help?

He used us.

And he used her. He used Renee. He knew . . . he knew. . . .

Yes.

The snake is in breach of contract, Harvey. What say we make him pay?

Can't be done. You know that. The arrangement wasn't witnessed, we don't have legal recourse—

Oh, for . . . would you listen to yourself? I didn't say we should take him to court, you wimp! I said we should make him pay.

. . . make him pay . . .

With his life.

Murder, you're talking about murder again.

As long as Gordon's around, Renee'll never come back, you know that. He won't let her. He'll keep her close to him and we'll never get a chance to be with her, to talk to her, to have her listen. You know that, Harvey. You know I'm right.

Still . . .

It's the only solution.

But . . . but we're talking about murder . . .

Wimp. Weak, useless . . . you can't decide, you can't commit . . . not even for her, you can't be strong. Fine. Flip it. Good heads, Gordon lives.

Bad heads . . .

Heh. You know what bad heads is, Harvey.

Go ahead.

Flip it.

TWENTY

EARLIER THAT NIGHT, WHILE JAMES GORDON was returning his wife to their home in TriCorner and the Penguin was removing the broken end of a cross-bow bolt from his thigh, the Batman recovered consciousness.

It wasn't the first time he'd ever been bludgeoned into darkness, but the moment he opened his eyes, he knew he'd been drugged, too. The fog in his head was deep, and beyond the lenses inside his cowl, the world seemed to quiver and tremble. He tried to move his arms and discovered they had been tied behind his back. His legs, however, were free.

He twisted, checking the strength of the bonds while trying to clear his head. It was still dark. With a squeeze of his glove he activated the heads-up display on the left lens, checked the clock, saw that it was 0403 hours. The HUD winked off, leaving the dim LED glow dancing on his retina for another few seconds. His head ached, and for a moment he felt a rising surge of nausea that forced him to stop moving altogether. He checked his breathing, began pulling in air steadily through his nose, feeling it fill his lungs, then letting it rush from his mouth. The sensation passed.

He shut his eyes, took another, deeper breath, and, twisting his wrists, slipped out of the ropes that held him.

Too easy, he thought.

He got to his feet and moved to the edge of the roof of the courthouse. Below him, the square was empty. There was no noise.

Drugged, he thought. The ropes were a token restraint.

This was a trap and I walked right into it.

But not a trap to capture me. My cowl's still in place, my equipment is still with me. Two-Face didn't want me prisoner.

Two-Face wanted me out of the way.

The surge of nausea this time had nothing to do with the blow to the head, or the remnants of the drug in his veins.

The Batman spared himself another ten seconds to clear his head, and then he began moving uptown, going from building to building using what Nightwing called the "rooftop express." It was slower going in the No Man's Land, but it served, and he knew it took him exactly seven minutes and twenty-eight seconds to make it from Civic Plaza back to the Upper East Side, to the territory he had claimed as his own.

He didn't like claiming territory, but he understood its merits in the NML, especially psychologically. The statement was everything, and ostensibly, those people who resided under a bat-tag had a reasonable assumption that they would be safe. It had worked well during the past month, and in a way the No Man's Land seemed uniquely suited to his crime-fighting persona. Before Gotham had turned to rubble, he had existed more as an urban legend in the popular culture than anything more. And while every night the number of people who could testify to his existence had steadily grown, compared to the millions of men, women, and children who lived in Gotham, it was simply a drop in the bucket. For so many people, he knew, he was nothing more real than the Bogeyman.

Before the NML.

Now, where the numbers were fewer and eyewitnesses were everything, more and more people knew the truth.

That translated to cachet in dealing with them, a trust. Those people who put themselves in his care, they did so believing in the myth. They knew nothing of the man.

He was at Muffo and Eighth when he knew there was a problem, and he began moving faster, toward the source of the light, where the fire was burning out of control in the distance. He flew past the EMS Barracks where he'd been meeting Batgirl, noting that it, too, was empty, and then, on the next block, he stopped short, registering what his eyes had seen on the brick wall twenty feet back. He turned and looked again, feeling his pulse beginning to beat at his temples.

The wall where he had sprayed the sign of the Bat, the wall that declared the block was his, protected by him, had been defaced. The yellow bat-tag had been painted over, replaced with another tag entirely.

Two-Face.

He resumed his path, trying to keep the focus, trying to push the fear away. But he felt it creeping at him, snaking around his spine— the lurking despair, that same haunting helplessness born in Crime Alley all those years ago. The sense that death was moving through the world, and it didn't care who it touched. The sense that pain rode with it, clearing the path.

He reached Peterson and Sixth, the ruins of the Eagle Cinema, and again knew that it was true.

He stood there for almost five minutes, staring at the fires burning in the streets. At the six bodies that had been strung up along the walls, the men who had been beaten to death or shot with arrows or otherwise murdered, all for the defense of their home, for his territory. He had known each of them, and knew that they had never known him.

He stared at the Two-Face tags that peppered the walls all around him, and at the words, painted in red, on the wall above the bodies.

TAILS, YOU LOSE.

As if it were some kind of joke, some sort of prank that Two-Face had played simply to get a laugh out of him, or at least a rise.

He had been holding his breath, and with a start realized that he'd been doing so for over two minutes now. He forced himself to breathe, returning to the basics.

He stood vigil for another hour and then, as dawn was threatening, set to work freeing the bodies from their confines. There was clear ground in Puckett Park, and he could inter the bodies there. It was the least he could do for them.

As far as he was concerned, it didn't matter if Two-Face had murdered them personally or had henchmen do it. They were dead.

Six more dead.

His fault.

And hers.

It was dawn before he had the last corpse in the earth, buried deep enough to be honored. His whole body ached from the labor, from the digging, and beneath the Nomex and Kevlar weave of his suit, he felt the sweat sliding around his body. All of him was exhausted, and it ran deeper than muscle and bone, and it surprised him somewhat. He was used to fatigue, had lived with it for most of his life, first as a result of horrible insomnia and then as an active decision, the commitment to two lives, one to be lived in daylight, the other in darkness.

He marked the graves with stones and promised himself that, when it was all over, when Gotham was restored, Bruce Wayne would pay to have the bodies exhumed and moved and buried properly, with all honor and consideration. But for now the stones would have to do.

He finished, straightened, and fixed his gaze to the horizon, ignoring where Batgirl had been hiding for the last hour, watching him. He had heard her approach though she'd tried to keep it silent, and twice while working he had marked her as she came close, almost found the courage to speak to him. Each time, though, she had retreated, and now he knew she was watching him from behind the broad oaks at the top of the slope.

He looked at the graves a final time, then turned and began heading north. Alfred would be with Dr. Thompkins, or at one of the northernmost caves. He would take some rest there and determine his next course of action.

No, that was a lie. He already knew his next course of action.

She was coming down the slope behind him, still at least fifty meters off. To pay her respects or her penance. It didn't matter. Both were worthless to the dead.

He stopped and without turning back, said to the Batgirl, "I trusted you."

And then he left her to stand over the graves.

PART TWO

ORACLE

PERSONAL
Entry #404—NML Day 176
1751 Zulu

Dear Dad—

Hindsight.

It's a bitch, ain't it?

If only we'd known. If only we could have known then, maybe . . . but maybe we'd just do the same damn things. Maybe it's fate.

That day, 145, it changed *everything*, didn't it? All of my maps had to be redrawn. Two-Face's territory doubled in one fell swoop, while Penguin lost almost all of his holdings. You made it all the way to the Park.

The Batman lost it all.

What a way to mark the middle of spring, huh?

I've been trying to reach him for the last seven days, broadcasting on his frequency twice an hour, but no response, nothing. Not even the Batgirl has answered my calls, though whether that's because she's out of a job or because she's not picking up, I don't know.

One of my agents, Charlie, he was on the ground there, told me that the Batgirl had saved his life.

But he told me the rest of it, too, how she had retreated, surrendering the territory to Two-Face. Charlie said she seemed to take it pretty hard.

"I think she was crying under that mask," he told me.

"Good," I said.

Is that cruel? Maybe.

I know who she is, and she has no right to that costume, never has. Six men died that night, six men who did nothing more than fight to protect their own homes, their own lives. Those six men . . . she had damn well better cry for them.

When I said what I said, Chas was still on the radio. He said, "You didn't see it. You don't know what it was like. She tried her best."

"Trying isn't enough," I said, and I cut the connection and caught my own reflection in one of my monitors.

Don't look a thing like the Batman, but I sure can sound like him, I suppose.

Maybe I am being too hard on her.

Maybe we're all just being too hard on ourselves.

Maybe that's why he's vanished again.

Cassandra was in here last night, had a note for me. I asked her where she'd gotten it, and after a couple minutes of charades with the map, I determined she'd been up in the MASH Sector with Dr. Thompkins.

The note was from Alfred Pennyworth, Bruce Wayne's butler—or gentleman's gentleman, as he prefers to be called. The note was short, basically bringing me up to speed on what had been going on at his end. He's been staying with Dr. Thompkins for the last couple weeks, assisting her in running the MASH unit. He says it's been busy up there, but the initial onslaught of injuries as a result of the "great claim jumping"—his phrase, not mine—has finally ended, and things are beginning to settle down.

Of the Batman's current situation and whereabouts he had little to offer, though I suspect he was being circumspect for fear that the letter fall into the wrong hands. He wrote only that he "has taken the loss of those territories claimed by him very much to heart, and is currently reevaluating his strategy with regard to the Declaration of the No Man's Land as a whole, and his modus operandi in particular."

He signed off wishing me the best, and saying that he expected that events would begin moving very rapidly now. He did not say why.

Maybe it's the change in the weather, the heaviness in the air, the rising humidity and the increasing heat. Whatever it may be, though, I feel it, too.

It feels like everything up until now has been a sort of preamble.

It feels like the real show is just about to start.

TWENTY-ONE

IT HAD TAKEN PRECISELY AS MUCH EFFORT to break into the No Man's Land as David Cain expected. The National Guard outposts, the tank barricades, the antipersonnel mines, all had been deployed to prevent people from escaping rather than penetrating. Certainly, they hadn't considered that anyone would spend the time, money, or effort to arrange a HALO drop. Or perhaps they had determined that anyone prepared to go to such lengths to get inside deserved whatever he had coming to him.

Cain fell for five miles before the city resolved below him, and through the night-vision goggles he was wearing, he made out Robinson Park, steering himself toward the reservoir at its northern end. He kept one eye on the altimeter, and at six hundred feet cut the cord to his equipment, kicking away the canister even as the water rushed up at him. At two hundred feet he deployed his chute, and at twenty he cut it away, too.

Then he was in the water, kicking to follow the rising of the bubbles, yanking the remainder of his drop equipment from his jumpsuit, letting it sink to the bottom of the reservoir in his stead. He broke the surface with air to spare, and swam quickly to the near shore, where he pulled himself onto the dry land, into the heat of the Gotham summer night. Without pausing Cain rose, making his way carefully through the thick undergrowth to where he estimated his gear to have landed. He walked carefully but quickly, cautious not to harm the abundance of greenery, the bushes, flowers, and trees that were unnaturally thick and lush. Where he found his path blocked he maneuvered to go around, and where he could not go around he went to his belly and crawled.

His intelligence had told him Poison Ivy was in the park; he had no quarrel with her, so he took care not to offend her by harming the green. From what he knew, Ivy eschewed all human contact, and was content enough to live and let live as long as her plants remained safe and strong.

Nonetheless, he found that his gear, still sealed in its black, ballistic canister, had broken two branches off an enormous pine when it had fallen to the earth. Working quickly, he hoisted the container onto its side, snapping open its main compartment, from which he armed himself with a single, silenced pistol, and a container that appeared to be nothing more than an aerosol can. Then, having done this, he moved the canister to his back, slinging the straps across his body, and made east as fast as he could.

He was in sight of the southern gate when the green around him came alive, suddenly, the branches of the two enormous oaks on either side of the exit gate dipping across his path with a furious cracking of wood and bark. He had been expecting this, though, and was ready. As the branches sprouted more branches, ends sharp as needles racing at him, he went into motion.

Cain pivoted, turning between the two extending spears with barely any room to spare, then dropped to his side, rolling toward the gate, bringing the aerosol up in his hand. He pushed the nozzle, spraying mist into the air around him, then pressed the second tab, causing the spark to fly.

The flames erupted instantly, the misted gasoline igniting everything it touched. The branches burst into fire, twisting crazily out of his way. He didn't stop, only pushed forward until he was out of the park, smelling the burning wood behind him, feeling the extra push of heat turn the remaining water on his clothes to steam.

He stayed stationary just long enough to find his bearings, then, certain he was oriented properly, began moving south, counting the blocks until he reached what he believed had once been Martin Luther King, Jr. Boulevard. He followed it south, the street empty and the night silent, and in under a minute saw the landmark that was his goal—the twenty-story tower with the clock face at its apex.

Cain moved to the side of the street, to the shadows, though he was certain no one had seen him thus far. He was paid to be cautious, however, and so he took the time to give the street a thorough visual scan. Two people were on guard outside the entrance to the Clock Tower, flanking the front door at either side. Not much of a deterrent, and certainly nothing that would slow him down should he decide to enter the building.

He considered his options, looking at the ruined architecture around him. His data suggested that the target would be at the top floor of the tower. Farther down on the opposite side of the street, there was another building still standing, but in sorrowful condition. Only sixteen stories tall, its front had crumbled in the earthquake, yet still the structure managed to defy gravity. He wouldn't be certain until he was inside, but he suspected the angle might well be workable.

Cain moved out of the shadow, turning at the corner and heading around the block, entering the building through a shattered window at the rear on the ground floor. Inside, he pulled the canister in after him, settled it once more on his back. He took the pistol from the holster on his thigh, screwing the silencer into place at the end of the barrel, and then slowly chambered the first round. There was a slight noise coming from above him, perhaps between floors, perhaps rats.

The employer had specified stealth first, and Cain meant to

oblige the request. He hated to do things twice. He had his reputation to maintain.

The stairs looked capable of taking his weight, and he ascended slowly, the gun out in front of him, held in both hands. On the second floor he noted which apartment doors were opened and which were shut, keeping a tally in his mind. He continued his count as he worked his way higher. Though the building looked abandoned, he knew better than to believe it so. This was Blue Boy territory, or so he had been informed, and there were plenty of people who would be eager to live under the illusion and memory of the Gotham City Police Department.

The sixteenth floor, he was disappointed to learn, had four apartments, and all the doors were closed. He removed the canister from his back once more, setting it carefully in the hall, then went to the first door, assuming that it would not be locked. He turned the knob slowly and it offered no resistance, and so he pushed back the door and made his way silently inside.

A man and woman were sleeping, half-nude, in the bedroom.

He shot them both twice in the head.

In the next room he found a man, alone, asleep on the couch.

He shot him twice, too.

The third apartment was empty.

The fourth apartment, the one with a view of the Clock Tower, the one he wanted, had another couple asleep in the master bedroom. He shot them, as well.

Then he returned to the hallway, hoisted the canister under his arm, and went back into the apartment, closing the door silently behind him, then locking it. Setting the canister on the floor in the center of the room, he then moved to the sofa, swinging it around so that its back was to the cracked window he wanted. He removed the cushions from its seat and experimented with their positioning. After a while, he moved the coffee table and other chairs around too, creating a pocket in the corner. He climbed into the space, kneeling on one of the cushions, looking out the window.

The angle looked good.

He went back to the canister and opened the main compartment, taking out the components of his rifle. The assembly was smooth and fast, taking him under a minute to complete. He loaded the magazine, slipped it into place, then set the rifle aside and removed the scope from its shock-resistant box. He had zeroed it only the day before, outside of Montreal, and hoped that the sensitive sight had survived the HALO drop unharmed. He bolted it to the rifle, then removed one more instrument from the canister. Then he climbed back into the sniper's nest he had made.

He took three range readings with the new device, marking them painstakingly in grease pencil on the laminated surface taped to the butt of the rifle. Then he adjusted the sight to match.

Content, he set the rifle aside and reloaded his pistol.

Finally, he lay back against the cushions, the pistol in his hand, his hand in his lap, and waited for the dawn to rise.

TWENTY-TWO

HE HATED HIMSELF FOR ALMOST ENJOYING what he was doing.

It had been depressingly simple to slip past Two-Face's guards, to penetrate the courthouse under the cover of darkness, to slip into Judge Halsey's chambers without alerting anyone to his presence. The only truly challenging part had been when he'd found Two-Face actually asleep in bed, and even that hadn't stopped him. He'd managed to bind Two-Face's hands and feet without waking him, and had the gag ready in his hand. It would be the gag that would give him away, he knew. It was impossible to gag a sleeping person.

The night beyond the window was dark and moonless. The Batman felt that was somehow appropriate.

In one swift move, he stuffed the gag into Two-Face's mouth. Then the Batman stepped back, watching coldly as the man he'd once known as Harvey Dent, the man he'd once called his friend, opened his eyes in horror and began struggling, pulling at the bonds that held him. He struggled for nearly a minute, straining violently at the ties holding his wrists and ankles, thrashing his head, the one already bulging eye seeming to surge all the more in the darkness and in desperation.

"Harvey," the Batman finally said.

Two-Face fell back against the bed, turning his head to the source of the voice. The surprise registered in his eyes, and he tried to say something that was lost behind the gag.

"I have a problem," the Batman said.

Two-Face made another noise.

The Batman moved silently around the room, then stopped at the bureau at the foot of the bed. On its surface was the silver half-dollar, and he picked it up, ignoring Two-Face's gagged protests. He held the coin between two fingers at eye level, turning it to look at each side, the smooth, worn surface that served as good heads, the representation of Liberty. Then the same face on the other side, only there it had been scratched and pitted, marred beyond all recognition. Bad heads.

"I think I finally understand its appeal, Harvey," the Batman said softly.

Two-Face's eyes widened slightly.

"There's no judge, Harvey. No court. No jury. There's no law anymore. Do you understand? There's no law anymore."

Two-Face didn't move, tracking the Batman's movement around the room.

"You murdered six men, Harvey. Six men I'd sworn to protect." The Batman moved closer, looming over the bed, glowering down at Two-Face. "Six men that I know of, and how many more have you killed who have no one to speak for them? Another six? Twelve? Twenty?"

He stepped back, looking once more at the coin in his hand. Two-Face's expression had changed, and the Batman recognized it as honest fear. For a moment, it gave him a glimmer of something like satisfaction.

"There's got to be a reckoning, Harvey," the Batman said. "What do you say? Should I flip it? Good heads, I let you go. Bad heads . . . "

Two-Face began thrashing again, then stopped suddenly as he caught the motion of the toss, hearing the sound of the coin, the slight tone of the metal as it was struck, the noise of the disk flipping through the air.

The Batman caught the toss with a snapping of his fist, looking at his closed hand as if he could divine the result by feel.

"Bad heads," the Batman repeated, spitting the words as if they were slick with grease, and then he turned and flung the coin, a move so fast and so sudden that Two-Face's muffled scream didn't begin until after the half-dollar had embedded itself, edge first, into the far wall.

The Batman leaned in suddenly, lifting Two-Face by the throat.

"Never forget how close you came tonight, Harvey," he hissed. "Never forget what you almost made me do."

Then he was gone, leaving Two-Face lying tied to the bed, pulling desperate breaths through his nose while he tried to force the gag out of his mouth with his tongue, tried to call for help.

TWENTY-THREE

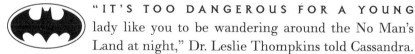 "IT'S TOO DANGEROUS FOR A YOUNG lady like you to be wandering around the No Man's Land at night," Dr. Leslie Thompkins told Cassandra. "You're sleeping here tonight, in my tent. No arguments."

Cassandra tried to explain that she needn't worry, that she really could take care of herself, but eventually gave up. Dr. Thompkins was a healer, after all, and worthy of respect. The last thing Cassandra wanted to do was insult her. There was no way to explain that she was only at the makeshift hospital and camp as a courier, running messages between Oracle and Alfred Pennyworth. It wouldn't matter to the doctor that Cassandra had already passed Oracle's message to Alfred, or that she now had Alfred's response folded safely in a pocket, ready for the return journey.

So she spent the night at the MASH encampment, helping Dr. Thompkins and Alfred with the patients there, following either one or the other of them around until quite late. She was astonished by the steady stream of people, men and women and children who made their way to the little camp, all hoping that the doctor could minister some aid.

Even more surprising than that, though, was Leslie herself.

Cassandra wasn't certain, but the woman had to be in her late sixties, at least, with hair that was both silver and white, and the clearest, palest blue eyes she had ever seen. She was a small woman, too, no bigger than Cassandra herself, and slight, with almost no muscle to speak of; the kind of person who looked like she could be tossed away in a stiff breeze. Yet Dr. Thompkins seemed invested with a boundless energy fueled from somewhere within. It was inspiring to simply watch her speaking with a patient, to see her render care so gently and so competently.

Dr. Thompkins would never hurt anyone or anything, Cassandra could tell that just by looking at her.

When they turned in that night, Cassandra tried to share that observation with the doctor, tried to pay her the honor as best she could. She waited until Dr. Thompkins had finished preparing the cot for her. Then, before the doctor could move out of the way, Cassandra stepped in, blocking her passage.

"I'm sorry?" Dr. Thompkins said. "Is there something more you'd like, dear?"

Cassandra shook her head, then presented both hands. With her right she made a fist, seating the face of it against the palm of her left hand, extending both in front of her at waist height. Then she bowed, looking the doctor in the eye.

Dr. Thompkins's wrinkled face wrinkled some more, and then she surprised Cassandra by returning the bow, saying, "You are quite a warrior, aren't you, dear? Thank you for the compliment."

Cassandra went to sleep happy.

The next morning, she woke before dawn and slipped out of the cot in the dark, making her way silently past Dr. Thompkins's sleeping form, until she was outside once more. The sky was turning pink, and a hint of the day's coming heat was already in the air.

Cassandra crouched outside the tent, pulling on her boots, and then she heard the movement to one side and turned quickly to catch its source.

The Huntress was watching her from beside the large tent, where the most serious patients lay.

Cassandra grinned and raised a hand, and the Huntress nodded in acknowledgment.

Boots on, Cassandra approached, arms out in an exaggerated gesture, trying to convey both that she was pleased to see the other woman and that she hadn't seen her in a while. It had been months since they'd crossed paths on the Upper East Side, and since that time Cassandra had found herself wondering what had become of the Huntress. Whenever she had tried to ask Oracle, Oracle pretended not to know what Cassandra was talking about.

"How are you?" Huntress asked softly.

Cassandra smiled and nodded, then gave her a thumbs-up.

Huntress smiled. "Good."

Cassandra indicated the camp, then pointed at Huntress.

"Me? No, I'm fine. I'm not hurt."

Cassandra shook her head, repeated the gesture.

"Oh, you mean what am I doing here?"

Cassandra nodded.

"I could ask you the same thing," Huntress said. "Just thought I'd stop by, make certain everything here was okay. I've been trying to keep an eye on the camp. What about you?"

Cassandra indicated herself, then made a walking gesture with the fingers of her right hand. Then she used her left palm as if it were a piece of paper, and mimed scribbling a note.

Huntress nodded. "Who for?"

Cassandra frowned, uncertain whether she should answer the question, if Oracle would be angry or not. Cassandra hadn't told her about the time she and Huntress had met at the end of winter, which had been all right because it really hadn't seemed to matter, then. But this was a question about Oracle specifically, and Cassandra didn't know what to do.

Huntress looked at her expectantly, and Cassandra finally nodded and pointed at her chest, making a small circle above her left breast. She tapped the circle, then did it again.

Huntress smiled gently, like a teacher with a favorite student. "I don't understand, hon."

With her hands, Cassandra drew a shield in the air between them. Then she tapped her chest again, made the circle again.

"Badge, is that what you're trying to say?" Huntress asked.

Cassandra nodded.

"Gordon has you running messages back and forth in the No Man's Land? He really has forgotten his priorities, hasn't he?"

Cassandra frowned. She didn't like having to tell the lie, and now she didn't like where the one-sided conversation was headed. And it was starting to get light, and she wanted to make it to Oracle's before the morning had progressed too far.

She made the running fingers gesture again, then pointed out of the camp, to the south.

"Got to run, huh?"

Cassandra nodded and shrugged.

The Huntress chuckled. "Not that you need the warning, but be careful. Two-Face is between us and the Blue Boys now, and he's not as permissive a landlord as the Batman was."

Cassandra made the gesture with her fists she had offered to Dr. Thompkins the night before.

Huntress returned it perfectly.

"Watch your back, kid," Huntress said.

After reading Alfred's note, Oracle wanted to work on Cassandra's lesson. They moved from the control room into the main space of the apartment, Cassandra watching while Oracle slid the false wall back into place. Cassandra took the seat Oracle indicated and waited while the other woman maneuvered the chair around to face her. From the coffee table, Oracle took a sketch pad and flipped it open to the beginning of the alphabet. They went through twenty-six sheets, each letter of the Roman alphabet, with Cassandra trying to mimic the sounds that Oracle made, matching the noise to the symbol.

"Good," Oracle said. "You're getting better. You've made a lot of progress."

Cassandra pushed the tip of her tongue against the back of her teeth. "T-aaans . . ."

"Thanks."

"Ta-ah nks . . ."

"Better. Okay, let's try something else." Oracle set the pad in her lap, turning to a new page and writing quickly with a large black marker. "Okay, try this one. This is a high palate sound. Stop."

"Sdaaa . . ."

"That's right, you're getting it."

"Ss-daa . . . ssddaa . . ." Cassandra tried, then turned quickly in her seat, attention now on the door to the apartment. There was a knock, and then the door opened, and the man she knew was Oracle's father was coming inside.

"Barbara, you shouldn't leave it unlocked," Gordon said.

"Who's going to break in, Dad?"

Cassandra got up, moving out of the way as Gordon passed her to hug his daughter. She could see Oracle's smile, how they both closed their eyes briefly. Her own father had only offered her a hug once, and that had been so many years ago, just before she had left. She felt both awkward and embarrassed watching them, as if she were intruding on something she had no right to see, and so she left, slipping silently out of the apartment and back into the hallway.

She could hear their voices, the soft tones, and she reached the stairs knowing that jealousy was dogging her steps. She wrestled with it in her mind all the way to the lobby, trying to see the emotion for exactly what it was. She didn't want to feel sorry for herself.

There were two extra Blue Boys in the lobby, bringing the total of guards to four. She didn't recognize any of them. The woman, the blond one who normally stood on guard, hadn't been there for days. Cassandra had meant to ask Oracle about her, where she had gone, but with communication being so difficult, it had been too much of a bother.

She stepped out into the summer heat and light, and saw her father across the street.

Her heart stopped for an instant, turned cold, and she froze on the steps, not believing it. She couldn't breathe.

It's not him, she thought. It can't be him, not here. He couldn't have tracked me here.

She stepped back into the lobby, pressing herself against the wall, then peeking around again with one eye.

The man was still walking along the broken sidewalk; he hadn't stopped, hadn't even looked her way, and Cassandra prayed he hadn't seen her.

He can't know I'm here, there's no way he could know that I'm here, she thought. He can't know, he can't . . .

He was entering one of the ruined buildings across the way, the tallest of them, now out of sight and inside. Walking with his head down, hands in his pockets, focused. She knew the look. She also knew that he didn't miss much, and that if he hadn't seen her already, it was by the same chance that had allowed her to see him first.

She edged back out of the lobby, clinging to the wall and then moving into the alley at the side, ducking behind some rubble. She couldn't see any movement from the building he'd entered. The windows facing the street had almost all been shattered in the quake, and most of them were now blocked with either scraps of boards or sheets, used by the residents to keep out the summer heat and the swarms of flies that moved in the streets like black clouds.

As she watched, the sheet hanging over the window on the end of the top floor moved barely. The glint of metal reflected just for an instant, then was gone.

There were voices coming from the Clock Tower, just inside the lobby. Oracle's father, telling the Blue Boys there that he was ready to go.

Her father! Cassandra thought, and then she was out of the alley, leaping back up the steps as Gordon and the other cops stepped outside. She scared them with her approach, two of the men stepping back and freeing their weapons from their holsters, and Gordon's surprise was alight all over his face. She didn't care, didn't think about it, just grabbed him around the waist, passing the Blue Boys on either side of the Commissioner, and then driving him back into the lobby, shoving him down and covering him with her body.

There was no sound of the shot, but the bullet hit the ground on a line with where Gordon's head had been only a second before, splintering the concrete of the steps. Cassandra pushed herself up, still holding the Commissioner, dragging him forcefully back into the lobby as more rounds were hitting the ground, each only an instant behind them until they were far enough inside to have cover, to block the sniper's angle. Cassandra let Gordon go, turning back to look.

One of the Blue Boys was already dead, shot through the throat. The remainder had pulled back, their weapons drawn, shouting to one another. One of them was trying to return fire.

Gordon started to get up and Cassandra caught him by the arms, shoving him back, toward the stairway. She indicated up with a finger, jabbing at the ceiling.

"Upstairs?"

She nodded vigorously, still poking the air above her.

Gordon shook his head, started to step forward, but another barrage of shots from outside peppered the ground, breaking into the lobby and snapping pieces of the marble tile, shooting them into the air. Cassandra moved directly in front of Gordon, then wrapped her arms around his middle, using her right leg as a brace, trying to keep him from continuing. He tried for a second longer, but Cassandra held her ground, and Gordon finally got the message.

"Fall back," he told his men. "Fall back."

TWENTY-FOUR

THE BODY LANGUAGE WAS ALMOST AS fluent as speech, and it filled in the gaps. The problem with trying to read Two-Face's lips, the Batman knew, was the left side of Harvey's face. So far, though, Two-Face had been obliging, ranting at the TallyMan in the outer office of Judge Halsey's chambers. From where the Batman was perched on the remnants of what had once been Gotham's Federal Building, his view via binoculars was unobstructed.

It had taken Harvey almost six minutes to break free from the bonds, twice as long as the Batman had estimated. He put the discrepancy down to two factors, possibly a combination of both. First, he had bound Two-Face to the bed more securely than intended.

Second, Two-Face had most likely been terrified by what had happened, and was almost certainly irrational.

The Batman understood that last factor more than he cared to admit. He had scared himself nearly as much as he had Two-Face. The coin had been, for one horrible instant, seductive. It had offered to take the responsibility away, and the offer had been a tempting one. So much of the No Man's Land seemed to now be resting on his shoulders, and the chance that somehow, someway, Batman could abdicate responsibility, that was a potent dream.

The fact was that the Batman didn't know what to do anymore, and once again, the despair that had consumed him after the declaration of NML threatened to pull him down.

Two-Face was pacing in the office, gesturing wildly, moving the coin back and forth in his hands. The TallyMan had backed away, giving his boss room to rant.

—tried to kill me in my own home he came into my own home and tied me to the bed he could have killed me he's lost his mind, he's—

And here the Batman lost the next couple of sentences as Two-Face turned away from the window, making further lip-reading, for the moment, impossible. TallyMan was nodding, trying to appease him, then moving quickly, almost like a spider, out of the way, as Two-Face approached the wall. The Batman watched as Two-Face revealed a safe secured behind the painting there, trying to calculate the combination as Two-Face spun the dial. Then the safe was open and Two-Face was removing stacks of bills, mostly hundreds from what the Batman could see.

Odd, he thought. Money in the NML. Why?

Two-Face had turned, stacking the money on the desk, and once more the Batman could read his lips.

—ective Montoya and if he thinks he can do that he doesn't understand what's going on here how there are some things a man can't stand I'll show him . . .

He had turned away again.

Montoya, the Batman thought. Detective Third Class Renee Montoya, member of the GCPD's Major Crimes Unit, the division tasked with handling "extreme" crimes, normally those committed by the lunatic fringe. Crimes committed by men like Harvey, or Joker, or Mr. Freeze.

Two-Face was continuing to remove bills from the safe, TallyMan helping.

Six weeks before Black Monday, the Batman had encountered Montoya and Two-Face in the rubble. It had been shortly after the quake, just before the National Guard had arrived, and looters had been running wild through the streets. The Batman had stumbled upon a group of citizens in Spanish Burnley who had mobilized their own grassroots rescue effort, moving from building to building, attempting to dig out those people still trapped. Montoya had been one of them, along with her brother. Two-Face had been helping, as well.

He'd been on one of his rare runs of "good heads," it seemed.

When the Batman arrived Harvey had panicked, defaulting to a coin toss, trying to determine if he should run or fight. Harvey had made it as far as the actual toss when Montoya had taken the coin from the air. She had completely ignored the Batman's presence then, focused entirely on Harvey. Somehow she had managed to convince him the toss hadn't been called for, that there was no decision to be made. She had convinced Two-Face to continue helping the rescue effort.

Batman had backed away then, still watching, warily. While Montoya seemed to have him under control, Batman knew that Harvey was dangerously unpredictable.

Yet that night, finished with their work, Harvey had voluntarily surrendered himself to Montoya. And she had brought him back to Arkham herself.

Batman had to admit, considering it now, that he'd never seen anything like it.

Two-Face had closed the safe, was moving back to the desk, still talking, this time faster. The coin made a silver streak along his knuckles as he rolled it over his fingers again and again.

. . . be that way, if he's here . . . should be . . . can't keep us apart then can he . . .

The TallyMan spoke.

He should have arrived by now . . . if he's as good as they say it's already been done.

Two-Face's grin was sinister.

Good . . . good he tries to break a deal with us he keeps me from seeing the woman I love . . .

Batman, for a moment, thought he'd read that wrong.

But Two-Face repeated it.

. . . she's stolen my heart I'm in love and he knows that and he'll pay for keeping us apart he'll pay for everything . . .

The last woman Harvey Dent had loved was dead, Batman knew. The last woman Harvey Dent had loved was his wife, Gilda.

. . . pay for it, never forget what he did after cane does Gordon she and I can be together and . . .

It was almost a literal shock, the mention of the name, and Batman lowered the binoculars quickly, stowing them back in his belt as he dropped out of his perch, his mind already snapping the pieces of the puzzle together. The money, the haste, the snippets of conversation. The fire last night in Robinson Park. Why Robinson Park, he wondered; why Robinson Park, of course, the reservoir. The only open area in the city, the only viable target for a parachute drop, and it would have to have been the reservoir because any drop would have been high altitude, low opening, a HALO drop, demanding not only a large target zone but one that could lessen the impact of landing.

Two-Face hadn't said "cane," Batman knew, already in motion, snapping out his grapnel and line, then jumping before the end was even anchored, heading west toward TriCorner. Two-Face had said "Cain" and everything made perfect sense now.

It didn't matter that Jim Gordon and he hadn't spoken for five months, and it didn't matter that, from all he had heard, Gordon considered him more an enemy than a friend.

What mattered was that David Cain was in Gotham City, and that David Cain was one of the most revered and precise contract assassins in the world. What mattered was that, for whatever twisted reasons in Harvey Dent's brain, Two-Face had managed to hire David Cain to murder James Gordon.

And if Cain was already in the city, there was a good chance that the Batman would be too late to do a damn thing about it.

. . .

"You know who he is, don't you?" Gordon asked. "I need you to tell me. Who killed one of my men today, who tried to shoot me?"

Cassandra looked helplessly from the Commissioner to his daughter, past the faces of the concerned Blue Boys who were now gathered in Oracle's apartment.

No, not Oracle, stop thinking like that, Cassandra told herself. Barbara. When her father is here, she's Barbara.

Cassandra reached for the sketch pad that had held her lessons from early that morning, and Barbara nodded, handing it over and giving her the pen. Cassandra worked quickly, drawing the circle and then blacking it in, leaving the negative space in the shape of a serpent's head. She heard the Commissioner talking to the other Blue Boys there, telling them to see if they could find a translator, and to double the guards at the perimeter. Cassandra wanted to tell him it wouldn't work, that it didn't matter. She hoped the picture would explain all that.

Finished, she handed the pen back to Barbara, then held the pad up so Commissioner Gordon could see the drawing. He took the pad, pushing his glasses up against his forehead to look at the picture clearly, and then sighed.

Cassandra could see he didn't get it.

Gordon replaced his glasses and dropped the pad back on the coffee table, saying, "We're getting nowhere with this. All we can do for now—"

"Dad," Barbara said, taking the pad up again. "I recognize this. I know what this is."

"And?"

"It's the mark of Cain. Interpol circulated a flier about two years ago. . . ."

"Cain? David Cain?"

"Yes."

One of the Blue Boys, the Latina, moved closer to the Commissioner, dropping her voice. "If that's true, sir, we need to move you to a secure location as soon as possible."

"Hold on, Renee," Gordon said, taking the pad back from Barbara and then turning once more to Cassandra. He tapped the picture. "Cain has no compunctions about killing women or children or teenaged girls. Why didn't he shoot you?"

Cassandra looked at the picture, then at Gordon. Then she looked at the coffee table, folding her arms across her chest.

"You know him," Gordon said. "Don't you."

She nodded.

"How?"

Cassandra blew out a long breath. With her right index finger she pointed at Gordon. Then she pointed at Barbara. Then she pointed at the pad, still in Gordon's hand. Finally, she indicated herself.

Barbara's voice was just above a whisper. "You're his daughter?"

Cassandra nodded and couldn't look at any of them, avoiding their eyes. It didn't matter; she could feel the stares, the heat and accusation in them. It didn't matter that she had never wanted to be like her father. It didn't matter that there had never been any choice. She was a killer, too, and try as she might, she had never been able to escape that.

Not even in the No Man's Land.

She heard the Latina speak again, the one Gordon called Renee. "Sir, if Cain's been hired to kill you, he won't stop until he finds you."

"He won't have to find me. He killed Donnelly this morning in front of this damn building. We're going to find *him.*"

Cassandra raised her head, saw that Gordon had turned to the door, his hand already extended to take the knob. She went to her feet as fast as she could, past Barbara, cutting in front of him before he could pull the door open, blocking it with her body.

"I understand what you're trying to do." Gordon turned to his daughter. "I need you to keep her here, Barbara. I don't want her out there trying to shield me."

"Dad, I—"

That was the last Cassandra heard, because by then she had opened the door herself, and was out in the hall, slamming it closed behind her. From her pocket she took her knife, popping the blade out with a press of the switch, and then jamming it into the lock. She pushed as hard as she could, then twisted, and the blade snapped, the tip remaining in the keyhole, jamming it shut. It wouldn't hold them inside for long, if at all, but she needed some way to keep it closed, to keep Gordon and Renee and Barbara from coming out after her. They didn't understand, they didn't know Cain, they didn't know how bad it could get, but Cassandra did and she wasn't going to let Barbara Gordon lose her father. She wasn't going to let that happen.

She dropped the broken knife and turned, and he was there, in the hall, behind her, pistol in his hand.

He didn't lower the gun, just used his left hand to motion her out of the way, his right hand holding the pistol level and steady.

Cassandra put her back to the door and shook her head, spreading her arms as if her weight alone could keep it shut.

Her father opened fire, five shots back-to-back that she felt dance past her, into the door around her torso. From behind her, inside the apartment, she heard yelling and Gordon's voice and the sounds of people diving for the floor. She heard no screams.

It all seemed to slow down for her then as the adrenaline poured in, and she moved forward, slapping the gun from Cain's grip. She was terrifying in her speed, and she knew that, because *this* was her strength, *this* was her language. These were the words her father had taught her, and she spoke fluently, her right leg snapping a kick that caught him in the middle, collapsing him double. Before he could straighten she had finished the sentence, a short burst uppercut that sent a spray of blood from her father's mouth and one of his front teeth into the air.

Cain reeled, staggering back from the blow, unable to get his guard up in time to block the flurry of blows sure to come.

But nothing happened.

Cassandra stopped, looking at the streaks of blood on her hand, remembering the other punch, the first one she had thrown almost a decade ago, the first time her father had urged her to speak.

It had been at a party. He had put her in a pink dress. He had sent her to see the man in the office, the one surrounded by bodyguards. Her father had said he would be outside.

He had told her to talk to the fat man behind the desk. No one would stop her, he had said. After all, she was just a ten-year-old girl in a pink dress. Not someone they should fear.

Just talk to him, her father had said.

So she had.

She had put her ten-year-old fist through the fat man's throat, and had been astonished at how, when she pulled it back, it was red and sticky and wet. The man had made noises, and so had the guards, and then the door had opened and her father was there and the red was on the walls and on the floors, and no one was moving. And her father was standing in the middle of the room and holding his arms open and smiling and she had known she had done just what he wanted. He was proud of her then.

But all of these men were dead.

Cassandra dropped her fist and looked at her father, so much older, his brown hair now silver, his smooth face now lined. He was still the man she had fled from all those years ago. He was still the man who killed.

She looked at Cain and felt the scream building inside her, the rage and the terror and the hatred and she opened her mouth and let it out all at once.

"Stop!" she screamed, feeling the tears splashing down her cheeks.

Cain dropped the gun, eyes wide. "What did you . . . " he said. "Did you just . . . you . . . can speak?"

She felt herself breathing wrong, too fast and too hard, her whole body shaking. She couldn't make the tears stop, either.

Cain reached out a hand, putting it in her hair, his stunned expression shifting to something closer to compassion. He whispered, "Can you . . . understand me?"

She started to nod, then heard the door behind her cracking, the sound of a kick trying to bust it open, and her father's eyes flicked away from her, hardening, and she saw everything returning, then. Cain wouldn't stop, not even for his own child.

And if Gordon came through that door, he wouldn't live.

Beyond her father's shoulder, she saw a window, cracked but intact. She liked that window. She had watched the sun setting over the park from it.

Her father was reaching for his gun again.

Cassandra tensed, then exploded forward, pitching her shoulder into his stomach, throwing her arms around his waist. He was too big, too heavy for her to grab, but she could push, and she did, and together they hit the window hard, and as the glass shattered she kept pushing, felt him move back and up, over the edge, his hands coming down on her back, trying to break her away from him.

Then they were in the air, falling with the shards, and Cassandra, for a moment, felt almost happy.

"Stop," she said.

TWENTY-FIVE

THE GUNSHOTS HAD WARNED HIM, AND Batman feared he wasn't in time as he swung onto the sloped roof of the Clock Tower. He'd secured the line, taking the route he always used to reach Oracle's control room, when the reports came. Five of them, almost too rapid, 10mm rounds, probably a Glock.

He turned with the noise, tracking it back along the roof, the line in one hand, ready to use it to swing out, then back, planning to enter the hallway through the window he knew was there. He hit the edge and then heard the glass shattering, looked down to see the bodies falling away from beneath him.

David Cain looked older, but just as he remembered him.

The girl he had seen before, and noted as one of Oracle's agents.

He jumped headfirst after them, feeling the line sliding along his palm, calculating the angle. They were falling away from the building, which gave him room to maneuver, to play the line, and he felt the air rushing past him, snapping at his cape. With his free hand he deployed the second grapnel, firing it at the building opposite as he caught up to them. He dropped the first line and with that hand grabbed at the two bodies still locked together, taking a handful of Cain's belt, hoping that the girl wouldn't let go. The additional weight tore at his arm, made the muscles in his shoulder sing, and it blew his balance, causing him to yaw wildly.

There was an available opening in the building, where the window had once been, but he knew there was no way he could get all three of them through it. They were still at least twelve stories up, more than high enough to kill any of them in a straight plunge to the concrete, and so Batman twisted on the line, gritting his teeth and taking the impact on his back. The blow seemed to rattle through his bones, along his spine, and it snapped his head back, too, cracking it against the brick façade. He brought his feet up and behind him, then pushed away from the wall in another attempt to make the broken window, this time swinging around for a better approach. His other arm had stopped singing and was now screaming from the weight of the two people. When he was close enough, he twisted, trying to heave Cain and the girl into the building.

It didn't work out as planned.

Cain pitched forward, but instead of going into the building, he stopped himself at the edge of the window, one hand holding himself in place, the other reaching to lift the girl, still hanging around his waist, into the room. But the girl looked up, and Batman saw in her eyes tears and fear.

Then the girl unclasped her hands from Cain's waist and continued her fall.

Batman let go and followed, once again in free fall, pitching forward like an Olympic diver, reaching for the girl. He caught her wrist with one hand, snapping out the cape with his other. The air couldn't fill it enough to stop them, but it allowed him to steer ever so slightly, and with three stories to spare they crashed through another window, breaking glass and wall, Batman trying to wrap himself around the girl, trying to shield her. He felt something tear into his leg, rolling as they fell into the room, and they hit the floor hard enough to drive the rest of his breath from his body.

The girl hadn't made a sound.

Batman tried to move, and then there was another cracking, and the floor gave way beneath him; the weight of his body and the girl's was too much, and they were falling again, crashing through drywall and floorboards and ductwork. The noise was sudden and terrible, and something hit his head again, and something else took what felt like a fair piece of meat out of his arm.

They crashed through the floor and into the basement with a splash. The water, brackish and black, was deep and cold and took the rest of the energy from the fall, and Batman kicked up to the surface, looking immediately for the girl.

She was already struggling out of the water, making for the spear of daylight visible above.

With a grunt, Batman followed after her, pulling himself up through the broken flooring, feeling his whole body protest with the effort. A visit to Alfred would be necessary as soon as he could find the time.

The girl had stopped and was looking back, though whether she was checking to see if he was all right or still following, Batman had no idea. When she saw Batman, though, she turned and sprinted out of the building, racing around to the front. He went after her, feeling his right leg threaten to give out beneath his weight.

She was in the street, staring up at the window where they had left Cain hanging.

But Cain was gone.

Batman tilted his head back, slowly scanning the buildings on both sides of the street, down one side and then back up the other, until finally he was again looking at the Clock Tower. He could see the tiny shape of figures at the broken window nearly twenty stories above, a tan overcoat discernible. One of the figures, he knew, was Jim Gordon.

The girl was pulling at his hand, silently imploring him to follow her off the street, toward the Clock Tower. She was pointing up, at where Gordon was still looking down at them.

Batman shook his head, breaking free from her grip gently. Clearly Cain had made an attempt on Gordon's life, one that had been blocked before he arrived, apparently by the girl. He gave her another look, saw the broad spread of the knuckles of each of her hands, how she held her center of gravity. She was looking at him with wide eyes, waiting, and he saw the pattern of her breathing, the measured control of an advanced martial artist.

He needed to withdraw, tend his wounds. Cain would be doing the same. There was time to spare. The girl had bought Gordon another day, at least.

He gestured for her to follow him, then made for Puckett Park.

TWENTY-SIX

"PARLEZ-VOUS FRANÇAIS?" **BATMAN ASKED.**
The girl looked at him blankly. They were seated
opposite each other, under one of the many oak trees
in Puckett Park, not more than a hundred yards from where Batman
had buried the bodies of those men Two-Face had murdered. It was
dark now, and the heat and humidity of the day had begun to mer-
cifully recede.

*"Sprechen Sie Deutsch? Nihongo ga dekimasuka? Vy govoritiye po
Russki? Hangookah hashimnigka? Ba heeayoo kahng noy deeyahng
Veeahdt?"*

The girl shook her head.

He used his hands to ask, Are you deaf, do you understand
signing?

The girl shook her head again, then reached out and took the Batman's hands, pushing his fingers into fists. Then she pressed her palms against the face of each fist. She pulled back and then repeated the gesture, harder, keeping her eyes on his.

Batman considered, then got to his feet and began performing the Push Hands drill from *Tai Chi Chuan*, going through each movement slowly. Before he had finished the first sequence, the girl was standing beside him, mirroring each gesture perfectly, timing her motions against his.

Batman stopped and looked at her, again grateful for the lenses in the cowl that shielded his eyes. He didn't want the girl to see the sudden pity he felt for her.

"I understand," he said.

She smiled hesitantly.

"I knew David Cain once, long ago," Batman continued. "More than twenty years past. I was a student of his."

The girl's eyes widened a fraction.

"He used to say that the only way to truly be a warrior was to make your actions as fluid and easy as your speech. He used to say that combat itself was a discourse, the finest form of conversation. At the time I thought it was hyperbole." Batman reached out, touching the girl's cheek. "I didn't realize he was insane enough to actually force that philosophy on another human being."

The girl nodded slowly.

Batman swiped at the earth with his hand, clearing a surface broad enough to work on. With his index finger he drew three symbols: a badge, a face with a line down its middle, and the serpent's head that was the mark of Cain. He drew an arching line, joining the mark of Cain to the badge, then another joining the split face to the mark.

"Two-Face," he said, tapping the appropriate symbol. "Hired David Cain to kill Commissioner Gordon. You saved Gordon's life." He circled the badge, then said it again. "You saved his life."

The girl's smile was genuine. She reached out and erased the line from Cain to Gordon.

"Yes," Batman said. "I want to keep that from happening."

The girl frowned, her brow creasing, and he could see that whatever she was thinking, she was having difficulty finding the means to articulate it. Finally, she brought her closed fist down on Cain, rubbing the symbol out.

"No," Batman said, and he quickly drew the symbol in again. "I won't kill him. I don't kill."

The girl's frown deepened and she redrew the line from Two-Face to Cain, then added arrow heads on either side of the link. She looked pointedly at Batman, then redrew the line from Cain to Gordon, dragging an X across the symbol for the Commissioner. Finally, she once again rubbed out the symbol representing Cain.

Batman calmly replaced it, saying, "I understand. Two-Face has paid Cain to kill Gordon. Cain won't stop until Gordon is dead. And you believe the only way to stop Cain is by killing him. I disagree. There is another way."

The girl held up her hands, as if asking for an explanation.

"The weak link is the money. If Cain isn't paid, he won't complete the contract, and Two-Face won't pay him until Gordon is dead." He got to his feet, looking at the girl. "Stay here. Whoever you are to David Cain, I don't want you two mixing it up again. In the morning, head back to Oracle."

She tugged on his cape as he turned, then pointed her index finger at his chest, the question on her face.

"I'm going to try and keep Jim Gordon alive."

The standoff had started during the night, four members of what had been Black Mask's cult, aimless and lost with his disappearance, taking hostages and parading them down Palmieri Way until reaching Central. Then they put knives to the throats of three innocents and began with their demands.

"We want the release of Black Mask!" their leader had shouted. "We want the release of Black Mask or these three die!"

Montoya would have laughed if she'd still had it in her to do so. It was utterly ludicrous, on so many levels. To begin with, she didn't know where Black Mask was. As far as that went, she didn't think anyone in the GCPD knew where Black Mask was either, and she didn't have the time or the inclination to look. She was far more concerned with trying to keep the Commissioner alive and as far away from Cain as humanly possible, and she honestly didn't have much faith in her ability to do so with only a handful of other cops beside her.

The word about Cain had spread like wildfire, of course, and now, to make matters just as bad as they could possibly be, the Blue Boys were two steps away from panic as a whole, their faith in Gordon's leadership shattered by this new threat. Montoya knew this, knew the cops who still had their nerve were few enough she could metaphorically hold them in her hand. She didn't have time to deal with the self-mutilated marauders gathered outside of Central.

But, of course, since the very last thing she wanted to be doing was negotiating her way out of a hostage situation in the rubble in the middle of the night, that was precisely where she had found herself.

When Pettit and his squad had finally showed up just before daybreak, she was almost happy to see them. She didn't even mind that Foley had come along to watch.

"No negotiations," Pettit declared.

Montoya sighed. "They've got hostages."

Pettit adjusted his cap, the same one he'd been wearing since Day 0. "No negotiations. These are terrorists. We don't negotiate with terrorists."

"Bill. What are you proposing to do?"

"We give them an ultimatum. QRT protocols. I'm in charge now." He faced the cult members. "You have until dawn to let them go. Otherwise you'll be shot."

"We want the release of Black Mask! We want the release of Black Mask or we'll kill them!"

"Yeah," Pettit muttered. "I heard you the first time, freak. Anderson?"

One of the men in the squad stepped forward. "Sir?"

"You and Lewis go up the block, come around back. I'll give you the signal when I want you to move."

"Yes, sir." He backed off and tapped another member of the squad on the shoulder, and the two men headed into the lightening night together. All of Pettit's squad were armed, sidearms and M16s.

"What exactly are they supposed to do?" Montoya asked.

"They'll shoot when the time comes."

"They have ammunition? You said we were out of ammunition."

Pettit ignored her, moving closer to the rusted husk of a crushed car, trying to get a better look at the Black Maskers and their captives. Two of the hostages were men, one of them barely out of his teens, the other on the far side of fifty. The other was a woman, and from the way the three hostages kept looking to one another, Montoya guessed they were a family. One of the few that had remained in the city as a unit.

The sky was beginning to bleed with color, driving the navy blue away, dripping gold light on the sides of surrounding buildings. Montoya saw the Black Maskers fidgeting, exchanging glances more and more frequently. The hostages had gone utterly silent.

"Time's up," Pettit said. Then, louder, he shouted, "I'm giving you one last chance to let them go, understand? One last chance. I'm counting down from ten. If the hostages aren't free when I hit one, we're opening fire."

"Free Black Mask!"

"That's the way you want it, fine." Pettit turned and motioned more of the squad forward, dropping his own rifle from his shoulder and snapping the rate selector switch above the trigger plate.

"You can't just—"

"You know what, Montoya? Shut up."

She felt the color racing into her cheeks. "Pettit! You can't—"

"What part of that didn't you understand?" Pettit brought the rifle to his shoulder, using the roof of the car as a support.

Montoya looked around, trying to find a solution, some support, anything. Foley was standing at the back of the squad, and he avoided her eyes. Pettit was now counting down, had already reached seven, and it seemed to her that he was actually speeding up instead of slowing down. The rest of the squad had their weapons up as well, all their sights on the Black Maskers. Montoya watched while the hostages were herded together in a tight group, and the Black Maskers proceeded to kneel behind them, using their bodies as a shield.

"This is crazy," she said. "Pettit! Stop, you'll hit the hostages!"

"Three," Pettit was saying. "Two. One—"

"What the hell is going on here?!" Gordon demanded.

Montoya turned, hearing Pettit moving as well, seeing the

Commissioner racing toward them from the end of the street. Bullock was with him, chewing ferociously on the stick in his mouth. She heard Pettit swear under his breath.

"What do you think you're doing?" Gordon demanded.

"Hostage situation, Jim," Pettit said. "You just broke my ultimatum, now they think they can push us around."

"Were you about to open fire?"

"We were on the count, Commissioner. You know as well as I do—"

"I don't give a damn if you were solving the national debt, Captain Pettit." Gordon shoved his glasses back on his nose with an angry thumb, glaring. "This is not how we deal with the mentally ill, and it sure as hell isn't how we deal with them when there are hostages at stake. *Nobody* is shooting anybody here until I say otherwise. Is that understood, Captain Pettit?"

Pettit blew out a long breath, and Montoya saw the muscles in the man's jaw tighten. The dawn light was making his skin look red, and then Montoya realized it wasn't just the light.

She saw what he was going to do, tried screaming, "No, don't!" but she was already a half-second too late to stop it.

Pettit spun and opened fire with the M16 from the waist, putting down a long burst. The noise was terrifying and tremendous in the dawn silence, and the barrage seemed to last a long time, and when Pettit came off the trigger, Montoya heard the rattling of spent brass on the ground.

The Black Maskers lay dead on the broken pavement outside of Central.

So did the family, the hostages.

"Don't compromise my leadership in the field," Pettit said softly.

Montoya felt the sudden, terrible need to vomit. For a moment she thought she would. She put a hand out on the wrecked car to steady herself.

Gordon and Bullock had moved past her, were staring down at the bodies. No one else was moving, no one in the squad, no one on the street.

Gordon looked back at where they were standing, Montoya beside Pettit, and he started to go for his gun, when Bullock grabbed his arm.

"No, Commish, don't do it," Bullock said quickly, fighting to keep Gordon's gun arm down. "Don't do it, it's not worth it."

Pettit had brought the rifle to his shoulder once more, had the barrel leveled at the Commissioner.

Montoya moved before considering, slapping the gun aside, and Pettit responded by swinging at her with the back of his hand. The blow snapped into the side of her face, high on the cheek, hard enough to put her on the ground, and when she could see again Pettit was pointing the rifle at her, scowling.

"Don't ever touch my weapon again, woman," he said.

Montoya thought it would be damn stupid to die this way, to die because Billy Pettit had lost it.

For a long second Pettit's finger stayed on the trigger. Then he came off it and stepped back, raising the rifle above his head and shouting.

"This is the only diplomacy left!" he cried. "The diplomacy of strength, the ability to back your words! We've been deluding ourselves for months, thinking we could survive by being soft.

"Well, I'm not deluded anymore. I know what has to be done."

He lowered the rifle, surveying the gathered men. Montoya, still on the ground, didn't move. The light in Pettit's eyes was one she knew. It was the light in Harvey Dent's eyes when he'd told her to run. It was the touch of madness.

"You can stick with him," Pettit said, gesturing with his free hand at Gordon. "With Jimmy's outmoded ethics and sense of fair play, his precious morality. You can stick with him, and you can die.

"Or you can come with me, and live."

He lowered the rifle, glancing down at Montoya again, his mouth curled in contempt. Then he stepped back.

Anderson and Lewis came around the car and joined him on either side. Then more of the squad—one man, then two, then four, then all of them—gathered around Pettit. Montoya stared, seeing Foley glancing from Pettit to Gordon, frightened. Then he dropped his gaze to his feet and fell in with Pettit's men, too.

"Right," Pettit said softly. "Nice knowing the three of you."

Then he led his men away, down the street, leaving Montoya, Gordon, and Bullock to stare after them.

TWENTY-SEVEN

 CASSANDRA, HAVING DECIDED WHAT SHE
was going to do, wasted no time in doing it.

Two-Face's men posed very little problem, really. Some of them
had guns, and those were the ones to be cautious of, but the rest were
only equipped with clubs and knives and the like, and she knew how
to deal with those easily enough. It took her less than two minutes to
work her way from the steps into the building, dropping each guard
with her hands or her feet as she came upon him, leaving them on
the ground, clutching at dislocated joints or fractured bones or, more
often, not clutching at anything at all, simply unconscious.

The guard at the bottom of the stairs, though, he had a gun, and
she moved at him quickly, tracking the weapon's movement, then

veering away before he fired. The one shot, she felt, would be enough, would do the trick, and she trapped the guard's arm at the elbow and then twisted until she felt the bone snap. She heard the doors opening above the atrium. She let the guard fall, glancing up to see a man with a horrible, split face.

Two faces, she thought, and bounded up the stairs, after him. Two-Face moved back, reaching into his pocket. Cassandra was only halfway up and trying to decide which way to go if he pulled a gun, but he didn't, he pulled a coin, flipping it quickly. Then he dropped the coin back into his pocket and ran.

She hit the landing, skidding around the corner on the marble floor in time to see the doors near the end of the hall slamming shut. There were another two guards here, each with a rifle, and she sprinted at them, then dropped to her back, sliding. Both fired and missed, and she flipped from the ground up, kicking the nearer of the two in the chest and then coming down on her hands, another flip, another kick, this one to the remaining guard's face. When she got to her feet, both were out cold.

She moved to the door, pushing it open, then stepping back.

The shots tore through the wood, hit the wall across the hall. She counted them, eleven, one after the other, and then there was a pause and she decided she would have to risk it. She went into the room low, diving toward the desk and then springing up, coming at Two-Face from his exposed side. She knew she was moving quickly now, perhaps as fast as she had ever gone, and she had the gun away from him with a bash at his wrist, then caught him beneath the throat, closing her fingers around his larynx.

There was another man in the room, in a funny hat. That man had a gun pointed at her, too. She didn't worry about him, moving Two-Face in front of her as a shield. With her free hand she dipped into his pocket, where she had seen the coin disappear. She showed it to Two-Face.

"You're gonna die for this, little girl," he managed to croak.

She shook her head and tightened her grip slightly, waving the coin at him.

"You, too? You're gonna flip on me, too?"

She frowned. The other man was still holding the gun on them. She gave Two-Face another shake.

"TallyMan," Two-Face said. "Drop the gun."

The man in the funny hat dropped the gun, and she saw it bounce onto the carpet by the couch, and next to it she saw a duffel bag. The bag was open, and in it were stacks of American dollars. Cassandra smiled. This made it easier, this made it so much easier.

She moved Two-Face with her to the couch, dropping the coin as she did, then smoothly lifting the bag. It was heavy, full of money, and that more than anything confirmed for her that it was what she had come looking for. She tightened her grip around the handles, backing toward the door, kicking the gun at her feet across the room.

"You're going to die for this," Two-Face said again.

She used her grip to spin him around, facing her, then drove her right knee into his solar plexus, letting go of his throat. Two-Face made a noise, doubling over, but by that time she was out of the room and running, sliding once more on the marble as she turned at the top of the stairs. She heard gunshots behind her, the screech of the ricocheting bullets, but she didn't stop, flying down the steps and through the atrium until she was out in the heat again, racing through the rubble, her prize tight in her hand.

It had taken Batman longer than he would have liked to find Gordon again, but shortly after dawn he located the Commissioner in TriCorner, passing the Kelso Blockade on his way back home. He was traveling with Montoya and Bullock, but no other support or officers, and Batman had to wonder why that was the case. The Commissioner certainly knew David Cain had targeted him, yet here he was, out in the open, with a minimum of protection.

He shadowed their movements south, staying slightly ahead of the small group, scanning. His leg still throbbed from the day before, and he had more bruises on his person than any one man had a right to, but his body was still doing what he asked of it, and he was satisfied with that. One less thing to worry about, the weaknesses of his own flesh.

He had determined that, after the Clock Tower, the next most logical place for Cain to strike would be at Gordon's home, and so with five blocks to spare Batman broke away from his shadowing, pulling ahead. Earlier that morning he had made a circuit around the house, seeing only the two guards on post at the front, a third in the garden around back. Again he checked the perimeter, confirming that all of the cops on post were still in place.

Stopping, the Batman positioned himself on the roof of a neighboring house, feeling the daylight heat center and increase on his motionless form. He felt exposed. Until the No Man's Land, the Batman had only appeared at night, a technique that helped maintain his terrifying reputation. Batman and daylight seemed somehow wrong, and it made him uncomfortable. He was perspiring slightly beneath the cowl.

Gordon and the others were at the end of the block, now, still coming forward, all walking in silence.

Batman turned his head, looking for a shadow to hide in, one that would offer some shelter from the heat of the sun. From his periphery he saw movement at the edge of the rooftop, the long shadow cast by the broken air conditioner there disrupted by another shape. He felt the rooftop vibrate beneath him with the footfalls, and he ducked, rolling back and springing up, David Cain's first four shots all missing him by mere fractions. The fifth caught him high in the center of the chest, and the Kevlar held, and the kinetic impact rattled through him as if he'd taken a brick to his heart. He staggered back, dipping his shoulder and rolling, forcing himself to resume breathing, and he heard the muffled sound of the silenced shots as Cain kept pulling the trigger.

He came up with Batarang at the ready, tossing it straight at Cain's head and knowing full well that his target would dodge the throw. Cain did, jerking his head out of the way, a quick snap of the neck, and Batman took his wrist, locked in his fingers and twisted, bringing his other hand down on the weapon. The gun flew free, clanging as it bounced off the air conditioner, then skittered from the roof, falling to the street.

The Batarang then arced back and slammed into the back of Cain's head, pitching him forward, and Batman used the momentum to flip the other man. Cain went over, twisting his wrist and reversing the grip, and Batman was in the air then, too.

They tumbled to the edge of the roof, Cain on his feet while Batman struggled to rise. Cain took another step, onto the ledge, and leapt, clearing the space between houses, trying to gain distance.

Batman followed, crossing the gap and coming down just behind the other man. Below, from the street, he could hear Gordon shouting.

Cain could hear it, too, and he rounded on Batman, growling, both hands coming around in an attempt to box his ears. Batman blocked with his forearms, and Cain brought his elbow around and up, a killing strike aimed for the temple. Another block, and then they began exchanging blows faster and faster, Cain alternating punches and kicks, each targeting a vital, each intended to kill, and Batman found himself almost entirely on the defensive. He fought for an advantage, breaking an opening and following it with a finger strike, trying to hit Cain between the eyes, trying to disorient him, to buy time. Cain took the hit, lowering his head so that Batman's fingers bounced off his scalp, and then Cain brought his head up again, trying for a head-butt. Batman dodged it, and for a moment they stood apart, the sun burning down on them, each pulling air down into lungs that were aching and empty. The humidity and sweat made Batman's eyes burn.

"I know you," Cain said between breaths, almost with a laugh. "Know all about you. Know your work."

"I know yours."

"It's an honor."

"Not the work."

"The meeting."

"For you."

"You can't stop me."

"Watch me."

Cain wiped sweat from his brow with the back of his hand, never looking away. Batman adjusted his balance slightly, forcing himself to remain focused for the attack he knew would come. From the street there came only silence, and he hoped that Bullock and Montoya had forced Gordon to cover somewhere.

"You've already lost," Cain said. "You just don't know it."

"We've time."

"Not enough. I won't stop. If you know me, you know that. I won't stop until the contract is canceled or fulfilled. You'll have to kill me." Cain smiled bitterly. "And you won't do that."

"I won't need to," Batman said, and then the attack came, a flurry of kicks that pummeled at him one after the other, forcing him to the edge of the roof, coming too fast for him to do anything but block again and again. Then he saw a pattern he recognized, one from long ago when Bruce Wayne had studied for a time with David Cain, before Bruce Wayne had discovered what David Cain really did for a living.

It was a *savate* sequence, left *coup de pied bas* followed by a right *coup de pied chasse*, and as soon as the second kick came Batman was ready, catching Cain's leg and using it to take the man down, hard, onto the tar roof. Cain grabbed at him, one hand closing around the back of the cowl, the base of the cape, and he tugged, and Batman went over him, into a roll.

He came up face-to-face with the girl he had left in Puckett Park. He spun back, preparing to defend again, and saw that Cain had returned to his feet but was now motionless, as well.

"Get out of here," Cain said, and Batman knew it wasn't directed at him.

The girl stepped around Batman, and he saw her expression from the corner of his eyes, the stone determination, the refusal to retreat. She was holding a small duffel bag, almost a gym bag, and on the humidity of the still air, Batman thought he smelled gasoline.

"Leave," Cain said. "If you can understand me, you must leave. This isn't your fight."

The girl dumped the contents of the bag onto the roof in front of Cain. Bills, bundles and bundles of them, and Batman knew intuitively it was Two-Face's money, and he knew why he was smelling gasoline.

If there was no money, then there was no payment for Cain. No payment for Cain, then the contract with Two-Face was null and void.

The girl had a book of matches in her hand, and in one fluid motion had torn a single one free, striking it against the rough pad, and then dropped it onto the bills.

The fire took instantly, the money crackling and curling in the heat.

The girl was crying.

The battle mask that David Cain had worn crumbled, and Batman saw tears in the man's eyes. He wasn't looking at the flames. Cain extended a hand to the girl.

She turned her back on him and walked back to Batman's side.

Cain stared at her for a moment longer, then seemed to slump, almost shrinking from within.

The girl looked at Batman, then took his hand in hers. She still wouldn't look at Cain.

Cain nodded, then turned away.

Batman heard him say, "Take good care of her."

Then Cain was over the edge and moving out of sight.

TWENTY-EIGHT

 GORDON WAITED IN THE GARDEN, working on the plot of vegetables in the far corner, knowing that sooner or later he would have company. His frown deepened as he dug out the weeds, tossing them aside, creating a small mound of the discarded greenery. Inside the house, Sarah was sleeping, still recovering from the bullet she'd taken during the Penguin offensive. Out front, Officer DeFilippis and Officer Witschi stood guard. Sergeant Weir had offered to take a post too, but Gordon had refused. There was no way he was putting a pregnant woman in the crossfire if he could help it.

Cain was gone, he knew that. But it didn't make him feel any safer. He had posts that were empty or staffed now by civilians who were eager to help, but who had no idea of what they were doing.

Pettit's defection was costing them dearly already, and he knew it would get worse. Before nightfall easily half of the remaining Blue Boys had left TriCorner to join the renegade. Gordon knew he would lose more men under the cover of darkness.

He was more scared than he had ever been in his life, he realized. More scared now than during the war, more scared than when Joker had kidnapped him years ago, trying to drive him mad. More scared than when he realized he was leaving his first wife because he no longer loved her, because he had fallen for a young and pretty detective named Sarah Essen.

Then he heard the voice.

"Jim."

He got to his feet, dusting himself off. Batman came out of the shadows from the far side of the garden, moving silently as always. Gordon felt the anger simmering in his gut begin to bubble.

"Leave," Gordon said.

"Cain's gone."

"Leave."

Batman didn't speak, didn't move. Gordon could barely see the man's features, what little there was to see that was not hidden under the mask.

"I didn't want your help," Gordon said suddenly, his voice rising. "Do you get that? I didn't ask for your help! I didn't want it with Cain and I sure don't want it now!"

Batman remained silent and immobile and, to Gordon's eyes, impassive.

"God dammit! Get out of my garden! Get out of my house!" Gordon moved forward, shouting in the other man's face, head tilted back to look into those blank, hidden eyes. "Leave!"

And then he hit him, one punch with everything he had that connected with Batman's jaw and turned the vigilante's head almost ninety degrees. The impact rode a shock up Gordon's forearm, made his knuckles ache.

Batman brought his head back slowly, looking down at him, and his mouth curved slightly, almost a frown, almost sadness. For several long seconds they stared at one another, and then, finally, Batman turned silently and moved back to the shadows.

Before he disappeared, Batman said, "Two-Face wasn't an ally you could trust."

"Neither were you," Gordon spat back.

But there was no response, no answer at all. Batman had already gone, taking the last word as he had a thousand times before, walking away just as he had all of those times when Gordon still had something to say. It was what defined their relationship; Batman was always gone before James Gordon had finished speaking.

There was a small, clay flowerpot with a tulip in it that Gordon had been cultivating for Sarah.

He kicked it across the patio without thinking, breaking it into a thousand shards.

The door from the house slid back, and Sarah said, "Jim? Jim, are you all right?"

"Fine. Go back to bed."

She shook her head and started down the steps, and Gordon saw she was barefoot, and moved to intercept her.

"Don't, you'll cut your feet open," he said. "I . . . I broke a pot."

She furrowed her brow, reaching a hand out and touching his cheek. "He was here, wasn't he?" she asked after a second.

"Yes."

"Come inside."

He followed her back to the bedroom, watched by candlelight as she removed her robe. The bandage on her side was clean as best as he could tell, the wound no longer seeping. She sat on the side of the bed, wrapping the blanket around herself, returning his stare.

"Our darkest hour," she said softly.

Gordon sat heavily beside her. "Yeah."

"I heard about Pettit. Bullock told me. Said that we're losing people."

"They think I can't protect them. They think . . . they think we won't survive."

"We will," she said, matter-of-factly. "They're wrong, and sooner or later, they'll see that. That's not what's bothering you, is it?"

"No," Gordon admitted. "What's bothering me is him. That . . . I thought I'd . . . he saved my life today, Sarah. If he hadn't been on that roof, we would have walked right into Cain's ambush. I would have died, Montoya, Bullock . . . all of us. You'd be here all alone if Batman hadn't been watching."

"And you resent that."

"He abandoned us. He betrayed our trust and now he's back, just like that, and he's baby-sitting me?"

"Do you really think that's what he was doing?"

"I don't know what he was doing."

"He was trying to keep a life from being lost. You know that. It's what he's always done." She leaned to the side, resting her head on his shoulder. "I've never been his number one fan. I disapprove of vigilantism, and I disapprove of him. But while I've had thousands of doubts about him, about your relationship with him, I've never had any doubts about one thing. No one dies if he can help it. No one."

"I'm just . . . so *angry*, Sarah."

"At him?"

Gordon removed his glasses, rubbing at the skin behind his ears, and then he laughed, softly. "You're good," he said.

"Am I?"

"Yeah, you are. I am angry at him. But I'm angry at myself, too. I was Commissioner of Police in this town for years, and all that time he was here, and maybe . . . maybe I grew to count on him too much, to rely on him too much. And maybe it's not what Batman did that's burning me so hard right now, Sarah . . ."

"It's what he didn't do," she finished softly.

"Maybe."

He wrapped his arms around her, buried his nose in her hair. It smelled slightly of mint, and he wondered how she could make it do that given everything else around them.

Alfred was in his tent at the MASH unit, alone, reading the volume of Browning he had packed before leaving behind the ruins of Wayne Manor many months before. Since Batman's arrival, he had spent much of his time with Dr. Thompkins, supplementing her medical efforts with his own meager skills. Staying in the encampment allowed Alfred company and relative safety, and also enough time and freedom to go where Batman needed him whenever he was required.

He had just finished rereading "Childe Roland to the Dark Tower Came" when he glanced up and saw the Batman standing just inside the entrance, the tent flap already closed and secured behind him. One look was enough to make Alfred's heart break. It was in the younger man's posture, he could see it, and it was as if the twenty-five years since that horrible night had contracted, as if the time had never passed at all.

Batman pulled back his cowl, revealing the haunted eyes of Bruce Wayne.

"You have the look of a man losing a war with himself, Master Bruce," Alfred said, closing his book and setting it aside.

It took Bruce a moment, as if he needed to focus, to remember where he was, and then he nodded. He moved to the bench opposite the cot, and as he sat Alfred could see it once more: that terrible weight pressing on Bruce's shoulders, so heavy it seemed it could push the man through the very earth and down to hell.

To the world, to those who knew, the Batman was a force, potent and mythic, and duly terrifying.

To Alfred, though, there were times when he was still an eight-year-old boy, demanding to know why the world had betrayed him so cruelly.

Somewhere outside a baby was crying in one of the other tents.

"I've lost my way," Bruce said, softly.

"Master Bruce . . ."

"It's all gone gray, Alfred." He looked at the butler helplessly. "The doubt and the confusion . . . I can't see the way any longer. The bodies keep piling higher . . . Pettit murdered seven people this afternoon and I wasn't there to stop it . . . I'm making mistakes, I can't trust my own judgment. I made an ally of Penguin, who betrayed me, I trusted a Batgirl when I should have known better and I . . . I just don't know how to do this anymore.

"I don't know how to fix it."

He looked just like a boy for a second.

"I saw Gordon." His voice was barely audible, almost less than a whisper, and Alfred had to strain to hear him. "I saw Gordon. I tried to talk to him. He told me to leave. He wanted nothing to do with me."

On Bruce's left cheek, below the eye, the beginnings of a bruise were evident, the skin starting to swell.

"Did the Commissioner give you that shiner?" Alfred asked.

Bruce barely nodded.

"You let him hit you," Alfred said.

"I let him," Bruce admitted. "He had made a deal with Two-Face, Alfred. Jim Gordon made a deal with Harvey Dent. It must have been for land . . . certainly it was how the Blue Boy offensive against Penguin was so successful. It's a theory. Whatever it was, I don't know the details, but . . ."

"Then it would be most unwise to speculate, would it not?"

Bruce squeezed his eyes shut. "With Two-Face, Alfred."

"Yes, sir."

He opened his eyes once more, the question still there, and it was the same question formed over the cooling bodies of his parents so long ago. It wasn't how; Bruce had never asked how. He had learnt that answer quickly.

Just why.

Alfred cleared his throat. "Might I suggest, sir, that now is the time to request some assistance?"

"No, it won't . . . I took help already and it cost six men their lives. I set out to do this alone, to save my city, I can't . . ."

"I hesitate to contradict you, sir, but you have never been in this alone, despite what you might think. You have, from the start, had me, had Oracle. You have always been, dare I say, dangerously hard on yourself, but even you must recognize there are some shortcomings that are not your own. No matter how much you may wish it to be otherwise."

"I failed."

Alfred made a noise of disapproval. "No, Master Bruce. You have simply yet to succeed. That is still your goal?"

"Yes."

"Then you need more assistance to achieve it, that is all. There is no weakness in turning to others for aid in times of crisis. If I may be so bold, not to do so would be arrogance of the highest order."

Something flickered across Bruce's face, the corner of his mouth turning slightly upward, and Alfred relaxed. That was better. That was the man returning to control himself.

"Not that I've ever been arrogant," Bruce said quietly.

"I would not presume to say, Master Bruce." He stood up. "I shall retrieve some first aid supplies from Dr. Thompkins's stores, and return shortly. You have injuries which need tending."

Alfred moved to the flap, tugging at the canvas ties and opening a sliver from the tent to the night. He looked back over his shoulder, seeing Bruce still seated on the bench, his forehead resting on clasped hands, already deep in thought.

"You would," said Bruce softly.

Alfred hesitated. "Beg pardon, sir?"

"You would presume to say, Alfred." Bruce didn't move, but the hint of a smile grew on his face. "You always did."

"I don't know what you're talking about," Alfred said mildly and continued out of the tent. Once alone and in the darkness, Alfred allowed himself a momentary, and very self-satisfied, grin.

Cassandra had slept on Oracle's floor, and woke as dawn came, light sneaking through the windows and splashing her face. She sat up, yawning, hearing the tapping from Oracle's keyboard in the Control Room. Getting to her feet, she stretched a long while, working out the stiffness in her muscles, then padded silently across the hardwood floor. Oracle was working busily at her terminal, fingers flying.

A noise came from the window behind her, and Cassandra turned to see Batman dropping into the room. He landed loud enough to make noise, and Cassandra realized he'd done so on purpose, a courtesy to Oracle, letting her know that he was now in her home. Oracle turned her chair, mastering her surprise quickly.

"Batman," she said. "Good morning."

He nodded.

"Something I can do for you?" Oracle asked.

He nodded again.

"Call them," he said.

PART THREE

ORACLE

PERSONAL
Entry #459—NML Day 233
1231 Zulu

Dear Dad—

For a while there, I really thought we'd lost him. Even after he'd been back, it seemed he was only going through the motions, that he wasn't . . . wasn't *himself*, if that makes any sense.

But three weeks ago the Batman I knew, the one I remembered, walked into my Control Room here, bright and early on a sunny Monday morning. Not that he was more talkative than usual, of course not, but the manner was different, the attitude. He'd made a decision. He'd caught his second wind.

It started with the call to assemble, which basically consisted of me tracking down Robin and Nightwing, getting messages to each of them, telling them to get their tails over here and pronto. Robin had been living in Keystone City, where his father had moved after Gotham was shut down, but the luxury of summer vacation gave him the free time, and he was able to get away. Nightwing, paradoxically, was harder to reach, even though he was only sixty-odd miles south of us, in Blüdhaven. But Blüdhaven, the primary repository for most of our refugees, has been hopping ever since Gotham shut its metaphorical doors. A town of roughly half a million had quadrupled overnight, and as a result of that, as well as the notoriously inefficient and corrupt Blüdhaven PD, he's been working pretty much 24/7 trying to keep a lid on the situation there. It took me almost a week before my cellular line and his schedule coincided long enough for us to exchange words.

"He wants you here, ASAP," I said.

"No kidding? This is the same man who told me to stay out of the way eight months ago?"

"Think so. Hard to tell with the mask."

"You're funny, Babs," he said. "I'll get there when I can. No sooner."

"I'll let him know."

"Do that," he said and cut the line, and I sat there for a couple of seconds marveling at how damn much alike he and his mentor were.

FYI—and I just realized I'm assuming things here, so I apologize—Nightwing is actually Richard "Dick" Grayson, Bruce Wayne's ward and, for lack of a better term, I guess, inheritor. Dick and Bruce, they have a strange relationship. It's almost like father and son, it's almost like friends.

Almost, but not quite.

They're so much alike and yet they're so different. Bruce never seems to smile, never seems to laugh, never does anything that appears impulsive or rash. Dick, on the other hand, is a gypsy rogue at his core, a born carny-kid, raised in the circus until his parents died and Bruce took him in. He's rash, brash, mercurial, passionate, and sometimes I swear he's living life on a perpetual caffeine-and-adrenaline high. That's sometimes. Other times he's brooding and taciturn and can make Batman himself look talkative.

Before he was Nightwing he was Robin, the first one.

The current Robin, that's a kid named Tim Drake, fifteen going on thirty, and I have to confess a great fondness for the guy. When someone says the words "all-American kid" I think of Tim, I just can't help it. He's razor sharp, rarely misses a trick, and could have been the high school jock if he'd wanted to go that route. As it stands, he's a computer geek like yours truly. He's also of that same single-minded determination that Bruce and Dick share; Tim wasn't picked to be Robin, he decided he wanted the job all by himself and went after it, and didn't really give Bruce much of a choice.

They form a bizarre holy trinity of crime fighting, in a way.

So that was the call to assemble, to bring them here and get the party started. It was going to take each of them about three weeks before they could get into the No Man's

Land. This didn't seem to bother Batman at all; he had other things to do, most of which he kept even from me.

It was clear he had a master plan, though. What it was, I didn't know.

For a couple days he had me hacking out of the NML, tracking fund transfers in a variety of numbered accounts in the Caymans, in Switzerland, in Metropolis and Fawcett City and London. I thought maybe they were Wayne Enterprises fronts, but it didn't take long for me to realize that wasn't the case. He wouldn't tell me whose money we were looking at, but there was a hell of a lot of it.

When I asked him why we were doing this, he said, "Land."

End of discussion.

Two other things of note happened before the gang arrived.

The first was more a change in manner and procedure, with Batman taking Cassandra with him on his rounds pretty regularly. She'd get back here before dawn—she was still sleeping on my couch—breathless and sweaty and eyes all aglow, looking delighted with whatever heads they had busted that night. I knew what he was doing with her, of course, and it was unspoken between him and me.

This time, he had my approval.

The second was that Batgirl contacted me, early one evening near the end of August. She came in on his frequency; I don't know how she managed to highjack it, but there she was.

"Oracle, come in."

I switched the voice modulator on and said, "What do you want?"

"Where is he? I need to talk to him."

"Don't know," I said, which was true. At that moment, I had no idea where Batman was.

"I need to talk to him," she repeated.

"Can't help you."

"I haven't seen him since that night Two-Face took the . . . our territory."

"Yeah, I heard all about that."

Silence for a second, then, *"I failed, I know that. I need to make amends. I need to talk to him."*

"You know what, kiddo?" I said. "You're smart, you'll get out of town while the going's good. He doesn't want to see you. He doesn't need your kind of help. You should take off that costume of yours and put on a different suit of clothes and maybe think about getting out of Dodge, that's what you should do."

"No. You want me to run, I won't run."
"You had your chance. It's over."
"Then I'll wait until I hear that from him."
"Your choice," I said, and cut the connection.
I almost felt bad for her.
But not quite.

TWENTY-NINE

HE WAS PROMPT, WHICH MERCY GRAVES, III appreciated. She hated tardiness, especially in business, and all the more so during covert actions. She planned to stay in Bogotá just long enough to accomplish her job, and then she would head back to the States. She had a schedule to keep, after all, one that her employer had established, and one he expected her to maintain.

Mercy Graves III did not ever want to disappoint her employer.

She saw the man enter—everyone in the restaurant saw him enter, to be frank. He was easily six and a half feet tall, if not taller, and comfortably over two hundred and fifty pounds, all of it muscle. His suit was light tan, linen, and well tailored, and he was far more handsome than Mercy had been led to expect from the photographs

she'd seen. She watched as he stopped to speak with the maître d',
then turned his head to her table. Mercy moved the briefcase from
where she'd set it on the empty seat beside her to the floor.

"Señorita Graves?" the man asked, offering a mammoth hand.
His voice was smooth and his diction precise, as if he had learned his
Spanish from books and tapes rather than in conversation. From
what Mercy knew of him, that had been the case.

She shook his hand briefly, appreciating the fact that he didn't
treat her like she would break. He didn't try to impress her with the
strength of the grip, either. He knew what he was capable of, and
didn't feel any need to prove it.

"Señor Bane," she answered, also speaking Spanish. "Thank you
for agreeing to meet with me. Is this a safe place to talk?"

"I own the restaurant," the man said, taking the empty seat. "We
will not be interrupted, and no one would dare repeat any conversation they overheard. And, please, it's just Bane."

"Very well."

"Would you like to eat first, or shall we move straight to business?" Bane asked, motioning one of the waiters over.

"I've a flight back to the States in just over an hour," Mercy said.

"You do not enjoy Colombia?"

"I have several appointments to keep."

Bane grunted and produced a large cigar, which he allowed the
waiter to light for him, then offered it to Mercy. She shook her head,
and Bane waved the waiter off, taking a couple of puffs and settling
back in his chair. The smoke was thick and aromatic and she felt it
insinuating itself into her hair and clothes. Mercy tried not to frown.
Business was business.

"You wish to hire me," Bane said.

"My employer does, yes. He feels that you are uniquely suited to
a task he needs completed."

"I am flattered."

"You should be. My employer is a very discriminating man. He
gave me very specific instructions with regard to you."

Bane arched an eyebrow, vaguely amused. "Such as?"

"I was to make our offer as compelling as possible."

He blew out another plume of smoke, eyes wandering over her.
She knew what he was seeing and, from the files she'd read before

arriving in Colombia, had a good idea of what he was thinking as well. His sexual appetite was notorious.

"And are you part of that offer?"

"I'm afraid not," Mercy said. "But I can guarantee your compensation would be worth the disappointment."

Bane laughed. "Very deft," he said. "You have my undivided attention now, Señorita Graves. Tell me what I can do for you and your employer."

"How much do you follow American politics?"

"Not at all. I am a citizen of the world."

"But you've heard about what has happened to Gotham City?"

Bane's smile vanished. He leaned across the table slowly, the cigar burning between clenched fingers. "If you know me, you know my interest in Gotham."

"The No Man's Land has turned into a political disaster," Mercy said calmly, ignoring the man's menace. "Easy to put into effect, much harder to undo. The President, the Congress, the Senate, they're debating the issue nonstop. It's only a matter of time now before the declaration is lifted, before Gotham is welcomed once more into the United States of America."

"I know all this." Bane grimaced, resumed leaning back in his chair, took another puff on the cigar, and looked around the room. At one of the other tables across from them a lovely brunette was speaking to two other women at her table. The brunette had been casting glances toward them since Bane had arrived.

"She wants me," Bane confided.

"She's DEA," Mercy said. "If you're not interested in what I have to say, I won't take up any more of your time—"

Bane raised his huge hand and waved it gently, motioning Mercy to stay put. He redirected his attention toward her. "No, no, don't be like that. Business, right? You haven't told me what you—pardon me—your employer wants."

"It's difficult."

"Then it will be more expensive. Please. Explain."

"He wants you to enter the No Man's Land within the next fourteen days. He wants you to proceed to the city recorder's office and the Hall of Records. He wants both sites destroyed, and all records that may still exist there burnt. Is that clear enough?"

"Admirably so."

"Good."

"Is there more?"

"Provided that you can accomplish these first goals, you would be paid an additional retainer to make yourself available to my employer until such time as the No Man's Land is officially ended."

Bane took a deep breath, straightening in his seat and then tapping ash from his cigar onto the empty bread plate in front of him. Mercy tried not to roll her eyes. Cultured and educated as Bane tried to be, his prison-bred manners still leaked out. In his heart, she knew he was a convict, a thug, and no matter how many layers of fine fabric he wore, that would remain.

"Your employer, he is a very powerful man," Bane said after some thought. "The kind of man who can buy and sell people as much as things."

"People are things. And like things, some are more valuable than others."

"My price for what he asks will be very high."

"I am permitted latitude in the negotiations, as I explained earlier."

"How much latitude?"

Mercy smiled.

"Try me," she said.

THIRTY

"PUDDIN'?" THE WOMAN ASKED. "WE going out today?"

Joker smiled sweetly and then bashed her over the head with the rubber chicken he was holding. He'd put a bar of soap in the chicken, and it made a pretty good club, and she wobbled for a second before sitting down on the steps beside him, giggling. Then she put her arms around his middle and tried to snuggle.

"Harley," he said. "Stop or I'll pick your nose with a power drill."

"You're just cranky because we never go out," Harley said, looking up at him, her eyes full of adoration. "You've been doing the same thing for months now, sweetie, just sitting here on these steps, rain or shine, looking down at the No Man's Land. We never go out anymore."

She thrust out her lower lip, pouting.

"We never went out to begin with," Joker said, wondering where he'd put his scissors.

"We could."

"Harley . . . if that hand heads any lower you'll be tying your shoelaces with your teeth."

She let go of him reluctantly, then sprang up and did a cartwheel down the steps, ending with a back-flip that put her on her feet once more. She smiled proudly at him.

"Getting better, aren't I, Mister J?"

He ignored her, then realized that wasn't going to do the trick, since he'd been ignoring her for what seemed like a darn long time at this point and here she was, still fawning over him.

After Two-Face had left him alone and Joker had taken charge of Arkham—which was really the way it was always *meant* to be, Joker felt—things had gotten quiet. He'd started his tenure as Arkham's new ruler by surveying his kingdom, making a complete audit of the grounds. He'd gone through all of the cells and storerooms, merrily looting his way along the empty halls. He found food in the cafeteria and plenty of drugs in the dispensary, and these things kept him happy and occupied for almost a month. As the winter continued, he took to trapping what animals he could find, then had hours of fun putting them through therapy. The opossum had been his most successful patient, and now was charming in its blood lust. His only regret had been the dearth of electricity, but he'd finally managed with a couple of car batteries from the garage, and even got some shock therapy going again.

When spring came he decided it was time to give the whole asylum a good cleaning, and so, with bucket and mop and hacksaw, he began scrubbing and polishing and cutting, trying to bring some glory and life back to the old place. When he heard the singing, he just paused in his sawing and, being who he was, completely ignored it.

Later that night, though, sleeping comfortably with the opossum beneath Dr. Arkham's big oak desk, he heard it again. This time, though, he was certain it wasn't himself who was singing, and after some investigation, tracked the noise to the nearest air duct.

It was a girl's voice.

Intrigued, Joker searched Arkham for the source. The singing continued off and on as he looked, the tune changing randomly. Sometimes it was a ditty from *Sesame Street*, other times it was songs he remembered from the radio. His favorite was when the voice sang Bugs Bunny's part from "The Rabbit of Seville."

It had taken him three days of looking before he thought he'd located the source—a door he'd never noticed before off the boiler room, with a fallout shelter sign faded and broken above it.

Being the gentleman he was, he knocked.

"Who is it?" the girl's voice trilled back.

"Land shark," he said.

"Don't want any," the girl answered, and the singing resumed.

Fair enough, Joker thought, and he headed back up the stairs and spent much of the next week contenting himself by moving all of the furniture from the offices into the cells and all the furniture from the cells into the offices, and by the time he'd finished he'd quite forgotten entirely about the girl. His next project was to try to build a Bat-Signal with which he could summon the one person in the world he most wanted to see, but halfway through the construction he got distracted and instead threw together what looked more like a bastardized version of Michelangelo's David, only this time *more* anatomically correct.

He'd been sleeping in one of the storage closets when he heard the singing again, and this time it was loud enough to wake him, and it was Billy Ray Cyrus to boot.

Putting his mouth to the duct, he shouted, "Knock it off!"

There was a very brief and merciful silence, and then the girl shouted back, "Make me!"

And then she started singing again.

Joker laughed and laughed and laughed, and decided he was going to rip her throat out and feed it to her. He got himself the fire ax from the wall and marched straight to the boiler room and began whacking away at the door. The singing continued and he whacked away in time with the beat and then, finally, the door had snapped open and he hoisted the ax over his head.

"I'll achy-breaky your heart!" he screamed into the darkness of the room. "I hate country music! It's not *funny!*"

Then he lowered the ax again because the singing had

stopped. He peered inside, seeing nothing. Absolutely pitch black in there.

And phew, did it stink. Bad. Like, really bad, like things had died in there and maybe someone had been using the space as a bathroom, too, for a really really really long time.

Then the girl came out, blinking rapidly, squinting against even the faint light of the basement. She was blond and pretty—well, Joker supposed she was pretty, but beauty was in the eye of the beholder, after all—and kind of short and just filthy, head to toe. He recognized her from his therapy sessions, though she looked different now that she wasn't crying or weeping or wailing about how ol' Dr. Arkham was going to keep them apart. She had on a doctor's jacket, and on the jacket was a nametag.

Dr. Harleen Quinzel.

Joker almost bust a gut laughing, because it was just too perfect. His own doctor Harley Quinn, how could he not like a broad with a name like that? And here she was, after oh so long, still in the asylum. His own doctor, and she had stayed behind just to be with him.

She squinted up at him, then looked over her shoulder, back into the fallout shelter where she'd undoubtedly been living for months.

"Saved," she said suddenly, and then, much to Joker's surprise and consternation, she jumped on him, wrapping her legs around his waist and her arms around his head, heedless of the ax in his hands. She kissed him, giving Joker a big blast of the stink from her body, the smell of waste that had accumulated in the stale air for so many months. Her tongue pushed past his lips like a quick slug, and she even rubbed herself against him in a manner he wasn't quite sure he didn't entirely dislike until finally he had to pry her away and toss her to the ground.

He menaced her with the ax. "Do that again and I'll split you in two, Harley."

She'd gazed up at him like a puppy, panting. "Whatever you say, Puddin'."

And that had been the start of it.

That had also been four months ago now, and Joker still didn't know what to make of her. Sure, she cleaned up all right, and she'd even gone so far as to make herself an outfit—well, more precisely, she had made herself several outfits, but cheerleaders and nuns didn't do much for him—but this one was good; this one made her look like, well, a harlequin. At times, he was almost in awe of her; she was so darn peppy and full of energy and sometimes even funny. But she was also sprung, totally bent, and he wasn't certain he liked that.

When she'd been Dr. Harleen Quinzel, when she'd been trying to cure Joker of his madness, she'd seemed much . . . saner. He'd had to work *very* hard just to get the edges of her psyche to crack during their sessions, and even when she had sworn her undying love in the weeks after the Cataclysm, Joker still hadn't been certain she wasn't trying to play games with *him*.

Now he knew.

The broad was bonkers.

Joker would have been delighted with his handiwork if she wasn't so damned annoying.

Worse, the more he abused her, the more she kept coming back. He'd even set fire to her hair at one point during the hottest day of summer and she had shrieked and run around the room until finally remembering to stop, drop, and roll. When the fire had been out she'd sat up and looked at him adoringly.

"Thanks," she'd said. "Needed a trim, didn't I?"

The next morning she'd made herself a headpiece for her little costume, complete with dangly bits and bells on the ends.

Joker supposed he could kill her, but each time he considered doing it something made him change his mind. Perhaps the nagging suspicion that she would thank him for doing that too, and what the hell was the point of murder if the victim didn't get the ultimate joke anyway? No, better to let her be, annoying as she was. Maybe she'd turn out useful.

Of course, she hadn't yet. She was still just plain old annoying.

He watched her work through another sequence of flips and jumps and kicks, punching at the air and crying, "Aiee!" and "Peanuts!" and sometimes "Oatmeal *this!*"

"Harl," he said at length. "What are you doing?"

She stopped, panting for breath, gazing at him beatifically. "Practicing, Mr. J."

"For?"

"The Ratman, Puddin'! You know he's out there somewhere. Sooner or later we're gonna go and get him."

Joker flew off the steps and grabbed Harley by the throat, driving her into the ground and then pinning her with his body. Harley's eyes bulged slightly as he tightened his grip.

"WE?" he demanded. "Did I hear you just say *WE?*"

She shook her head.

Joker let go, sitting back. Harley needed an extra couple of seconds before she could sit up, too, coughing slightly. Then she tried to nuzzle the back of his neck.

"Batman," Joker said. "You know, he hasn't been to see us?"

"Uh-huh," Quinn murmured, nibbling on Joker's collar.

"That's just darn rude, really, that's what that is. Not coming to see us. After all the trouble I've gone through to make this place presentable, not even so much as a note, not a card, not even a telegram. Not even a smoke signal." He squinted at the horizon, feeling Harley moving around behind him, wrapping her arms about his middle. "See, look. No smoke."

"No smoke," she murmured in his ear, then licked his jaw.

He frowned, punched her lightly in the face, and went back to staring at the city below them. Then he sprang to his feet and began marching purposefully toward the front gates. Halfway there he stopped, looking back to see Quinn still sitting on the ground, staring after him mournfully.

"Well?" he demanded. "What are you waiting for? *You're* the one who keeps saying I never take you anywhere!"

She bounded after him, and together they descended into the No Man's Land.

THIRTY-ONE

THE BOY WONDERED HOW LONG HE was going to sit on this rooftop, waiting for Batman to finally show up, trying to keep the resentment from taking hold. It wasn't easy. He'd come a long way in response to a single request, an E-mail from Oracle on his computer back in Keystone City, a message saying, simply, "Tim—he wants you to meet him, Labor Day, warehouse at the corner of Moench and Hama, sunset."

Tim Drake hadn't hesitated, dashing off a response saying that he was on his way, and then he'd lied to his father about taking a road trip to New York with two of his friends, Tony and Mike. Tim's father, delighted to hear that his son had actually succeeded in making friends in their new hometown, had agreed without reservation. It had taken slightly more manipulations to get Tony and Mike to cover for him—a story about the girlfriend he'd left behind when he moved out of Gotham, the girl who now lived in New York, that he just *had* to see, but the boys understood that. He was covered.

Getting through the blockade, that had been harder. Dodging the National Guard patrols on the far shore, then scaling the underside of the Brown Bridge, avoiding the mines until he'd reached the broken center. He wore his work clothes by then, in full Robin mode, and had used the grapnel to swing across. At the lowest point of the swing, he'd felt his cape brushing the water, could swear he'd seen the mines floating in the Gotham River below him. He'd nearly fallen from the wet spars upon landing, pulling the muscle along his shoulder trying to keep from taking the tumble. But he had done it, he had done what Batman asked, and he had been on the warehouse roof even before the sun had begun to set.

Now it was dark, and there was no sign of the man.

"He could at least be prompt," he muttered to himself.

"Why change a pattern?" Nightwing said from behind him.

Robin turned to see Nightwing's patented smirk, breaking into a grin. "Dude! How long you been listening to me mutter?"

"Dude. About twenty seconds, tops, I swear. How you been, Tim?"

"Can't complain, or more fairly, I shouldn't complain. But I've been waiting for this, man. Been hoping he'd call."

Nightwing nodded, the smirk now gone. "Me too."

"What took him so long?"

"Who knows? You know how he is. Tells us to stay out of Gotham, out of his way, vanishes for months. Then he has Oracle call and he expects us to come running."

"And we do."

"And we do," Nightwing agreed. "He'll tell us what he wants when he's ready."

"If he shows up."

"He'll show."

"I already have," Batman said from behind them.

Robin saw Nightwing frown.

"Glad you both made it," Batman said. "Robin?"

"Yes, sir?" Robin said, straightening. He wanted to say he was glad to see him, too, that he was glad to be there. He wanted to say a lot of things, actually, but Batman's look was dark and focused, and Robin thought it might be better to wait.

"Head to the Clock Tower, wait with Oracle. Nightwing and I will join you shortly."

"So that's how we're going to do this," Nightwing muttered.

"Yes, sir," Robin said.

"Nightwing, you're with me," Batman said, and then he turned and was off the roof in one swift move.

"Catch you later, Tim," Nightwing said, following.

Robin sighed, watching them disappear into the rubble. Then he turned and made for the Clock Tower, as ordered.

The Black Maskers had left St. Vincent's intact, and as she had every night since Two-Face had stolen their territory, Batgirl lit candles for the dead at the front of the ruined church. She went to her knees and prayed quickly, silently, for each of the men she had failed. Then she rose again and left, leaving the flickering lights burning behind her. The candles would be gone when she returned the next night, either burnt down to nothing or blown out and taken, but it was too much effort to sit and guard them, and it didn't matter. God, she was certain, understood the sentiment, knew the gesture for what it was.

Batgirl worked her way south, through the darkness and silence, climbing rubble until she was back on the rooftops. She took her time, looking carefully and telling herself she was watching for trouble as much as for Batman. She saw no signs of either. It had been quiet in her sector for over a month now, most of the gangs long since having withdrawn. Billy Pettit and his Blue Boy defectors, now calling themselves the Strong Men, had taken over ten square blocks farther west and south from her position, and their brand of law had leaked into the surrounding neighborhoods, creating a buffer.

Pettit, she thought for a moment.

She had watched him and his crew working the streets earlier in the week, and she still wasn't certain what she thought of them. The populace in their territory seemed to be doing very well indeed, safe and fed and protected. From what she'd heard, there were no troubles at all in his territory. The worst that she'd seen for herself was

Pettit threatening to cut a boy's hand off for stealing, a threat that had gotten the kid to return his ill-gotten goods without further protest.

At the old brownstone on Moldoff Avenue, above where Huntress had placed her tag on the side of the alley, Batgirl stopped and dropped off the roof, landing on the fire escape, then slipping through the window into her apartment. The building had endured the quake with little damage, and no one had dared to approach it since the No Man's Land for fear of feeling the bite of one of Huntress's crossbow bolts.

She stopped to light another candle inside, the sole source of illumination, then stepped back and pulled the cowl from her face, breathing in the air, heavy with the sudden burst of smoke and burning wax. Cowl in her hands, she stared into its empty eyes for a moment, feeling the thickness of the material that covered the lower part of the mask.

"Heavier than you thought it would be," Batman said.

She whirled and there he was, standing in the corner as if he owned the whole apartment. Beside him, draped over the back of the couch, was her Huntress costume, laid out carefully and not where she herself had put it before heading out. It was a statement, and one that she thought was unnecessary, and she felt heat rising in her cheeks at the implicit humiliation.

Not only did he know, the exposed costume seemed to shout, he had *always* known.

From the doorway to the kitchen she heard the other voice, the one she'd spent too much time and energy dreaming of hearing again. "Helena," Nightwing said.

She felt the heat in her ears now, and for a moment she was grateful for the light of the candle and the protection it offered. At least they couldn't see her clearly, she thought.

And then she remembered Batman's cowl and how her own masks never worked quite right. They had NVG that worked, and she knew they both were seeing every thing, every detail, and that there was nowhere to hide.

And no point.

Helena Bertinelli felt her heart racing in her chest and she tried to keep her voice soft as she said, "What now?"

"Six people are dead," Batman said, coming forward slowly. "My fault as much as yours, Huntress."

She swallowed, trying to find her voice. She wished the heat would stop. She wished she didn't feel like hiding.

"You want to keep that cowl?" Batman asked. "I have to be able to trust you. I have to know that you'll follow orders, that you'll do whatever it takes to get the job done."

"I tried—" she began.

"Trying isn't enough. You were to stop Black Mask and his cult out of sight of the Clock Tower. Barring that, you were not to be seen. You failed. I told you to protect our territory, our people, but Two-Face now holds that land. And six more bodies are in the ground."

The heat snapped suddenly hotter, and she realized the cowl was still in her hands, that she was twisting it tighter and tighter. With sudden rage she hurled it at him, and of course he caught it as if he'd known she would do that all along. It only made her angrier.

"And you blame me!" she spat.

"No. I hold you responsible. As I hold myself."

"You think I don't know what happened? You think I can just forget they're dead?" She was moving forward, getting in his face, her voice rising. "You think I can sleep at night? For three months before you got here I fought for this city, I fought as the Bat because somebody had to! And for three months since Two-Face played us all as fools you've ignored me, avoided me, *punished* me! You think I don't know it's my fault, Batman? Do you really think I don't know? There were sixty, seventy of Two-Face's men there, dammit! What was I supposed to do?"

She felt the movement behind her, Nightwing coming closer, and she shut her eyes, hearing Batman's response.

"More," the Dark Knight said simply.

She almost laughed.

"You lack discipline. You lack control. You're too emotional. If you want to remain with me—with us—you'll have to fall into line, otherwise you're out. That's the way it has to be from now on. With us, or alone."

Helena glared at him, feeling a new humiliation. With *us*, with me and Nightwing and Oracle and the rest, and of course he knew, he knew what had happened in this same apartment over a year ago, and that was why Nightwing was there. So he could see, too, so Batman could show his prodigal son the mistake that had been made, how unworthy she was of him.

"That's the way it has to be," Batman said, turning away.

She moved to follow, demanding his attention. "Dammit, look at me! Your way! The only way and nothing else will do! I bow to you or I'm nothing, is that it?"

Nightwing had moved around in front, interposing himself between Helena and the Batman. His expression was pained, and he reached out to stop her.

"Huntress, think——"

"Keep out of this! You may submit to him because you want to," she snapped, moving around Nightwing as he grabbed at her wrist. With her free hand she pushed her next words at Batman, who once again was facing her, his expression stoic, jaw set as if cut from glacial ice. "But I don't take orders and I certainly don't take them from you!"

"That's the problem," Batman said.

"No, not mine. Not anymore!"

"Huntress," Nightwing said softly.

She yanked her wrist free from his grip, not bothering to look at him, glaring at Batman. "Don't touch me," she said.

Nightwing backed away, silent. For a long moment none of them said anything more, and Helena realized that her eyes had begun watering, that tears were starting down her cheeks, and the humiliation that had, for a moment, been buried behind her rage, reared up again. She turned away, putting her back to both men, moving to the window.

"I won't be what you want, Batman," she said, and her voice surprised her, thick and low, and she had to clear her throat before she could say the rest. "Don't ask me. I can't."

"Then stay out of it," Batman said. "You'll only get in the way."

She felt his cape brushing past her, saw him disappear through the window the way a shadow flees from the rising sun. Nightwing followed, then stopped halfway out, one foot still in her apartment, one already on the fire escape.

"Helena," he said softly.

"Get out," she said simply, suddenly empty, suddenly utterly tired. "Just . . . go away."

Nightwing opened his mouth, then shut it, and then he was gone.

Helena stood alone in her apartment, watching the shadows cast by her single candle dancing along the wall and floor. She brushed at her eyes with the back of her hand, felt her heart slowing. Then she remembered the humiliation again, and it all came back, as savage and present as before. Fingers almost shaking, she pulled at the collar of her suit, freeing the cape, finding the snaps that hid the zipper along her shoulder. She yanked, pulling the shell of Batgirl away from her own skin.

She saw the Huntress costume laid out on the couch, where Batman had placed it.

She stared at the costume on the couch for a long time.

I won't be what you want . . . can't.

Then stay out of it. You'll only get in the way.

I can't do that, either, she finally thought, and began to change clothes.

Nightwing caught up with Batman a block away, where he found the other man standing motionless atop the ruins of Vincenzo's Fine Foods, staring down at the city. Swallowing his frustration, Nightwing vaulted up to where Batman was waiting, settling gracefully beside him. He followed the gaze, trying to spot what Batman was looking at, and after a second realized that Batman was looking at nothing in particular, but rather the city as a whole.

"You handled that well," Nightwing said, dryly, and when Batman didn't respond, added, "You can't push her like that and expect her to just play along."

"I know," Batman said.

"Then you know she won't 'stay out of it.' She'll go rogue. She won't stop."

"Yes."

"Oh, I know that tone. That's the 'I have a plan' tone."

"Yes." Batman paused, and when he resumed, his voice surprised Nightwing, because it no longer sounded the same. It no longer sounded like Batman.

It sounded like Bruce Wayne.

"I made a mess of it, Dick," Batman said, softly. "I tried pretending things were the same, that only the terrain had changed. I knew what I was working for—Gotham's redemption—but I didn't know how to get there. What's happened in the last couple months, with Gordon, with Two-Face, it woke me up."

"I don't know what happened with Gordon and Two-Face," Nightwing said.

"It's irrelevant right now."

"But that's why you finally summoned us?"

Batman nodded, setting his shoulder square once more, and Nightwing knew that the moment had passed, that nothing more would be revealed. He resisted the urge to press, to make Bruce say more, admit more. But he knew better than anyone how pointless that would be. Bruce would share what he wanted to share, when he wanted to, and that was that. It didn't matter if Dick was angry or feeling taken advantage of. It didn't matter that he resented like hell being made to witness the humiliation of Helena Bertinelli. It didn't matter that he'd known damn well what was up the moment they'd arrived at the apartment, the apartment he remembered better than he thought he would.

Bruce was finished for the time being. Anything more would have to wait.

"Let's go," Batman said, already throwing his jumpline for the next roof. "Oracle's waiting."

ORACLE

Dear Dad—
He apologized.
Batman apologized.

Not in so many words, of course, and not in such a way that you could take it to the bank if you were so inclined to try. But he admitted to being wrong, and that's about as rare a thing as . . . well, as if you were to admit *you* were wrong.

Robin arrived first, and I introduced him to Cassandra, gave him the short explanation of who she was and why she was in my inner sanctum. They took to one another pretty well and pretty quickly, and it made me remember how young Cassandra really is.

About an hour later, Nightwing and Batman showed up, and the moment they came in I could tell it hadn't gone well. I knew where they'd been, and I knew what they were doing; Batman had been kind enough to let me in on a small part of his plan, since he needed my help—and permission—to accomplish it. As a result, I knew that Batman would be paying Huntress a visit; that he took Nightwing along with him was unexpected, but not, on the whole, surprising.

Batman stayed quiet while I introduced Nightwing to Cassandra. Nightwing was suspicious of her, and even a little bit hostile at first, but it was clear that his real anger was for his mentor. I could see it in his posture, that he was willing to argue, that nothing Batman said was going to be just taken at face value.

"I need your help," Batman said.

Took the wind right out of Nightwing's sails, let me tell you. Left Robin absolutely speechless.

Batman asking for help.

I saw it cross their minds then, saw it on both Robin's and Nightwing's faces. The unspoken conclusion; if Batman needed their help, the situation must really be bad.

Then Batman went on.

"I thought I could do this alone," he said. "I was wrong."

Nobody said anything. Even Cassandra seemed to understand that something important was being said.

"No one person can do this alone," Batman said. "No Man's Land is too big, too dark, and too wild to be tamed by any lone will. I thought that I could play the game by the old rules, that if I was a gang lord, a warlord, who was bigger and badder, I could save the city. All I needed to do was to rule stronger and better than the rest of the gangs.

"I didn't understand what that decision would cost me, and now I know that the price is too high, the compromises required too great. I cannot, I *will not*, fight on their terms any longer.

"We're changing the rules from now on. The only way to bring Gotham back into the light is for us to work together.

"All of us."

Understand, Dad, I've known Batman for a number of years now.

I have never in all that time heard him say as much at once. I doubt that I ever will again.

It was quiet for a while after Batman stopped speaking, Robin and Nightwing exchanging glances. Then Nightwing indicated Cassandra, who was still waiting patiently.

"By us you're including her?" he asked.

Batman nodded. "You can trust her," he said, and then he proceeded to explain why that was the case.

He told them everything he had learned about Cassandra. He told them about Cain, about how the assassin had raised her to be the perfect fighter, the ultimate killer. He told them about her rebellion, her revulsion at having been trained to murder, about her commitment to life. Batman explained that Cassandra had rebelled against Cain, and fled from him, coming to the No Man's Land in the hope that he wouldn't find her here. He explained that Cassandra had worked for me since the start of the year, as one of my agents and couriers.

"She is as well trained, as well disciplined as any of you," Batman said. "She will *never* take a life. She will *never* surrender a fight. She would rather die than see an innocent be hurt."

"You're so certain," Nightwing said.

"Of her abilities, absolutely. Of her heart, positively."

Nightwing looked unconvinced.

"I agree with him," I said. "You can trust her. She saved my father's life, twice. I can vouch for everything Batman has said about her. She can do the job, she knows what it takes."

Nightwing crouched, bringing himself to eye level with me, searching my face. "Babs?"

"She has my blessing, Dick," I said.

That was what did it, I think, because Nightwing sighed and almost smiled. It was easier for him to accept my opinion on the subject than Batman's, for some reason. Maybe because he understood where this was going, and he understood where it put me. We were talking about another Batgirl, and he knew me well enough to have guessed my reaction to the last one.

"Give it to her," Batman told me.

I took the bundled costume from where I'd stowed it beneath the console, handing it over to Cassandra. She took it hesitantly, eyebrows raised with the question.

"Honor it," I said. "It is a sacred trust. Remember that."

She nodded reverentially, then stepped out of the Control Room to change. While we were waiting for her to return, Batman explained his current course of action.

"We bide our time," Batman told us. "A plan is in motion. For it to work, the rest of the players need to make themselves known. We won't win Gotham back by simply working our way down the island, breaking heads. We need more than that, influence from the outside, and I am reliably informed that is coming."

"No kidding?" Robin asked.

"Bane is in the city," I said.

The stunned looks I got from Robin and Nightwing were almost gratifying. Both remembered what had happened the last time Bane had met Batman in Gotham, and their memories were justly bitter ones. It had taken more than a year for Batman to recover from his injuries, and a lot of heartbreak and anger was still wrapped up in the memory. It wasn't something I wanted to dwell upon, either, not wanting to follow the thoughts to the resentment at the end of the line. Batman could walk again, was as strong as he ever was, and for that I was sincerely grateful.

No reason we should both spend our lives in wheelchairs, after all.

"Why is he here?" Nightwing demanded. "What's Bane after?"

"Trying to grab some land for himself?" Robin asked.

"I'll handle Bane," Batman told them.

Nightwing rounded on him. "You're not going up against him again, not alone!"

"I don't intend to," Batman said. "Your concern is noted. I'll be careful."

"I'll come with you."

He shook his head. "You and Robin and Cassandra, I've got very specific tasks in mind for you. You'll start by cleaning up the West Side, shutting down the minor gangs still working there. Oracle will give you the briefing as soon as Cassandra comes back."

"She's back," Robin said.

We turned to see her, standing in the doorway, dressed in the costume. It was based on my original one, but I'd modified it for the No Man's Land, even going so far as using the same mask design that Huntress had adopted. The whole outfit was coal black, so dark that the cape seemed like a liquid shadow hovering behind her. Only the belt and the symbol on the chest stood out, each in their yellow. I'd kept those colors muted, though, the bat itself only in outline rather than the yellow disk that Batman himself wore.

"Ready?" Batman asked her.

Our new Batgirl nodded.

It was hard to catch, and I think the others missed it. I didn't.

Batman, for a second, smiled.

"Let's get to work," he said.

THIRTY-TWO

BANE KNEW WHAT SHE THOUGHT OF him, and he was eager for the opportunity to prove her—and her unnamed employer—wrong. When he had come to Gotham the first time, he had come with the sole intent of destroying the Batman, his self-manufactured demon, his nemesis. He had come to claim what he felt was his destiny, his legacy—that of being the greatest man, the most powerful man, in the world.

This time he had no such motivations. This time it would be professional, and he would show Miss Mercy Graves that when Bane was hired to do a job he did it completely, and he did it well.

It was a matter of honor as much as pride, and both mattered to him more than anything else in his world, now. More than money or women or status or infamy. He was, he felt, the epitome of the self-made man; in fact, it had been precisely that which had made the Batman the object, at one time, of his hatred.

Bane had been born at the bottom of life's pit, as far as he was concerned, robbed even before he was born, of his future. In his native Santa Prisca, one of the many minor Windward Islands, the law was brutal and archaic, and it visited the crimes of the fathers upon the sons. In his case, that had been almost entirely literal. His father had been found guilty of a capital crime while Bane was still growing in his mother's womb. As such, after his father's execution, she too had been sentenced to prison, and it was into the prison, into custody, that Bane was born. He came into the world to suffer for his father's crimes, sentenced to spend the rest of his life behind bars.

The prison life had been brutal, his mother dying when Bane was only eight years old, finally broken, beaten to death by the warden who no longer wished to avail himself of her charms. That hatred then passed entirely to him, and Bane was forged by the harshest reality he could imagine for anyone. That he survived was miraculous. That he thrived was unbelievable.

Bane taught himself to read, and he read everything he could. Half his time behind bars he lived in his mind, honing it; the remainder he lived in his body, growing stronger. Before he was in his twenties, he ruled the prison's inmates. He had already resolved to escape.

The opportunity came with the men in white coats and their illegal experiments—the project they called Venom. Selected for treatment, Bane received controlled dosages of the Venom itself, a drug that was part synthetic steroid, part pure adrenaline, and as addictive as anything in creation. It took his enormous strength and amplified it.

But Venom robbed him of his mind, ultimately, driving him to the insanity of addiction.

Then he had escaped Santa Prisca, his eyes turning to Gotham. . . .

Ancient history, now. He was his own man again, free and in command of his destiny, and if there was any question of that, the payment he would receive for the job he was to do in Gotham would remove it. Finally, he would have the control he wanted, and he would punish the wicked.

He would visit the crimes of the fathers upon the sons.

But that would come later. For now he had plastique to mold and detonators to assemble, weapons to load, and body armor to tailor.

"How is it coming?" Miss Graves asked.

"Almost prepared," Bane answered. Now that they were in Gotham, they spoke English, and Bane was careful with his diction, enunciating each word precisely. "Another hour. Then I will be ready. I will begin tonight."

"Good." She stopped at the table where he had set out his charges, taking one and examining the wiring on the detonator. "Recursive, very nice. Timer and remote detonator."

"I thought it would be best to plan a redundancy." Bane finished soldering the last connection, setting the iron down and then flipping off the electrical generator. Miss Graves had been able to supply everything he had required, almost effortlessly, and when they had arrived in the No Man's Land, he had been pleased to see a workshop already prepared for him.

She had surprised him by insisting on accompanying him into the No Man's Land, and his protests had fallen on deaf ears. His opinion of women in general had never been very high, and he had thought, at first, that Graves would be a liability, following along only to make certain Bane did as he had promised.

She had quickly proven him wrong outside of the No Man's Land, though, when they'd been stopped by a random National Guard checkpoint. Miss Graves had rolled down her window, presented her license with a smile, and then produced a pistol. She had fired four times, one shot for each of the weekend warriors, all to the head, then exited the car and begun moving the bodies away from the road almost before Bane had realized what had just transpired.

Clearly a woman to be reckoned with.

She had led them into the island via a tunnel from the northern part of Gotham County, and Bane had seen the signs of recent work, had known the tunnel was a new addition, quite possibly prepared for their use alone. It gave him confidence that their employer was sincere in his support.

Bane snapped the nine-volt battery into place on the detonator, then used a voltage meter to check the connections. All lights were green. From over his shoulder, he heard Miss Graves make a small sound of approval.

"I'll be away most of the night," she said. "I have other business to attend to. If you have any trouble, we'll meet back here at dawn."

"There will be no trouble," Bane said.

"There's a woman here to see you," Garrett told the Penguin.

They were in his apartment, or, as Penguin insisted on calling it, the "private chambers," in what had once been the Davenport Towers. A lot of work had been put into making the ruined space livable, and Penguin's rooms, in particular, were lushly decorated. Thick Oriental rugs and antique wooden furniture, all salvaged from around town, filled the rooms. There were paintings on the walls, several Garrett himself had carried at Penguin's request from the ruins of the Gotham Museum of Fine Art, crafted by people who had died a long time ago and who, apparently, were only known by a single name like "Rubens" or "Cézanne" or "Mondrian." Books were everywhere, all hardcover, and most of them old.

Penguin himself was lounging on what Garrett had learned was referred to as a "daybed," wearing a fancy silk robe called a "smoking jacket," and puffing away at the cigarette in its holder. The bandage on Penguin's thigh had been removed weeks ago, and his injury had healed well enough, but Penguin still insisted on elevating the leg whenever he was seated. On the table next to the daybed was a glass of something dark and red, but whenever Garrett called it wine, Penguin sneered.

Penguin didn't look up from the book in his hand. "This concerns me exactly how, Garrett, my boy?"

"Um . . . she told me to show you this," Garrett said, handing over the business card the woman had given him.

Penguin took it absently, still engrossed in his book. He was reading a fairy tale, Garrett thought, and it must be a good one, because he was totally into it. At least, Garrett assumed it was a fairy tale based on the title. He couldn't imagine a book called *The Prince* being about anything else. Except maybe music.

Penguin finished the page he was reading and flicked a glance at the card in his hand, then did a double take, dropping the book on his lap. He hastily put his monocle back in place, looking at Garrett with something like alarm.

"Is she still outside?"

"Yes, sir, Mr. Cobblepot."

"Then usher her via the ingress, lad, hurry, hurry!"

Garrett stared blankly.

"Bring her in!" Penguin clarified, rising and adjusting the robe—no, "smoking jacket"—then quickly cinching the belt tighter around his belly.

Garrett moved back to the door and opened it, letting the woman in and watching her walk as she passed. She was nice to look at. Most of the women in the No Man's Land, like most of the men, were filthy and didn't really care how they dressed. This broad, she was in an open overcoat and a black skirt and wearing a white blouse that Garrett thought might be silk, because it clung to her body in a nice way, showing off her shape just a bit, but not like she was trashy. She was tall, too, his height if not a little taller, and she had broad shoulders. It was the legs, though, that he went back to because they were really something, they went all the way up.

The woman extended her right hand toward Penguin, saying, "Mr. Cobblepot, thank you for seeing me."

"Miss Graves, is it?" Penguin took the hand, but instead of shaking, bowed and kissed it. "A delight to receive such an august visitor, I assure you." He let her hand go gently, then indicated the couch—no, Garrett corrected himself, "love seat"—opposite the daybed. "Please, take a seat. Coffee? Port? Brandy? I have a modest selection of cigars as well, if you are of a type to enjoy the richer tobaccos."

Miss Graves sat, adjusting her overcoat. "No, thank you."

Penguin smiled, moving quickly to the armchair—no, Garrett remembered, the "Louie Cans"—by the love seat, joining her. "If I had but known you were coming, I would have prepared a more suitable reception, I do apologize."

"Think nothing of it."

Penguin's smile grew broader, and for a couple more seconds Garrett saw that he was just looking her over again, taking his time. "So, what can I do for you?"

"Not for me," Miss Graves clarified. "For my employer."

"Yes, I recognized the name on your card. I had no idea he was interested in Gotham."

"I didn't say he was."

"Yet here you are. Two plus two, my dear, must equal four."

"The equation he has in mind is more one plus one," Miss Graves said. "He's willing to compensate you handsomely for some very minor help."

"Indeed? My attention is yours, entirely."

"We wish to, shall we say, rent some space from you. Your sector is one of the most stable in the No Man's Land at this time, and a large portion of the land is of no use to you."

"For what purpose?"

Miss Graves glanced at Garrett.

"He's trustworthy," Penguin said. "He wouldn't dare speak out of turn, would you, my lad?"

"No, sir, Mr. Cobblepot," Garrett said.

She gave Garrett another brief looking over, then nodded, turning her focus back to Penguin. "We wish to move a large amount of material into the No Man's Land, over one hundred tons' worth, actually. We would require several of the warehouses along the Miller Docks as a holding area for these items. Further, we want the locations guarded, twenty-four hours a day, seven days a week. Finally, we demand discretion. No one is to know what we are doing. No one is to enter those warehouses without my authorization."

Penguin leaned back in his chair, removing the cigarette holder from his mouth, plucking the dead butt from its end. He dropped it into the silver ashtray on the table to his right, then motioned for Garrett. Garrett brought the tortoise-shell box and opened it, and Penguin selected another cigarette, taking his time. Miss Graves watched, unimpressed.

After Garrett had lit Penguin's new cigarette, Penguin said, "Well, you certainly have piqued my curiosity, Miss Graves. For instance, I'm now pondering how anyone could move one hundred tons of anything onto this island."

"That's my problem, not yours."

He nodded, agreeing with her. "Nonetheless, if one can bring that much of anything into Gotham, one must be capable of moving in the opposite direction, so to speak."

Miss Graves sighed. "I am a busy woman, Mr. Cobblepot, and I am not interested in playing a game of semantics." She leaned forward, putting her arms on her knees and looking Penguin in the eyes. Garrett saw that she was really a blond, that her roots weren't dyed or anything. "I can transport goods onto and off the island, securely, and without interference. If you think you can discover my methods, you're welcome to try. But should you do so, my employer will respond in kind."

Penguin didn't say anything for a second, and Garrett thought that just maybe some of the color had drained from his cheeks. "I think the one plus one equation is far more equitable," he said, finally.

Miss Graves leaned back against the love seat. "I thought you might."

"I will want . . . compensation for my help."

"Of course. In addition to a rental fee which we can, of course, negotiate. The market for luxury items—jewels, precious metals, fine art—continues to be strong in the world outside of No Man's Land. I can arrange for the transport and sale of those items you've acquired in the past year. And I can see that the proceeds from those sales make their way, cleanly, to any account of your choosing."

"What's your cut?" Penguin asked, and his voice was uncharacteristically blunt to Garrett's ears.

Miss Graves almost sneered. "Nothing. We have no interest in taking any pieces of your pie."

"No, you have a pie of your own, yes?"

"Yes. Do we have a deal?"

"Let's talk about rents, shall we?" Penguin said. "Garrett? Make some coffee, would you? I think this may be a long night."

THIRTY-THREE

 SO FAR IT WAS GOING SWIMMINGLY except for a single thing.

No Batman. Whatsoever.

None, nada, zilch, zero, the flying rat was nowhere to be seen.

Joker knew in his bones—especially in his elbows, but also in his scapulae—that the Dork Knight was somewhere in No Man's Land. He'd seen the signs, for God's sake, the tags on walls in the shape of a bat. He'd heard the talk. Somewhere in the carnage and broken buildings, along the decrepit streets and tortured boulevards, somewhere out there the Fatman was waiting for him.

But it had been a month now and nothing.

It was starting to bug him. Not much—there was time, there was forever, in fact, but he felt neglected.

Harley didn't understand.

"But Puddin', Ratman always beats you up!" she'd exclaimed when he had tried to explain it to her.

"You're missing the point. It's a running gag."

What could he expect from her anyway? She's dressed up like a harlequin and keeps talking about how they should make babies at some point. Babies. Like he needed that trouble, changing the oil on a squealing child on top of all the other many duties he had found himself with. He'd been working hard as it was. The thought of more work, that just made his skin try to crawl away.

Psychiatrists, he thought. Go figure.

Other than the Batman, though, he had to admit things were good. Even from atop Arkham, looking at the No Man's Land, he hadn't realized how bad it was on the ground, how much fun could be had. He and Harley had started out together almost a month before, taking their time on the road down from the asylum, eventually wandering into Burnley, where people screamed when they saw him and ran away in a really funny fashion.

Sometimes they ran so scared they fell down and rolled and hurt themselves really badly, and then Joker would wander over, taking his time about it, and offer them a hand up. Depending on his mood he'd be friendly and solicitous or outright hostile, and sometimes, just for kicks, he'd tell Harley to do a trick.

Harley, he had discovered, had tricks. One of her favorites involved a rusty cheese grater and a stapler. It didn't always work, mostly because people didn't tend to sit still for that sort of thing, but it gave Joker a consistent laugh, and he figured in time Harley would have it down to a science.

Another thing had happened, too, and frankly it helped his self-esteem.

It had gone down like this.

About two weeks after leaving Arkham, Joker and Harley had gone up to the old Gotham Knights Stadium. It was almost October, after all, and Harley, it turned out, was a baseball fan. So they went to see if the Knights, in fact, had a chance at all of winning the pennant. They'd arrived to find the stadium all but empty and barely still standing, at which point Joker had been willing to leave. Harley had pouted, dragging him by the hand through the team entrance, then out onto the diamond. While Harley ran the bases, Joker had picked through the dugouts, looking for a really good set of cleats.

"Oh, God," he heard, and turned around to see a tall and skinny man peeking from around the corner of the hallway that led back to the locker rooms.

"Hey," Joker said. "Know where I can find some really good cleats?"

The man turned and ran for it.

"Harley!" Joker screamed, then began his pursuit. The man made it down the hallway, then turned right, knocking open a door, Joker right behind him. They entered the visiting team's locker room, and Joker skidded to a stop, taking in all that was around him.

There were about fifteen other men in there aside from the tall and skinny one, and it was clear they'd turned the space into their own little clubhouse. There were open crates of salvaged goods, the odd weapon scattered around. A rather nifty-looking baseball bat, with spikes on the broad end, was leaning against the locker right beside Joker. He picked it up, checking its weight, then cocked his head at the crowd, most of whom were already backing away from him.

"Wanna play Three Flies Out?" he asked.

One of the men, who had a really entertaining nose, said, "We don't want any trouble with you."

Joker smiled and nodded. "Fair enough. I don't want any trouble with *you.*" He'd pointed the bat at tall and skinny. "He didn't answer my question, though."

Nose looked at Skinny. "Answer his question."

"He wants cleats," Skinny said.

"We don't have cleats," Nose told Joker.

"Oh, you must have cleats," Joker said, and he hopped up on the bench and brought the bat down onto Skinny's head, hard. There was a very satisfying wet and crunchy sound, and Skinny had fallen to the floor. "And a batting helmet," Joker had added.

Nose started backing away, and the other men tried moving around for the exit. Joker watched them, grinning as Harley appeared in the doorway, wearing a catcher's mask. She had a shoe on each of her hands, and waved them at the faces that were coming her way.

Nose turned back to Joker. "We don't want any trouble with you."

"Cleats," Joker said, and he swung again, catching the nearest of the men alongside the face. He fell down, screaming, with a lot of blood rushing out of him. "Ought to do something about that. Maybe a styptic?"

"Mr. J! I found your cleats!" Harley waved her hands at him.

"Cleats, Harl. Not spikes. Those are spikes."

Harley looked at the shoes on her hands, then punched at the nearest face. The man with the unlucky face staggered back, clutching at his eyes.

The other men backed into a corner.

"Please," Nose said. "Whatever you want."

"You mean aside from cleats?"

Nose nodded quickly.

Joker thought, then did a quick count of the men. There were twelve of them without any obvious injuries. Plus himself and Harley, that made fourteen.

"You got uniforms?" Joker had asked.

Nose hesitated, then started nodding frantically. "Can find some, I know where some are."

"Harley, go with Nose here and bring back all the uniforms you can find."

"Okay, Puddin'."

Joker occupied himself while awaiting their return by practicing his swing at the air. That bored him after three swipes, so he started swinging at Skinny again, noting with some pleasure how easily some parts of the man broke and how difficult it was to really tear off others. Then Harley and Nose came back, each with an armful of clothes.

"Put 'em on," Joker told Nose and the rest of the men.

There had only been thirteen uniforms. The one man who hadn't managed to get himself a jersey and matching pants began frantically searching the empty lockers.

"No, no," Joker said. "I'm sorry, but I'm going to have to cut you from the team."

The man tried for the door, and Harley blocked him with one of her fancier kicks.

"Baseball is a team effort," Joker told the man. "And you're just not pulling your weight."

Then he beat him to death with the bat. Finished, he turned back to address the rest of the roster.

"Gentlemen," he said. "You represent our national pastime. With me as your GM, we will surely win the Super Bowl this year, returning the Stanley Cup to its rightful place in Gotham. And now, our team mascot, Miss Harley Quinn, will lead us in a short prayer."

Harley cleared her throat, drawing herself up to her full height. "Joker is God," she said.

The men gaped, stunned.

"Amen," Harley encouraged.

"Amen," they muttered.

"That's hardly team spirit, boys," Joker said, hefting the bat.

"Amen," they said, louder.

"Better. Okay, now let's go on out there and play some ball."

That had started his gang. Of course, almost all of the original team got cut, but Harley was great at recruiting new players, and the roster had now nearly tripled. Several days back Joker had given up on trying to keep all of his boys in uniform. As it was, he knew he was doing something right, because wherever they went people screamed and jumped up and down and made a horrible fuss.

His boys, he thought, looking at them. Much better now than on that opening day at Knights Stadium. Those players then, they really hadn't had any interest in the game. But these new ones that Harley kept finding, they were his kind of people. They didn't argue, they did what they were told, and all of them had quick wrists and a mean stroke with their bats.

With this team, he figured he could get all of Gotham behind him.

"I just want to know what's happened to her, that's all," Nightwing said.

"Why don't you go by her apartment and find out?" Oracle answered, focusing on the monitor in front of her. Code streamed by on the screen, numbers flying quickly past as her eyes tried to track the incoming information. "You know where it is, after all."

Nightwing sighed heavily. "I went by. She wasn't there."

Oracle's eyes stopped their back-and-forth for a moment, then resumed. "Oh, well."

"You know where she is, don't you?"

"Maybe."

"I'd appreciate it if you told me."

"Don't you have work to do? Doesn't Batman have you investigating something?"

"Yeah, the warehouses on the Miller Docks. Already checked them out. They've been cleared, Penguin's got men guarding the locations. Nothing's inside. Must be expecting a delivery."

Oracle tore her attention from the monitor, looking up at Nightwing. "How many warehouses?"

"Six," Nightwing said. "Babs, look, tell me where Huntress is and I'll get out of your hair."

"Why do you want to know?"

"Because I'm worried about her."

"Oh?"

"Yeah, oh. What's that supposed to mean, oh. Oh what?"

Oracle shook her head. "Just oh."

"It's not what you think."

"You don't know what I think, Dick," Oracle said mildly, tapping away again at the keyboard.

"Actually, you're broadcasting it pretty loud. You don't like her. You don't like that I like her—"

"So you admit it."

"Admit it?" Nightwing threw up his hands in frustration. "Admit that I like her? Of course I like her, Babs! I think she's basically a decent person who's trying to do the best she can."

"She's a murderer and quite possibly insane."

"That's harsh."

Oracle spun her chair around to face him, the color in her cheeks rising slightly, as if trying to match the red of her hair. "No, it's a fact. She's a killer. She has a vendetta thing going. Maybe you're not up on the facts, Dick, but I am, because that's my *job* here. Helena Bertinelli isn't wearing a costume because she wants to do what's right for the people of Gotham. She isn't wearing that getup of hers because she's out for justice. She wants revenge, plain and simple."

"Did she kill anyone while she was Batgirl?"

Oracle closed her mouth, glaring.

"Well?" pressed Nightwing. "If she's as nuts as you say, why didn't she?"

"She kept it under control, that's why."

"Uh-huh. And that makes her insane how, exactly?"

"You want to know where she is, Dick? I'll tell you. I got a report from Vanessa this morning, and another of my Eyes, Alex, he confirmed it. She's on the Upper West Side. She's in with Pettit and his Strong Men. The martial law brigade. Apparently she's playing on their team now."

Nightwing frowned darkly, turning away and moving to the stained-glass window, looking out past the shadow of the hands on the clock face beyond. "Dammit."

"Not so rosy now, is it?"

He shook his head slightly, almost not listening. There was a plan, he knew there was a plan, and that Batman had put it in motion, but what it was . . . he hated not knowing. But when he'd asked Bruce he'd received only silence in response—the traditional answer that Nightwing remembered since childhood. Sometimes it honestly felt as if nothing had changed between him and Batman. Nothing at all.

"Dick?"

He blinked, saw that Oracle was watching him with some concern.

"I was just . . . I am hard on her," Oracle said slowly. "But, you've got to understand, I think it's warranted."

"It is warranted. That's not what concerns me."

"Then what?"

"Batman," he said, and that was the only answer necessary.

THIRTY-FOUR

PATIENCE WAS THE KEY, AND BANE
knew that, and so he took his time before making the
first move. A lot of time, almost two weeks' worth.

Miss Graves, he noted, seemed perfectly content with this, allowing him to proceed at his own pace and staying out of the way. She
had something going on with the Penguin, he had gathered that
much, and he suspected he knew what that was. But it didn't concern
him, and thus he devoted no energy to confirming his suspicions.

Most of the initial work was surveillance. The target location
was in the center of Two-Face's southern territory, near City Hall.
And though the Hall of Records itself was not heavily guarded,
there were many men in the area, and several were armed, and he
knew they would respond in kind to his actions once he began. For

that reason, among others, he planned carefully, caching weapons at strategic locations, mapping his routes, and calculating his best angle of attack.

Only when he was certain he had accounted for all of the variables did he begin, and as the mid-October evening descended he rose from his cot in the warehouse workshop that had been his home for the last several weeks and began dressing. He had a costume, his traditional outfit for actions such as these, but put it aside in favor of more utilitarian garb. This was, in his mind, a military operation, almost commando work, and he dressed accordingly. He wore his mask nonetheless. Concealing his features was a conceit, but he knew the psychological value it would provide.

"You're ready?" Miss Graves asked.

"I am. You will not see me for the next couple of days. This will take some time."

"Very well."

She watched as he armed himself, as he hoisted the mammoth pack onto his back. Bane took a moment, adjusting the straps and distributing the weight. He was carrying over two hundred pounds of equipment, a weight great enough for even him to feel its effects. After making certain it was seated properly, he made for the exit. Miss Graves followed.

"May you have good luck," she said.

"Luck will play no part in this."

The covert infiltration was flawless, and Bane was inside the Hall of Records before darkness had completely fallen. In an empty office he stowed the majority of his gear, and then with a gun strapped to his thigh and a knife in his hand, he began making his way silently through the halls, working from the top floor down. He encountered no one until reaching the ground level, where Two-Face had posted guards at all of the entrances. Bane had expected as much.

Returning to the office where he'd left his gear, Bane began gathering the explosives he had made. Patiently he began wiring each floor, starting with the top and again working his way down. There was no rush, and haste, he knew, would lead to a mistake. He had the luxury of double-checking his work, even, and so he did.

By dawn he had completely wired the upper floors of the building, the guards below blissfully unaware of his presence.

Shortly after daybreak, the guards were relieved by their replacements. Bane watched as the old departed and the new settled in, then he returned to the office for the third time and, after barricading the door, lay down for a nap. He felt good about his progress and certain in his hiding place and safety, but nonetheless it was hard for him to fall asleep. He ached for a good woman or a fine cigar or some rich, rare brandy, and his mind wandered among such thoughts for a good hour before he was able to calm it enough to truly sleep.

It was dark when he awoke, and he sat up in the office, listening carefully for almost two minutes before assuring himself that all was as it should be. Using the NVG from his bag, he gathered the two submachine guns and reconfirmed that each was fully loaded. Then he put the pack on once again, the detonator in his pocket, and snuck back into the hallway, guns in each hand.

The same guards from the night before were at their posts again. Without preamble, Bane descended the stairs and opened fire.

None of them reacted in time to return the shots, and the hallways echoed briefly with the sounds of dying men and the rattle of spent brass. Then there was nothing more but silence.

Slinging the guns, Bane searched the bodies. One had a radio, and he took it, hooking it to his belt in order to monitor any transmissions that Two-Face might broadcast. According to his surveillance, he would be safe until dawn, when the relief arrived. Finished with his search of the cooling bodies, he moved the corpses out of the main hall, dumping one after the other inside the nearby men's room.

He used four more explosives to mine each of the doorways into the building, running nearly invisible tripwires back and forth across the thresholds to prevent any entry. Then he armed the devices. Anyone trying to enter via a doorway wouldn't have time to regret the decision.

He moved to the basement level, where the actual records had been kept. There were, he knew from reviewing the blueprints Miss Graves had supplied, eight separate rooms that housed the mainframe computers, and the electrical data that was now useless in No Man's Land. Another four rooms—almost cavernously huge— housed the hard copies. Bane took the mainframe rooms first, going from computer to computer, systematically removing the platters of digital tape, setting each aside. When he had finished with the machines, he moved onto the hard copies.

This took most of the night, moving down the rows and rows of files, opening each drawer, starting from the bottom, and dumping its contents to the floor. It was tedious and repetitious, and Bane didn't much enjoy the task, but it had to be done, and he knew it had to be done this way. Records safe inside their filing cabinets might survive what was to come, and the instructions from Miss Graves had been absolutely clear.

When he was finished with the second room of hard copies, he turned and surveyed the scene, and for a moment he marveled at the amount of paper spreading out before him. It completely covered the floor, in places almost two feet deep, and the scent of it was pleasant and almost overwhelming.

There was one set of records he had retrieved personally that he had yet to add to the pile, though, and he held them in his hand for a moment longer before opening the thick file and leafing through the contents. Technically, what he held was only one small part of what was, relatively, a much larger set of records.

Wayne.

He flipped it open, leafing through the contents. Birth and death certificates, titles and deeds, the annotated history of a dynasty. Stretching back to the late 1600s, Waynes had lived in Gotham City before it was called that.

The final copies were, of course, the birth certificate for Bruce, followed almost immediately by the death certificates for Thomas and Martha.

Bane allowed himself a moment of commiseration, then banished it entirely. Bruce Wayne had, at least, known a father and a mother, proud people who had left him a legacy. He, on the other hand, had never known a father at all, and his own mother had been less a parent than the prison's whore who sometimes paid him extra attention.

With a flick of his wrist, he sent the files fluttering to the ground, then moved purposefully out of the room, back to where he had left the platters of digital tape. He then broke each spool apart with his bare hands, letting the celluloid strips spring wildly and uncoil.

He checked his watch and noted that it was already past five-thirty in the morning. With a heavy sigh he moved out of the base-ment, back up to the floor where he had stowed his gear. Phase One was now entirely completed, and with time to spare. He dragged the pack to the stairs, then lifted it, returning once again to the lobby where he began assembling the machine gun, mounting it on its tri-pod. He carefully removed and then refolded the belt of ammuni-tion, making certain all of the links were smooth, that there would be no kinks in the feeding of the rounds.

His watch now read eleven minutes past six. He sighed, then set-tled back to wait.

The relief arrived precisely at eight, as they had the morning before, and Bane lay flat on the floor, covering his head as the doors opened. The explosion came next, the concussion of the blast rolling back into the building and over him, and he could feel it through his thick muscles, deep in his thick bones. He rose quickly and moved to the machine gun, taking in the cloud of smoke and dust, pieces of masonry, wood, and marble still finding their way to the ground.

The dust cleared and no one was in the doorway. He saw a piece of a leg just beyond the entrance, presumably a segment of the man who had first tried to enter.

The silence stretched. Outside, Bane saw daylight filtering down through the floating dust, showing the dance of the motes. Pausing momentarily, he caught a breath of the autumn air from outside.

Someone stuck his head around the corner cautiously and with-out hesitating, Bane shot him.

Phase Two had begun.

Christina Weir screamed.

"Push," Essen urged.

"With all due respect, Lieutenant," Christina said, gasping for air, "go to hell."

Essen nodded and said, "That's good, just remember to breathe. And push."

"I am pushing!"

"And you're doing great. Breathe. Andy?"

"Uh," Officer DeFilippis said.

"Keep holding her hand."

"Uh-huh."

"Touch me and I'll kill you," Christina said, then winced, then hollered again. "Oh, God, this is killing me."

"You're doing great, Chris, you're doing fine, you're almost there. I can see the head. Just another couple of—"

"This hurts! Oh Jesus God dammit ow oh dammit how did I let you do this to me?" Christina tilted her head back, looking up at Andy, reaching for his arm. "I swear you're going to pay for this, I swear to God."

"I love you," Andy said.

Christina hollered again, her hand almost white from the strength of her grip around his arm, almost sitting up in bed, and her expression changed suddenly and she fell back, pulling long breaths from the air, blinking rapidly. Andy put a hand on her brow, wiping her hair back, murmuring to her.

The baby started to cry.

Essen took the blanket Montoya handed her, swaddling the newborn gently, then looked up at where Christina and Andy were both staring at her, and she thought it was almost cute, how both of them had the same stunned expression, the same look of absolute wonder in their eyes. Christina was still trying to catch her breath.

"It's a boy," Essen said. "A perfect little boy. Congratulations."

Later, outside of the bungalow that Weir and DeFilippis were now using as their home, Essen joined her husband. It was evening and cool, the edge of an autumn crispness in the air, and she slipped her hand into his, giving it a squeeze.

"A boy, huh?" Gordon said.

"Yup."

"And everything is good? "

"Looks that way. All his fingers and toes are there, at any rate."

Essen brushed her hair back off her face. "In a week or so we can have someone take them up to Dr. Thompkins, have a real doctor look at their work."

"Good idea. So, this kid have a name?"

"A mouthful of a name. Justin Michael DeFilippis-Weir."

"I'm impressed."

"Yeah, just imagine yelling that from your front porch."

Gordon let go of her hand, putting his arm around her shoulder instead. "Not what I meant. From all the shouting going on in there I wasn't certain if it was a birth or an interrogation."

"Well, rubber hoses can be used in both situations, as I'm sure you know," Essen joked. "So it's understandable that you'd become confused."

They began walking toward their home. After a minute, Essen said, "You know, I think that's the fourth kid I've delivered in my career as a cop. Four. Wow."

"I never have."

"No?"

Her husband shook his head. "No. Almost all of the cops I know, they've delivered at least one child, or been present for at least one delivery in the field. Not me. I keep missing out."

"Children," Essen said softly.

He stopped, moving his hand to her shoulder and looking in her eyes. "We agreed when we got married. You regretting that decision?"

"No," she said. "I've got you, and that makes me happy."

"You're happy?"

"Right now? Yes. I'm walking home with my husband, the Commissioner of Police for the city of Gotham. We're safe, we've got a roof over our head. We're surviving. You told me a while back that you were afraid with Pettit gone we'd crumble. Well, it's been months, and here we still are. I'm happy. I'm proud."

She moved forward and kissed him on the mouth, feeling the familiar scratch of his mustache, and he responded in kind, wrapping his arms around her tighter and pulling her in close. They stayed in the clinch, lips together, and she felt her heart beginning to race and the same sense of wonder that, after so long, he could still excite her like this, still make her feel as young and strong and potent as he had all those years ago, when they'd first met.

From down the street, she heard Bullock shouting, "Woo-hoo! You kids knock that off! There's laws against that!"

She broke away from her husband long enough to turn and spot Bullock and Montoya a couple doors down, sitting on the stoop, side by side. Montoya was laughing, and Bullock was waving his arms as if to say, please, no more.

"C'mon," Jim whispered in her ear. "We can go back to our place and do that thing people do when they want to make babies."

"Except without that baby-making part."

"Whatever you want," he said, and his breath on her neck made her shiver involuntarily.

She ignored the catcalls and hoots from Montoya and Bullock, taking her husband by the hand and leading him the rest of the way home. Then she didn't have to lead him at all.

He was careful not to wake Sarah when he rose the next morning, just before dawn. He slipped on his glasses and his clothes, quietly opening the door to the bedroom before stopping and looking back, seeing her asleep still, listening to the gentle song of her breathing. He let himself smile, and for the first time in months didn't feel guilty that he could.

Things were bad, sure, Gordon knew. But not impossible.

Hell, even in No Man's Land people were having babies. If that didn't prove that life would triumph no matter what, he didn't know what did.

He moved into the kitchen, finding a half-empty can of Sterno with which he started a fire to heat some water. Back when they'd taken Penguin's land south of the park, in one of the caches, they'd found some vacuum-sealed French roast, already ground, and he used a little of it now to make himself a cup of coffee. He took the cup with him out to the garden, planning to watch the sun rise.

He'd settled on the bench, watching the dawn beginning to bleed over the horizon, when he heard the voice right behind him. The hot coffee scalded the back of his hand when he started at the noise.

"Jim."

From the corner of Gordon's eye, he saw Two-Face standing just behind him, to the left. He had a gun in his hand, not quite pointed at Gordon's side.

"What do you want?" Gordon said tightly.

"Your turn to fulfill our bargain," Two-Face said softly, and it wasn't the voice Gordon expected. It was almost imploring. Almost hopeful.

"Our deal is off, has been for months. Long over."

"For you. Two people make a deal. Two people end it."

Gordon turned slowly, facing him, holding the mug with both hands. Worse came to worst, he'd fling the hot liquid at Two-Face and hope that would buy him a few seconds. He glanced at Two-Face's free hand, and was vaguely relieved to see that the coin was nowhere in sight.

"You tried to have me murdered," Gordon said. "You hired David Cain to do the job. You think I don't know?"

"That had nothing to do with our bargain. That had to do with Renee."

"What?"

"It's not important right now," Two-Face said, leaning down. Gordon heard it again, the note in his voice. Close to desperation. "You have to help me, Jim, like I helped you. I've got a lunatic on the loose in my territory. He's holed up in the Hall of Records, killing my men. I've lost half my troops to this animal. You have to help me."

For a moment Gordon marveled at Two-Face's ego, how he could toss out words like "animal" and "lunatic" without a moment's pause. Then it struck him that anyone who could send Two-Face running for help had to be bad news, indeed.

"You owe me," Two-Face hissed.

"I owe you nothing."

"Damn you, Jim. I need your help!" Two-Face was almost pleading.

"No."

"I could kill you, you know that. Half of me wants to."

"Then you'll kill me."

"You're a cop, you're the law. This man is committing murder in my sector. You have to do something."

"I stopped being a cop months ago. I stopped being a cop when I shook hands with you." Gordon felt the fatigue clawing at his back, knocking away what dim pleasure still remained of the night before. "You'll get nothing from me."

Two-Face snarled, bringing the gun up, and Gordon flung the coffee at his face, diving out of the way. The shot came, pinging off the patio, whistling past Gordon's side, and he rolled, reaching for the nearest suitable weapon, coming up with a hand trowel from the potting bench. Two-Face was shaking his head, the hot coffee rising off him with steam. From beyond the garden voices were shouting an alarm.

Gordon lunged, bringing the trowel down as if it were a knife, and Two-Face barely backed away from the blow, then brought the pistol down, hard, going for Gordon's neck. The metal scraped the edge of Gordon's ear, burning a short track of pain along the side of his head, and for a second Gordon saw nothing but heat, bright and white, and when he got his vision back Two-Face had the gun pressed to his temple, the coin ready in his other hand.

But before Two-Face could flip, Gordon heard his wife, shouting, "Drop it!"

Two-Face froze.

Gordon turned his head to see Sarah in the doorway of the garden, an oversized sweatshirt and nothing else on, her service pistol in her hands.

"Drop it and move away from him or I'll kill you," she said.

Two-Face let go of the gun and backed off. Then he turned and went for the wall of the garden, up and over it in a matter of seconds, and Gordon was wondering why Sarah hadn't fired, scrabbling for the gun that Two-Face had dropped on the ground. Sarah was at his side then, helping him up.

"You had him," Gordon said, feeling his ear with one hand, the sting where the flesh had been torn. "You had him, why didn't you shoot?"

Sarah made a nervous laugh, more of relief than fear, snapping open the cylinder on her revolver. Gordon could see the six empty holes.

"I haven't had bullets in over two months," she said, then took him by the arm and led him back into their house.

THIRTY-FIVE

"WANT TO SEE WHAT POWER REALLY is?" Pettit asked Huntress. "Want to see how you get things done in the No Man's Land?"

"Show me."

Pettit adjusted his cap, then motioning her to follow, led the way down a flight of stairs and into the basement of the building he was using as his headquarters. The area was remarkably clean and free of debris, and she followed him down a hallway to a room marked STORAGE. Pettit used a key from his pocket to open the door, pushing it back and allowing her to lead the way in.

The room was filled with large storage containers, almost like giant lockers, but these were wood framed and walled with chain link. Each container was filled with a variety of things, presumably objects put into storage by the original tenants of the apartment building, from cardboard boxes to old exercise machines to broken pieces of stereo equipment. Huntress took it all in, then looked at Pettit, who moved past her, heading down the narrow corridor between rows. At the end he took a left and unlocked another door.

Inside this room were crates stacked upon crates, some covered with tarp, others exposed. Pettit shot Huntress a grin, then yanked back a tarp and pulled open the container that had been concealed beneath it.

"Used to live in this building, you know," he said, reaching into the crate. "Couldn't get back here as often as I wanted to when I was playing coward along with Gordon and the rest of those wimps. Now, though, rules are different. See what you think."

He tossed her a small box, no bigger than a pack of cigarettes.

They were bullets. Twenty-two caliber.

She looked at the box and looked at Pettit and found herself without voice.

He misunderstood, his grin getting bigger. "Yeah, that's right, Huntress. I've got twenty-two, thirty-eight, forty-five, I've got nine-milli, I've got NATO standard."

"How . . . how much?"

"Figure I've got a bullet here for every man, woman, and child in Gotham." He took the box out of her hand, dropping it into the pocket of his coat. "This is how we're going to get our point across."

"Pettit."

His expression changed, the smile fading as he registered her tone. "Huntress, we've already had this conversation. We had this conversation when you first showed up here. This is war, remember. And we're soldiers."

And war is hell, she thought.

Foley came through the door before she could say anything more, breathless, saying, "Bill! Bill, there's—"

"I told you not to interrupt me," Pettit said, glaring.

Foley nodded, glancing at Huntress in apology, then turning his gaze back to Pettit. "Something's going on in Two-Face's sector. He's pulled all of his men out of the northern section, and there's word of a major firefight going on there. Been going on for over a day now, something like that."

"Two-Face against who?" Huntress asked.

Foley shook his head.

"Doesn't matter," Pettit said. "Hugh, get the boys together and get them armed. Anyone who's taking down Two-Face is doing us a favor. We'll head over there and take a look around."

"Right," Foley said, and was gone.

Pettit tapped one of the crates. "Want one?"

"I don't use a gun."

"Right, right." He gave her a grin she wasn't certain she liked. "You change your mind, you let me know."

As the last sunlight vanished from the sky, Batman used his jumpline to cross Civic Plaza, skirting the courthouse and then alighting on one of the cracked gargoyles adorning City Hall. He switched on the starlight lenses in the cowl with a squeeze of his glove, scanning the area below that led to the Hall of Records.

Two-Face's men had pulled back. For the most part, it seemed to him, the battle had ended. Sporadic gunfire sounded from farther away, another part of the territory, but he knew it wasn't Bane, and right now, Bane was the priority. He fired off the line again, leapt, and swung to the next building, landing easily on the flat roof, then crossing to the access door. There was no question that Bane had trapped the entrance; Batman was certain he had, in fact, trapped all of the entrances.

He picked the lock quickly, then attached his line to the door and retreated around the side of the accessway. Any bomb would be directed by the nature of the architecture, and his observation thus far had confirmed that Bane was using a low-yield explosive, possibly less than an ounce of plastique for each device.

He brought up his cape as a shield, preparing to use it as a bomb blanket as he had so many times in the past, and yanked on the line in his hand. The door snapped open but nothing followed, no alarm or detonation.

Dropping the line, Batman edged his way around the side of the accessway, peering with one eye into the darkness. Still nothing. He switched the cowl lenses to infrared and, finding no heat signature, switched the NVG on again. Still nothing.

No, he thought. No, I don't believe you for an instant, Bane.

Flicking the NVG off, he reached into his belt and removed a miniature halogen light, slipping it around his right index finger and turning it on. Then he crouched at the edge of the open doorway and cautiously began playing the light across the opening, left-to-right, then right-to-left, gradually working his way higher and higher. His intention was to sweep the whole doorway before even beginning to attempt an entry.

He hadn't raised the light more than six inches from the floor when he caught the bare reflection of the fishing line. He allowed himself a grim smile.

Better, he thought.

Using the light, he traced the network of lines with his eyes, following the crisscrossing pattern until he was certain he'd found the leading end. From the first aid kit on his belt he removed a small pair of clothing shears, and then calmly cut the line. The tripwires collapsed like a spiderweb set on fire.

Using NVG again, he checked the stairwell, and now convinced it was clear, made his way into the building.

There was another, similar booby trap at the bottom of the stairs. Once again he methodically traced the lines and cut the lead.

Then he was inside, standing in the long hallway in the dark. He rotated from NVG to infrared once more, scanning carefully, and then, again using the light, began making his way forward. From outside he could still hear sporadic gunfire, but it was much more distant now, almost otherworldly.

He took a step, then another, walking slowly down the hallway, finger light playing methodically along the floor and walls ahead of him as he went. All the same, he nearly missed the tripwire, not registering its existence until his boot had already hit it and he felt the barest pressure against his step. There was a soft clicking noise, metal closing on metal, somewhere to his right. He froze, his leg in the air, midstep. The line was all but invisible until the light hit it, and then the halogen beam turned it into a thread of silver, running the width of the hallway at ankle level; no more than three inches high, it looked like.

You've primed a bomb, he told himself. Very well done.

Now let's see you get out of it.

Foot still in the air, he swung the light along both sides of the hallway, looking for the detonator, trying to hold himself steady. Odds were that any more pressure on the wire would trigger the bomb. Any less would probably do the same.

It took him seven seconds to locate the device, a matte black box that had been inserted into one of the air vents in the baseboard. The grating over the vent had been replaced, so that only the line was exposed, the device itself protected from any tampering.

He felt perspiration beginning to slide down his back. His right calf was beginning to ache.

No way to access the detonator without changing the pressure on the line.

Wonderful.

He began checking the pouches on his belt, one at a time, carefully, looking for something to substitute for his foot, at least temporarily. Rebreather, too big, too bulky. Laser torch, too small. Smoke pellets, much too small. Miniature camera, almost, not quite. Skeleton keys, no. Tear gas pellets, too small. Power source for suit, too big, too difficult to access. Digital recorder, too bulky. Jumpline, useless. Plastique, too little . . .

Can of yellow spray paint.

Spray paint.

Lid on can of spray paint.

This might work.

Carefully he removed the spray paint from his belt, separating the cap from the canister. Then, controlling his breathing, feeling the ache climbing in his leg and feeling his pulse beating at his temples, he began lowering himself with his left leg, bending forward slightly. He needed both hands for this, and the light on his finger danced along the hallway as he moved, alternately illuminating and hiding the tripwire. He felt his center of gravity shifting, his balance beginning to ebb.

How much pressure is on the wire, he wondered. Not much, can't be much, less than a pound, easily, less than half that. Weight of the can versus the pressure of the wire . . .

He set the cap on the ground, flat, then slid it forward until its edge rested against the tripwire. The sweat was starting to leak from beneath the cowl, he could feel it sliding along his jaw, then down his neck. Canister next, placed behind the cap to hold it still. Has to be perfect, he thought, has to be perfect, no margin for error . . .

He moved his foot back, away from the line.

The tripwire didn't move.

He took a deep breath and that was when he realized he had been holding it for over a minute now.

Still not finished. Bomb's still primed.

He went to the vent, looking in at the detonator. It was a simple, functional circuit-with-explosive device, and he saw where the blasting cap was wired into the plastique. The unit was powered with a nine-volt battery.

Using the laser torch from the belt, he set the beam as narrow as possible, then fired, burning out the circuit. Then he tugged the wire free from the unit, hearing it snap loose, and there was no explosion and he was still breathing and fine, and he got back to his feet, vowing that he would be more careful.

It took him another seven minutes to clear the hall on that floor, finding two more devices, which he deactivated as he went.

Knows I'm coming, he thought.

On the second floor he found four more, and deactivated those.

The gunfire from outside had stopped.

He entered the lobby cautiously, finger light off, again rotating from NVG to infrared. He found fading heat signatures, the residual glow from the piles and piles of spent brass. Over a thousand rounds had been expended in the lobby, he determined, most of them .50 caliber. The machine gun itself was unattended on its tripod just beyond the reception desk, still shining with heat.

He stopped in the middle of the lobby, listening hard.

"Batman," Bane said, somewhere in the shadows. "I know you are here, my friend."

"Bane."

"I am flattered. You remember me."

"You do yourself a disservice. How could I forget you?"

Bane's laugh was soft and bounced along the bullet-scored marble floors, echoing from the stairwells. "How indeed? But here you are. Ready for more of the same?"

"I see no need to repeat history, Bane. Right now you and I are about even."

"Tied, you mean," Bane clarified. "And in a draw there are no winners."

"And no losers." Batman began moving again, this time lightly, watching his step. Soundlessly he reached the stairwell leading down into the basement archives, and when Bane spoke next he knew he was heading in the right direction. He began making his way down the stairs, rotating views, finger light still off. As he neared the bottom, he saw the faint glow of electric light spilling on the floor.

"We are not men who accept our defeats," Bane was saying. "In fact, we defy them. You and I, we are of the same world. We have made ourselves as much as we have been made. You know this is true."

Batman stepped into the hallway and there Bane was, waiting for him, unsurprised.

"You may not believe me," Bane said. "But it is good to see you again."

"I wish I could share that," Batman said, taking in the chaos around him. "You sure you got everything down here?"

"Doesn't matter. The whole basement is wired with incendiaries." He held out his right hand, palm open, showing Batman a small silver box. "One flick, it's all on fire."

"Radio controlled?"

"With you in the area, I am always very careful." Bane slipped the box into the pocket at the side of his belt, then adjusted his stance, centering his mass and squaring his shoulders. "Whenever you are ready, Batman."

"Who said I'm looking for a fight?"

Bane cocked his head slightly. "Why else are you here?"

"What's he giving you for all of this hard work, Bane?" Batman asked quietly. "It's not simply money, is it?"

Bane laughed again. "No, not simply money."

"Then what?"

"What does it matter?"

"I want to know what it's worth to your employer. I want to know how much of you he's bought."

Bane wagged a disapproving finger, coming up from his fighting stance and relaxing once more. "Not bought, Batman. There is no need for an insult like that. My services have been purchased. Not my heart. I am as easily bought and sold as you."

"My apologies."

"It is worth a great deal to him. It is worth enough that when I am finished here, Santa Prisca will have a new ruler." Bane gestured gently with both arms, as if taking in the world. "Me, of course."

"Of course. Santa Prisca. You drove a hard bargain."

"He could pay it."

Batman nodded barely. "Absolutely."

Bane squared his shoulders once more, bringing his hands up, ready to fight.

Batman turned around and started back up the stairs.

"Excuse me? Where are you going?"

"I'm leaving," Batman said, without looking back.

"Leaving? You're just going to walk away from me?"

"Yes." He stepped out into the lobby, checking it quickly to see if anyone else had entered the building while he had been in the basement. He could hear Bane's boots on the steps, coming up after him.

"You are playing games with me, yes?"

"No. Sorry to disappoint you."

"You've lost your nerve, that's it, isn't it? You are afraid you cannot defeat me a second time."

Batman didn't stop, heading for the front doors, noting that they had been blown clean off their hinges at some point. Bane came around in front of him, blocking the passage with his bulk.

"You will not simply walk away from me," Bane said. "I deserve an explanation, if nothing else."

Batman stopped, looking squarely at Bane. "Do what you've been paid to do and then get out of Gotham," he said. "Our fight is for another day."

He tried to move forward once more.

"I think perhaps our fight is now," Bane said mildly, and then sent a quick left jab to Batman's head, following with a body punch to the middle. The jab missed, but the body blow connected, the punch sinking deep into Batman's gut. Batman pitched forward suddenly, doubling from the blow, his hands out, brushing Bane's waist.

Bane stepped back and waited.

Batman righted himself, catching his breath.

"You win," he said. "Happy?"

Bane shook his head, laughing again. "I broke more than your back. I broke your spirit, too." He moved out of the doorway, gesturing to the outside. "Please, our business here has ended."

Batman moved through the doorway silently, then stopped.

"Remember what I said," he told Bane. "Finish the job and then leave."

"I shall take it under advisement," Bane said.

Without another word, Batman moved into the night.

From atop the wreckage of the Gotham First National Bank, Batman kept watch on the Hall of Records, the detonator he had palmed from Bane in his hand.

He considered for a long while, looking at the silver box in his hand.

What if I'm wrong, he thought. What if . . .

No. You have to make him feel it's safe to proceed. You have to bring him and his money here. And he'll only do that if he believes the way is clear. If he believes all the records of the past have been destroyed.

Nonetheless, he had to make certain, and he switched on the commlink in his cowl, saying, "Oracle?"

Her voice answered in his ear almost instantly. "Batman? What's your status?"

"Hall of Records, just confirming the situation. It's checked out."

"Robin and Batgirl just got back from the West Side, they're awaiting further orders. They say the Xhosa have retreated."

"Tell them to stand by. Oracle?"

"Yes, Boss?"

"The files. They're secure?"

There was a pause, and he assumed the question had taken her by surprise. "Still have them on my system. Sent duplicates to the WayneTech Crays in London and Hong Kong, hidden in the system, so there are copies off-site, as well. You want me to do anything with them?"

"Not yet."

"Why are you asking?"

Doubt, he thought. But he didn't say it, because he knew he never could say it, that they could never hear the word from his lips. Batgirl and Robin and Oracle and even Nightwing.

"Good work," Batman said. "Out."

He closed the connection. Then he pressed the stud on the silver box in his hand.

Almost instantly, flames began dancing in the lower windows of the building, spreading fast. Whatever accelerant Bane had chosen, he had chosen it well. In under a minute the fire had spread to the first floor, and its glow was beginning to illuminate Civic Plaza.

Batman waited until the whole building was burning before dropping the detonator and walking away.

He could feel the heat on his back.

He imagined, for a moment, that it was what hell felt like.

ORACLE

Dear Dad—

It's quiet again, and I've finally found some peace in which to write.

Autumn is ending. Maybe it's that, the new chill in the air, the bite of the coming cold off the Gotham River and the Atlantic Ocean. Maybe that's what is keeping us silent.

Or maybe in the wake of Bane's one-man war against Two-Face, the whole of No Man's Land is nervous again.

There was a lot of blood spilled at City Hall. A lot of Two-Face's men died, and in the course of three days, the No Man's Land's mightiest warlord fell from his perch, crashing into near anonymity. My Eyes haven't seen hide nor hair of Dent since the Hall of Records went up in smoke, and neither Nightwing nor Robin has mentioned seeing him, either. Batman himself has remained silent on the subject. All he would confirm was that Bane escaped the blaze. He added nothing more.

Pettit and his Strong Men took losses, too, trying to corral the fleeing members of

Two-Face's crew. It led to more fighting, and people fell on both sides. My agent Charlie saw some of it, said that Huntress was in the thick of it with Pettit's boys. From what he says about it, my interpretation is that she wasn't very happy to be there, but that may just be Nightwing's influence rubbing off on me more than anything else.

Doesn't matter, she's still with them, and the Strong Men, as of now, are still the safest cordon in the city next to you down in TriCorner.

I've had this feeling, though, Dad . . . like things are on the verge of changing, that we might be nearing the end of the tunnel. It's not that I can see the light yet—I can't—more that I just know the light is there, a little farther ahead, attainable.

Problem is that, until I see that light, I'm still in the dark.

This is what I know now, and it's mostly gleaned through my own analysis, conversations with Nightwing, Robin, and (kinda) Batgirl, then supplemented by reports from the Eyes.

First off, almost all of the minor players have been removed from the board, either through their own actions or, in the last two months, by direct movement against them by either Pettit's Strong Men or our guys. Nightwing, Robin, and Batgirl have pretty much been working their way through the city, sector by sector, treating symptoms as they encounter them.

Of the name players, only Penguin seems to have any power base left, and he's been remarkably quiet. His sector has remained firmly under his control since Two-Face's double-cross so long ago. Apparently, he has no interest in increasing his holdings. This makes perfect sense to me, actually. Penguin's never been much for the kind of power games the No Man's Land encourages. He'd much rather—you'll forgive me for this—line his own nest.

Two-Face, in the wake of Bane, has a handful of men left to command, far too few to actually hold the land he'd claimed. He's lost all of his northern chunk, which has already been reclaimed by Batman and the rest of our little "squad." Further, he can no longer hold onto all of his southern sector, as I'm sure you've discovered. By all reports, he's pretty much retreated to the area around Civic Plaza, and doesn't venture out. Rough estimates are that he has between ten and twenty armed men, and that all those civilians who had been living in his territory have long since fled.

So the wild card, as always, is Joker.

Maybe that's why the city seems so silent.

We all know he's out there, we hear the reports, second- or third-hand, rumors of madness along the West Side, stories of bonfires and baseball games and stranger things still. Rumors abound—Joker has started a cult, à la Black Mask; Joker is breeding rats with which to infect the city with bubonic plague; Joker has become a cannibal; Joker is married; Joker is organizing a militia and planning on attacking fill-in-the-blank. No confirmations on anything at all, and no idea how many people he may have gathered to his side. Vanessa reported a rumor that he's traveling with a woman who wears a costume of her own, but there's been no visual confirmation of that.

All rumors, and that only makes it worse.

Nightwing's spent much of the last week searching for him, with Robin and Batgirl helping. They've found some locations where it's possible Joker had stayed, at least for a while . . . mostly evidenced by the discovery of several corpses. The problem, as I'm sure you know, is that Gotham is a big place to begin with; the No Man's Land has just made it all the easier to hide inside, and as a result, he could be almost anywhere and we would never find him.

Unless he wanted us to.

That seems to be what Batman is counting on.

He was here a couple nights ago, and Nightwing brought up the situation, saying, "Joker. What are we doing about him?"

"Nothing," Batman said. "Ignore him for now."

We all gave him stares, even Batgirl. She didn't know who Joker was yet, but I'm sure she'd noted the tension each time the name had been mentioned around her, and she certainly knew something was up.

"Ignore Joker?" Robin asked.

"He'll come looking for me. Right now there are other priorities."

"But—" Nightwing said.

"No. If you encounter him notify me and continue monitoring the situation. Gather what intel you can, numbers, capabilities, so on. But otherwise do not engage him unless the life of an innocent is at risk. Leave him alone. He'll come to me."

And that was the end of that discussion.

As for the plan . . . well, I wish I could be certain I understood it, but here again Batman has been tight-lipped. The destruction of the Hall of Records was not the blow it seemed to be at the time, I know that much. The reason I know that much is because way back when Mr. Wayne went to Washington and we could all read the writing on the wall, he contacted me and said that I had to make duplicates of all the titles and deeds— yeah, that's right, *all* of them—for Gotham and the surrounding area. Preferably scans, he said, but duplicates however possible.

"Is that all?" I'd asked, sarcastically.

"Don't worry about birth and death certificates," he'd said, as if I'd been serious. "Those are duplicated as a matter of course elsewhere. Just make certain you get every deed, every title."

I had thought he was just trying to cover his own interests; after all, Wayne Enterprises itself was built primarily on real estate money, diversifying from there. But he was adamant, all of it.

Took some doing. Took a lot of doing, actually. Took all of the Eyes I had at the time. working twenty-four hours a day, for over a month.

But in the end, I had computer copies of everything Batman had asked for, digitally encoded, locked away on my system and encrypted like you wouldn't believe. I'd pretty much forgotten about them until Batman called that night when the Hall of Records went up in smoke. He came to see me the next day to talk about them.

"I have a project for you," he said. "It's going to take a lot of your time and energy, but it has to be done, and done flawlessly. I cannot stress this enough."

"Have I ever let you down?" I asked him.

"Each of the files needs to be imprinted—in effect, forged. You need to turn them from unauthorized electronic duplicates into notarized computer copies."

My jaw felt like it actually dropped into my lap. "We're talking about over one million records," I said.

He just looked at me, that steely impassive face beneath the cowl, and I could almost hear him thinking, So? What's your point?

"Whose notarization?"

"The government's. These need to be their copies."

"Doesn't the Library of Congress or someone already have these copies?"

"They've been destroyed."

"By?"

He shook his head just barely. "Later. Can you do it?"

"It'll take time."

"How long?"

"A month, at the very least. I'll need to write an optical character recognition routine that can identify the text in each scan, and then I'll have to create an entirely separate program, one with a semi-intelligent logarithm to identify variations in the actual documents. Then I'll have to code a new routine entirely to replicate the digital fingerprint that the government uses for such documents. I do all that, we'll be able to modify them as we see fit, but any modification beyond the official notarization in the code for the scans, I'll have to go in and do that manually."

"The last won't be necessary. We're not changing the records. We're preserving them. Keep me informed on your progress."

"I'll need Tim's help," I said.

"Fine," he said. "Just make it happen. And soon."

"Why the rush?"

He left without answering. I contacted Tim, and he and I set to work. We'd been at it for about a week, serious code-raiding, hacking at its finest, when Batman returned and dropped another piece of the puzzle in our laps.

"I need a sat-phone link to Lucius Fox," he said.

Tim swung around from the terminal he'd been working at, giving Batman a curious look, then bouncing it over to me. I didn't even bother to shrug. Batman wanted a satellite phone call to the CEO of Wayne Enterprises, that was relatively easy to accomplish, and a break from the drudgery of the last week. I pulled up my tracking information, set my telemetry, then punched up the number Batman gave me.

"Gonna be a minute before the connection comes online," I said. "Can't track the satellite to maintain the connection. We have to take the window as it comes."

"How much time?"

"You'll have seven minutes, tops. Then the signal will start to break up."

"That'll do," Batman said.

"That's a D.C. number, isn't it?" Tim asked. "Lucius is in D.C.?"

Batman grunted, taking the handset. "Put him on speaker when he answers," he told me. "And give me some background. Côte d'Azur."

"Beach?" I asked.

"Hotel swimming pool. And give me Kitty and Lise."

I grinned. This was, in fact, much more entertaining than coding. I switched to a third terminal, the one I use for audio/visual, and got some background noise running. Then I loaded up the voice routines for Kitty and Lise, making certain that the giggling girls sounded appropriate.

Tim slid his chair over, watching what I was doing, now grinning. "Can I be one?" he whispered.

"Lise," I said, and linked his keyboard.

The sat-phone connected and began ringing. It was nearly midnight our time, which meant it was midnight in D.C., too. I made certain all my levels were set, the sounds of the fictional pool now coming from my A/V speakers, complete with background murmur and the odd clinking of glasses.

There was a click, and then Lucius Fox picked up the phone, sounding mildly irritated. "Hello?"

"Lucius!" Batman said, and there's no real way to describe the effect of hearing him switch into full Bruce Wayne mode while wearing the cape and cowl. It's amusing and alarming at the same time.

His voice changed, of course, went higher and much more bubbly, and his posture altered with it. It was like watching Bruce Wayne dressed up as Batman, and I know that that sounds like precisely what it was, but it's so much more than that. Bruce doesn't dress up as Batman. Batman dresses up as Bruce. That's the only way I can think of putting it.

"Bruce?" Fox said from the speaker. "Where have you been? I've been trying to reach you for weeks. Melinda said you were in Cabo—"

"No, no, not for a while now. I'm in France, I think. I think it's France. Nice is in France, isn't it? I'm in Nice." He moved a finger at me, and I took that as a cue. From one of the speakers came Kitty's accented voice, drippingly French, asking Brucie if he was going to get another bottle of champagne.

"Nice?" Lucius asked. "Why are you in Nice?"

"Uh," Bruce said, vapidly. "Dunno. Seemed nice. Nice seemed nice, that's it."

From Tim's speaker, Lise told Brucie to put more lotion on her back.

"Who is she, Bruce?" Lucius asked, with a sigh.

"Oh, uh . . . not sure, actually. But she's real nice, too."

More giggles from our speakers. Batman motioned to turn it down, and we lowered the voices, then had our electronic girls begin a discussion about the pleasures of swimming in the ocean versus swimming in the hotel pool.

Batman was saying, "So, look, Lucius, reason I'm calling is I met this fellow, didn't catch his name, but we were talking, and I told him I was from Gotham. Which I was, you know, or suppose, still am, but since Gotham is now No Man's Land—"

"I know where you're from, Bruce," Fox said, the hint of exasperation in his voice.

"Right, right, sorry. But he said, see, this guy, he said that he'd owned land in Gotham and that he'd just sold it. Said that he was surprised anyone was still buying the land, but he said he got rid of it, no problem. Had this offer from some company or something, and he jumped at it, he said, just to get rid of the land, because he said it was now all worthless and he'd—"

Fox finally managed to break in, saying, "Wait a minute. This guy sold his land *after* the No Man's Land began?"

"Yeah, that's what I mean, see, that's why I thought it was odd, because, right, he can't do that, can he?"

"No. No, he can't. All of the Gotham real estate is in limbo right now. Can't be bought, can't be sold."

"So we still have our land?"

"We still have our land. Hmm . . . Bruce?"

"Uh-huh?"

"You remember this guy's name?"

"Nuh-uh. Just some guy."

There was a pause over the line as Fox thought about what Bruce had been saying.

Tim had Lise resolve to try the pool, and I kicked up a large splashing noise to convey that she had fallen into the pool.

"I'll look into it," Fox said. "Thanks for letting me know."

"Is it important?"

"Maybe. We're in a delicate position right now, Bruce. I've been doing as you asked, and so far we've managed to cobble together a fairly strong coalition to lobby Congress. A lot of the larger businesses in the country have rallied around Wayne Enterprises, citing the economic crises created by the loss of Gotham. Right now it's Marifran-Holby Industries, Zellar Manufacturing, S.T.A.R. Labs. I've got another meeting in the morning at the White House to plead our case."

Batman didn't respond.

"Bruce?"

"Huh? What?" Batman said. "Oh, sorry, Lucius. There's this blond girl and she's kinda . . . waving at me . . . at least, I *think* she's waving. . . ."

"You didn't hear a thing I said." Lucius sighed. "Look, tell Melinda where you'll be, all right? That way I can contact you?"

"Sure."

"We're getting there, Bruce. Don't lose hope."

"I've got faith in you, Lucius. Gotta go. I just figured out what the blond is doing, and I think she needs my help."

Batman flipped the switch, killing the connection. For a moment longer, the sounds of the pool and the two digital bimbos continued, then I turned them off, as well.

"Real estate?" Tim asked.

"Land is everything," Batman told him, and it was Batman again, no sign of Bruce Wayne ever having been in the room, let alone the building. And never, ever, under that mask.

It took me a couple days after that before I really began piecing it together, before I realized who it was Batman was waiting for.

And it's brilliant, Dad. It really is.

Because the one thing that will save the No Man's Land, that will restore Gotham, is the one thing that even politics cannot resist.

Money.

A lot of money.

Now, getting that money into Gotham, that's the trick.

THIRTY-SIX

HUNTRESS STOOD ON THE ROOF OF THE apartment building that the Strong Men used as their base of operations, looking down over the sector, feeling the rain dripping off her cape and hair. She liked the smell of the rain, the sweet musk that rose from the asphalt below and made the city seem clean. The streets were empty, most of the populace inside and staying dry.

At the end of the block was P.S. 221, and in the gymnasium there Huntress knew Pettit was putting his men through their paces, as he did every morning unless there was a fight to be had. When she had first joined the Strong Men, she had attended one of the sessions, more out of curiosity than anything else. P.S. 221 had been one of her schools, before the No Man's Land; she had taught there twice a week, leading a special education English class for at-risk children. The school had given her a faint sense of belonging.

That had evaporated when she had seen what Pettit had done to the gymnasium. Inside he'd created a drill instructor's dream, an obstacle course through which he drove his men for hours. Then he'd split them into pairs to work on their hand-to-hand skills, and then an hour for weapons maintenance.

Gave a whole new meaning to vocational school, Huntress thought.

From where she was standing she could see the guards posted around the sector, the checkpoints on the streets where comings and goings were diligently noted. There were times when Huntress thought she was living in Cold War Berlin as much as the No Man's Land. She suspected that was exactly what Pettit was trying to conjure.

She wasn't even certain why she was here, anymore. She didn't feel particularly needed, and for the most part even less liked. In the last month, she'd made connections with precisely none of the people in the sector. Only Foley and Pettit made efforts to talk to her, and the more time she spent talking to them the more she realized she didn't particularly like either man, but for different reasons.

Foley, she thought, wasn't an entirely bad sort. Simply ill-equipped for the loss of civilization that had happened in Gotham. He was a social creature, good with people, and his main function among the Strong Men seemed to be that he was the conduit between Pettit's force and the general populace, bringing the concerns and requests of the one to the other. Huntress had watched the previous evening as Foley made the rounds, moving from building to building, checking on the occupants while carrying a salvaged clipboard in his hand and a broken ballpoint pen. He'd made a list of needs and concerns, presenting them to Pettit.

She respected Foley for that. The man knew what he was good at, and he was using it to try to help. He may not have been much of a policeman back in the day—she didn't really know, and wasn't prepared to try to speak to such a claim—but he sure as hell knew how to be a public servant. He smiled when he talked to the people under their care. He listened and nodded, and he made whoever he was talking to feel that they, indeed, mattered.

Pettit didn't do that. Pettit, Huntress suspected, wasn't as much concerned about what the people wanted for themselves as what he wanted for the people. He hated being opposed, rankling whenever the slightest criticism was leveled at his decisions or actions. Twice since the Two-Face incident he had raised his voice to Huntress when she had dared to disagree with a proposed course of action. Each time she had taken it, swallowing the anger, keeping her responses mild.

It bothered her that she had done so. She talked back to Batman, for God's sake; she had no trouble following her own decisions, her own mind. Why was she willing to let Pettit push her around?

"There must be something *really* interesting about the rain," Nightwing said from behind her. "You've been standing out here for over an hour."

She resisted her first instinct to whirl and face him, feeling her heart kick-start in her chest and the heat rising on her cheeks. He'd caught her completely by surprise, and she felt savagely embarrassed, and that first sensation opened the door to the memory of how she'd felt when "unmasked," and the humiliation rose again as strong as it had at the time.

She heard him moving closer, the splash of the water beneath his feet.

"What do you want?" Huntress asked, keeping her eyes straight ahead, and that wasn't enough because now she saw him at her right side, standing in her peripheral vision.

"Just taking a look around."

"You've been watching me for an hour." It wasn't a question, just a fact said to disprove the lie. "He send you to make certain I wasn't fouling up his plans any further?"

"No, I'm here on my own."

"Oh, so he let you off the leash, did he?"

Nightwing blew a sharp breath out his nose. "Didn't come here to mix it up with you, Helena. Just wanted to check out the situation, see how you were holding up."

"Never better."

"Glad to hear it."

"And how are you?"

"We're making do. The Upper East Side is secure down to the

Fashion District. Burnley's still a mess, but we're taking it a little at a time. Most of the gangs have given up on their territorial claims up there. Too busy trying to survive, you know how it is."

"Sure."

For a while they said nothing, just listened to the sound of the rain.

"Helena," Nightwing said softly. "I'm sorry about what happened."

"Don't be. It was my fault, I failed. I should have known better when I started, I'd never be able to do it his way."

"You've been doing it his way for months now. You didn't need the Bat for it."

She shook her head. "Is that why you're here? You wanted to apologize for your boss freezing me out?"

"You could have—"

"No, I couldn't have, and you know it." She turned to look at him. "Nice of you to stop by, but there was no need, okay? What's done is done."

He studied her, and even behind the lenses of his mask she could feel the look, and it made her tense, made her heart start bounding in her chest once more.

"You're not alone," Nightwing said. "That's all I wanted to say."

She watched him go, his graceful leap surefooted in spite of the rain, jumpline thrown, and then he was on the rooftop across the street, and then he was out of sight. She felt the rain drip down her neck, and it made her shiver suddenly.

"What do you know about it?" she whispered, and then continued watching the street.

Cassandra had been checking the MASH Sector as a matter of course, adding it to her rounds as Batgirl, on her own accord. She'd been working alone for most of the last couple of weeks, though sometimes Nightwing would join her in the late hours of the night, and they would patrol silently through those territories that now sported clean new bat-tags. Each night, if she was close enough, Cassandra would end with a stop by Dr. Thompkins's tent, silently looking in on Leslie. Oracle had explained the purpose of the mask

Cassandra now wore, that it was there to protect those she worked with as much as herself. There were people who knew the faces beneath the masks, Oracle had said, and those people could be trusted. But it was best to always be prudent, to avoid compromising the identity.

Cassandra had understood, and had been willing to accept whatever sacrifices were required for her new job. Still, when she had learned that Dr. Thompkins was one of the people who knew the truth, she had been relieved. She liked Leslie.

That morning, Cassandra found Leslie inside one of the tents, holding a baby. Two of the Blue Boys, Weir and DeFilippis, watched as Dr. Thompkins completed her exam.

"I'm happy to say that Justin is a healthy little boy," Leslie said, handing the baby to the man. "Even his weight is good, and frankly I'd have expected some malnutrition. I don't know how you and Chris did it."

"The old-fashioned way, doctor," the man said.

The woman, Christina, reached for her son, saying, "We had a lot of help. When Commissioner Gordon found out, he made certain that I was getting first crack at the food and supplies. Kept telling me I had to watch what I was eating."

Dr. Thompkins nodded. "You two are members of a very select club. With the addition of Justin here, that makes over thirty infants born during the No Man's Land, at least that I'm aware of. Yours is certainly the healthiest I've seen."

Cassandra watched as both parents beamed, then moved out of the way as good-byes were exchanged and Dr. Thompkins walked them out of the tent. Cassandra followed discreetly, watching as the parents and child joined a group of four other men and women, then left the camp, heading south. For a moment Cassandra considered following them, just to make certain that they would all reach their destination without trouble. But the sun was up now, and Leslie was coming back her way, extending a hand in greeting.

"Hello, dear," Dr. Thompkins said. "Long night?"

Cassandra nodded.

"Have you eaten? I was about to join Alfred for my breakfast."

Cassandra shook her head, indicating with her hands that she had to be going. Dr. Thompkins's face softened. Cassandra then pointed at the doctor, then used her hands as if cradling a baby.

"Do I have children? No, dear, I don't."

Cassandra walked with the doctor to Alfred's tent, where the old man was waiting with a pot of tea. He tried to offer Batgirl a cup, but she refused, again gesturing with her hands that she had to be going. Leslie gave her a hug before she left.

Cassandra was about a block out of the camp when she saw the group of men coming around the corner. The one in the lead looked kind of like a clown, and she was marveling at that when she realized he was also carrying an ax. Walking beside him was a woman, small and dressed in a costume all her own, different from the leader or the men who followed. She wore red and black and white, and her face was painted to look like a theater mask.

The men following, they all had clubs and axes as well.

She ducked into a ruined storefront, finding cover and watching the street as they went past. The clown was whistling, swinging his ax at the air as he walked. She could see from his grip that he knew how to use it as a weapon, not a tool.

Joker, she realized. That is Joker.

She slipped back onto the street, saw the mob moving away, heading straight for the camp. Cassandra looked up, checking the tops of the surrounding buildings, then used the line from her belt to get onto the nearest rooftop. She ran, moving to get ahead, but as fast as she went, Joker and the rest were already in the camp when she arrived.

They stood in a line outside of the largest tent, where Leslie tended the most injured.

"All right, you malingerers!" she heard Joker shouting. "Everybody up and at 'em!"

Alfred had already come out of his tent, Leslie just ahead of him, and from their expressions Cassandra knew it was bad whatever was about to happen, and she knew she had to do something. She had all sorts of things inside the belt Oracle had given her, tools for a situation like this, and without stopping she reached for the compartment at the left, dropping six of the tiny pellets held there into her palm. She launched herself off the rooftop, flinging them out and down at the line, and the rising sun made her shadow stretch on the ground beneath her, crossing Joker's men.

The pellets hit the ground, bursting with a sudden flash and bang, and as Cassandra landed she saw the line of men falling back slightly, stunned by the noise and light. She rose already in her turn, reaching for the nearest man, disarming him without stopping, then rising to face the rest. The girl with the painted face was tumbling at her, already almost upon her, and Cassandra was surprised by the speed with which she had responded. The girl threw two kicks, laughing, and Cassandra blocked both, then gave one of her own.

She was all the more surprised when the girl dodged it.

"That's enough, Harley!" Joker shouted.

Harley stuck her tongue out at Cassandra and moved back to where the clown was standing. The rest of Joker's men were recovering from the flash and smoke, but none of them were moving to attack.

Cassandra waited, wondering why they had stopped.

Joker moved forward, ax across his shoulder. "Right, well, hey," he said to her. "You look the same, but different. Long time. How you been?"

Cassandra didn't move.

"Oh, okay, so now you're coy, that's fine. Listen, Batgirl, no offense, but you're not the response I was looking for."

Cassandra tried to think of the best way to get the ax out of his hands.

"All right, fine, I understand. Second-stringers. Well, if that's how he feels, we're gonna forfeit the game, toots. Get it, got it? Good!" Joker turned around, motioning to his men. "He's fielding the substandard team, boys, and I'm not going to play that game. Let's go."

Dumbfounded, Cassandra watched as Joker and the others walked calmly away. She didn't understand. It didn't make sense. She didn't know what to do.

She looked at Alfred and Leslie, and both wore expressions much like her own.

Just didn't make sense.

She would try to ask Oracle or Batman about it later.

THIRTY-SEVEN

WHEN HE MOVED HIS HAND AWAY HE saw the coin was showing bad heads.

No two ways about it, Two-Face thought, and dropped over the wall into the garden. Beneath his feet, leaves from the plum tree crackled slightly, and that's when Gordon heard him, but it was already too late. Two-Face was on him before the Commissioner could speak, catching him by the hair and punching viciously, once, twice, three times. Gordon's glasses broke in the middle, the two halves falling onto the patio, and Two-Face kept punching until Gordon was limp, unconscious in his grip.

He rolled the Commissioner over and put the handcuffs around his wrists. Then he took the badge from Gordon's shirt and used it to weight the note he'd written. He left the note and the broken eyeglasses on the potting shelf, then hoisted the unconscious cop over his shoulder in a fireman's carry and moved back to the edge of the garden, crushing the dying tomato plants as he did. Quickly he heaved Gordon onto the wall, then followed up after him, dropping into the dark alley on the other side. He pulled the Commissioner back down, then threw him over his shoulder once more.

At the mouth of the alley, he took the radio from his pocket and switched it on. "TallyMan," he said.

"Boss?"

"Now."

"Gotcha."

Two-Face turned the radio off again, then dropped it to the ground.

He wasn't going to need it again, he knew.

However it was going to end, he knew it was over.

As the shots started echoing through TriCorner, Two-Face took his prisoner to the courthouse.

Garrett held the case and stood by the Penguin's side, waiting in the warehouse. They were surrounded by crates and crates, some of them, it seemed, stacked nearly to the rooftops, and all covered by tarps. He didn't know what was in the case he held, and although he was curious, it had been made clear to him that he wasn't supposed to even ask, let alone consider looking himself. That was okay, though; he'd gotten this far by not knowing too much, and the way Garrett figured it, if he kept it up, he might get out of No Man's Land alive.

At eleven exactly, at least according to the watch that Penguin had given Garrett, Miss Graves arrived. She came through the side door and emerged from between the stacks of crates, coming from the opposite side of where the oil lamp was burning atop one of the boxes. Even though the light was dim, Garrett could see that she was still dressed pretty much the same, and that made him glad. It meant he could get another look at those legs.

"Cobblepot," she said.

"My dear Miss Graves." Penguin reached for her hand and, as always, planted a slight kiss on the back of it. Garrett thought that

Miss Graves was maybe getting a little tired of Penguin always doing that. "A delight, as always."

"What did you want to see me about?"

"We have fulfilled our part of the agreement. Now it is time for you to fulfill yours."

"We honor our agreements, Mr. Cobblepot. Provided, of course, that you have done precisely as we required."

Penguin touched his breast with his left hand, as if he had just been knifed. "Dear lady! You wound me! Already you have moved over one hundred tons of material into my warehouses. Flawlessly executed deliveries, detected by no one—"

"You're certain of that?" Graves demanded. Her eyes were cold.

"Madam," Penguin said. "If the information has leaked, it has come from your own camp, not mine."

"You had better hope so."

Uh-oh, Garrett thought. That sounded like a threat.

He looked at Penguin, and from Penguin's reaction determined that, in fact, a threat was precisely what it had been. Penguin's smile vanished into a thin line. "Garrett, give her the case," he said.

Garrett offered the case to her, but she held out a hand for him to stop. "Open it first, please. I want to know what I'm carrying."

Penguin nodded, and Garrett flipped the attaché on its side, supporting it with one hand while he snapped back the latches with his other. Then he opened the lid and turned it, showing the contents to Miss Graves. The jewels inside shone in the lamplight. She reached into the case, sliding the contents about, and the sound of the metal and stones was soft and eerie.

"Fine," she said, and Garrett closed the case once more, then handed it to her. She looked at Penguin. "I'll have these sold immediately and the funds transferred to your Swiss account."

"I have evaluated the contents very carefully," Penguin said mildly. "Market value should fetch in excess of four point four million dollars. Any less transferred to that account, and I shall hold you responsible."

"You won't be shortchanged. Good night, Mr. Cobblepot."

She left the way she had entered and didn't look back.

Penguin sighed. "Garrett, my lad, I think I'm in love."

"She's, um . . ."

"Hot."

"Hot, right. Hot."

There was a noise from above them and Garrett looked up,
thinking that the last time he had heard a noise like that he'd gotten
pretty badly beaten up by Batman. Then he thought that if he hadn't
thought that, maybe it wouldn't be Batman coming to beat him up
again, but by then it was too late and Batman had, in fact, landed
right in front of them, and already had Penguin by the front of his
fancy coat.

"Garrett!" Penguin said.

Oh, nuts, Garrett thought, but he knew who paid his bills, and so
he took a swing, tried to make it a good one.

Batman didn't even move, and for a second Garrett thought that
he might get away with it. Then he got hit in the side with a kick,
and when he pulled himself from the warehouse floor he saw that
Batman hadn't arrived alone.

"Don't get up," Nightwing told him, sounding surprisingly
friendly. "It's really not worth it."

"Call him off, Oswald," Batman said. "Or else you might get
hurt."

"That's enough, Garrett," Penguin said quickly.

Garrett nodded, massaging his sore ribs. Nightwing was leaning
with his back against the crates, looking at him almost apologetically.

"Let's talk, Oswald," the Batman growled.

"Now, my masked friend, I really do not think we have anything
that needs discussing."

Batman lifted Penguin off the floor in one move, placing him at
eye level on a nearby crate. With his free hand, Garrett saw the
Batman grab the nearest tarp and yank it down. Revealed in the
lamplight was a gigantic cement mixer, like the kind used at major
construction sites.

Garrett stopped rubbing at his ribs for a moment, staring in
stunned silence. He didn't know what he'd thought Miss Graves was
moving into the No Man's Land, but he was certain he'd never considered she might be into cement mixers.

"Who is she?" Batman demanded.

"No idea," Penguin said quickly.

Batman leaned in closer, and Garrett heard the solid thud of Penguin's back hitting the crate hard. "I'll ask once more, Oswald."

"Batman, please . . . I think you'd agree that my business is my own? This really doesn't concern—"

"The case Garrett gave her. I know what was inside it, Oswald. I know she's your pipeline out." He adjusted his grip on Penguin, lifting him off the crate and holding him a good three feet off the ground. "Now I want to know what she's bringing in and why. I want to know who she is. And I'm losing my patience."

"She's never given her name as more than Miss Mercy Graves," Penguin said in a rush, his legs working in the empty air, trying to find purchase. "For the last thirty days or so I've been assisting her in moving large quantities of various materials into these warehouses, as you can see. Construction supplies, mostly, easily one hundred tons so far, and more is on its way. She and her employer are planning on some large scale urban renewal, I believe, and—"

"Batman," Nightwing interrupted. "Transmission from Oracle."

"It can wait."

"Two-Face is attacking TriCorner. The Blue Boys are losing."

For a half-second longer, Batman kept his grip on Penguin before letting it go, dropping the man to the floor. Garrett looked quickly to see if Penguin was all right, then turned to try to find Nightwing and Batman again.

But they were already gone.

"We've just been upstaged," Penguin explained.

The fighting woke her, and Detective Montoya fumbled out of her bed and into her clothes, racing onto the street in time with the rest of the bungalow, nearly jamming up on DeFilippis in the doorway while trying to get outside. Gunfire echoed dangerously nearby.

"That Kelso?" DeFilippis asked.

Montoya nodded. "Stay with Chris, I'll find out what's going on."

She started running up the block, hoping that she wouldn't trip and fall on her untied shoes, had made it to the next corner when she heard Bullock shouting her name. She skidded to a stop.

"Essen wants you!" Bullock shouted. "The Commish is gone

and there was a note, something. She wants you at the house right now!"

"What the hell is going on?"

"Looks like Two-Face's boys have popped a gasket, they're attacking every checkpoint. We're gonna have to fall back." He spat the stick from his mouth. "Go! Essen is getting frantic."

Montoya headed the other way, racing to the house. The gunfire was more sporadic, and she hoped that meant that Two-Face's men were low on ammunition, or even out altogether. She doubted any of the cops had rounds left. When Pettit had abandoned them, he'd taken what remained of their bullets with him.

Essen was in the doorway, and she pulled Renee into the front hall, pressing a piece of paper into her hand. "Read it," she said, then moved back to the window, checking the street.

The paper was crumpled and dirty and hard to read in the darkness. She smoothed it against her palm quickly, trying to make out the words.

It read—

I've got Gordon.
If Montoya isn't at the courthouse at dawn, he dies.
—Two-Face

"What the hell?" Montoya asked.

"I don't know and I don't care," Essen said quickly. "And I don't know what else we can do. I can't and won't order you to go, Renee. There's no guarantee that this isn't his game to get two hostages instead of one."

"But if I don't . . ."

"Yeah, I know."

"You need me here."

"One person isn't going to make much of a difference at this point. Two-Face doesn't have a lot of men left, but if they're armed, we're going to lose this fight anyway. You being here means one more person dies instead of maybe two more people living if you go."

"I'm not leaving you."

"I said I wouldn't order you, Renee." Essen turned to face the detective. "So I'm going to ask. Please. If you can save Jim, do so. Whatever has got Two-Face so fixated on you, whatever it is that went down all those months ago and brought Cain to town, let this end it. Please, let this end it."

Montoya felt the paper in her hand crumpling as she made a fist. The gunfire had stopped for the time being. There was no noise from outside, and above the line of broken rooftops, she could see the hints of color playing on the edge of the night sky.

"I'll go," she said.

THIRTY-EIGHT

THERE WAS NO ONE GUARDING THE territory as Renee Montoya made her way to the courthouse off Civic Plaza, and the first rays of sunlight were shining in the cold, damp morning as she climbed the steps. She could still smell the fire from over a month back, when the Hall of Records had burnt down. The doors to the courthouse were wide open, and the foyer was empty.

Montoya stood for a couple of seconds on the broken marble floor, looking around her, then shouted, "I'm here!"

Her voice echoed through the halls of justice with no answering response.

After another second's pause, she started up the stairs, making for Judge Halsey's chambers. The door was unlocked, and when she pushed it open the room was much as she had remembered it. She stepped inside, checking the corners, feeling the nervousness inside her blossoming into a much greater fear.

The door at the other end of the chambers opened, and Two-Face entered, carrying a bundle of clothes in his hand. He stopped when he saw her, and Montoya watched as the two halves of his face warred with one another for expression. The scarred side looked as if it loathed her; the unmarked half looked overjoyed.

"Renee! You came, I'm so glad."

"I had to," she said, trying to keep her voice strong. "You didn't leave me much choice."

"I'm glad anyway."

"Where is he, Harvey?"

"Jimmy? He's fine, don't worry about him, he's not dead yet."

"Yet."

"Well, he hasn't been convicted yet, so killing him before the verdict, that's premature."

"It's . . . premature?"

"We're going to have a trial, Renee."

"A trial."

"Yeah. Jimmy's the defendant. You're gonna be the bailiff." He tossed the bundle onto the couch. "Put those on and we can get started."

She stared at him, then at the clothes.

"I'll wait outside," Two-Face said, and slipped back out, shutting the door behind him.

Montoya spread out the bundle, and confirmed that, in fact, she was looking at a bailiff's uniform. She glanced back at the closed door, hesitating, the idea of undressing in the chambers suddenly far more frightening than anything else had been before it. But there really was no other option, and she recognized that. Even as she stood there, staring at the clothes in her hands, she knew that Blue Boys were fighting and dying in TriCorner. The only chance she could see was to play along with Two-Face, to try to get him to call off the offensive. Maybe she could save the Commissioner. Maybe she could save Essen and Bullock and DeFilippis and Weir and . . . so many people, and if this was the only way . . .

She undressed quickly, feeling horribly exposed, then pulled on the uniform. It was clean, but a little big, and when she tucked in the shirt, the tails almost touched the tops of her knees. She fastened the belt, then the tie around her throat, then the shoes. As she was getting the hat settled on her head, there was a gentle rap at the door.

"Ready?" Two-Face asked.

"Ready," she said, wondering what she looked like. There were no mirrors anywhere.

He opened the door for her and she exited, and then he began walking with her down the hallway.

"Looks good on you."

"Thanks."

"How have you been?"

"I've been better, Harvey."

He laughed softly. "Yeah, I'm sure you have. Me, too, actually. Me, I've been a lot better. That maggot Bane really punched my ticket. Got nothing left. Of course, that's when people get the most desperate, so it all works out in a way, I suppose."

His tone was staying the same, level and conversational, but Montoya heard the current beneath it, the voice of Two-Face rather than Harvey Dent trying to reach the surface.

"Why am I here, Harvey?" she asked. "I don't understand what it is you're trying to do."

"I told you already. We're going to have a trial. I used to love the law."

He stopped suddenly, and Montoya saw that they were now outside of one of the criminal courtrooms on the second floor. Two-Face reached to open the door, then stopped, frowning. His voice was much softer when he spoke again.

"You're here because you're a good cop. You're here because I wanted to see you. This is about what Jimmy did, Renee. This is about what I did, Renee. Justice must be served. Revenge must be had."

He put both hands to his head, briefly, as if fighting a sudden and savage migraine, then turned the knob and threw open the doors. It was one of the courtrooms that Montoya had testified in on numerous occasions, and she took it all in almost on instinct. The galleries and public seating were a mess, the benches broken and overturned, some crushed by pieces of the ceiling that had fallen during the quake. Beyond the gate, though, where the defense and prosecution tables stood, it was a different courtroom—clean, polished, and swept. Even the jury box looked to be in good order. At the back of the room, opposite where they had entered and behind where the judge would sit, a cracked relief of Justice hung on the wall, split almost perfectly down the middle.

No wonder he likes this room, Montoya thought.

Sunlight was falling through the missing eastern windows, and dust floated in the air.

At the defense table, Commissioner Gordon sat in cuffs, dressed in an orange convict suit. On the back of the jumpsuit was stenciled the Gotham City Department of Corrections logo, and then the letters GCDC-PRISONER. TallyMan stood beside him, his revolver leveled at Gordon's head.

"Commissioner," Montoya said, moving forward, past Two-Face. He didn't try to stop her, and she knew that was because he had nothing to fear. She didn't have a gun and she hadn't bothered trying to bring a knife. There was no way she was going to fight her way out of this, and he knew that.

Gordon turned his head to her, and she saw the bruises on his face, the dried blood around his nose and mouth. His glasses were gone, and as a result of that, or the beating he had obviously received, his eyes seemed to have difficulty finding her.

"Renee?"

"I'm right here, sir," she said, coming through the gate and then crouching at his side. Beyond his shoulder she could see TallyMan giving her a look she'd have paid for a chance to shove back down his throat. "Are you all right? Do you know where you are?"

Gordon nodded vaguely. "Two-Face explained it. Said there was going to be a trial. My trial."

"That's right, Jimmy," Two-Face said, moving to the prosecutor's table. From his pocket he removed the coin, setting it on the wooden surface with a solid click. From beneath his arm he removed his automatic and set that on the table, too. He focused on Montoya. "Bailiff, please take your assigned position."

Montoya rose and glared at him. "No," she said, her anger giving the words fuel. "No, I won't help you, Harvey. This is sick. This is evil, and there's no point. You've already found him guilty, this is just a sham—"

"Bailiff!" he growled, and there was no mistaking which of his two voices was now in control. His right hand went to the butt of the pistol, fingers wrapping around it, still keeping it on the table. "Take your assigned position or I will hold you in contempt."

"No! No, I don't want to play your games!"

"This is not a game, Detective Montoya!" Two-Face was almost spitting, and she could see his fingers turning white from the strength of his grip around the gun. "This is a matter of justice!"

"You've already reached a verdict. This is a show-trial, nothing more."

"This is an impartial proceeding! You don't believe that?"

"No, I don't."

He grabbed the coin off the table, showing it to her, eyes flaming. He brought the gun up, pointing it at the floor. "I'll prove it to you. TallyMan?"

"Yeah?"

"You kill anyone today?"

"Couple cops."

"How many?"

"Three, I think. Well, maybe only two."

"Fine." Two-Face looked pointedly at Montoya, then back to TallyMan. "You're charged with two counts of murder in the first degree. How do you plead?"

"Uh . . . "

Two-Face pointed the automatic at TallyMan. "How do you plead, TallyMan?"

"Not . . . uh, not guilty. What are you doing, man? This isn't—"

"Shut up!" He flipped the coin, catching it in the same hand and then showing his open palm to Montoya. "Which is it?"

She looked at the scarred face of the coin in his palm and felt her mouth go dry. She didn't want to say anything, knew there was nothing to say.

TallyMan, apparently, did too, because he didn't speak either. He tried to bring his gun up to shoot Two-Face, and then there was the report, horribly loud in the open courtroom. TallyMan's head snapped back and he staggered, still on his feet, unsteady and already dead. Against the far wall, sticking to the faded mural of Gotham City circa 1730, Montoya saw the splash of blood.

TallyMan hit the ground and didn't move again.

"Bad heads," Two-Face said. "Guilty."

Montoya looked down at TallyMan, then at where his gun had skidded beyond the gate, resting in the shadow under one of the benches. No way to reach it without getting herself and the Commissioner killed.

"Bailiff," Two-Face said gently. "Please. Take your assigned position."

Gordon whispered, "Do it, Renee."

She shook her head once more, but moved all the same, crossing to the witness stand and standing between it and the jury box. Two-Face smiled. Gordon didn't move.

"Good," Two-Face said. "All rise. Court is now in session."

Gordon, the only person actually seated, struggled to his feet.

"In the matter of the people versus James W. Gordon, the charges are breach of contract, negligent homicide—multiple counts—and dereliction of duty. A plea of not guilty having been entered by the defendant, I have set a trial date for now. The defendant will note, if found guilty the sentence will be death.

"Death to him, to his family, and to all those under his protection.

"As there is no jury sitting for this trial, no opening statement is required.

"The prosecution then calls its first witness, Gotham City Police Detective Third Class, Renee Montoya."

He motioned with the gun for her to take the stand and, casting another glance at Gordon, she did. The Commissioner was glaring at Two-Face, jaw clenched shut.

"State your name for the record."

"You know my name, Harvey," she said.

"For the record, if you please."

"Renee Montoya, GCPD Detective, Third Class."

"What the hell are you trying to prove, Harvey?" Gordon asked suddenly, voice rising.

"Order in the court!"

"Dammit, no! You're going to kill us both——"

"This is going to be a fair trial!"

"Right," Gordon said, rising, almost spitting in his anger. "Fair. You'll kill me, you'll kill her, you'll kill my wife, my people——"

"You broke the law! *Your* law, Jimmy! Guilt must be punished——"

"And innocence?" Montoya asked.

Two-Face and Gordon both looked at her.

"If he's found innocent, then what happens, Harvey?" she demanded.

Two-Face shrugged. "He's free to go, of course. His wife, his family, his sector, all free."

"Not good enough. What about me?"

"Renee . . . " Two-Face began.

Montoya cut him off. "You let me go. And you turn yourself in. You surrender yourself to our custody. That's fair."

"I'm on trial, too?"

"You know exactly what you've done," she said.

Two-Face looked at the coin, then back to Montoya. He nodded. "So be it. May we proceed?"

Gordon reluctantly took his seat once more. Two-Face approached the witness stand, the gun in one hand, coin in the other.

"Detective Montoya, how do you know James Gordon?"

"He's Commissioner of Police. He's my boss."

"And how long have you known him?"

"Little under four years."

"Is he a good boss?"

"The best."

"So you like working for him?"

"I do."

Two-Face turned back to the defense table, leaning down to put his ear near Gordon's. "You can object any time you like, Jimmy," she heard him saying.

"Will it do any good?" Gordon growled.

"It might." He straightened and moved once more to Montoya.

"Detective Montoya, please describe your relationship with James Gordon."

Montoya almost threw up her hands in frustration. "For crying out——"

"*Answer the question!*" Two-Face screamed.

It took Montoya a couple of seconds before she could recover her voice. "He's my boss," she managed. "He's—"

"Boss?"

"—my friend, I—"

"Friend?"

"Objection!" Gordon shouted.

Two-Face grinned, still looking at Renee, and she could see it in both eyes, he was having the time of his life; so far, he was having a blast.

"Good call, Jimmy," he said, and then he flipped the coin and read the result quickly. "Overruled."

"Of course," Gordon muttered.

"Let's continue," Two-Face said. "We've got a lot to get through, Detective."

It was almost comical it was so surreal, Montoya thought. Out beyond the courthouse, her friends were fighting and dying, and here she was in an all but destroyed courtroom, playing lawyer with Harvey Dent. And the greatest irony of all was that Harvey Dent was a good lawyer. A damn good one.

He was suave and quick and charismatic, split personality and deformity notwithstanding. Montoya had been cross-examined by the best in her years on the force, but never by an attorney like Harvey Dent. One question and then another, and suddenly the whole line had turned and she would find herself out on a limb, having said something she'd had no intention of sharing with him at all.

Because what Two-Face was after was really very simple. He was after the truth. He wanted only for her to confirm that Gordon had sent her to him and asked for his help.

"You disapproved of his sending you to talk to me?" Two-Face asked.

"Yes."

"Why?"

She hated herself for saying it, knowing it would give Two-Face exactly what he was looking for, but it came out anyway. "We're cops. You're a criminal. Working with you is morally and ethically wrong."

Two-Face nodded sagely. "It is, in fact, illegal. Did you want to talk to me?"

Montoya hesitated, swallowing. He was switching back and forth too fast for her to keep up with now, and she was certain the next question, the next answer would be the one to send him careening over the edge.

"Detective?" Two-Face asked. "Answer the question, please."

"No," she admitted.

"Why not?"

"You scare me."

That stopped him midpace, as he was facing the box full of imaginary jurors, and he swung his head around to look at her, and she didn't know what to make of his expression or the look in either of his eyes.

"What?" he asked, and it wasn't his lawyer voice, it wasn't his madman voice, it was . . . just a man, she thought.

"You scare me," Montoya repeated.

He looked at her for a long while, for over a minute, and still she couldn't make out his expression and she was afraid to say anything more. Finally he turned back to the jury box, waving in her direction with the gun in his hand.

"No further questions," he said softly. "You can step down, Detective Montoya. The people thank you for your testimony."

He returned to his table and took his seat, putting his head in his hands. Montoya left the witness stand, and for a moment didn't know what she should do. She could see where TallyMan's gun still lay on the floor, hidden beneath the benches. Gordon was squinting at her.

She moved toward the defense table and Two-Face, without looking up, said, "Where are you going, bailiff?"

Montoya stopped cold. "I'm not certain where you want me. . . ."

The coin in his hand seemed to shiver with the strength of his grip. He was almost whispering, his voice hoarse, when he said, "Resume your assigned position." Then he cleared his throat, straightening in his chair again, adjusting his tie. "The people call James W. Gordon."

Gordon took the stand.

. . .

"You were responsible for the people of this city!" Two-Face said. "You set events in motion, Commissioner!"

Gordon didn't move, glaring at the figure in front of him, trying to focus. His head throbbed, his bones hurt, and every moment he stopped to actually think about what was happening beyond the courtroom, his insides seemed to melt into some sickening mixture of guts and heart.

Sarah, he thought. Oh, God, Sarah.

"You abused your office, your power, your command! You broke your agreement with Two-Face. You refused aid to Two-Face when he called upon you, when he begged for your help while under attack by Bane! How many men died because you refused to honor your agreement? Can you even answer that question, Commissioner?"

Gordon shook his head, and it struck him then that there was a method to the madness, a truth to it beyond, perhaps, what even Two-Face imagined. Maybe he deserved to be on trial.

He had caused men to be murdered. He had given orders sending others to their deaths, in the name of his quest, his belief that Gotham could be saved, if only by his will alone. Even now, all those men, all those women, even the children—and he thought of Chris and Andy and Justin—were in peril, maybe dying, maybe already dead.

All because of his decisions, his choices, his actions.

Pettit was right, he thought. I'm too soft for the No Man's Land. I still have a conscience.

He looked at Two-Face glaring back at him, and all James Gordon could think at that moment was that, indeed, an accounting was required. And if his was to be now, then that was, perhaps, as it should be.

"You're guilty as sin, Gordon," Two-Face was saying. "And you know it."

Gordon watched the other man return to the prosecution table, smiling smugly.

"I rest my case." Two-Face raised the coin in his hand, looking over it at him and Montoya. "Don't think we're going to need this to determine the verdict, huh?"

Gordon saw the gun coming up, blurry in his sight without his glasses, and he thought that he was sorry he hadn't said farewell to

Sarah and Barbara, and that he really had left a hell of a lot undone and unsaid in his life. He heard Two-Face say the word "guilty" and he expected the bullet, and then Detective Renee Montoya, dressed as a bailiff, was in front of him, shouting.

"No! You can't do this! You can't do it like this, Harvey!" she was saying. "What about his defense? He's entitled to a defense, dammit!"

Dent shook his head, and Gordon thought he sounded almost sad when he said, "No defense. No one to speak for him, Renee."

"He can speak in his own defense," she retorted.

"Can't do that. He's not a lawyer. I'd have to declare a mistrial."

"Then I'll do it."

"Same problem, Renee," Two-Face said, raising the gun again.

"You can't do this! You told me you loved the law, Harvey! How can you pervert it this way? In this courtroom, in Judge Halsey's chambers, how can you do this? Don't you see?"

He stopped once more, and the look he gave Montoya was sorrowful, and Gordon saw that Dent honestly couldn't see another option. "No one can speak for him, Renee. Don't you understand?"

"You can," Gordon said. "I want Harvey Dent to defend me."

The shock rode across both sides of Dent's face like a searchlight ranging the night sky. "Dent? For . . . the defense?"

"You have to, Harvey," Montoya said. "You're the only one who *can* defend him."

Two-Face looked from Gordon to Montoya and back again, the conflict raging in his expression. He stepped back, eyes frantically searching the courtroom, and then he remembered the coin in his hand, and without another word, gave it a toss.

It was the longest coin toss of Gordon's life; it seemed that the silver half-dollar danced through the air forever, audibly flipping end over end. The sun gleamed off the good head as it crossed the shaft of light from the window, and for a moment the polished side threw a reflection against the face of Justice on the wall. Then Dent's hand had closed around the coin once more, and his fingers were coming apart, and he was reading the result, and there was no expression on his face, none at all.

Then he pointed the pistol at Gordon again and Montoya started to open her mouth, but Two-Face said, "You may step down, Commissioner."

He lowered the gun, staring at the coin in his hand.

"Harvey?" Montoya asked.

Dent shook his head, waiting for Gordon to move from the witness stand. Montoya saw him struggling to get up, moved to help him, and her hands were sure on Gordon's arm, and she guided him back to the table. It was easier this time, Gordon thought. He was getting more steady on his feet.

"The defense calls its first and only witness," Dent said. "Two-Face."

Gordon and Montoya watched as Dent took the stand, seating himself, the gun still in one hand, coin in the other. He surveyed the room, and for a long moment there was nothing else, no noise, no motion, just Dent on the stand and the two police watching him.

Then Dent shut his eyes and put his hands to either side of his head. Very faintly, they could hear his voice, barely make out what he was saying.

". . . did it you did do it you blackmailed him you did do it . . . did not no . . . yes did you did, you did . . ."

And then he fell altogether silent, and the only sound in the courtroom was the creak of the chair as Two-Face continued to rock gently, back and forth, on the stand.

Montoya quietly moved away from Gordon's side, stepping over TallyMan's body. She retrieved the dead man's revolver, checking the cylinder, then giving Gordon a nod. There were rounds still live. She searched TallyMan's body, finding the keys to the handcuffs, and quickly unfastened them from Gordon's wrists.

"Go," she said softly. "I'll wait here."

"I'm not leaving you alone," he whispered back.

"Go. Find out if your wife and Bullock and the others are still alive. I'll be okay here." She looked at where Dent was fighting his own madness, and Gordon saw the compassion on her face, and he thought that she was a hell of a good police, that she could care so much for someone so insane. "He won't hurt me."

Gordon turned, making his way to the doors quietly.

Just before he stepped out, he heard Two-Face's voice, almost a child's sob.

"The defense . . . rests . . . not . . . guilty . . ."

THIRTY-NINE

 HALF BLIND, HALF NUMB, AND ALMOST out of his mind with the lurking fear that it was too late to do anything, James Gordon ran for his home. On Schnitzer Avenue he took a bad spill, catching the edge of a pothole, and his right ankle, unable to support the sudden shift, went out from beneath him. He shredded the left forearm on the jumpsuit, felt the burn and sting of the abrasion. Still, he got up and kept moving.

The smell of smoke was strong as he hit the bridge, and he barreled past the Kelso Blockade, certain that the only reason he wasn't seeing the bodies of his people was that his glasses were gone. Coming down Bonafe he saw three buildings in flames, the fires in their dying stages. One of the buildings, he knew, had held twenty of their population, all gathered together under the same stable frame. In the winter, the building had been insulated, and kept them warm.

He realized it was raining, but he kept running.

There were no guards outside of his home, not a cop to be seen anywhere on the street, and he stumbled through the open doorway, his lungs raging for air, and when he tried to call his wife's name he broke into a coughing fit that left him doubled-up. He tried again anyway, wheezing it.

"Sarah! Sarah!"

There was noise from the garden, the sound of a door opening quickly, and he turned toward it, lurching down the hall past the pictures on the walls. There was the blur of a shape and then he saw that it was her, and he felt the relief whip out of him, and he said her name once more, falling into her arms.

Neither of them could speak for a minute, and neither of them wished to.

"Jim," Sarah finally said in his ear. "Oh, I was so worried, I thought I'd lost you for good."

"No," he said. "No, never, never lose me. Never."

He broke out of the hug long enough to look at her face, now close enough to see her clearly. "Two-Face . . . he lost it . . . just, lost it completely. . . ."

She was nodding. "I know. I know. But . . . Renee? Is she all right?"

"She's fine, she's still with him, she's . . . I'm sure by now she's put him under arrest, probably has him locked up in the holding cells. We'll need to send people over there, to help her, before more of his men get back. If we still have people. If we . . . how many did we lose, Sarah?"

She started smiling, pulling him toward the garden. "None. We won."

"My eyes aren't any good, don't tell me my hearing has gone, too."

"Your hearing is fine, Jim. None. We didn't lose anyone." She slid the door back, guiding him through the opening. "We had some help."

Gordon came down the steps, then stopped. The garden was full of people, and without his glasses it was difficult to distinguish the faces. Bullock was there, and DeFilippis and Weir and Leonhardy, and others, the two boys who'd shown up so many months ago, Paolo and Nicky, the Cassamento family, who had been in TriCorner for three generations and who sure as hell weren't planning on leaving just because the government had told them to do so.

But those weren't the shapes, the blurred faces that stopped him.

It was Batman.

And Robin.

And Nightwing.

And a woman, a woman dressed as Batgirl.

Sarah was behind him, and she said, "They came as soon as they heard."

Batman moved forward.

"All right," Gordon said. "Let's talk."

Night was falling before everyone had left, by which time Gordon had changed his clothes, cleaned his wounds, and found his last spare pair of eyeglasses. Word had come back from Bullock that Montoya had Two-Face in custody, and that City Hall could now be added to their list of territories. The rest of Two-Face's mob had dispersed, and Gordon presumed that the other vigilantes were taking care of that business while Batman waited for him in the garden.

Sore and stiff, the Commissioner went back outside, and when he saw that Batman was still there, the anger he'd been carrying, the anger he'd thought he'd finally lost, came back.

Someone had lit a fire in the barrel, setting it in the middle of the patio, and the flames made Batman look alternately more demonic and more human, depending on their cast. He had turned when the door opened, and Gordon descended the stairs knowing he was being watched. But Batman's expression stayed as impassive and unknowable as ever, and that only gave the anger in Gordon's gut another push.

He sat on the bench, easing his sore body down, trying to keep the weight away from his right ankle. The pain in his body had diffused, moved to claim whole territories, as if it, too, had learned the law of the No Man's Land.

Batman didn't move, watching him.

I'll be damned, Gordon thought, if I'm going to speak first.

For nearly an hour they said nothing, each man putting their eyes anywhere but on one another. The fire crackled in the barrel, the flames dancing, occasional sparks fluttering skyward into the clear early winter night.

"Your garden," Batman finally said, and Gordon saw that he was cupping a chrysanthemum gently in the palm of one gloved hand. "You've done a fine job with it."

Gordon nodded, heard himself saying, "We had some trouble in the summer. An infestation in the vegetable bed." He indicated the bare spot of earth by the back door, feeling his shoulder throb with even that slight movement. "Had to tear everything out to keep it from spreading. Saved some of the crop, though."

After a second Batman said, "That's good."

"We got some nice carrots out of it," Gordon said. Then he added, "Tomatoes, too."

Batman nodded.

Gordon sighed, removed his glasses, rubbing the bridge of his nose. In a way, he thought, it was like trying to talk to his first wife when they both knew the marriage was ending, and neither of them had been willing to concede that divorce might be an answer. The anger was abating again, but he knew it would be back, and he knew that, at least for him, at least then and there, it was not only justified, it was righteous.

Batman had let him down. Batman had betrayed his trust.

He put his glasses back on, sighing without meaning to, saying, "It's been a long year."

"It has," Batman agreed.

There was another silence.

"Jim," Batman began, but stopped when Gordon cut him off.

"Are we friends?" Gordon asked, looking at him. Where Batman stood beyond the barrel, the light made the ears on the cowl look as they were designed to look, like the horns of a winged demon. Even the lower part of the vigilante's face looked supernatural.

"Yes," Batman said. "We're friends."

Gordon thought about that. "Damn odd. I don't . . . I don't have many friends. I don't have many people I trust. But I trusted you."

Batman didn't move. Nothing on his face changed but the fire-light.

"I trusted you," Gordon repeated, louder, getting to his feet. The chill had caught him, and the fire was warm, and he moved closer to it for the heat. "You saved my wife and protected my people. I'm grateful for that, don't think that I'm not."

He thought he saw Batman nod, just barely.

"But that's not enough," Gordon said. "You say you're my friend. But I don't think you really have friends."

Again, there was no answer. Gordon could feel the gaze on him, though, knew he had his attention, that Batman was listening, and would continue to listen. He looked down at the fire, used it to warm his hands. He'd scraped his palm when he'd fallen, and the heat felt surprisingly good.

"When the NML was announced, Sarah and I tried to leave," Gordon said softly. "A moment of weakness, of fear. I wanted to run away, find a job in some other town where I could do what I do best, where my wife and perhaps my daughter, too, could be a little safer. I tried to abandon the sinking ship."

He looked up from his hands. "Everywhere I applied I was turned down. It wasn't that I was asking for much, mind you. Not like I expected to be Chief of Police in Dallas or Commissioner in Central City, nothing like that. I'd have taken a detective job if it'd been offered. I was that scared. That desperate.

"No one would hire me. They didn't want a cop who needed an urban legend to do his policing for him."

He looked back at his hands, almost smiling at the memory. Batman remained still.

"They laughed at me. Some of them were kind enough to do it to my face. Most did it behind my back. And I started to wonder, after a while, if maybe you were laughing at me, too."

"No," Batman said.

"Really?" Gordon leveled a finger at him. "You use me. You've been using me for ten years."

Batman's voice was tight. "Or vice versa."

Gordon grinned. "Absolutely. Because I thought we wanted the same thing. I thought we wanted our city—this city—to be safe. That's what I thought, Batman. I thought we were in this together."

Again, there was no response.

Gordon suddenly felt the anger erupting, and he almost shouted it, demanding, "Where the hell were you?"

No answer, no response. Not even the slightest change in his features but those caused by tricks of the light.

After a minute, Gordon said, "That's why I don't believe we're friends. You don't respect me. You don't trust me. That whole fiasco a couple years back, after Bane had been to town and all those rumors were circulating that you'd been defeated, broken. And you vanished, and I had to deal with that parade of pretenders under that cowl, what was it, two of them? Did you think I wouldn't notice? Did you really think I was that stupid?"

"No," Batman said.

Gordon came around the barrel, moving his face in close. The firelight reflected in his lenses. Batman met his gaze without hesitation.

"You have your secrets," Gordon said. "I've never pressed you for them, never. Maybe I should have, instead of letting you turn me into your . . . your . . . whatever it is you see me as."

The edge of Batman's mouth turned down, and Gordon realized that he'd hurt him, finally, without meaning to, and for a moment he didn't know what to think, what to feel.

"You're my partner," Batman said.

Gordon started to laugh, turning away and putting the distance between them once more, feeling the heat from the fire fading. The breeze bit at him through his shirt.

"Don't blow smoke at me," he said.

"It's true."

"It's what you'd like to think, I'll accept that. But that doesn't make it true." Gordon spun back, suddenly furious. "Partners are equals, Batman! When have you *ever* treated me as your equal? Partners tell one another their plans. Partners keep each other informed. And they sure as hell don't walk out on you in the middle of a sentence!"

Batman's head turned away, slightly, as if he was looking into the fire. Gordon caught his breath again, feeling his lungs stinging once more from the day's exertion. The scent of the smoke was sticking in the back of his throat.

Then something in Batman's posture shifted, and Gordon saw it and for a moment couldn't think of a way to explain it or define it or even name it. It was as if the vigilante, the demon at the fire, had suddenly shrunk, and for a clear moment then James Gordon saw absolutely the man beneath the cape and the cowl, the man who had fought on Gotham's streets, every night it seemed, for over ten years. Gordon saw the pain that drove him, and he saw the loss.

"I've . . ." Batman began. "I've never been good at saying goodbye."

Gordon found himself without words.

Batman kept looking into the fire. "You're the best cop I've ever known. And I've known a lot of cops, Jim. There's no man or woman living that I respect more than you."

He turned once more to face him, and Gordon saw the posture shifting again, the man resolved to action.

"But as you said, saying so isn't enough. The words don't mean anything. They don't fix the damage. They don't rebuild the trust. Actions speak louder than words, and my actions haven't spoken to you at all. That's my fault."

Gordon realized what Batman was doing a second after the motion started, saw the vigilante's hands coming up to his cowl, the fingers slipping beneath the edge of the mask. He knew the rest of the action then, he knew what would happen next, and he turned away, and put his back to the other man.

There was just the sound of the fire. And then Batman's voice, and it was different, softer. "Jim."

Gordon shook his head, saying, "Put it . . . put it back on."

"It's the only thing I can give you other than my word," Batman said softly. "When the world abandoned Gotham . . . I had to find my reason again, my purpose."

Gordon shut his eyes.

"I need our partnership," Batman continued. "We can save Gotham. We're so close, Jim. We can bring it back from the edge. This is the only thing I can give you. Me, my identity."

"I don't want it, dammit!" Gordon said. "If I wanted to know who you were, I could have discovered it ten years ago. And for all you know, maybe I did. Maybe I do know. But that's not the point.

"Put it back on."

He heard nothing from behind him, just the crackling of burning wood. He opened his eyes, looking at the back door of his house, the reflection of the fire in the glass.

Gordon turned around, taking his time, and when he saw Batman, it was with the cowl back in place and the man he knew and had known for over a decade again standing before him. The relief replaced the remnants of the anger.

"You need my help, huh?" he asked.

"You and your people's."

"Figured it wouldn't be just me alone. We should plan."

"Tomorrow. Sunset?"

"Here?"

"Agreed."

"I'll be waiting," Gordon said.

Batman nodded and headed for the rear wall, Gordon watching him go. But Batman stopped before ascending, turning to look back.

Gordon thought he might even be smiling.

"Have a good night, Commissioner," Batman said.

"You, too, Batman."

Then he was over the fence, and Gordon was alone again in his garden, warmed by the fire.

PART FOUR

ORACLE

P E R S O N A L
Entry #631—NML Day 310
1953 Zulu
Italics indicating entry amended on NML Day 364—2333 Zulu

Dear Dad—

The end of No Man's Land.

I'm still not certain when Batman saw it, when the pieces locked together in his mind and the plan took its final shape. He must have had doubts, he must have wondered if it was going to work at all, but you could never tell it from looking at him, you could never tell it from what he said. Even when events began accelerating, even when the media descended and the construction started and Gotham burst to frenetic, crazed life, he remained as staid and steady as before.

It was as if he had known all along, as if there had never been the slightest doubt. And maybe he did see it all.

All of it save for one thing. The one thing none of us could have anticipated.

We didn't know what it would cost us.

. . .

Dear Dad—

It started with a phone call, Lucius Fox trying to reach Bruce Wayne and dialing the number for Bruce's personal assistant, Melinda. The call originated in D.C., and Fox thought he was calling Melinda in Kingston, Jamaica, and the signal bounced back into the States, through another three routers, before it even reached the Clock Tower. I was finishing the file upload with Tim when the phone started ringing, and for a moment we both just sat there, trying to figure out what that damn noise was.

Then it hit Tim, and he shouted, "Phone!"

I whipped the chair around, checked the incoming signal, then booted my program for Melinda's voice. When I answered, Lucius came over the speakers, loud and clear.

"Melinda Beaumont," I said.

"Melinda, Lucius." He was in a hurry, nearly breathless. "Is Bruce there?"

"You know better than to ask that, Mr. Fox," I said. "I'm really not sure where he is right now. He had a one o'clock tee-time, so I assume he's on the green now."

"Can you page him?"

I laughed.

"Right," Lucius said. "What was I thinking? All right, tell him that I've got news, big news. It's not over yet, not by a long shot, but we won our suit in Federal Court. He'll want that explained, but the quick version is—"

"The No Man's Land has been found unconstitutional," I finished. "Took them long enough."

"That's it, that's right. And yes it did. The government is, of course, appealing the decision, planning to take it to the Supreme Court, but that's really not important because what I'm holding in my hand right now is a message asking me to be at the White House in twenty minutes. The President wants to meet with the coalition leaders to talk about an exit strategy for the NML."

I tried not to cheer.

"Can you get the message to him, Melinda?" Lucius asked. "I know Bruce will be over-joyed. If all goes well, he'll be back home by Christmas."

"I'll send someone out for him now," I said. "Thanks, Mr. Fox, that's great news."

His sigh made the speakers crackle. "Not over yet," he repeated. "But we're close."

I hung up, turned to Tim, who was grinning ear to ear. He gave me five and did a little dance in the Control Room, ending with a whoop, fist in the air.

"What are you celebrating?" I asked. "We've still got work to do."

So we went back to it.

That was the start.
Like I said, we didn't know how it would end.
And I can't stop crying, Dad. Typing this now, and I can't stop crying.

FORTY

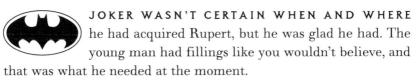

JOKER WASN'T CERTAIN WHEN AND WHERE he had acquired Rupert, but he was glad he had. The young man had fillings like you wouldn't believe, and that was what he needed at the moment.

"Too many sweets when you were a kid, eh, Rupert?" Joker said.

Rupert nodded and made a gurgling noise. Joker grinned and put the tinfoil antenna in his mouth, then walked around the man, positioning his head and arms for the best reception. Harley had found the pocket television who knew where, and they'd taken the batteries from some kid's Game Boy. The television worked, but finding a signal was proving to be a real pain.

It was, in fact, Harley who had suggested that they make an antenna, but it had been Joker's idea to use Rupert.

Satisfied with the work, Joker went back to his La-Z-Boy and sat down, motioning for Rupert to raise his right palm, where the television was now resting. Joker grunted and sank back in the chair, scratching his nether regions, feeling that the gesture was appropriate. Yes, he was surrounded by a group of violent and antisocial thugs who would do his bidding with but a word, and yes, this was no living room he was in but rather an abandoned slaughterhouse, and yes, Harley was a far cry from Donna Reed. But there was nothing more satisfying in Joker's mind than sitting back in a comfy chair to watch the television after a long day's work looking for people who needed a good killing.

The reception, however, wasn't all he had hoped for. "Harley," Joker said. "Change the channel."

She bounded out from the area she had claimed as the kitchen, still in her harlequin costume but now wearing a yellow and pink floral-print apron. "Anything you need, Puddin'," she said, bending in front of the television and turning the tiny dial. She waggled her rear at Joker as she did so.

"Stop there, on the news," Joker said.

Harley did as asked and backed away, beaming. Then she slid around to behind the chair and began running her fingers through his hair. Joker thought that ignoring her for the time being was the funniest response, and so he focused on the small screen.

They'd picked up NewsChannel, in the middle of a broadcast from Washington, D.C., and on the screen a thirty-something black woman was speaking to the camera while standing outside of the Capitol. A caption on the screen said that her name was Laila Illes, and that she was "live."

Joker thought that was a riot, and started laughing so hard he almost missed the good bit.

"Word tonight in a shift on the government's No Man's Land policy," Illes was saying. "Seen by detractors far and wide as a dramatic failing of American domestic policy, the decision to create a federal No Man's Land around the remains of Gotham City over ten months ago has been called everything from misguided to downright unconstitutional. In the wake of the ruling by the Seventh Circuit Court of Appeals, a new groundswell of support has arisen, with congressional leaders and members of both houses suddenly inundated with calls, E-mails, and letters demanding swift action."

The signal started to fade, and Joker nearly lost the last part of what Illes was saying. He motioned Harley forward again, to stand by Rupert and adjust the cant of his head. The signal got somewhat better, but not much.

". . . closed-door sessions at the Capitol tonight and rumors of meetings at the White House. We'll be following this story . . ."

The signal went out again, but Joker no longer cared. News was, for the most part, not funny and quite boring, unless it was about ethnic cleansing or people acquiring anthrax. He sprang up from the chair, looking at the gathering of his boys, almost all of whom were ugly as sin and bright as mud.

"Who wants to watch *The Punkmatics?*" he asked.

Harley squealed in delight and began jumping up and down, saying, "Me! Me! *Meee!!!*"

He turned to give her a punchline, but Rupert then dropped the television, setting up a much better joke.

Joker looked at the man, the tinfoil antenna still in his mouth, his neck tilted back, his arms still extended. The tiny television was shattered at his feet.

All of his boys were dead silent.

Joker grinned at Rupert. "Hey," he said, crouching to begin cleaning up the mess. "Accidents happen, right?"

Rupert nodded, still afraid to take the now-useless antenna from his mouth.

Joker picked through the broken television until he found what he wanted, a nice sliver of the broken screen, almost an inch and a half long. He picked it up gingerly, clapping Rupert on the back with his other hand, then waggling his eyebrows in a Groucho Marx fashion at his boys. They were his audience, after all, and even though it was a small turnout for such a good show, they deserved his best efforts.

You had to treat the audience with respect, Joker knew.

"We were watching that, you know, Rupert. And poor Harley, she was really looking forward to *The Punkmatics* and everything." Joker pushed Rupert's head level with his empty hand, forcing him to look at where Harley was sobbing uncontrollably, using the corner of her filthy apron to wipe her eyes.

Rupert made a noise around the antenna in his mouth that Joker took to mean he was sorry.

"Oh, I am, too, Rupert, I am, too. But the problem is, now we have no entertainment for the evening, and after Harley went to such trouble to make dinner." Joker gestured to the food that Quinn had spent the last two hours carefully burning to an absolutely inedibly charred state. "And you know how girls get."

Rupert barely nodded, eyes wide with fear.

"So now we have to come up with another show. Any suggestions?"

Rupert made a muffled sound, one syllable and pathetic.

"Kill you?" Joker exclaimed. "That's a *great* idea!"

And so he did.

"You assured me there would be no mishaps," Miss Graves said coldly.

"You had my assurances, indeed," the Penguin answered smoothly. "But a woman such as yourself knows that there are no guarantees in life. Even less so when there is a Batman lurking in our midst."

Garrett said, without thinking not to, "You got that right."

They both looked at him as if he'd just taken a leak on their shoes.

Miss Graves sighed, taking another long look around the warehouse. "It's ultimately irrelevant, I suppose," she said. "We've accomplished what we set out to do. Secrecy is no longer vital."

Penguin perked up. "May I infer from that statement that your employer will be arriving shortly?"

"You can infer what you like, Cobblepot. Our business here is complete. Thanks for your assistance."

Penguin gave her his most charming smile, which Garrett thought really only made him look all the more like a short fat round guy with a long beaky nose. "My dear, I'd hate to think our association was to end on such a sour note. Perhaps there are other services I can facilitate for you and your employer? Certainly, if I have divined the situation correctly, there will be a need for . . . security, shall we say? I can provide you with guards for those locations you choose, at a reasonable price, to boot."

She sighed, then made a slight gesture to the open warehouse doors, as if beckoning someone inside. "That won't be necessary, Mr. Cobblepot," she said. "As you can see, I have taken care of that myself."

Bane came through the door, walking calmly to Miss Graves's side.

Garrett thought he heard Penguin swallowing, but he might have missed it, because his heart was beating awfully loudly in his ears.

"Is there a problem?" Bane asked, softly.

"I don't think so," Mercy said mildly, not looking away from Penguin.

"Yes, well," Penguin began, then stopped, then coughed discreetly into his hand. "Have a very pleasant day, Miss Graves. Garrett? Let's retire."

Garrett thought about saying that he was only twenty-eight and really didn't think he was in any position to retire, but Penguin had already started moving out of the warehouse. Garrett caught up to him quickly, and they left without looking back.

"Big things are afoot, my lad," the Penguin said as they began walking back toward the Davenport Towers. "Great doings, indeed."

"Yeah, something's definitely up," Garrett agreed.

Penguin chuckled. "I smell an opportunity, and I have an idea. Get ten of our lads, Garrett. I've a special task for you and them."

Garrett had a thought, then, one that came upon him suddenly and surprised him with its insistence. He puzzled at it for a while, walking with Penguin in silence. At least, Garrett was silent; Penguin began talking about Miss Graves, describing her in detail.

"Mr. Cobblepot, sir?" Garrett asked just before they arrived back at the Davenport.

"Yes, Garrett?"

"You, uh . . . you're not planning on, like, trying to horn in on Miss Graves's action, are you?"

Penguin smiled broadly, in some surprise. "Garrett! You're learning! And here I'd thought you'd remain a Neanderthal forever!"

Garrett didn't smile at the compliment. "Maybe that's, um, a bad idea, Mr. Cobblepot, sir."

Penguin's smile disappeared and he poked a long and bony finger at Garrett's middle. "Leave the ideas to me, Garrett. You're not equipped for thinking."

Garrett had to admit that was true.

But the thought kept nagging at him, anyway.

Miss Graves changed while Bane kept an eye on the door, stripping between boxes in the warehouse and then putting on her suit. She took a certain amount of pleasure in putting on the clothes, not because she found them more comfortable or even more functional —in point of fact, they really weren't; the skirt, though it came to her lower thigh, was tight enough that it restricted some movement, and the black nylons inevitably ended up torn. But they were what her employer had picked out for her to wear, from the under garments to the accessories, and he was not a man to be argued with, and she understood, in part, the purposes behind it.

The first was, simply, the statement. Image was everything.

Second, it was about control.

She understood these things, and since she liked her job and was honestly happy in it she didn't complain. Unlike most of the people in her employer's organization, she had his ear, and he would listen to her. For that reason, she chose her criticisms very carefully, loath to abuse the privilege.

She tucked in the white silk blouse, then pulled on the black waistcoat, buttoning it completely to her throat. She stepped into the shoes last, then smoothed the lines of the fabric with her hands. The cap she left off—it was a beacon, and she wouldn't wear it until he had arrived.

Putting her overcoat back on, she took out the last accessory for the outfit and gave it a thorough, but quick, examination. Although he had chosen it for her, she had to admit she agreed with the decision. The pistol was small and sleek and as black as the clothes. She screwed the matching silencer onto the barrel, then slipped the gun into the customized holster at the small of her back. The holster had been made to accommodate the weapon with and without the added silencer, as well as to conceal the pistol perfectly against her body.

It was unspoken that she was always to look her best in his presence. Unsightly lumps beneath her clothing were unforgivable.

Finished, she joined Bane at the door, saying, "You're to stay out of sight, is that understood?"

"Perfectly."

"There will be media, a lot of them. If you show up on camera we will disassociate from you. It will void the agreement with my employer."

Bane let out an exasperated sigh, then said, "You do not need to concern yourself with me, Señorita Graves. I think I have proven already that I know what I am doing, and that I know how to do it."

"You have, and my employer commends you for it. But neither he nor I wish to see anything compromised at this late stage."

"Your *employer*," Bane said, pushing the word with something close to mocking, "has nothing to worry about from me."

"I'm delighted to hear it." She adjusted her coat once more, tucking the hat beneath one arm. "I'll contact you when you're needed."

"I look forward to it."

From his perch fifty yards from the warehouse, Nightwing watched the woman leave. Bane stayed in the doorway for a moment longer, then went back inside, shutting the sliding doors behind him.

Nightwing keyed his commlink. "Oracle, she's on the move."

"Gotcha. Batman says to follow her but to be discreet."

"Am I ever anything but?"

She laughed. *"You're asking the wrong person. He's the guy you have to please, remember?"*

"Don't I know it. I'm moving."

"Be advised, I'm hacked into the National Guard Air Network, and I've got five incoming. ETA looks like about twenty minutes. National Guard has already warned them off."

Nightwing didn't immediately respond, vaulting from the ruined rooftop he was running across down to the ground, using a sagging awning as a breakfall. "Likely to shoot?"

"Doubt it. They know who the passenger is."

"Keep me posted."

"Will do. Oracle out."

He'd lost sight of her for a couple of seconds, and he put on some extra speed, tumbling expertly from the awning and then springing up through the open side of another broken warehouse. The smell of the ocean was strong even though he was still fifteen blocks away from the water. The sky was clear and bright and cold.

He saw her again coming off Moldoff, making for Grant Park, and after another block he was certain that was her destination, but then she stopped and Nightwing thought, for a moment, that she had seen him shadowing her. But she didn't look back, and though he couldn't see her expression, he sure could read her body language, and she was pissed.

He raised his eyes and looked in the direction she'd been facing, saw that in the park ahead of her there were ten men or so working in a group. He instantly recognized the short man supervising them, without needing to see the nose or monocle to make certain he was right.

He keyed the commlink again. "Oracle. She's headed for Grant Park. Penguin's there."

"Stand by," Oracle said.

He used the opportunity to vault to another rooftop, then ran the length, leapt, ran, and leapt again until he was atop the building closest to the park. The last leap nearly cost him, though. As he came down he could see that a portion of the roof had given way. He twisted in the air, came down on his hands and sprang up over the gap, feeling the boards beneath his palms cracking and giving way. He landed on his feet, crouching near the edge, hoping that the rest of the rooftop wouldn't collapse. It wasn't the fall that worried him; he fell as a matter of course, had done so since before he could walk. It was the noise. He didn't want to give himself away.

Oracle came back on his commlink. *"Boss says that Grant Park is the most viable landing site, probably will be used as the base camp. As for Penguin, he doubts Cobblepot was invited to the party. Says to stay out of it unless it gets really ugly."*

"Confirmed."

Somewhere across the city, he could hear the sound of helicopters.

. . .

Mercy Graves III swore under her breath when she saw him, contemplated shooting Penguin and his subordinates then and there, but then decided she wouldn't have enough time to dispose of the bodies before the media arrived. She continued forward, one hand still holding the cap, the other thrust deep in her overcoat pocket. She moved the cap from beneath her arm to the inside of the coat, where it could rest against her belted middle. There was a pass-through in the right-hand pocket, designed to allow her to reach under the coat while it remained closed, and this she did, pulling the pistol from its holster, keeping it against her leg, hidden, as she approached.

Penguin's primary buffoon, Garrett, saw her first, and she gave him marks for that. He at least knew how to keep his eyes open.

"Shake a leg!" Penguin was telling the working men. "We're on a schedule here!"

She stopped behind him, nodding slightly at Garrett, then taking in the action before her. Penguin had ten men working the park, hastily pruning back bushes and sweeping the old paved paths, raking at the piles of dead leaves that had fallen from the trees. One of the men was even repainting the park benches.

She felt herself getting angry.

Garrett nudged Penguin, and he turned, looking up at her and beaming. "Darling!" Penguin exclaimed. "Just lending a hand. Hoping to greet the employer fortunate enough to have you."

He reached for her left hand, and she saw again the lascivious leer, and she kept her face blank and let him take it. When Penguin kissed her hand, he moved in closer than he had in the past, bolder. She thought he smelled vaguely of fish, but knew it was just her imagination.

He lingered over her hand, looking up at her after pecking it. "Don't suppose you would consider working for me, my dear?" he asked sweetly, and she supposed that he imagined that it sounded seductive.

Again she had to fight to keep her expression blank, because in truth, the offer made her want to laugh. If he truly knew who her employer was—and she had no doubts now that he did—he was deluding himself willfully. All Penguin could offer her was modest money and meager power and, potentially, the promise of whoring herself. None of these interested her. She was richer already than he would ever be; her power was far more pervasive than Penguin imagined, and what she could not influence, her employer could, without so much as leaving his office; finally, her body was, and always had been, her own. No man had access to it, and no woman. Her employer understood that, and respected her for it.

"I can offer you many perks," Penguin said, still holding her hand.

She sighed and moved the gun from against her side to level with her hip, which put the barrel just above Penguin's collarbone. Garrett hadn't even realized what had happened until after she'd begun speaking.

"Get your men out of here right now or I'll kill you," Graves said. Not a threat, she was careful with her tone. A simply factual recitation, but not a threat. If not A, then B.

Penguin dropped her hand and looked up at her, and she saw that the lust had gone from his eyes and that he was now smiling at her almost dopily.

"You're perfect," he said. "You know that?"

She almost smiled. She wasn't, in fact, perfect.

But she was damn close, and she knew it.

Penguin backed away, looking at Garrett, still smiling. "A change of plans," he said, mildly. Then he raised his voice, shouting to the others. "The lady has asked us to leave, gentlemen! Let us depart in haste!"

He offered her a small bow, and with Garrett at his side, left the park, the rest of the men following, carrying their tools with them.

She could hear the helicopters, and she moved to the edge of the clearing, standing on the wet grass, unbelting her overcoat. She slid the gun back into its holster, returned her cap to beneath her arm, and looked up, tracking the progress.

There were five of them, four news copters led by one that she recognized, gleaming white and slightly larger, and even in the air it made its intentions known. The downdraft from the blades buffeted her briefly as the helicopters flew over, and then the lead bird began to hover, turning in the air until it faced her. She began moving toward it even before it settled onto the ground.

The other copters were landing too, but being far less ceremonial about the procedure, which didn't surprise her. She could see the markings on the different helicopters, WGBS, WGMC, CNN, NewsChannel, and with the blades still turning their doors began sliding open, reporters and camerapeople pouring out, busily setting up their shots.

At the white helicopter, she opened the front passenger door, acknowledging the pilot with a brief nod of her head, then removing her overcoat and laying it properly on the seat. Then she shut the door and moved alongside the passenger's compartment.

She put the chauffeur's cap on her head and gave her waistcoat one last tug, just to assure herself that she looked as she should.

Then she slid the door open and offered her hand to the passenger, saying, "Welcome to the No Man's Land, Lex."

"Mercy," Lex Luthor said, climbing out of his personal LexCorp chopper. His smile was small, and his eyes gleamed, and she knew he was pleased with her work. He looked good, too, his tailored suit making him appear even stronger and fitter than Mercy knew he was.

Luthor waited until Mercy had slid the door shut, turning his bald head slowly, taking in the park. The media began heading their way, already shouting for comment.

"Lex! Lex—"

"—government approval of your presence—"

"—LexCorp's involvement will be—"

Luthor's smile grew, his public face settling comfortably into place. "Well, Mercy," he said. "Are we ready to rebuild Gotham City in our own image?"

"Yes, sir," she said, and she was smiling, too.

"Then let's get started."

ORACLE

PERSONAL
Entry #692—NML Day 327
2046 Zulu

Lex Luthor.

The richest man in the world.

Founder and CEO of LexCorp.

If people have totem animals, then Luthor's is the great white shark. He has that same focused intensity, the same directed purpose. He is power personified; the power of money, of business . . . and of greed.

Living in Metropolis, controlling his empire from "the City of Tomorrow," he had always found Gotham beneath his notice. But suddenly he was here, in person. Suddenly Metropolis's second-favorite son was standing in front of the cameras, a champion of Gotham City, a foe of the No Man's Land.

Within twenty-four hours of his arrival, Luthor had transformed Grant Park into his base of operations, with over two hundred LexCorp personnel arriving and nearly twice that number in support services. They flew in on helicopter after helicopter, bringing equipment and people, and the flights continued throughout the night and into the next day, with more and more arriving from outside the No Man's Land. They built tents, including an executive Quonset hut for Luthor himself, and a huge military-style one they labeled HUMAN RESOURCES. They brought medical supplies and food, gasoline-powered electrical generators and construction equipment from bulldozers to backhoes. They erected huge arc lights to illuminate the surrounding area, and LexCorp security patrolled the grounds, armed with MIGs and .45s.

The media dubbed it Camp Lex, and they were eating out of his hand.

The day after Luthor arrived, he held a press conference, which he started by reading a statement he had prepared.

"The No Man's Land is a disgrace," he told the cameras, and his righteous indignation transferred perfectly through the medium. "An embarrassment, a betrayal of the fundamental precepts this country was built upon! To deny citizenship, existence even, to our own people is nothing less than criminal!

"For the better part of a year politicians have squabbled and lawyers have debated. They've squandered time and resources, spending more money to justify doing the *wrong* thing rather than simply making it *right!* And all the while, the soul of Gotham—its people—suffered."

He paused, giving the cameras a good beat with which to zoom in for a close-up on him or to swing around for reaction shots. He was selling it beautifully. I watched on my A/V monitor, using my NewsChannel hack to pick up the live feed; even I believed it, and I knew what he was really up to. But Luthor was that good, that charismatic and that passionate, and the fact was, people wanted to believe him. They wanted to believe they were doing the right thing. If he was taking the lead, giving them a chance to feel good about themselves, they were going to jump at it.

"Well," he said, after a weighty pause. "LexCorp says enough is enough. We have committed ourselves to rebuilding Gotham City. Starting today.

"Starting now."

There was a round of applause, loudest from the LexCorp employees gathered there. When it died down, Luthor started taking questions from the reporters, picking out the ones he wanted to answer from the barrage being thrown his way.

Wasn't what LexCorp was doing illegal, someone from CNN asked. *After all, entering the No Man's Land was a criminal offense, wasn't it?*

"I will not be beholden to an immoral law," Luthor answered, and again he played his righteous indignation card, and again it trumped everyone watching. "Nor should any of us be. This is a government that listens to the people, is it not? The No Man's Land is *wrong,* it is as simple as that! I will not stand idly by while my fellow men and women suffer and die. It's time for us all to speak out, to stand up, and declare that we want what is right. If that's criminal behavior, then, yes, I've broken the law. If the government wants to press charges, they can talk to my lawyers."

That got a minor round of applause and some laughter. LexCorp's legal division is well known for its hardball tactics, after all. Messing with them would be like walking through Arkham dressed like . . . well, Batman. Asking for trouble.

But there was more to it than that, more than most of the media knew; like the fact that Luthor had dozens of politicians in his pockets, and literally hundreds more who owed him favors. Like the fact that Luthor wasn't above blackmail as a business tactic, and either had, would find, or could make, dirt on anyone who proved a problem for him. And the media didn't know that he used these tactics as a matter of course.

Another question. This one about jobs and construction, referencing the Human Resources tent that, by observation alone, was signing up over one hundred people an hour to the LexCorp payroll. The cameras showed the long line of Gothamites approaching the tent entrance, the queue ranging out of the park and stretching for several blocks, men, women, even some children, entering in their filthy rags and with hope in their eyes.

And out the other side of the tent they came, now with a pair of new coveralls, a yellow hard hat, and a bag of winter clothes and food, proud new members of the LexCorp family.

"We will employ anyone who wants to work, within reason, of course," Luthor told the media. "We're here to give them the tools and support they need, nothing more. It's their city, after all."

Follow-up question, from NewsChannel. *What do you get out of this, Lex?*

Luthor laughed. "Are you kidding me? Aside from the benefits of helping my fellow man, even *I* can't buy this kind of PR!"

They all loved that, and it ended the press conference on a big laugh, with the cameras centering once more on the reporters, now all smiles and jokes. *No Man's Land, what's the big deal? And that Luthor, ain't he a hoot?*

Gimme a break.

"He's spinning it as a humanitarian gesture," I told Batman when he stopped by the Control Room that evening. "Which I suppose is the best way to play it. I've hacked the newsfeeds for Metropolis, Chicago, and New York, and the PR value is stunning. It's every network's lead story. They're all rushing to get their best correspondents into the No Man's Land and on the ground. The public support has been overwhelming. They're calling him the millennium's greatest philanthropist."

"Good, it should keep him busy so the real work can get done," Batman said. "Bruce

Wayne spoke with Lucius Fox earlier today. Apparently, the President is willing to consider reopening the city if certain criteria are met."

"Those would be?"

"Infrastructure and basic services need to be restored to a quarter of the island before the government is willing to allow people to return to residency. The Army Corps of Engineers, in concert with LexCorp, Wayne Enterprises, and a handful of other major businesses, will spearhead the rebuilding."

I grinned. "That's good news."

"They're setting a deadline. If the city cannot meet the standards the government sets by New Year's, Gotham will remain closed. If it can, New Year's Day will see the official end of the No Man's Land."

"You don't look happy about it."

"Still a long way off." He tilted his head to the nearest terminal. "Have you uploaded?"

"Tim and I still need a little more time. Give us a week."

"Robin's going to be busy."

"Doing what?"

"Surveillance."

"Then it's going to be more like two weeks before I'll be ready to send the files out."

"No. Wait."

I tried to hide my confusion. "Why?"

"Minimum exposure. The records need to be kept secret until I need them. I'll let you know."

"I live to serve."

He looked at me sharply, then muttered something about Alfred. I hid my grin behind the monitor.

"Joker," he said. "Where is he?"

"I don't know."

He positively scowled. "He's being very quiet."

"Maybe he's occupied."

"No. He's waiting for an opportunity. Have your Eyes keep a special watch out for him. His encounter with Batgirl and Leslie has me nervous. He's getting impatient. He's going to lash out soon."

"Will do. Where are you off to?"

"To pay a visit to the great philanthropist."

FORTY-ONE

HUNTRESS STOOD ON THE ROOF, LOOKING at the distant glow of Camp Lex as evening began to fall. Clouds were rolling in off the Atlantic, pushing cold air ahead of them, and she expected there would be more rain that night, if not snow by morning.

She heard the door behind her open, and the footsteps approaching, and then Foley, saying, "Thought you'd be up here."

"I was hoping to be alone."

"Bill wants to talk to us. About the Luthor thing."

"Tell Commandant Pettit that I'll be down when I'm damn good and ready," Huntress said, without looking away from the lights.

Foley didn't say anything, but he didn't go away, either. She tried to ignore him.

"I think Bill's losing it," Foley said.

The admission, not the statement, caught her off guard, and for a brief second she wondered if this wasn't some sort of test on Pettit's part. Send Foley up to talk to Huntress, see what she says, see if she's still with us. But when she looked at Foley's face she could see the sincerity there, the honest concern, the nervousness. Foley wasn't a good liar; his intentions always showed on his face.

"Don't get me wrong," Foley said, misinterpreting her look. "All the people here, we've got three hundred plus people living in this sector, and they're safe and warm and . . . he's kept them safe, you have to acknowledge that, you know? He's kept *us* safe."

Huntress looked back at the glow to the east. Where the sun would rise, she thought. Camp Lex, Gotham's sudden sun.

"I don't know if I trust him anymore."

She turned and started toward the door, and after a second Foley followed, anxiously.

"You're not going to tell him what I said, are you? You're not going to do that? Huntress?"

"I'm not going to tell him anything, Foley." She stopped outside the door, not yet opening it.

"I'm telling you because I thought you'd understand, I thought you'd seen it, too." He searched her face for a confirmation, a hint of some validation from behind her mask.

"I've seen it, too," she said, softly. "And he can't know that, can't know that either of us think this."

Foley nodded, agreeing. "You're the only one left that I've got any faith in, Huntress."

Somehow, it didn't make her feel much better.

She sighed, then said, "All right, let's go see the General."

"They can't just walk away from us!" Pettit shouted. "Not after all we've done for them!"

Then he picked a box of ammunition off the desk and threw it at the wall, sending the rounds bouncing everywhere in the room; the sound of the brass pinged off the furniture. Huntress moved her left hand to her right wrist, just assuring herself that the launcher was still there, where she wore it, for the comfort of knowing. It was there, but it didn't help.

She, Foley, and Pettit were in one of the apartments in the building, the one that Pettit had dubbed as the armory. There were guns everywhere, pistols and rifles and submachine guns and boxes and boxes of ammunition. A variety of military equipment was scattered about as well, helmets and jackets and vests.

"Luthor is offering work and shelter, warm clothes, money," Foley said, trying to soothe Pettit. "They're responding to that, to the chance to rebuild their homes. You can't blame them, Bill."

Pettit muttered something, spinning to put his glare on Huntress. "This keeps up we're going to have no one left!"

"Calm down, Bill," Foley urged.

It was the wrong thing to say, and Huntress actually saw Pettit's face turning a shade of crimson before he rounded on Foley. "Who the hell do you think you are, telling me to calm down? How many walked out on us yesterday, Hugh? Do you even know that, can you give me that figure?"

"Only fifteen, but—"

"Only? That's thirty hands just went AWOL, Foley! You damn fool!"

"You can't blame him for that," Huntress said. "They heard about Luthor, they went to go take a look."

"We're talking about *our* people here! Am I the only person who gets that?"

"Right: *people*," Huntress said sharply. "Not prisoners."

"You don't get it." Pettit moved to the desk. "We're a unit, Huntress. We rely on one another. When people walk away like that, they weaken the whole, they reduce us, our strength, our capabilities."

"They'll be back by nightfall, I'm sure," Foley said.

"They want to live, they had damn well better be!"

He went out the door with a slam.

Huntress looked at Foley, and knew that she was mirroring the expression on his face.

He's losing it.

Luthor enjoyed his meal alone in his personal hut, dining off bone china laid out upon a linen tablecloth over the oak table he'd had flown in and then assembled that morning. The meal was prepared by his staff chefs and served to him by Mercy while he read the latest edition of *The Financial Times*. He started off with a 1929 Château d'Yquem with which he chased down his foie gras. He followed the appetizer with a half-bottle of Montrachet, of which he had only one glass with his arugula, goat cheese, and walnut salad, by which time he had finished reading the first paper and had switched to *The Daily Planet*. His main course, over the newspaper, was a top sirloin cut of Waygu beef encased in cracked black pepper, and served beside a mixture of miniature vegetables with grilled polenta, which he savored with a glass of bordeaux, the 1929 Château Petrus. When he had finished the newspaper and the meal, he had a final dish of mixed cheeses—Camembert, chèvre, and a Stilton—served with an assortment of biscuits, fresh fruit, and bread. He closed the meal with a small glass of a 1962 Taylor Fladgate.

As he sipped the port he said, "Update, please, Mercy."

She responded immediately. "The surrounding twenty blocks have been secured per your order. South to Andru, east to the water, north to the Sprang river, and west to Goodwin Boulevard. The perimeter is secure, and we have twenty additional LexCorp guards in plainclothes patrolling the immediate area around the park."

"Continue."

"Cobblepot has repeatedly expressed a desire to do business with you, although I have explained the situation to him *twice* already. He is nervous about losing so much of what he perceives as 'his' territory to you. I can send Bane to talk to him, if you think it's necessary."

Luthor took another sip of port, then gestured Mercy over. She produced the humidor and opened it, and Lex took his time in selecting his cigar, finally deciding upon a hand-rolled H. Upmann, made especially to his standards in Havana, Cuba, with a fifty ring-size. Mercy cut the cigar, then handed it back and provided the flame.

"What do you make of him?" Luthor asked as he got the cigar going.

"Cobblepot?" Mercy seemed surprised at the question. "He wants to be you, Lex. He doesn't understand that he never will."

Luthor blew out a column of smoke. "As long as he keeps out of the media spotlight, we'll let him play. Soon as he steps too far, he and I will talk. What else?"

She replaced the humidor on his desk. "We signed up four hundred eighty-eight laborers in the last twelve hours, all of whom will be joining the major workforce at first light. By tomorrow night we'll be ready to have work crews running twenty-four hours a day. Finally, NewsChannel reported this evening that, according to their latest polls, public opinion has swung twenty-three points in your favor. Margin of error for the poll is plus-or-minus five, as to be expected. Not coincidentally, LexCorp stock jumped twenty-six points."

Luthor smiled around the cigar, leaning back in his chair and folding his arms behind his head. "Excellent, Mercy. You may turn down the bed."

"Certainly, Lex."

He watched as she cleared the table, taking the half-empty wine bottles and dirty dishes outside, returning in under a minute to prepare his bed. She took the leather easy chair by the foot of the bed, turning it so that she faced the entrance to the hut, drew her pistol, and then sat, waiting.

He took his time with the cigar and the port, thinking, and acknowledged that he felt quite good about the last couple of days. His people in Washington had confirmed that an executive order was forthcoming that would allow entry to the Army Corps of Engineers and the business coalition, and he had no doubts that the New Year's Day deadline would be reached. Gotham would reopen on schedule.

His Gotham.

After finishing the port, he switched on his laptop computer and skimmed the enormous volume of E-mail that had been forwarded from his Metropolis office. It took him roughly half an hour to reply to those that warranted his immediate attention; the rest of the mail he bounced to the appropriate subordinates with a note saying that he was not paying them so that he could do *their* work. He logged onto the Nikkei Index next and tracked stock movements for another ten minutes, more for the entertainment value than for any need to increase his own wealth.

Then he was ready to sleep. He changed into his silk pajamas—just the bottoms, he never wore the tops—stripping down and then pulling on the pants as if Mercy wasn't there. It was the way it was done, the way it had been done every night since he'd hired her. For a brief time his vanity had plagued him, and he wondered why she didn't want him. When he realized she didn't want anyone, instead of seeing it as a challenge, it had come as a comfort. No one would ever be able to blackmail or influence her with sex. It made him all the more certain he had been right in hiring her.

"Lights, Mercy," he said, slipping between the sheets and shutting his eyes.

"Good night, Lex," she said softly.

He heard the click and felt the lamps switch off.

Then he slept.

What woke him was a nightmare speaking his name. His heart racing, he opened his eyes to see the shape at the foot of the bed, looming over him, and he started, first upright, then back against the headboard.

"Luthor," the shadow said. "Let's talk."

It was then that Luthor realized who it was, and he glared at the Batman, then looked past his left to where Mercy was in the chair, unconscious. He looked at the Batman, who was returning his glare without the slightest hint of intimidation.

"I hope you didn't hurt her permanently," Luthor said. "Good help is very difficult to find."

"She'll live."

Luthor swung his legs out of the bed, reaching for the robe draped over the footboard. "Delighted to hear that," he said, getting to his feet. He pulled the robe on, then faced the Batman and glared into the hidden eyes. "Is there a point to this visit, or are you just planning on looming ominously at me all night?"

The Batman's mouth did something that Luthor suspected might be a sneer, and he took a step closer, moving in complete silence. Luthor met the stare and held it.

"I know what you're planning," Batman said. "You're not in Metropolis now. This is my city."

"For now," Luthor said. "I'm here on a humanitarian mission, vigilante. Unless you can prove otherwise?"

Batman smiled but stayed silent.

"You're bluffing. If you had anything you wouldn't be here

threatening me." Luthor could see the easy chair past the Batman's shoulder, Mercy beginning to stir.

The Batman moved another step closer, and there was no space between them. Luthor still didn't look away. In his peripheral vision he could see Mercy quietly getting to her feet.

"This is not a threat, Lex," the Batman said. "This is a warning. You don't want me to take you out. And your bodyguard there doesn't want to start anything."

"Don't bother, Mercy," Luthor said, and he made what he felt was his only mistake in the conversation then, because he looked to her when he said it. She nodded and Luthor saw another motion from the corner of his eye, turned back to address the Batman, and saw that he had vanished.

Utterly.

He didn't get back to sleep that night.

FORTY-TWO

JOKER SWUNG THE SCYTHE AT BATMAN'S
head, screaming his frustration at the top of his lungs.
The blade cut neatly just above the cape, and his follow-
through almost hit Harley, but she ducked and bleated, "Yeep!"

Joker watched as the head bounced off the racks of costumes on
the far wall, spurting stuffing, then hit the floor and came to a stop.
Several of his boys were apparently very interested in something on
the floor. He looked back at the remains of the costume display—and
it wasn't a nice display, it really didn't look a thing like Batman at
all—and felt himself coming over all teary-eyed. He dropped the
scythe and threw an arm around the costume dummy's shoulder,
whispering where the ear would have been.

"I just don't know what to do to get your attention, I just don't know what to do, Bats. You don't come out to play, you're not around, it's like . . . it's like you're ignoring me. All I ever see are your brats, the second-stringers, the wannabes. Ratgirl and the Boy Blunder and that other one that no one knows the name of."

"Nightwing," Harley offered.

Joker kicked her in the shins without looking, still speaking to the imagined Batman. "I'm starting to take it personally, I really am, and I know I shouldn't because I know that personally you just wouldn't take anything anyway, not even from me, but, really, just look at the situation here. What am I supposed to think?"

The dummy remained strangely silent.

"You're *useless*, you know that?" Joker told the dummy, turning and brandishing the scythe at his gathered boys. "I ask you, what do I have to do to get some attention in this burg?"

Now his boys were *really* interested in the floor.

"Well?" he demanded. "Criminy jeepers here, kids, gimme something!"

The boys were as silent as the decapitated dummy.

Joker turned away in disgust, tossing the scythe over his shoulder, and he was strangely vindicated to hear that one of his boys was now making very wet and bubbly sounds. Harley was looking at him adoringly, and the last thing he wanted right then was to be adored by her, so he grabbed her by the fluffy white ruff around her neck and used it to see if he could get her face to turn red, even under all that white makeup she insisted on wearing.

"I don't get no respect, *that's* the problem," he told Harley. "Geez, listen to me, I sound like that fatso, that comedian, what's-his-name . . ."

"Dangerfield?" Harley croaked.

"No, you idiot!" he screamed. "The *other* one, the *fat* one . . . Bullock! That's it! Bullock!"

He dropped Harley as quickly as he'd grabbed her, staring mournfully at the decapitated dummy of Batman.

"It's just not fair," he said petulantly.

"Aw, Mr. J, don't talk like that," Harley said hoarsely. "You're the best, Puddin', and you know it! You rock! And . . . and if they can't see that themselves, well, then . . . we just got to make 'em see, that's what we got to do! We got to make 'em see!"

Joker wiped at his nose with the edge of his jacket, sniffling. "Really?"

"Oh, yeah, of course! Absolutely! Isn't that right, boys? Boys?"

The boys agreed that, in fact, it was right and true. They did this quietly, trying not to be noticed, but Joker saw the reactions and it perked him up instantly.

"The problem, Puddin'," Harley went on, "is that you've been out of the spotlight for too long, that's the trouble. We got to get you back in the spotlight."

Joker grinned, reaching for Harley. He twisted her ear painfully until she made a noise like a cat falling into a garbage disposal. Then he let go, thinking about something she'd said. Something about his back—no, no, not his back, but about . . .

"Spotlights!" Joker exclaimed.

He knew where he could find some of those, yes indeedy.

"Mercy, let's hear it."

"It happened again last night, Lex. Around oh-three-thirty at the Taylor Street site, where the crews were clearing the ground for a new foundation."

Luthor scowled.

"Joker showed up," Mercy continued. "Everyone ran—"

"That site was guarded!"

"The guards panicked, Lex. By the time I was on-site Joker had left."

Luthor's scowl deepened. "Continue."

"Our equipment was destroyed. No fatalities."

She watched as her employer rose from the table, crossing to the entrance of the hut, looking out. A light snow was falling, and outside, across the compound, in the mess tent, Mercy could see LexCorp employees gathering for dinner.

Without turning around, Luthor said, "That makes it every night this week. He's out of control and he's costing us time and money. Take care of the problem, Mercy."

She smiled. "Already on it, Lex."

. . .

Robin was being snowed upon, which he wouldn't have normally minded if he could move. But he had been told by Batman to maintain a static surveillance post over five days ago, and so he had to stay still, or at least, relatively still, which to him was practically the same thing. Batman was good at staying still. Even Nightwing could do it if he really needed to. But Tim Drake liked to move, and he liked to talk, and he liked to be with people.

He did not like spying. He especially did not like spying on people he was kinda fond of, and he had to include Huntress in that list. He understood why Batman felt the way he did about her. She *was* pretty dangerous, he knew that. She had killed people, after all. Not like the Arkham crowd, not like the criminals who used to run the Gotham streets, but yes, she'd put on a costume and then she'd taken lives while wearing it.

That was a hard thing to get past, even for Tim.

But he kinda liked her, and now, after watching her and Billy Pettit's Strong Men for five days, he'd reached a couple of conclusions. One of them was that she deserved better than this. She shouldn't have to baby-sit Billy Pettit and not even know that was exactly what Batman had wanted her to do way back when he'd stripped her of the Batgirl mask.

Robin rubbed his gloved hands together, then checked the receiver and headphones, making certain the bugs were still functioning. The levels looked good. Across the street, in the building Pettit used as his headquarters, he saw lamps being lit in one of the rooms. He put the headphones on and brought the binoculars up, saw Huntress pacing back and forth like an animal in a cage.

He lowered the binoculars to turn up the volume, and saw that Batman was standing beside him.

"Wondered if you'd come by," Robin said.

"Anything today?"

"I placed all the microphones as you ordered and they've all checked out okay. Reading loud and clear. Other than that, nothing."

"And Huntress?"

Robin glanced back at the window, trying to think of the best way to speak his mind. "She went outside a couple times today, patrolling the perimeter. I stayed out of sight, she didn't see me."

"Not what I meant."

"I know what you meant. Best that I can tell, she's not a happy camper."

Batman extended his hand for the binoculars, and Robin handed them over. Batman spent almost a minute scanning the building, and Robin saw that in the room where Huntress was, another figure had joined her. The light was bad, and even using NVG he wouldn't be able to make out the features, not without the optics, but he thought it looked like Pettit.

"Receiver on," Batman said. "I want to hear them."

Robin pulled the headphone jack out of the unit, then flipped the speakers on, keeping the volume low. The voices came through with slight distortion and a little static, but it was easy to make out the words and who was speaking them.

"*—aren't prisoners, Pettit! They should be free to come and go if they like!*"

"*They're my people! Every time they leave this sector they leave us weakened! That's a tactical risk I cannot and will not allow, Huntress. I want checkpoints from now on, nobody comes in or out of here without my permission!*"

"*Are you mad? We're not the bad guys here! We've got an obligation to protect the people in this sector, that's it, that's all we set out to do!*"

"*You don't like it, you can leave . . . maybe Batman will take you back . . . if you beg him . . . but maybe it's time you faced facts, sweetheart. You've got nowhere else to go.*"

There was the sound of a door slamming, and Robin could see that Huntress was alone in the room once more. Beside him, the binoculars still up, Batman hadn't moved.

"*Dammit.*"

Her voice sounded very small over the speaker.

Batman lowered the binoculars, handing them back and then switching the speaker off. "She'll make it," he told Robin. "She's strong."

"I hope you're right."

Batman's expression tightened, but he didn't respond directly, saying, "What are the numbers on Pettit's men?"

"Fourteen as of now, all trained by him. They're like some sort of Special Forces wannabe unit. Most of them were GCPD, I think."

"If she tries a coup . . . ?"

"She can't take them all out, and the only person who might consider helping her is Foley. Even that's a maybe." Robin glanced back at the building, where Huntress was still in silhouette by the window, her head down. He thought maybe that she was praying. "Pettit will kill her if she challenges him. That's my assessment."

"Understood. You should get out of the snow, head to the Clock Tower and get some rest. This will keep for the night."

"Where are you going?"

"I have some baby-sitting of my own to do," Batman said.

Then he was gone, leaving Robin to wonder if his mind was truly that easy to read.

FORTY-THREE

THEY'D BEEN DOING IT FOR LONG ENOUGH that everyone knew their parts and was pretty good about sticking to them, except for Harley, who, Joker had noticed, had an irritating tendency to ad-lib. He'd talked to her about it twice already, and he really hoped it would stick this time.

The guards went down easily, all of them blinded by the lights that surrounded the construction site, and so it was easy to get in close and bash them over the head with one of the many blunt and heavy objects lying around. The boys did this quietly, which Joker appreciated, because it kept the workers from noticing. Whenever the workers noticed, they'd run and scream and then Joker would have to content himself with simple property damage.

He'd been doing this for eight nights now, and what he really wanted was an innocent victim. More than that, of course, he wanted Bats, but in lieu of Bats he'd take some poor schmuck who'd just been in the wrong place at the wrong time.

That was the essence of humor, after all. Timing.

Once all the guards were down, Joker gave Harley a shove out into the light, following closely behind. He'd been working with props a lot lately, but was trying to keep it simple tonight. Just Boo-Boo the Rubber Chicken Surprise, that was it.

Harley recovered her balance and did a couple of cartwheels up to the edge of the pit where the workers were busy working. Joker thought they were digging a foundation, but foundations were boring, so maybe it was a mass grave. That would be good, a mass grave, he thought.

"Ladies and gentlemen!" Harley was shouting. "Back by popular demand for his eighth consecutive night, the one . . . the only . . . *Joker!!*"

Joker bounded out of the shadows, making certain the lights caught his good side, his arms up, waving Boo-Boo the Rubber Chicken Surprise. "Thank you, thank you so much for coming!"

". . . and his lovely and talented assistant, Harley Quinn," Harley added.

Joker hit her in the nose with Boo-Boo, saying, "No ad-libs!"

The workers, of course, were now screaming for him. Or because of him. He was never certain which it was these days. The boys were moving in to exercise some crowd control, which was good, because certain members of the audience were trying to get away. Of course, those were the ones that caught his notice, in particular a female one, in dirty blue coveralls and a yellow hard hat, and he thought, hey, she has red hair! And so he jumped into the ditch in front of her, blocking her way and then showing her Boo-Boo.

The woman backed into the side of the ditch, and Joker knew a captive audience when he saw one, so he leaned in and said, "Hey, great to be here tonight, and what's your name, doll?"

She had trouble getting her tongue to work, it seemed. She said, "L-l-l-lo-lor-lori . . ."

"Lori!" Joker exclaimed, then stage-whispered to her, "You ought to see someone about that stammer, kid."

Above, Harley giggled.

Joker showed Lori Boo-Boo the Rubber Chicken Surprise, and she tried to back farther away but now, since she was trapped, all she could do was move her head back farther and farther until her hard hat came off and she was pressed against the freshly cleared earth.

"It just so happens," Joker said, "that I can help you with that st-st-stammer of yours."

"No . . . no, please . . ." Lori said.

"No trouble at all." He showed her Boo-Boo's surprise: inside the rubber chicken's mouth was a pair of really nasty old scissors. Joker snipped at her a couple times, not yet cutting, hoping she'd pick up her cue.

"Please," she said. "Please, please don't do this to me, please . . ."

"Louder," Joker said. "Like you mean it. Scream, too."

Her eyes were frantic and almost dumb and she clearly didn't get it, so he put his mouth to her ear, still holding the scissors over her face.

"Between you and me, Lori," Joker whispered. "This has nothing to do with you, you seem like a sweet kid, the kind of girl I'd take home and feed to Mother. But, you see, I've got to get his attention somehow, and I'm pretty much out of ideas."

"God oh God please don't I'm begging you please . . ."

And then he saw the shadow falling over him and he immediately forgot about Lori, straightening up and turning and saying, "Finally! I was beginning to think that you didn't love me . . ."

It wasn't him.

It was Bane.

". . . anymore?" Joker finished. "Oh, this is gonna hurt, isn't it?"

Bane lifted him by the collar, cocking his right fist back.

"Yes," Bane said. "It is."

And Joker felt the familiar hot sensation of a fist colliding with his face, and the world went all silly for a little bit, and then he was on his back looking up at the stars, and Bane was coming out of the ditch after him. Joker still had Boo-Boo in his hand, and he tried to readjust his grip so he could stab or snip with it, but Bane was already lifting him up again.

"I don't think you're very funny," Bane said.

"Well, you know, comedy's tricky that way——"

He was in the air again, then on the ground, and this time it took longer to get the world sorted out again. He'd lost Boo-Boo.

He was looking up a woman's skirt at her nasties, her knickers, her underthings, her unmentionables.

He giggled.

"I see London, I see France . . ." Joker began, then stopped when the woman pointed a gun directly at his face.

Bane yanked him back to his feet, turning him to face the woman. She was blond and big and wearing a lot of black, and she was pointing the gun right at his face. Joker felt blood swimming in his mouth, and he swallowed it, savoring the taste.

"You stand when you speak to a lady," Bane told him.

"Of course, of course. And the lady might be?"

The woman smiled at him. "All you need to know is mine is the last face you're ever going to see. No one messes with Mr. Luthor's business——"

"That's enough of that, toots," Harley said, and Joker saw that his harlequin had a great big gun of her own pointed at the mean woman's head. "You let him go or I'll put a whole new breeze through that airhead of yours."

Joker giggled. "Ain't she a pip?"

The woman with the pistol and the unmentionables frowned, then lowered the gun. "Let him go, Bane," she said.

Bane let him go.

Joker dusted himself off, retrieved Boo-Boo, and headed for the shadows, stopping to check that Harley was following him.

"Been fun!" he said with a wave, and then he and Harley disappeared into the darkness.

Bane returned to Camp Lex with Mercy, but they parted company at Luthor's hut. He had yet to speak with the man in person, and each time he'd gotten close, Mercy had prevented it, restricting access. Bane understood this, but it was both annoying and insulting. Here he had given Lex Luthor some of his best work—at least, to Luthor's knowledge—and still he was being treated like a costumed lunatic, a tool to be discarded.

There was a distinct lack of respect there, Bane felt.

He went to the trailer that had been supplied for him, away from the main camp and out of the eyes of the media. He was cold and looking forward to having a brandy and going to sleep, and he was thinking of just those things when he closed the door behind him and switched on the light to see Batman waiting for him.

"An unexpected surprise," Bane said. "To what do I owe the pleasure? Are you here for our rematch?"

"No."

"No, I did not think so. You were watching tonight when the clown gave his performance?"

"Yes."

"Yes. Of course." Bane reached past him and took the bottle of brandy on the counter and a glass, then moved to the couch. He sat and poured himself a drink. "I would offer you one, but you would decline it, I have no doubt."

"I appreciate the gesture."

Bane chuckled and took a sip, feeling the alcohol burn in his sinuses and mouth. Batman, it seemed to him, looked almost relaxed. That made Bane feel strangely good about himself. Here, at least, was a man who gave him respect.

"You know, it took me a while to figure out what you were up to," Bane said conversationally. "After that whole fiasco at the Hall of Records. You could have just told me to set off the explosives; I was planning on doing so anyway."

"I needed to get a look for myself. Had to get inside."

"I understand, trust me. As I said, it took me a little while to figure it out."

"But now?"

"Now I know. The fact that you're here confirms it. I haven't told Luthor, if that's your concern."

"I didn't think you would have."

Bane smirked into his snifter, then took another, larger sip. "You do me an honor, Batman."

"I've come to repeat what I told you that night," Batman said. "Leave while you can. You know what I'm planning. You must know that when I'm finished, Luthor won't be honoring his deals with anyone, least of all you."

"I had been coming to the same conclusion." He set the empty glass down and refilled it from the bottle. "I'll be leaving in the next couple of days."

"Good."

Bane laughed, then raised his glass to Batman. "To your good health and good advice, Batman."

ORACLE

PERSONAL
Entry #723—NML Day 336
0603 Zulu

Dear Dad—

The announcement came yesterday, a press conference in the Rose Garden at the White House. The President was there, and Lucius Fox, and a handful of other business-men. Alex, the Eye who has been watching Camp Lex for me since Luthor hit town, said that LexCorp put it on speakers all throughout the park, broadcasting the voices into the No Man's Land, loud as they could.

Those who didn't hear the conference in person heard the news soon enough.

I watched it on my NewsChannel hack, Robin and Batgirl with me.

It started with standard media babble, and then the Press Secretary made an open-ing announcement, saying that a decision had been reached with regard to No Man's Land. Then he handed over the podium to Lucius Fox.

There were honestly tears in Lucius's eyes.

"I'm pleased to announce that the President signed an Executive Order at ten-thirty

Eastern Standard Time this morning declaring immediate aid and relief to the No Man's Land," he said, wiping his eyes. "Wayne Enterprises is proud to be one of the many businesses that helped to make this happen. At the present time, access to Gotham City will be limited to deliveries of emergency supplies, equipment, and personnel. The Army Corps of Engineers has been mobilized and will be arriving in Gotham within the next twenty-four hours.

"The goal is to return basic infrastructure and services by January I, New Year's Day, at which point the President has assured us that the No Man's Land will be revoked, and that Gotham City will once more welcome her children home. . . ."

Then Lucius had to stop because he was so choked up, and the LexCorp representative stepped forward, began fielding questions alongside the President himself.

But none of us were really paying attention at that point, because we were all hugging one another and shouting, and even Cassandra was managing to make a little noise, squeaks and rasps.

"Yes!" she managed, mimicking Tim.

I got on the radio, called Nightwing, and told him the good news. He tried to take it like Batman, I think, tried to keep his voice and tone level, but the relief crept in anyway. He was delighted, and we could hear it.

I was switching channels to call Batman himself when Cassandra stopped her celebrating and pointed behind me. Tim and I looked, and there he was.

"We did it!" I said.

"No," Batman said. "We did *some* of it. Now we do the rest."

The helicopters woke me this morning, and it was like nothing I'd ever seen before in my life. So many of them they filled the sky.

The Army Corps of Engineers came first, of course, leading the way; there had to be over sixty of their copters in just that first wave, big ones, small ones, all of them towing giant crates or sections of prefab buildings or huge tanks full of I don't know what. . . .

Then the private sector followed, the Wayne Enterprises and S.T.A.R. Labs and LexCorp people, all flying in after them.

From the window, if I use my binoculars, I can see the soldiers on the other side of the Gotham River, taking down the razor wire. There are naval minesweepers clearing the river. The 234th Combat Engineers battalion is building a pontoon bridge from the mainland. There's a line of people gathered on the road on both sides of the river . . . survivors of the No Man's Land cheering for the construction, and opposite them a crowd of people up from Blüdhaven and wherever else, all coming to get work and help rebuild our city.

Never seen anything like it.

But the wildest thing of all just flew past ten minutes ago, and it's so strange, so surreal, and so perfectly Luthor I just have to share it.

I just saw a LexCorp chopper fly by carrying a giant Vermont pine tree, a hundred feet tall if an inch. The quintessential Christmas tree.

Christmas is coming, Dad. You believe that?

I'd completely forgotten. Even with all this talk of New Year's Day, I had forgotten what came first.

Alex just called in to say that the tree is being set up in the middle of Camp Lex. You have to hand it to Luthor; he knows how to use his symbols.

There's a rumor spreading that my section of Old Gotham may have power by the end of the week. I can't tell you how excited that makes me. Maybe, if they get everything up and working in time, if I've got electricity and even running water, I'll see if I can get a message to you and Sarah, and we can spend Christmas Eve here, together. I'd like that.

I think we'll have something to celebrate.

FORTY-FOUR

IT WASN'T THE SOUND OF THE HELICOPTERS that woke Sarah Essen, although some part of her mind was aware of the noise as it began to grow in the distance. It was Jim, suddenly turning in his sleep, his agitation rising, and he was mumbling and it was his voice that brought Sarah fully from her dreams. The chill of the bedroom wrapped itself tightly around her bare skin as she sat up.

Then she really heard it, in the distance, the sound of all those rotors.

She rose from the bed, hastily pulling on a pair of sweatpants and shirt, and even the carpet was cold beneath her feet. Essen went to the window, and the noise was growing louder, and she heard Jim waking, as well.

The glass of the bedroom window was cold and covered with condensation. She wiped it with her hands and looked up at the lightening sky, and she gasped audibly.

"Sarah? What is it?"

She could barely find her voice. "Jim . . . oh, Jim, I think . . . I think it might finally be over . . . I think it's the end."

The bed creaked as he rose from it, and she felt the warmth of him as he wrapped his arms around her from behind, resting his head against hers. Together they stood in their bedroom, watching the sky.

"Army Corps," Gordon said at one point. "They were in the war. Those guys are amazing, Sarah. They can make a hydroelectric dam out of a toothbrush, you give them enough time."

"This the same military that pays ten grand for a screwdriver?"

"One and the same, yes."

She laughed, and he laughed, and they both knew it wasn't that funny at all, but it felt good. To Essen's mind, she hadn't honestly laughed since before the NML started.

When they saw the Christmas tree, they laughed again.

"We should go spread the news," Gordon said.

"Like everyone in this town isn't looking up right now just like we are."

"Well, then we should get outside and provide positive leadership. And maybe find out exactly why all these helicopters are here."

"There's no rush," Essen said, taking hold of her husband's hands and keeping them firmly in place around her. "Let's watch for a while."

Joker stood and stared out the window of Wicked Wendy's Costume Emporium, looking at the helicopters flying overhead. They had started arriving before dawn, and he had gone to the window then and stayed there, looking up, and now, three hours later, they were still flying overhead and the noise was enormous. He knew why the helicopters were coming, and it posed a great problem to his mind.

The expectations had suddenly and drastically risen, and he honestly didn't know if he was up to the challenge.

Reflected in the cracked glass, Joker saw Harley tiptoeing toward him. The boys were nowhere to be seen, probably playing cards or jacks or one of those damnable collectible card games somewhere in the back of the shop. He frowned, and Harley took that to mean he was unhappy, which he was, but not at the helicopters, which he could tell was what she thought.

"Puddin'?" Harley had to shout over the noise from above, but she still managed to make it sound like he was, in fact, her favorite dessert treat. "You been standing here for hours now——"

"Touch me and I'll feed you your arm," Joker told her. "Can't you see that I'm thinking?"

In the reflection, he saw Harley drop her arms, then her chin, looking at her booted feet. "I'm real sorry they're gonna end the No Man's Land without you, Mr. J."

Joker whirled from the window and pounced on her, riding Harley to the ground, and in the process upsetting a stand of novelty wigs which toppled over, throwing the synthetic and multicolored fake hair across the floor. Joker straddled her and Harley immediately smiled broadly and began to shimmy her hips around in a tight circle beneath him, but she stopped when Joker closed his hands around her neck.

"Idiot!" he hissed. "They're *not* ending it without me, Harley, haven't you been paying any attention at all?"

"Choking . . . me . . . "

"I know," he said dismissively. "It's an invitation, Harl. A challenge! A dare, even! Look at all the trouble they're going to to save this rathole of a city, all the time and energy and money they're pouring into this wreck! They've even told me where, when, and how Gotham is to be saved!"

He looked at her, waiting for her to get it, but she was turning a little blue around the lips and her eyes were bulging, and it was pretty clear to Joker that she wasn't truly listening. He unclasped his hands and rolled off her, idly picking through the discarded wigs before him. One of them was the same green as his hair, sort of baby-poop green, and he picked it up, momentarily distracted by the color, then sniffed it experimentally. It smelled a little musty, but nothing like crap.

"I can't disappoint them, Harl," Joker said quietly. "Really. It's a built-in audience, a once in a lifetime chance. I mean, before, you know, I could really grab this town by its short-and-curlies, but now the stage is so much bigger, the whole world will be watching Gotham. I've got to do something that will just blow their shorts off, something that will leave them stunned and begging for more."

He stared hard at the wig, then looked around to see if there were any purple jackets in sight.

Harley coughed a couple times, then tried to reach for him again, saying, "Baby, I—"

All at once it hit him, the perfect idea, the only way to go. He dropped the rug and did a backward somersault into her, and for the first time since they'd met Harley actually recoiled, throwing up her hands and trying to make herself as small as possible.

"Sorry," she said. "I'm sorry I didn't mean—"

He grabbed her by the shoulders and kissed her, putting his tongue into her mouth, then into her nose, then into her right ear.

"Harley," he said excitedly. "You are the greatest, you know that?"

He sprang to his feet.

"We have to get the boys together, we've got a lot of work to do. Oh, this is going to be *brilliant*, they'll be talking about this one for years!"

He started laughing.

Harley was looking at him quite strangely.

Didn't matter.

Joker had the plan, now.

Batman be damned. This was going to be better.

This was going to get them *all*.

The MASH Sector exploded into frenzied activity almost immediately upon the arrival of the Army Corps of Engineers, and the next morning Cassandra arrived in plainclothes to see men and women in uniform busily building more tents, moving equipment into place, running back and forth. Dr. Thompkins was standing in the middle of the compound, talking to a group of men in uniform, and she saw Cassandra approach.

". . . medical facilities," one of the uniformed men was saying.

He had a friendly face, a little round, and almost the same skin color as Cassandra herself. "I'm impressed that you've managed to do as much as you have here, Dr. Thompkins. We thought we'd be arriving to find the situation much worse."

"It was worse, much worse, outside of this sector," Leslie said. "There were many people who died simply because they couldn't reach us for aid. We were fortunate, Dr. Zahedi. Malnutrition was actually our biggest concern, but once the gardens started producing, and then the park, most people were able to balance their diet."

"I'm frankly stunned." Dr. Zahedi glanced around the compound, noting Cassandra and offering her a friendly smile. "Your list of critical cases is much lower than I expected, as well."

"Yes, since the major fighting died down. For the last couple of weeks, in fact, it's been mostly treating infections, the odd cuts and bruises, a couple of deliveries."

"Deliveries? People had babies in the No Man's Land?"

Leslie's smile was brilliant. "The nights got cold, Dr. Zahedi."

Dr. Zahedi laughed. "All right, then. Tell us what to do, we're here to help."

While Leslie and the doctor talked awhile longer, Cassandra watched the work going on about her, feeling strangely content. Almost everyone was smiling.

Cassandra saw Alfred, and tapped Leslie on the arm to say goodbye, then made her way over to the old man.

"Hello, m'dear. How are you today?"

She smiled and wrapped her arms around him in a hug. She did it quickly, the way she did every movement once she had decided upon it, and it caught him by surprise. Then he patted her on the back and tried to free himself.

"Yes, I'm glad to see you, too," Alfred said. "Is this simply a social visit, dear? Or is there something I can do for you?"

Cassandra shook her head, then put the index finger from each hand at the corners of her mouth, pulling down on one end and pushing up on the other, making a crazy face.

Alfred looked at her with confusion for a second, then his face smoothed and he said, "No, no, dear. We haven't seen Joker."

Cassandra nodded, then shrugged, indicating that the question had been adequately answered.

"Master Bruce sent you to ask?"

She shook her head, then mimed wearing a headset.

"Oracle."

She nodded.

"Well, tell Oracle that we haven't seen any signs of Joker since you were here to stop him that last time. But I am keeping an eye out, and I will inform you if we see any hints."

She looked at him curiously for a couple of seconds, wondering how he could think that she would be able to tell anyone anything, then realized that he hadn't meant strictly speaking. She smiled again, but it faltered and then faded when she saw Alfred was now frowning and no longer looking at her. She turned to pursue his gaze, trying to find what was upsetting him, but beyond the soldiers moving back and forth and the patients leaving the different tents, she saw nothing but the city. She tapped him on the elbow and put the question on her face as best she could.

"Hmm?" Alfred said. "Oh, no, dear, don't concern yourself. Just an old man thinking."

She indicated that he could continue and that she would be glad to listen. She was, after all, a gifted listener.

"Joker, my dear. You don't know him very well. He's the worst of them. When he's quiet, like he is now, it's normally for a very wicked reason." He put his hands on her shoulders. "You be careful."

She nodded.

Alfred forced a smile back into place. "Very well, then. Off with you. I have much work to attend."

Cassandra departed, wondering what, exactly, was so dangerous about Joker.

ORACLE

P E R S O N A L
Entry #781—NML Day 344
1250 Zulu

Dear Dad—

I'm writing to you from my newly powered apartment! There were soldiers working on the street all day yesterday and today, and fifteen minutes ago the lights came on and all around the block I heard people cheering.

Lights!

I'd forgotten how much I missed being able to see, you know?

Been over eight days now since the ACOE arrived and all the rest, and it's going far better than anyone imagined. It's been the sounds of heavy machinery day and night, voices from below. A couple of the more derelict buildings on the block have already been knocked down and cleared—I'm stunned by how fast it's moving, but I suppose all it takes is time, money, and manpower. If you have any two of those three, you can get a lot accomplished. If you have all three, you can get a lot accomplished a lot faster.

Word is that LexCorp is now trying to run power along the whole of the East Side, and the 132nd and 98th Combat Engineer Divisions arrived in the city yesterday, setting immediately to work on sewage and water treatment. That's over five thousand Army personnel on the ground in Gotham at this very moment, and that doesn't include the thousands more that have come in from Blüdhaven and other cities to aid in the construction. Some of the media estimates put the total "emergency" labor force at over 30,000 people, but personally I think that's a conservative estimate; I know for a fact that Wayne Enterprises itself has hired over 10,000 men and women from all along the coast and ferried them into the city on their own dime. The estimate certainly doesn't include the number of people who actually remained here during the NML and who, now, are working on the construction as well.

Building inspector came through the day before yesterday, and I had a hell of a time convincing him that he didn't need to check the walls up here. Last thing I want is some federally funded yokel discovering my base of operations. But he was pleasant enough and in the end gave the Clock Tower a clean bill of health, calling it one of the only buildings he'd seen in the last week that didn't need major repairs to its structure. I acted surprised and delighted by the news, though the delight part was fairly honest. Frankly, I've never had any concerns about the integrity of this structure; one of the many faiths I've placed in Bruce Wayne.

Speaking of which . . . I know Batman's been to see you about the Joker thing, how no one can find him. He's had Nightwing, Robin, and Batgirl combing the city every spare moment they get, but still nothing. I know you've had those people you can spare doing the same thing, but until you're officially police again, you've got your hands full with all your other obligations.

There's a piece of me that's sure this can't be good, that Joker is up to something and up to something big. Since Bane left town there have been no further attacks on any of the construction sites, and I've heard nothing from any of my Eyes about other activities that might be attributable to the clown.

Wait and see time. And if you think that makes me nervous and tense, you can just guess the mood Batman is in.

The files, incidentally, are all ready and waiting for his word to upload. He's picking his moment, though I'm not certain exactly when that will be. Probably around Christmas.

Speaking of . . . got the note from DeFilippis, and I'm glad to hear that you and Sarah will be joining me for dinner. I sent him back to you with another note . . . you guys are going to have to bring the fixin's, I'm afraid. All I've got left are MREs and a variety of freeze-dried entrées, none of which seem appropriate for Christmas dinner.

Looking forward to it, have to tell you.

FORTY-FIVE

 PENGUIN HAD SENT THE REQUEST FOR THE meeting by courier, and his note had been insistent. It had mentioned the media, and had requested that Luthor meet him at the warehouse off Colby at noon.

"I can handle it alone," Mercy had told him.

"No," Luthor had said. "I'll come along. He should see what he's truly up against."

Leaving Camp Lex without the media noticing took a little doing, but wasn't impossible, and Mercy covered Luthor as they left the Quonset and worked back through the park, around where the one-hundred-foot-tall Christmas tree stood, still bare, waiting to be decorated. No one noticed as they slipped from the camp onto the street, and for a while they walked side by side in silence, Mercy scanning the terrain for any potential threats.

"Any news?" Luthor asked.

"We've been suffering minor thefts of material."

"Who's doing it? The bird?"

"I don't think so. Most likely people who don't believe that the No Man's Land will be ending in the next few weeks."

"What's been stolen?"

Mercy took her personal data assistant from her pocket, called up the report. "Crates 2117 and 2118, most recently."

Luthor started laughing, and to her ears he sounded genuinely amused. "Won't they be surprised."

"Lex?"

"They're worthless, Mercy," Luthor explained. "Children's toys that I had shipped in to go under the tree. Dolls, cars, the like. Don't worry about it, just have the head office send in another shipment of the same."

They had reached the warehouse, the doors open, and through them Mercy could see Cobblepot and another five of his men, including the big one, Garrett. She scanned the surrounding area quickly, confirming that there were no surprises in store for her employer. At the distance, she couldn't be certain that Penguin's men weren't armed, but it didn't truly concern her.

She let Luthor lead the way inside, staying close to his side. Penguin gave them a broad smile, and she felt his eyes wandering over her once again. He had his umbrella with him. She noted that two of the men were, in fact, armed, Garrett and another, their holsters clumsily concealed beneath their winter coats.

"Cobblepot," Luthor said. "You wanted this meeting."

"Indeed I did, and may I say what a delight it is to meet such an august presence. It is truly an honor, sir." Penguin made a little mock bow.

Luthor looked bored. "What do you want?"

"Ah, you are a direct man! I appreciate that, I sincerely do, no time for chitchat. Very well." Penguin adjusted his monocle, stepping forward slightly and craning his head back to look Luthor in the eye. "I want a piece of the pie, my friend."

"The pie?"

"Indeed. Whatever your angle is, I want a share. A modest one, but a share nonetheless. I have donated to your service my time, resources, and effort, as I'm certain you know. Now I feel that a broadening of the partnership is in order."

Luthor smirked, looking down at the little man. "You think so?"

"Absolutely, sir."

"And if I refuse?"

"Then you will leave me no choice but to shatter your philanthropic image by going to the media and explaining to them exactly how you and your associate did business with me, a known felon, during the darkest days of the No Man's Land."

Penguin smiled and spread out his palms, as if his argument was foolproof and justly compelling.

"I'm afraid you would leave me no alternative, sir," Penguin finished.

For a couple of seconds, Mercy thought Luthor might actually be considering what Penguin had said, still staring down at the man.

Then, without bothering to look at her, Luthor said, "Mercy. If you please."

"Happily, Lex," she replied, and slammed her fist into the nose of the nearest of Penguin's men, shattering the septum and driving a wedge of bone into the man's brain. She followed with a quick kick between the legs of the next one, then moved onto the third, punching three times in quick succession—solar plexus, thorax, and throat—the last blow of which crushed the man's windpipe.

The remainder of Penguin's guards only then began to react, and the two with guns tried to index their weapons, but they were woefully slow. Mercy kept moving, snapping a quick kick to Garrett's stomach, knocking the man down, out of breath, then moving to the final two. She took the one with the gun first, catching his wrist and snapping it down. The man screamed as bone shattered. She finished with him by slamming her forearm up and across his face, feeling more cartilage crackle and splinter.

The final guard had managed to take a stance, and she let him try to hit her, blocking the three punches he threw with her left arm, then striking him in the right ear. The guard cried in pain, recoiling, and it left him wide open, so Mercy finished with a sequence she'd learnt as a child: six quick blows, alternating hands, into the man's gut and chest. She turned away from him, snapping her elbow back and into the base of the guard's chest, just below the ribs, to the xiphoid process, finishing him off.

Garrett was on the floor, and had managed to get the gun out of its holster, was trying to get a sight on Mercy. She kicked him sharply in the wrist and the weapon went skittering away, across the floor. Then she bent down and put her hands on either side of the man's head.

" . . . bad idea . . . " Garrett muttered.

She nodded barely to him, asking, "Lex?"

"Do it," Luthor said.

She pushed and pulled at once, and snapped Garrett's neck. The man fell forward heavily, his eyes glazing.

Mercy straightened her coat and looked at Penguin, who stood dumbfounded, staring at his dead and wounded men.

"Don't ever threaten me again, Cobblepot," Luthor said. "Or else you'll get another taste of my Mercy."

Then he turned and left, with her following in his footsteps.

The man from the Department of Justice was waiting for them on the steps of Central. Behind him, soldiers and workers were busily tending to the building, checking wires and fixtures on the exterior, clearing the debris from the quake and their own efforts, and the noise of the saws and hammers and drills was familiar and comforting. Someone had already repainted the doors in the dark blue of the GCPD.

Most of his remaining officers were there, too, waiting on the wide steps that led to the entrance. Montoya and Bullock and DeFilippis and even Weir, holding her little boy.

Sarah whispered in his ear, "Welcome home, Jim."

"Welcome home."

The DOJ man came down the steps, extending his empty hand. In the other he held a large manila envelope. He shook hands with Gordon, then with Essen, then stepped back and gestured to the building.

"Like what you see?"

"It looks beautiful."

Bullock, on the steps, chuckled. "Hey, now, Commish. Beauty's in the eye of the beholder."

"You calling me ugly, Harvey?" Essen asked.

"Perish the thought, Lieutenant!"

The gathered officers laughed, and the man from the DOJ grinned, saying, "If we can get down to business?"

"By all means," Gordon said.

The DOJ man opened the envelope, removed the sheaf of papers inside and then handed them over to Gordon. "James Gordon, on behalf of the Attorney General of the United States, I hereby present your new charter, reauthorizing you as Commissioner of Police for the City of Gotham."

Gordon took the papers, saw the seal of the United States Department of Justice on the charter, and the surge of emotion through his breast took his breath for a second. "Thank you," he said.

"As of now, your police force consists of those officers who remained with you during the No Man's Land. We'll have more volunteers for you after Christmas." The man grinned. "Welcome back. Nice to be in control again, huh?"

"You have no idea," Gordon said.

"Let's go in," Essen said. "Take a look around while it's still quiet inside."

"That's an idea. You know that as soon as word gets out that we're back in business, we'll be swamped."

Gordon led the way, the rest following, entering to find the main desk already in place and tarps covering the floor. The smell of fresh paint and sawdust was strong, and people were on ladders, running lights along the ceiling. Each of the cops with him stared and grinned, and Gordon turned to look back at them and saw that each, to a person, was wearing a badge.

For a moment, he felt pride for his people, the same pride he had felt when they'd stood on this same roof almost a year ago, resolved to stick it out, resolved to do what was right. Then he thought of Pettit and Foley.

He wondered what they had done with their shields.

. . .

Pettit took a swing at Foley and missed, and Huntress had to move quickly to keep the two men separated, pushing her way between them, facing Pettit.

"Cut it out!"

"No!" Pettit shouted around her, still reaching for Foley. "You will attend, do you understand? Everyone will attend!"

"It's Christmas, for Pete's sake," Foley said.

"I know! That's the point, dammit! Christmas Eve, and we're having a dinner, is that clear? In the gymnasium and *everyone* is going to be there, and we're going to spend it together, got me?"

Pettit pushed himself away from Huntress roughly, pacing back and forth on the street. Several of his men were watching nearby, and Huntress couldn't read anything in their expressions. But when she'd moved to stop Pettit, she'd seen some of them tensing, a couple of the hands dropping closer to the sidearms, and it made her stomach all the more nervous.

"You can't keep them here if they don't want to stay," Foley said. "Not on Christmas, Bill."

"I sure as hell can! What I *can't* do is allow our numbers to keep being whittled away like this. I *can't* allow our morale to be constantly eroded by propaganda and false hope! The No Man's Land isn't over! It's not going to *be* over!"

He stopped, breathing quickly, and Huntress saw the clouds of condensation billowing out of the man's mouth, his eyes scanning around him frantically.

"Yeah," Pettit said softly. "Yeah, that's it, we'll have our Christmas feast in the gym. It'll be good. Everyone will come. Everyone. Attendance will be mandatory for the sector."

He turned to look at Foley, and Huntress almost relaxed because Pettit finally looked calm.

"That's what we're going to do, Foley. And if you've got a problem with that . . . " Pettit said, and Huntress felt the tension racing back into place because he was reaching for his gun and she was putting herself once more between the two men.

"Hey! *Hey!* Easy, Bill!" Foley cried, backing away.

"Back down, Pettit!" Huntress snarled. "Now!"

Pettit held the gun still for a second longer, and Huntress didn't like the look in his eyes at all then. He looked almost satisfied, as if Foley's fear and Huntress's anger were what he had been after all along. Then he holstered the weapon and adjusted that damn cap he always wore.

"See you there," Pettit said. "Both of you."

She watched him turn, the rest of his Strong Men following as he made for the apartment building.

"God," Foley said quietly. "Oh, God, he's just . . . he's losing it, big time. Isn't he?"

Huntress nodded barely, watching the last of the Strong Men disappear into the building.

"You could . . . you could probably make it out of here, you know," Foley said hesitantly.

"No. I'm staying," Huntress said firmly, more anger in her voice than she'd wanted. "You're right, he is losing it—if he ever had it to begin with, if he hasn't lost it already. He's too dangerous, now. He's going to snap."

She looked down at her hands, at where the launcher was strapped to her forearm and the crossbow, folded down, was strapped to her thigh.

"And when he does, I'll have to stop him," she said.

ORACLE

P E R S O N A L
Entry #803—NML Day 354
2314 Zulu

Dear Dad—

Tomorrow is Christmas Eve.

I haven't been this excited since I was little, and I don't know why, but it honestly does feel special. Maybe it's because there's just been so much this year, so long since there's been anything, any way to celebrate, that since the opportunity now exists, I want to embrace it. Maybe it's because, since Gotham is in such a sorry state, the spirit of the season is honestly evident. No advertising, no crass commercialization. Just an honest wish for Peace on Earth and Good Will Toward Men.

Or maybe I'm just hoping you got me some really good presents.

That's a joke.

I am stunned by the progress that's been made in the last couple of weeks, by the amount of construction that has been completed. Gotham is, of course, a far cry from being even a ghost of what it once was, but there's life on the streets again and hope in the air, and I have no doubt now that we're going to make it. And I'm not the only one who thinks that way, I know . . . Nightwing, Robin, Cassandra, all of them are possessed of the same budding optimism.

Even Batman seems almost willing to accept it. I think he would accept it, if it weren't for Joker.

Joker. Still missing in action, still hiding somewhere in the city, planning something.

First time in almost two weeks that I saw Batman was this afternoon. He looked haggard, and that's something, as you know. When it shows on him, then you know it's taking a toll.

"Still nothing?" he asked.

I shook my head. "You're sure he's still in the city?"

"Positive. He wouldn't leave. He's planning something, probably for New Year's, probably for the Eleventh Hour. He'll try to sabotage the opening, most likely."

"Makes sense. Luthor's already announced plans for a big blowout at the Babylon Towers. He's already got people making certain the building will be ready come New Year's Eve."

Batman didn't say anything, staring at the wall behind me for several seconds.

"Boss?" I said. "You want to get some rest yourself?"

"No. No, Alfred's planning a Christmas dinner for tomorrow evening, I'll get to rest then." He looked at me again, as if remembering that I was actually in the same room, then tapped the top of my monitor. "Upload the files."

"Now?"

"Within the hour."

"Consider it done. Can I assume you're ready to take Luthor on?"

"Not me," he said. "Lucius Fox. Bruce Wayne will be watching."

FORTY-SIX

IT HAD BEEN A LONG TIME SINCE HE'D walked as Bruce Wayne, and for several minutes after Alfred had left, he sat on the edge of the bed in the apartment, looking at himself in the mirror, trying to remember how to do it. The clothes were right, he saw that, the Armani cut perfectly, the Ferragamo shoes on his feet shined to a rich luster. He tried to put the grin on his face, the vaguely vacuous one that was in its way just as effective as the cowl.

Alfred tapped on the door, saying, "Master Bruce? Mr. Fox is here."

"Be right there," Bruce said.

"Very good, sir."

He got to his feet, watching his reflection move in the mirror. He adjusted his posture, lowering his chin just a bit more, bringing his shoulders in slightly. Slouching barely. He tried the grin, and thought it looked stupid.

Bruce Wayne, he thought. Bruce Wayne Bruce Wayne Bruce Wayne Brucie Bruce Bruce . . .

He sighed and thought about golf and pretty girls and expensive champagne, and then he opened the door and moved into the main room of the apartment, among the mixed furniture where Alfred was diligently unpacking their temporary home. The apartment was the penthouse suite at the Dallas Arms, a Wayne-owned building that had survived not only the quake and Black Mask, but the depths of the No Man's Land itself. Work had been done on it, of course, getting the windows replaced and the power squared away, and the luxury of it bothered him. It seemed very wrong that he should live in this comfort while so many still went without power.

But that was part of Bruce Wayne, too, and the fact was that he had opened the whole building to residents, rent free. This one and a dozen others, and Wayne Enterprises was sponsoring more construction, more temporary housing every day.

Lucius was waiting in the living room, holding his leather barrister's case, wearing a suit and looking vaguely irritated at having been kept waiting. Bruce thought he looked older, his hair just a little grayer. He looked healthy nonetheless, and Bruce realized that he was truly glad to see him.

"Lucius!" The moment the name was out of his mouth he knew he'd gotten it right, that he was Bruce Wayne again. He took two long loping strides forward, offering his hand and clapping him on the shoulder at the same time. "Wonderful to see you, just wonderful to see you! How have you been? How's your wife? How're the kids?"

"Bruce, fine, thanks. We're all fine. They're staying in New York for the season. Didn't want them moving back to Gotham until everything was official."

"Of course, of course. Got to take care of your family. So, what's this about?" He gestured at the couch, then half fell, half flopped into the empty armchair opposite it.

Lucius sat, opening the case and removing a sheaf of papers. "You remember when you called me from Nice?"

"Nice?"

"In France, Bruce."

"Right, yeah! That was Cissy, I think. Alfred?"

"Master Bruce?"

"Nice. Was I with Cissy or Missy or . . . who was that?"

Alfred curled his lip slightly. "Who can remember?" he said. "Mr. Fox, would you like a cup of tea?"

"Thank you, Alfred."

"And I'd like some hot chocolate," Bruce said. "With sprinkles. And the little marshmallows, this time."

"Very good, sir," Alfred said, tightly, and moved into the kitchen.

Lucius pushed the papers at Bruce, who took them with some hesitation, as if they might require his thought. "You told me someone was buying Gotham real estate, remember?"

"Did I?" Bruce said, looking attentively at Lucius and not the papers in his hand.

"Bruce," Lucius said patiently. "Take a look at what I just handed you, would you please?"

Bruce shrugged and began flipping through the papers. What he saw gave him great satisfaction, and he took pains to keep that from showing on his face, instead showing Lucius only idle interest, then confusion, then boredom. After all, he was looking at nothing but legal documents, what looked to be deeds and titles. And after all, Bruce Wayne could hardly be counted on to notice that there were two copies of each document, one from the Library of Congress—courtesy of Oracle, of course—and the other a forgery of the same, saying that Lex Luthor, or LexCorp, or one of LexCorp's subsidiaries, was, in fact, the owner of the same land.

"Well?" Lucius asked.

Bruce furrowed his brow, then looked toward the kitchen. "What's taking Alfred so long? Alfred?"

"Yes, Master Bruce?"

"What's taking so long?"

"I'm melting the chocolate as we speak, sir."

"Good."

"Bruce," Lucius said again, harder. "What do you think?"

"I think it's a lot of paper, Lucius. I don't know what you're try-ing to show me, I'm sorry, I'm . . . I'm missing it, I guess."

"What you're holding are copies of the official deeds to various properties in Gotham."

Bruce's eyes lit up. "Oh! So . . . uh . . ."

The light faded.

"You're also holding duplicates, claiming that those same prop-erties are now owned by LexCorp in one fashion or another."

Bruce looked at him blankly.

Lucius sighed. "What that means, Bruce, is that Luthor has been buying up Gotham real estate. Except I did some checking, and it turns out that he never paid anyone any money for the land. Yet he has all of these deeds that say he's the sole owner."

"Well, where did the other ones come from? The real ones?" Bruce looked alarmed. "I heard that all the records were destroyed sometime during the year, that someone burnt them all up!"

"That's right. But I found copies that had been filed with the federal government before No Man's Land began. Somehow Luthor neglected to look for those; either he didn't think about it or he didn't find them. Because with what I've got, we can prove he's committing fraud."

Alfred returned from the kitchen with a tray, offering Lucius a cup of tea. He gave Bruce his hot chocolate in a mug that said, I ATE THE WORM IN TIJUANA. Bruce took the mug in both hands and sipped, and then had to hide his surprise; Alfred had honestly melted choco-late to prepare the drink.

"So, what do we do now, Lucius?" Bruce asked, wiping the hot cocoa mustache with the back of his hand.

"We confront Luthor."

"We?" Bruce looked alarmed.

"Don't worry, Bruce," Lucius said with a sigh. "I'll do all the talking."

Luthor received Bruce and Lucius in his luxury hut, offering them seats. His bodyguard, Mercy, stayed in the room by the door. She was watching them carefully and Bruce could tell she knew what she was looking for, and so he leered at her legs for a couple of minutes while the three men exchanged pleasantries. The woman ignored him, which was the result Bruce wanted.

"Now, then, gentlemen," Luthor said. "What's so urgent it couldn't wait until morning?"

"If I may, Bruce?" Lucius asked.

"By all means," Bruce said, sneaking another gaze at Mercy's legs.

"We were updating our records this past week in preparation for Wayne Enterprise's return to Gotham," Lucius said. "And we came across some incongruities."

"Incongruities?" Luthor's brow creased slightly. "Of what sort, Lucius?"

"I was hoping you could answer that, actually."

Lucius removed the papers once more from his bag, sliding them across the table to Luthor. Luthor went through the pile quickly at first, flipping the sheets, one after another, and then he slowed abruptly and went back, and Bruce saw the man's brow crease again, this time more profoundly.

Bruce cracked his knuckles noisily, and Lucius shot him a dirty look. He stopped.

Luthor took almost twenty minutes, going through the whole stack in silence. From outside, Bruce could hear the sounds of people working, the odd break of an engine starting or stopping nearby.

Finally, Luthor said, "Indeed."

"I'm not certain what to make of them," Lucius said. "If they're accurate, it implies that your interest in rebuilding Gotham is less than philanthropic, to use the media's term. I'd hate to think that were the case, Lex."

Luthor's face was blank, but Bruce could see the wheels spinning beneath the bald head, the darkness filling the man's gaze. "These could all be a fraud," Luthor said. "Someone planted these in an attempt to make me look bad."

"Most likely. But I did some checking, trying to make sense of the matter, you understand, and best as I can tell, none of those titles has actually traded hands. So the options are that either someone is, indeed, trying to make you look like a villain . . ."

"Please, go on," Luthor said, darkly.

Lucius shook his head. "I'd hate to even speak it, Lex. It's really incomprehensible to me that the other could be true."

"That I would have forged these titles?"

"You would?" Bruce asked, shocked.

Luthor gave him a look that would have made the Batman proud.

"Of course he wouldn't," Lucius said quickly. "Bruce, *think*, please. Mr. Luthor is the richest man in the world. He doesn't need to steal land when he can buy it. The only plausible explanation here is that someone is trying to slander him."

Luthor nodded, then forced a smile into place. "I want to thank you for bringing this to my attention, Lucius. I'll have my people look into it immediately. I'd hate for the media to hear even the slightest whisper of this."

"They won't be hearing anything from us, Lex," Lucius assured him.

"Do you mind if I keep hold of these?" Luthor indicated the papers with a gesture. "Might give my people a lead."

"Go ahead." Lucius got to his feet. "I've got copies if you need more."

"Do you?"

"Several," Lucius said. "Just in case. Bruce?"

Bruce got up, grinning. "Nice place you got here, Lex," he said.

"Glad you like it," Luthor said tightly. "Mercy, please show them out."

Mercy moved to the door, opening it.

"Thanks for seeing us," Lucius said.

Luthor didn't respond, but Bruce thought Mercy looked mighty angry as he passed her on the way out. Before she could shut the door, though, he turned and stuck his head back in, looking at her with his most charming grin.

"Don't suppose you've got a date for New Year's?" he asked her.

"I'd rather dance alone, barefoot, on broken glass, than dance with you, Mr. Wayne," she answered sweetly.

Then she shut the door in his face.

He almost hurt himself trying to keep from laughing.

. . .

When Bruce returned to Luthor's hut later that night, he returned as the Batman. Once again, he roused Luthor from his sleep.

"I told you this was my city," Batman whispered, holding his hand over Luthor's mouth and keeping him pinned to the bed. "You press any claim to any property in Gotham, I'll make certain the documents Lucius Fox found go straight to the press. I will make certain your reputation is destroyed. Do you understand?"

Luthor nodded, his eyes shouting hatred.

"I want you out of my town by New Year's Day," the Batman said.

He checked to see that Mercy was still unconscious in her chair. She was.

Then the Batman left like a bad dream.

FORTY-SEVEN

 "GIVE ME THE KNIFE," DICK SAID.

"Absolutely not. Sit down."

"How many times do I have to say this. I'll carve, you sit."

"Certainly not. It wouldn't be proper."

"Give me the knife."

"I reiterate, absolutely not."

Dick Grayson reached for the carving knife, and Alfred deftly moved it away. Dick tried to reach around the butler's body, and Alfred gently elbowed him in the gut.

Leslie Thompkins laughed, looking the length of the table, past where Cassandra was seated, to the head, at Bruce Wayne. Somehow, Alfred had managed to put together a substantial spread, two bottles of wine, a fresh loaf of bread, a fresh salad, mashed potatoes with gravy, even stuffing. The crystal of the glassware shimmered in the apartment light.

"Do they do this every year?" Leslie asked.

"Every year?" Bruce said, and there was a hint of a smile on his face. "They do this every meal."

"Master Dick," Alfred said, sternly. "If you do not sit down right this minute there will be no supper for you."

"If I don't get to carve I don't want to eat," Dick said, again reaching for the knife.

Alfred once more fended him off, attempting to cut the bird.

"Thanks for joining us," Bruce said to Cassandra. "I'm glad you came."

She nodded, then said, "Stop."

Alfred and Dick froze. Leslie covered her mouth in surprise.

Cassandra grinned, reached across the table, and took the carving knife. Then she set about cutting the bird.

Andrew DeFilippis left Central just before dark on Christmas Eve; he was exhausted but the closer he got to his temporary home in TriCorner, the closer he got to his bride-to-be and their little boy, the faster he found himself going. He'd even managed to score some presents for their first Christmas together, and though they weren't anything fancy, he hoped they'd bring joy. He'd finally found a ring for Chris, and he was already imagining the look on her face when he gave it to her, the way her eyes smiled suddenly, with lovely crow's feet, and her cheeks turned pink. Their son had inherited that smile, and it had given him more joy in the last couple months than he'd ever thought he'd feel, especially in the No Man's Land.

For Justin, he'd found a teddy bear, soft and clean, and as big as the three-month-old himself.

DeFilippis reached the house and stepped inside, calling, "Chris?"

No answer.

He frowned and moved forward down the darkened hall, feeling for the switch. Power had been returned to TriCorner earlier that week, and with it had come electric heat, and the temperature change from the outside had him sweating inside his jacket. His fingers found the switch and the lights came on, and he looked into the living room and didn't see any signs of Chris or Justin.

Maybe with Montoya, he thought, but he called her name again. "Chris?"

There was a soft sound from the kitchen, like something banging against a cabinet.

Andy felt the fear clambering up his spine suddenly, and he drew his gun and put his back to the wall, making for the corner and the kitchen. The lights were off in the room.

He peeked around the corner.

Chris was on the floor, in a pool of blood, a huge gash opened on her forehead. He said her name once more, this time without realizing he'd done so, and then was on his knees and at her side, putting his arms around her and praying that she was still breathing, that her heart was still beating. He tried to lift her up, and she made a noise of pain, and when he pulled his hands back they were covered with her blood. He could feel the torn fabric of her shirt at her back, the rough edges of her skin where Chris had taken a knife.

He screamed for someone to help him, pushing hair away from her face, saying, "Chris, Chris, oh, God, don't leave, don't do this . . ."

Her eyes opened and her mouth moved and he couldn't understand what she was saying, had to put his ear by her lips. Then he heard the whisper.

"Justin . . ."

Then Bullock was there, and Montoya, and then Bullock left, shouting for more help, for someone to find a medic, saying they needed to transport wounded, that there was an officer down. Montoya crouched, began checking Chris's wounds, using her own shirt as a bandage, trying to stop the bleeding.

Andy just sat there on the floor, watching as the woman who had made No Man's Land worth surviving seemed to fade away before his eyes.

This has to be the worst Christmas dinner of my life, Huntress thought. And I've had some awful ones.

But nothing beats this one, nothing.

She looked across the gymnasium, where the tables had been set up in rows, the eighty-plus men, women, and children still in the Strong Men sector all seated opposite one another, eating overcooked turkey in silence. If there was joy to be found, she couldn't see proof of it on a single face.

At the head table, Pettit ate in silence, flanked by Anderson on one side, Foley on the other. While almost everyone else looked down at their meals, Pettit kept his head up, glaring at the people spread out before him. Of his fourteen Strong Men, eight were present at the meal. The remaining six were on guard duty outside, each wearing a silly Santa's cap that Pettit had handed them earlier in the evening.

God alone knew where he'd found those.

At least no one had tried to sing any carols.

I can't do this much longer, she thought. I can't stand this much longer.

She looked across the head table, saw that Foley had looked up from his plate just enough to meet her gaze. His expression was sympathetic, and she remembered that he had family somewhere outside of Gotham, and that just made her mood worse. Foley should be with his family. He shouldn't be alone.

Alone. Dammit, but she hated how alone she felt at that moment.

The radio on Anderson's waist crackled, and though the volume was low, the sound carried through the gym, echoing.

"... *four repeat, post four, I've got a visual. I've got a visual, someone's out there ...*"

Everyone in the room stopped eating, every family turning their attention to the head table.

"... *Joker* ..."

Huntress felt her insides freeze.

The effect throughout the room was immediate, and universal, the horror covering each face as if the people were caught in a crashing wave.

"... *post six Joker attacking post* ..."

And then the moment passed, and the panic hit, and all of a sudden every family was rising from the tables, parents grabbing for their children, and the noise started, voices beating against one another. Everyone began moving for the exits, and Huntress headed quickly to the closest set of doors, the main doors, her mind racing.

If the Joker was outside, she couldn't let these people leave. If the Joker was outside, he'd kill every last one of them.

Pettit was shouting orders to the men at the tables. "I didn't say this meal was finished!" he was screaming. "Nobody leaves until I say they can go! Nobody! Block the doors!"

His men were running to block the exits, their weapons already slung. The crowd was backing away again, massing in the center. One of the babies started wailing, and then another one, and Huntress saw couples clutching one another for comfort and safety.

Pettit's men began locking the doors, barricading every set but for the main entrance, where Huntress stood.

"Don't panic!" she shouted. "Everyone! Stay calm!"

They seemed to be listening to her, and then there was a burst of gunfire from outside and people screamed and ducked instinctively. Huntress turned to see Foley had made it to her side, Pettit coming right behind. There was nothing coming over the radios from outside.

There was another brief silence, and Pettit opened his mouth to give an order, and then they all heard Joker shouting from outside the gymnasium.

"'Twas the night before Christmas, and all through the digs, not a creature was stirring, not even the PIGS!!" Joker cackled madly, then made loud oinking noises. "Hey, Billy! You in there? Pig pig pig pig!!!"

Pettit's face flushed almost crimson. "Anderson!" he shouted. "Get second squad up here, now!"

"Yes, sir," Anderson said, then turned to gather the men.

"What the hell are you doing?" Huntress demanded, blocking the door with her body. "If you go out there he'll kill you."

"Get out of my way, Huntress," Pettit growled. "It's time someone put that lunatic down once and for all."

"Dammit, Pettit! Can't you see that's just what Joker wants you to do? He's trying to draw you out!"

"He's challenging my control, making me look like a fool in front of my people. No one does that to me, princess. No one. Got it?" He spun to find Anderson again. "We ready?"

"Yes, sir," Anderson snapped, adjusting his grip on the M16 in his hands.

Pettit nodded and faced the small windows set in the main doors, looking through one of them. Huntress peeked, too.

Joker was standing about thirty feet from the entrance, in the rubble near the end of the block. There was a woman with him, the one she'd heard rumors about—Harley Quinn.

On the ground in front of them were the bodies of three of Pettit's guards, dead in a pool of their own blood. Quinn was wearing one of the Santa hats.

"You've always been all talk and no walk, piggy!" Joker exclaimed, and then he turned around and dropped his pants, mooning the building.

Pettit dropped back down, muttering. "I'm gonna kill him. I'm gonna do what should have been done to that lunatic years ago."

"Pettit—" Huntress began.

"What you and Gordon and Batman never had the guts to do, understand?" Pettit went on. "I'm gonna kill him once and for all. I'm gonna end that maggot's reign of terror."

From outside, they heard Joker calling, "Watcha waiting for, Billy Boy? Losing your nerve? Or is it that poor widdle Biwwy is just another *wimp cop* like Gordon and the rest of the Pork Factory?"

"Rifle," Pettit said, extending his arm. Anderson immediately supplied him with one. "On my count, ready?"

"Yes, sir."

"Think this through, Pettit!" Huntress urged. "It's a trap, it's got to be."

"You get out of my way right now, woman," Pettit said. "Or so help me I'll drop you where you stand."

He gave her a shove, clearing the doorway, and she let him go, trying to prioritize, to figure out what course of action she still had open. The whole situation was in a nosedive now, she knew it, and she knew it was a trap. If she tried to keep Pettit inside, she'd end up dead. There was no doubt in her mind that he'd order his men to open fire on her.

Pettit was counting down from three.

Huntress looked at the mass of terrified faces gathered in the room.

Beside her, Foley whispered, "He's going to get us all killed, isn't he?"

Pettit had reached one, was going for the door, the men following after him.

"Not if I can help it," Huntress said. "Not while there's a breath in my body."

And the door was open, and Pettit and the Strong Men were pouring out of the gym and into the night.

Huntress rose and followed.

FORTY-EIGHT

IT HAD STARTED SNOWING.

Joker and Quinn had vanished.

Pettit dropped into a crouch by the nearest pile of rubble, motioning the men to spread out. "Yeah," he murmured. "Figures you'd run and hide. Who's the coward here, huh? Anderson!"

"Sir?"

"Bring the squad up and spread out. Find that . . . that . . . clown."

"Yes, sir," Anderson said.

Huntress watched while the men moved into the darkness, weapons to the ready. She moved closer to where Pettit was kneeling, hearing someone behind her and looking to find Foley had exited, as well. The doors to the gym had swung shut.

Pettit brought the rifle up, using the rubble as a brace on the barrel. Huntress scanned the surrounding terrain and immediately felt another wave of despair. There were just too many places to hide, too many nooks and crannies and shadows to make any search effective.

"Come on, come on," Pettit was murmuring. "Come on, clown, give me a shot."

Foley was crouching beside Huntress now, and they exchanged glances. There was only the sound of the snow falling, nothing more, and the silence seemed to grow and stretch as if fed by Huntress's own fear.

Then she saw movement, just ahead of her, at the edge of the spilled light coming from the gymnasium. Behind a line of rubble, she caught the barest movement, and she thought maybe it was the top of someone's head. She started to open her mouth when she heard Pettit moving the gun. He'd seen it, too.

Then the head popped up, and Joker waved at them.

"Got you, you son of a bitch," Pettit said, and he fired, the report from the rifle tremendously loud, echoing and reverberating along the silent street.

In the dim light, through the falling snow, Huntress saw Joker's head blow open, his body falling back behind the rubble.

Pettit lowered the rifle and shot a smug grin at Huntress, eyes shining. "Wasn't so hard after all, was it?"

Huntress didn't say anything, starting to rise to move toward the body.

From behind the rubble she heard Joker's voice drifting their way.

"Nice shot, Billy Boy!" Joker called. "Want to try for two?"

She glanced back at Pettit, and saw the smug look had vanished to a single point of fury. She turned again and took a step back, stunned, as Joker climbed over the rubble again, waving his hands quickly.

Before she could speak, Pettit had fired again. The bullet hit Joker in the chest, spinning him like a cheap top. He hit the ground, blood pouring from his mouth.

Huntress heard Pettit say, "Sure."

Then another Joker sprang from behind the rubble, tumbling

over the body of the one Pettit had just shot, and Huntress realized what was happening, turned back to Pettit, shouting, "No! Don't shoot—"

But Pettit did, firing again, and Huntress saw Anderson hit the ground, the green wig falling atop his ruptured skull. She ran back to Pettit, trying to block him, but the rifle was still up, and she heard Joker cackling from the darkness and Pettit was firing again, and again, and then finally she had grabbed the rifle.

"You're killing your own men!" she screamed at him. "It's not him!"

Pettit yanked the rifle free from her grip, shouting, "Get off of me! I'm going to kill him, I'm going to kill him!"

Foley grabbed her by the shoulders as she tried to reach for Pettit again, saying, "Don't, don't, Huntress . . . he's gone, he'll kill you . . ."

"That was Anderson!" Huntress shouted. "You're killing your own people!"

Pettit ignored her, raising the rifle again, shooting again and again and then there was the sound of the hammer falling dry, and he was out of bullets, turning his back to the rubble and starting to reload. Huntress couldn't breathe, felt like she was hyperventilating, and she looked across the empty ground to where the multiple Jokers had been coming, body after body fallen on the ground.

"Thinks he can play games with me, I'll show him how we play games," Pettit was muttering, fumbling round after round into the clip. "Thinks he can make a joke of me, thinks he's a comedian, see how funny he is dead . . ."

"You're killing your own people," Huntress said again, barely whispering.

"He's not listening anymore," Foley said. "He's not even hearing us."

She shook her head, glancing back at the closed gym, seeing the faces in the windows, watching.

"Can you call him?" Foley asked. "Call Batman?"

"I can't. I don't know how." She faced him. "Get out of here, Hugh. Get to Central, get Essen or Gordon, somebody. Get help."

Foley nodded, started to move, and Huntress saw the motion from the corner of her eye, from the line where the Jokers had been rising, and she dived into Foley, bringing him to the ground as the machine-gun fire raked the earth beyond them. Bullets whistled over their heads, careening off the cracked pavement.

Joker's laugh floated around them with the snow.

"Go," Huntress said, rolling off him.

Foley got to his feet, began a crouching run in Pettit's direction, Huntress following. There was another barrage of machine-gun fire, and again they hit the deck. Pettit was slamming his reloaded clip back into his rifle, and as Foley got to his feet once more, he glowered at him.

"Where the hell do you think you're going?" Pettit demanded.

"He's getting backup," Huntress said.

"He's what?"

"This is crazy, Bill," Foley said. "We need help. I'm going to try to get to Central. See if you can hold off Joker until I get back."

"I said nobody leaves without my permission!" Pettit screamed, and before Huntress could move he had dropped the rifle and drawn his pistol and shot Foley through the head.

"No!"

Foley hit the ground like a bag of wet flour, eyes open, dead.

She was at his body instantly, and everything else faded away then, Pettit, the gymnasium, Joker, all of it, and she was looking down at the dead man. The man who had only wanted to spend the holidays with his family.

Pettit had dropped the pistol, taken up the rifle again, once more looking for a chance to kill Joker.

"You're . . . you're as mad as Joker is," Huntress whispered. "As sick and as evil and as wrong . . . "

And she was on him before thinking to move, knocking the rifle away, screaming.

"You bastard!"

She hit him, hard, again and again, battering his face and feeling the bone shift and crack beneath the blows. She took him by the collar and threw him against the rubble, barely thinking, still screaming at him.

"Foley trusted you! He trusted you to protect him!"

She punched him in the gut, doubling him over, then yanking

his head back once more. She threw him at the gym, against the doors, then grabbed him again, knocking the hat from his head and grabbing him at the neck, spinning him around. Back to the door, she punched him once more in the stomach.

"They all did, all your men! All the people here! *We* all did!"

She rammed the launcher on her right wrist beneath his throat. All it would take would be a twist of her hand and she'd drive a metal spike into his brain, she'd kill the son of a bitch where he stood. Pettit's eyes wandered, dazed, blood running down his face.

"You're the worst of us, you know that, Pettit?" Huntress hissed at him. "And I know how to solve at least one problem. You're a dead man, Billy——"

There was a shot, and Pettit's eyes began filling with blood and his head pitched forward, and suddenly Huntress was holding entirely dead weight.

"Couldn't have put it better myself," Joker said.

Over Pettit's head she could see him, still holding the gun, wisps of smoke flying away from the barrel. Quinn was beside him, the automatic rifle from one of Pettit's men now slung over her shoulder.

And behind them were at least twelve men, maybe more, thugs to the last of them. Joker's boys.

Huntress dropped Pettit and stepped back until she felt her boots hit the door of the gym.

"We're just here to gather some things, and then we'll be going," Joker told her. "Babies, in particular. I understand there are something in the neighborhood of four of the little cherubs inside, are there not?"

She didn't answer.

"You're, um . . . blocking the door, toots."

"I know," Huntress said.

Joker looked legitimately surprised. "Oh, you've got to be kidding me! You're not seriously thinking of taking us all on?"

She didn't answer.

"It's just you versus us now, kiddo! That's you versus twelve of us, not counting me and my worst girl, here. And thanks to Billy Boy, there on the ground, I'd like to stress that we're now armed."

She didn't move.

Joker sighed, throwing one arm around Harley and pulling her with him as he backed away.

"Well," Joker said. "It's your funeral. Kill her, boys."

She had been fighting crime for a long time, and she knew as it began that she was at the best she had ever been.

She knew she didn't have a chance, and she didn't care.

Before Joker's boys had even begun to move, she'd dropped three of them with shots from her wrist-launcher, spikes burying deep in shins, arms, knees. She went into motion, never losing track of the door, pulling the cape from behind her neck and whirling it as a shield, disarming man after man, raining fists and forearms, punches and kicks. She flew and dived and tumbled and rose and she didn't stop, even as the sweat stung her eyes and the cold air burned her aching lungs.

Huntress fought, not as if her life depended on it, but as if the lives of everyone in the building behind her did.

She took on all twelve of Joker's boys, and she beat them all, and as the last one fell, clawing at the ground to get away, she turned from the door and felt her leg explode in a sudden numb heat, and she hit the ground hearing the report, and she knew she'd been shot. She used the door to pull herself upright again, put her back to it for support.

Joker stood only ten feet away, his pistol pointed at her.

"You're good," he said. "She's good, isn't she?"

"Very good," Quinn agreed.

"Yup," said Joker, and he shot her again, this time in the chest.

Huntress fell to her knees, feeling the blood beginning to bubble up into her throat. She opened her mouth, saw it staining the snow in front of her. For a second she couldn't remember where she was, and then she saw him again, and he was talking to her.

"It's funny," Joker mused. "See, I wouldn't keep shooting you like this if I didn't have all these darn bullets. But who knew that Pettit had so many of the little buggers? I'd swear that psycho had a bullet for every man, woman, and child in Gotham!"

She tried to tell Joker what she thought of him, Pettit, and the bullets, but when she opened her mouth the only thing that came out was more blood. It was getting very hard to breathe, too, she couldn't get enough air. She tried to stand up, feet slipping in the snow.

"And since I won't be using the bullets on the kids, you know," Joker continued, "I figure these ones, well, they're all yours."

Huntress forced herself upright, feeling the chill of the metal door against her back. It felt very cold.

"Here," Joker said. "Have another, cutie."

He shot her again, and this time she barely felt the impact, the sting, but her left side felt funny, suddenly, and she was on the ground again and wondering how she had gotten there if, in fact, she'd just been standing up. Her arm wouldn't move, and the world seemed to be turning very shaky.

Joker was in front of her, and she felt something hot pressing against the side of her head.

"Tough little thing, aren't you?" Joker asked.

Huntress heard a sound like the key turning in a lock, but she knew that wasn't right. The door wasn't locked, was it?

"It's been fun," Joker said.

Oh, right, Huntress thought.

I'm going to die.

FORTY-NINE

JOKER WAS PULLING THE TRIGGER when the Batarang hit his hand, knocking his aim away, and the shot missed Huntress and buried itself in the side of the building. He recoiled, yanking his hand back and looking up and finally, after all this time, there he was.

Batman, coming to punish him.

And that other one, Nighty-Knight or . . . Nightwing, that was it, Nightwing.

Nightwing seemed really upset about something. He was shouting, "Huntress!"

Didn't bother Joker.

"What took you?" he asked.

Batman grabbed him by the jacket, and he would have been will-ing to take the punch if it had come, but it didn't, because Harley, bless her twisted little Carol Brady soul, opened fire with the assault rifle then. Batman let him go, diving to the ground and then going for Harley. Nightwing was busy trying to save the other girl's life, so Joker took the opportunity to get the bomb he'd made out of his pocket, arm it, and throw it onto the roof of the gym.

"Now that we're all here," Joker said. "Time to bring down da house!"

Harley was already on her keister, Batman coming back his way, but Nightwing knew his lines and shouted, "Bomb!"

Batman, glaring, veered off and up, going for the roof of the building.

Joker, laughing with unrestrained glee, grabbed Harley by the arm and ran for it.

She felt like she was swimming in something hot and sticky, and she opened her eyes to see Nightwing looking down at her, and she wondered how he'd snuck up on her again. There was something she had to tell him, too...something important, but her mouth was filled with copper and wasn't moving right.

"... baby ..." Huntress managed to say. "... wanted to take ... the babies ..."

"Hold on," Nightwing told her. "We're gonna take care of you ... hold on."

She felt the pressure in her side increase and with the pain came more focus, and she remembered suddenly where they were, what had happened. Above her, Nightwing turned his head briefly, and she managed to follow his gaze and saw Batman was standing only a cou-ple feet away, holding something metal and plastic in his hands, tear-ing it apart angrily.

"Joker was after the babies," Nightwing said.

"Get her to Dr. Thompkins."

"... Batman," Huntress croaked.

He moved closer, looking down at her, that face once again empty of anything.

"Happy . . . now . . . ?" she asked.

His hand came down, and she felt the slight brush of his touch against her forehead.

"Rest," he said. "Good work, Huntress."

Then he turned and she knew she was losing consciousness. She heard Nightwing saying, "Congratulations, Helena. That's his highest praise. Honest."

Then there was only darkness.

Essen thought she would cry when she unwrapped the present her husband and stepdaughter had given her. In addition to the meal, the joy of being together, the fact that they had managed to even present her with a gift, made her speechless.

That it was a gift such as this, that made her want to weep.

"You like it?" Gordon asked.

She nodded, saw Barbara grinning.

It was a picture in a beautiful golden oak frame, an eight-by-ten photograph of the three of them, taken almost two years earlier at the end of the season. They'd all gone to watch the Knights play, and the picture caught them on that afternoon, preserving the moment perfectly. The slight sunburn from a day in the park, the huge smiles each of them wore beneath their Gotham Knights baseball caps. Their family.

"I love you, Sarah," Gordon said. "Merry Christmas."

"I love you, too," she said, and kissed him, and kept on kissing him until she heard Barbara moving in her chair and realized that, potentially, she was embarrassing her stepdaughter.

Then she saw that Barbara was looking at the shadow coming toward them, and she saw it was Batman.

"Jim," Batman said. "We have a serious problem."

"Merry Christmas to you, too," Gordon said mildly.

"Joker attacked Pettit's camp. Pettit and Foley are dead. Huntress held Joker off, but she's in critical now and may not make it." Batman kept his gaze on Gordon, and Sarah noticed that Barbara was listening as closely as any of them. "Joker was after the infants. He's kidnapped babies from all across the No Man's Land—"

"Dear Lord," Gordon said.

"Do you think . . . did he take Justin?" Essen asked.

"I don't know," Gordon said. "God, let's hope not."

"It's his statement," Batman said. "He wants to murder hope."

Gordon nodded, and there was no joy left in his face, in any of them.

"I'm gathering my people," Batman continued.

Essen was already on her feet, her husband now joining her. "I'll get as many officers as possible, have them assemble at Central," Gordon said.

"We'll meet you there," Batman said.

As Batman was moving out the window, Essen made for the door, her husband on her heels. She looked back at Barbara, who was watching them leave, eyes full of concern.

"Don't worry, Babs," Sarah said. "We'll handle it."

"I know you will," Barbara said.

Nightwing could hear Oracle over his commlink, ordering him to Central, ASAP. He ignored it, carrying Huntress's limp body as carefully as he could into the MASH camp, ignoring the stares and the people, moving straight for the largest tent.

"Leslie!" he shouted, and the desperation in his voice made him shout again, louder. *"Leslie!"*

Alfred appeared in the doorway, and his face blanched. He reached out, trying to take Huntress from Nightwing's arms, but he refused, pushing past the old man until he could lay the woman down on an empty table. Leslie was there, her sleeves already rolled up, working on another woman, a blond that Nightwing recognized as one of Gordon's cops from before the No Man's Land. A man was holding the woman's hand, looking both relieved and worried all at once. Leslie turned to see the new patient, and for a moment there was no expression on her face other than horror at the sight in front of her.

"Good God! What happened?" Leslie turned her head, shouting. "Doctor Zahedi!"

"We've got her now, lad," Alfred said.

"Don't let her die . . . you can't let her die," Nightwing said.

"We'll attend her as best we can," Alfred said. "You have an emergency of your own to deal with now, I think."

"Alfred, please . . ."

The old man touched his shoulder, gave it a squeeze. "We'll do all we can."

Nightwing shut his eyes, nodding, then turned away, heading back out of the tent.

Batgirl was waiting for him.

"Central," Nightwing said. "We're supposed to go to Central."

She began moving south without another word.

Nightwing cast a last glance back, then followed.

Please, don't let her die. . . .

It had taken Robin longer to arrive than the rest of them, because he'd been having dinner with his father at their new house just north of the city. Luckily, Oracle's call had come in after they'd eaten, and he was able to duck out of his room and into the snowy night, then steal onto one of the helicopters departing the nearby National Guard staging area.

He was afraid he was going to be too late, all the same, and was almost relieved to see that, although Gordon and Essen and most of the cops were already outside of Central, Nightwing and Batgirl had only just arrived. Batman and Gordon were talking, and Robin joined the group silently, catching sight of the faces all around him, the expressions of strained concern.

Nightwing looked miserable, his costume stained with blood. Robin wanted to ask him what had happened—all Oracle had said was that Joker had stolen babies—but Batman started talking.

"Oracle ran some quick checks," Batman said. "And LexCorp is missing seventy pounds of Semtex."

"Which means Joker can make a hell of a big explosion," Gordon said. "We've received a total of thirty-six missing persons reports in the course of the night. All infants, including Sergeant Weir's baby."

"She was attacked in her home this evening," Essen added. "She's at the MASH Sector now, in stable condition."

"The parents must be going mad," Montoya said.

"We're going to find those children," Batman said.

From above and across the street, they heard Joker's shout. "I don't think so!"

All of them turned to see him on the opposite rooftop, waving down at them. In the nightlight he was little more than a silhouette. He had a Santa cap on his head, and the voice was unmistakable.

"Here's how it's going to play, kiddies," Joker yelled gleefully. "'Twas the night before Christmas, and all through the town, little babies were hidden by Gotham's king clown! As Christmas Day neared and the sun it did rise, either Bats found the kids, or the kids . . . well . . . they dies!"

Batman already had the grapnel out, firing the line up and at the rooftop, bellowing, "Go!" as he rose into the air. Joker had turned and was already out of sight beyond the rooftop.

Robin looked at Nightwing.

"Fan out," Nightwing said.

And they began the search.

It was Bullock's suggestion to check the abandoned day care centers, and Montoya thought that was an excellent idea.

Problem was there were over two hundred of them in Gotham before the No Man's Land, and they didn't know where to start. But that being the case, and figuring that Joker couldn't have had much time, they started in the area around Central, working out in a box pattern northward toward the park. They tried to be quick about it, moving from location to location, knowing that time was working against them and working hard. Joker's deadline wasn't a joke. Wherever those kids were, unless they were found, they'd be dead come dawn.

The snow fell steadily as they searched, one derelict building after the other, running through the streets, finally commandeering an Army jeep to help with their transport.

By four in the morning both of them were tense, frustrated, and feeling the panic grow. It wasn't just them, either. They had radios, one each, and over them they heard Gordon or Essen or other cops calling in, offering what little news or theories they had. So far, nothing.

It was Bullock who saw the sign.

HAPPEE CLOWNE DAYCARE.

He stopped the jeep and he and Montoya got out, drawing their guns and running low for the door. The place was a mess, not yet officially condemned, but certainly uninhabited. The door itself looked like it was barely on its hinges.

Harvey held out three fingers for the count, then two, then one, and together they put their boots against the door in a sharp kick, sending it flying off its hinges.

Inside was darkness.

Montoya pulled her flashlight, used it to support her weapon, and when the beam hit the rows and rows of eyes, she almost dropped it in surprise.

"Holy . . . " Bullock said.

There were dolls everywhere. On the floor, in the cubbies, on the shelves, even suspended from the sagging ceiling by strings. Toy dolls, their eyes open and glassy, reflecting the light.

"Looks clear," Bullock said, looking around for a light switch.

Why dolls? Montoya thought, and then she knew why, and she was grabbing her partner and pulling him out of the door.

But not before Bullock had thrown the light switch, and the explosion knocked them clear off the steps, across the sidewalk, and into the street. Montoya landed in the snow, feeling the air rush out of her as the concussion from the blast rolled over her. Her ears were ringing. She shook her head to clear it, feeling like it was full of wet laundry, then reached for Harvey, who was pulling himself upright using the fender of the jeep.

"Joker's way ahead of us," Montoya said.

"Maniac even did his Christmas shopping. You okay, pard?"

"I'm fine."

"Then let's keep looking."

Robin was glad to have Oracle in his ear. Not only did she keep him company, but she kept him informed of what else was going on. Batman was still after Joker; Nightwing, Batgirl, the cops, all the rest, they were looking for babies.

Where do you hide babies in a city like Gotham? Robin thought.

"Oracle?"

"Go ahead."

"I'm thinking a nursery."

"Sounds like a plan."

So Robin checked nurseries. For hours. One after the other.

And then, outside of Li'l Bud's Nursery, he saw a sign in a broken window that made him think it might be worth a closer look. The sign had been drawn by hand, and said, BABY'S BREATH—BUY ONE, GET ONE FREE.

"Oracle," Robin said. "Think I might have something."

"Be careful. It's most likely a trap."

Robin took his time with the door, checking it for trip wires carefully before pushing it open; he almost expected an explosion anyway, but nothing happened. The interior of the shop was empty, all of the shelves bare but for a register on the counter. Another sign was propped there, saying, WAKE UP AND SMELL THE ROSES!

Cautiously he made his way across the floor, watching his feet, until he reached the counter. He leaned over it slowly, trying to look behind, and then climbed onto the counter for a better view.

"Robin?"

"Yeah . . . I'm . . . there are a bunch of dolls here, under the counter . . . the kind with mouths, you know, that you can stick a bottle in . . ."

"Mouths?"

"Yeah . . . and . . . it looks like a tank of some sort, running from the dolls. It's a canister of some kind—"

He reached down to lift one of the dolls.

"Joker Gas," Oracle said. *"Mask on, Robin!"*

He stopped, straightened, and got the gas mask from his belt, slipping it on. Then he leaned back down and reached for the nearest doll.

And sure enough, from the mouth of each one came a cloud of green vapor. Joker's patented poison gas.

"Robin? Robin? Answer me!"

"I've got it," he said, yanking the tube from the canister and switching it off angrily. "You were right. It was a trap."

"Any clues?"

"Nothing."

"Keep looking."

"Yeah," he said.

He was beginning to be afraid they wouldn't pull this one off.

DeFilippis had demanded to go back on active duty, and Gordon and Essen took the officer with them in their group, the three of them searching high and low. Chris was as safe as she could be, and the only thing the young officer could think now was that he had to find their son. Damn Joker and his games, the bastard had stabbed the woman he loved, had stolen his child.

He had to do something.

By four in the morning they had searched every playground in the western half of the city, including the smaller recreation areas at the fast-food restaurants. It was the fast-food places that had given him the idea then, that they should check Discovery Domain. It had been on his beat before the NML, one of those facilities where parents could take their preschoolers to run and play. When DeFilippis suggested it, both Gordon and Essen agreed it was a logical location to look.

The place was in serious disrepair when they arrived. Shining the beams from their flashlights around the cavernous space, they could see three slides, a merry-go-round, a couple of jungle gyms, and a tent where the floor was covered with plastic balls that kids could jump around in.

The three of them made their way forward, and then Gordon said, "Stop."

They all stopped.

"Look." The Commissioner shone his light into the tent.

There was a sea of tiny hands and feet jutting out from the surface of plastic spheres.

DeFilippis surged forward, thinking that his son was there, suffocated or suffocating, and he heard Essen shout, "Don't!" but he did anyway. She grabbed him from behind, yanking, and he fell back into her and they both went to the ground. Essen swore, pushing him away and then shining her light at the ground.

"Look," she said. "Tripwire. It's a trap."

"They're dolls," Gordon said.

DeFilippis caught his breath, nodded, feeling foolish.

Gordon patted him on the shoulder, giving him a hand up. "Stay off my wife," he cautioned. "You've got a woman of your own."

DeFilippis grinned.

"Damn," Essen said, getting to her feet. "My radio's busted." She held out the broken unit, crushed in the fall.

"Temporary equipment." Gordon sighed. "Lovely. Breaks when you drop it."

"Or land on it."

"Head back to Central, get another one," Gordon said. "I don't want any of us out of communication for too long."

"I'll call in as soon as I'm ready to rejoin you," Essen said.

It took a while, but by four in the morning, Batman knew he wasn't chasing Joker.

Joker was never in such good shape. Joker was never this fast or nimble, or this willing to keep running.

Which meant it had to be Quinn in the costume, decoying for Joker.

The options were clear, then. Either he continued to pursue, hoping to catch her and extract Joker's location out of her, or he could abandon the chase and start from scratch. It was an easy choice to make, and so he continued after her, racing along the rooftops and alleyways, trying to close the distance. Over the earpiece in his cowl, he heard the radio traffic between Oracle and the rest of his team; heard about the Joker Gas in the nursery; heard Nightwing and Batgirl visiting Camp Lex and discovering that the giant Christmas tree had been decorated with more dolls, only those dolls had been incendiary, and the fireball had been visible throughout the city; he heard about the efforts of the police, the traps; and he knew that no one had found Joker yet.

The trouble was that Quinn was fast, if indeed it was Quinn. And since her goal seemed to be running, not fighting, she was making it very difficult for Batman to get in close. They skirted Robinson Park on the south edge, and he pursued her across the Sprang River, into the Fashion District, and then, finally, at a construction site only fifteen blocks from Camp Lex, things began to go his way. "Joker" started to climb, and Batman easily got to the high ground first, then leapt down.

This close, he could confirm it wasn't Joker. He moved to block her progress.

She tried to kick him.

He caught it, punched her once, hard, in the face, and then let go of her leg.

She fell backward, and the wig came loose, and the makeup had smudged when he'd hit her, and he could see it was Quinn, the girl he'd been hearing so much about.

"We've never met before," he hissed as he picked her up by the front of the jacket, holding her out in front of him. "The way this works is you tell me what I want to know."

Her mouth did a strange little dance, almost like a hula. "Or?"

"Or . . ." and he pivoted, still holding her, and dangled Quinn over the edge of the scaffolding.

She looked down and screamed.

He pulled her back in, close, and he put everything he had into his voice, all the menace, all the rage. "One chance. Where. Is. He?"

". . . Central . . . he hid the babies at Central he thought that would be funniest if all the babies were at Central and please don't kill me I don't want to . . ."

But the Batman had already dropped her back onto the scaffolding, was now jumping, using the cape to slow his descent, trying to get Oracle on his commlink.

"Joker is at Central," Batman said. "I'm en route."

"*Understood,*" Oracle said, and then she began broadcasting on all channels, all bands, so everyone with a radio could hear her. "*Joker is at Central, repeat, Joker has the babies at Central. All personnel respond . . .*"

FIFTY

THE VOICE CAME OVER GORDON'S RADIO.
He listened.
He looked at Officer DeFilippis.
He said, "Sarah."
And he started running.

The precinct was empty and dark when Sarah Essen arrived. She stopped inside the entryway, switching on the main lights and then shaking the accumulated snow from her hair, brushing it from her shoulders. The heat had been left on, and it made the snowflakes melt quickly, sent the water trickling down the inside of her shirt.

The radios were kept in their own room off the hallway behind the main desk, and Essen made directly for them, leaving the door open behind her. The water on her shoes made her soles squeak with each step. She stepped into the radio room, dropping her broken one on the table and reaching for the first in the rack, pulling it out and switching it on.

Nothing happened.

Essen turned the radio in her hand and found that the battery pack had been destroyed by some sort of sharp object, either a knife or a screwdriver having punctured the unit. She set the radio down quietly and pulled another, and found that battery pack in the same state, too.

All of the radios had been sabotaged, and when she realized that, the nervousness that had been building inside her opened, blossoming into fear.

Then she heard the crying of a baby.

She stepped quietly out of the radio room, drawing her weapon and holding it in both hands. She checked the hallway carefully. No one was visible.

She heard it again, and there was no doubt this time, it wasn't her mind playing tricks on her. Somewhere in the building a baby was crying.

Still holding the gun in the low-ready position, Essen began walking silently in the direction of the noise. It had come from nearby, she was certain.

The door to the basement was open.

There was no reason for the door to the basement to be open. There was nothing in the basement. The basement hadn't been finished yet.

At the top of the stairs she stopped, looking down. There was light coming from below, dim. She heard what sounded like small animals padding around on dirt. She heard the sound of a voice, but none of the words.

She went down the stairs as quietly as she knew how, the gun raised now, and at the foot of the stairs she stepped off, then turned into the main room of the basement, her shoulder against the wall.

The babies were there, and she didn't need to count to know she had found all thirty-six of them, and in a way didn't it make a perfect kind of sense? Joker wanted a statement.

What better one than murdering thirty-six infants right beneath the noses of the police?

None of the babies had been injured yet, as far as she could tell. Some were sleeping on the earth floor, others crawling clumsily around, still more just sitting still, watching the strangeness of the world, calmly trying to master the intricacies of vision. A couple were looking at the man who was comforting the crying baby.

Joker stood in the center of the room, his back to her, rocking a child gently in his arms.

"Shh," he was saying gently. "No, no, it's okay, little guy, it's okay. You won't feel a thing, I promise. And you'll thank Unky Joker when it's over, trust me on this, I know what I'm talking about . . . most of the time."

He raised the baby in both hands, putting him against his shoulder and crooning in its ear.

"Tell you a secret," Joker said softly. "Big secret, biggest secret there is. It's this: Life is the biggest joke of all. You're just gonna get the punch line sooner . . . that's it, right there, little fella."

Essen put her sights on the base of his skull.

"Freeze," she said, and her voice was strong and clear and she was proud of that. "GCPD. You're under arrest, Joker."

Joker turned slowly, lowering the baby from his shoulder to rest in the crook of his left arm. The baby was a little boy, olive skinned and wide eyed, and tear-tracks had dried on his cheeks. Essen recognized the infant. She had delivered him. Justin Michael DeFilippis-Weir.

Joker was staring at her, and he wasn't smiling.

It was the first time she'd ever seen him without his smile, and it made the marrow freeze in Sarah Essen's bones.

"Put the baby down," she said. "Gently. Do it now."

Joker stared at her.

"Do it, Joker."

Very slowly, he began to crack a smile. "Oh," he said softly. "It's the police. Hmm . . . I'd like to report a crime . . ."

He began to walk toward her, stepping heedlessly through the infants crawling around his feet. His right hand dipped into his jacket and came out with a pistol of his own.

". . . she tried to shoot me," Joker said softly. "And I dropped the baby."

Essen slammed the hammer back on her pistol with her thumb, readjusting her aim. "Stop! I mean it——"

"No," Joker said. "I *mean*, she *rushed* me . . . and I dropped the baby."

He was close now, and still holding Justin in the crook of his left arm. He brought his gun up level with the infant's head, cocking it slowly.

She was staring right at him, he wasn't more than three feet away, and right then Sarah Essen knew what would happen next, and in that instant she felt suddenly, effortlessly calm. There was only one thing left for her to do.

She just hoped she could do it.

"Or maybe . . ." Joker said. ". . . I just . . ."

He dropped the baby.

Essen let go of her gun, pitching forward, arms out, and she caught Justin well before he hit the ground, landing on the hard earth floor of the basement on her knees. It didn't hurt. The baby looked at her, blissfully unaware.

Joker had his gun pressed to the side of her head, just inside her ear, at her temple.

She carefully set the baby down.

"Merry Christmas," Joker said, and he pulled the trigger.

The sun was just starting to rise as the Batman landed in front of Central, the jumpline automatically respooling on his belt. He had already started up the stairs when he heard the sound of men running, turned to see Gordon and another cop coming from behind.

The look in Gordon's eyes told him everything he needed to know.

He started moving once more and saw that Joker was now in the doorway, leaning against the frame, smiling. In his right hand he was holding a pistol loosely, which he dropped onto the snow-covered steps at his feet. Then he began making his way down the stairs, headed for Batman.

"I surrender," he said happily.

With his peripheral vision, Batman saw Montoya and Bullock

and another officer rushing into the station. Gordon was making his way slowly toward Joker.

It's stopped snowing, Batman realized.

More people were around them, gathering at the foot of the stairs. He heard Robin arrive, and then Nightwing landed, Batgirl with him. More police volunteers ran up, stopping short when they saw the tableau. The sunlight was beginning to gleam off the fresh snow, making everything seem exposed, too bright.

Montoya and Bullock came out of the station, stopping at the head of the stairs. Detective Montoya was crying soundlessly. Bullock looked as if he had lost a member of his family.

Behind them, another officer appeared, holding a small infant in his arms.

"Commish," Bullock began, and his voice caught. "Jim . . . I'm . . . I'm so sorry . . ."

"She's dead," Montoya said.

Joker was looking complacently at Batman.

Gordon drew his revolver and whipped it once along the side of Joker's head, sending the clown sprawling across the steps. "Animal!" Gordon screamed.

His voice bounced off fresh snow.

Gordon used both hands to support his gun, proper shooter's stance, leveling the barrel at Joker's head.

Batman remained motionless, watching.

Joker, on his back, dabbed at the blood coursing down the side of his face, then looked with a smile from Batman to Gordon.

"Commissioner!" he exclaimed. "You'll be hearing from my attorney!"

Joker wiped at the blood again, smeared it across his face, and then got slowly back to his feet. Gordon cocked the pistol.

"Jim," Batman said.

"He's gone too far," Gordon said simply, his voice dangerously calm. Tears had begun running down his cheeks, fast, fat drops that shivered at the edge of his jaw before falling to the ground. "He paralyzed my daughter, my little girl . . . he . . . he murdered . . . he *just murdered* my bride, my . . . my Sarah, my friend . . . my . . . my love. . . ."

Batman watched Gordon squeeze his eyes shut, as if by closing them the Commissioner hoped to change the reality, to make it different, to make it all go away.

It wouldn't work, Batman knew. He'd tried it once, too, when he was very young.

Joker was grinning from ear to ear now.

Gordon opened his eyes. The determination was there, the outrage and the anger pushing him forward. He didn't look away from Joker, refusing to see Batman, to see anyone else around him.

"Too much," Gordon said. "Too much . . . too far . . ."

"We've all gone too far," Batman said. He raised his hand, gesturing to the crowd of people now around the steps, the police, the vigilantes, the parents of the missing children. "Look at them. Look at *us*. They can't take it anymore."

The barrel shivered slightly in Gordon's hands.

"It's time to bring our people back, Jim."

Gordon wiped quickly at the tears on his cheeks, then adjusted his sights again, barely breathing. His finger was coiled on the trigger.

"I won't stop you," Batman said.

Gordon nodded slightly, as if acknowledging the words, or perhaps another voice from somewhere else entirely. Then he took a deep breath, letting it blow out his nose.

"You and the missus never had kiddlins of your own, didja?" Joker asked smugly.

Gordon pulled the trigger, dropping the sights an instant before the round fired. The report thundered across the snow-covered steps of the precinct, seemed to echo throughout the city.

Joker fell back, clutching at where his left knee had once been. Blood was rushing down his calf, over his shoe, into the snow. He screamed in pain, then abruptly shut his mouth, sitting upright and opening his eyes wide in understanding.

"Hey!" Joker said. "Hey! I get it! Like your daughter, Commissioner, oh, that's *good*, that's really *funny*!"

He began to laugh uncontrollably.

Gordon put his gun back into its holster, turning his back on the building. "Bullock," he said hoarsely. "Montoya. Arrest him. Charge is murder."

He began to walk down the stairs, slowly, taking each one at a time, and Batman saw Gordon slowing, saw him sag, and then he moved, catching his friend before he could fall.

"I've got you," he said.

The sob came out of Gordon all at once, devastated, the sound of a breaking heart.

Batman held him in the daylight, feeling Gordon's grief rocking his own body.

"I've got you," he said again.

EPILOGUE

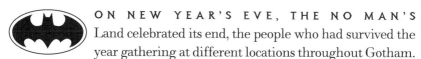 ON NEW YEAR'S EVE, THE NO MAN'S Land celebrated its end, the people who had survived the year gathering at different locations throughout Gotham.

At midnight, fireworks exploded in the sky, a shower of flame and sparks and color that marked not only the dawn of a new era, but the rechristening of an old city. In her bed in the MASH Sector, the explosions woke Helena Bertinelli long enough for her to realize that she was still alive.

At Central, someone threw a switch, and the bright silhouette of a bat painted the clouds, tracking back and forth in the sky. Everyone who saw it cheered. Everyone who saw it knew what it meant. Everyone who saw it knew the truth.

And almost everyone saw it but for two men and one woman.

· · ·

At midnight on New Year's Eve, Jim Gordon and his daughter Barbara opened a bottle of champagne at the grave site of Sarah Essen-Gordon, loving Wife, Friend, and Officer. They drank a toast to Sarah, and another to Gotham, and a third to the future. Then they held one another while each wept tears that they thought would never stop.

Outside of Gotham City, on the grounds where once had stood Wayne Manor, and where it would soon stand again, Bruce Wayne visited the family grave site deep on the estate. He carefully cleared the overgrowth from all of the headstones and markers, paying special attention, as always, to that of his parents.

"I'm home," he said.

ORACLE

PERSONAL
Entry #893—January 1 (NML +1)
0545 Zulu

Dear Dad—
I'm looking back now, trying to dry my eyes.
You said to me tonight, "I don't think the hurt will ever stop."
You're right.
It won't.
Just ask Batman.

I've been thinking, and I can never show this work to you, and for that I'm sorry. When I started out, I thought of this as a chronicle of the No Man's Land, and now I realize it's both more and less than that. But what I recorded in the name of posterity no longer needs my testimony.

Sarah will be remembered in far better ways than this narrative.

We keep in our hearts, after all, the true record.

So you will never see this.

But if it's any consolation, neither will the Batman.

I'm going to finish this half-bottle of champagne by my side and drink one last toast to Gotham and another to Sarah.

Then I'm going to delete this file.